A TASTE OF EDEN

A SWEET, SMALL TOWN ROMANCE

TINA NEWCOMB

DEDICATION

To my sister—through the years, laughter, and tears, you've always believed in me.
Love you bunches, Holly Hertzke.

CONTENTS

Carolyn West Richmond pushed the pile of clothes down with one hand while yanking the zipper with the other. The new suitcase didn't hold much, but she couldn't risk taking her own.

She hurried to the spare bedroom and reached for a collapsed cardboard box from underneath the bed. Unfolding it, she secured the bottom flaps with duct tape she'd shoved between a stack of sheets in the linen closet. Quickly, she filled the box with new clothes and shoes she'd hidden in garbage bags labeled "give away" in the back of the guest room closet. Leaving her daily wardrobe behind would buy her a few more precious hours.

Running into the master bathroom, she tripped on the edge of the rug and smacked her hip against the corner of the vanity. *That's going to leave a bruise.* The thought almost made her laugh. Almost.

She opened a drawer. Mascara, moisturizer, concealer. These items could be bought on the road. Her goal was to travel light. She started to shut the drawer, changed her mind, and grabbed the concealer. After checking that both toothbrushes were aligned in the holder, she hung two clean bath towels and straightened the rug. The used towels went into the hamper. She left the room, but returned to run a wet paper towel around the already spotless sinks.

In the bedroom closet, she placed a stepladder under the attic opening, slid the door to the left, raised the insulation, and groped around blindly until her fingers clasped a strap. She lifted a small backpack from its spot, tamped the insulation back into place, and positioned the door evenly before climbing down and stowing the ladder. Halfway out of the closet, she hesitated, went back, and ran a hand over the carpet to erase any indentations. Unzipping the backpack, she shifted through the stacks of twenty-dollar bills wrapped with currency straps—her ticket to freedom.

The phone rang and she froze. She glanced around the bedroom, searching for the hidden camera she'd always suspected but could never find. The phone rang again, the harsh sound echoing through the quiet house. She had no choice but to answer. "Hello?"

"Why do you sound breathless?"

"I…ran for the phone." Carolyn put a trembling hand to her forehead. *Stay calm.*

"I called a minute ago. You didn't answer."

Liar. "I was cleaning—running the vacuum. I didn't hear the phone."

"What are you vacuuming?"

Stupid answer. Now I'll have to vacuum, and there's no time.

"Carolyn?"

She glanced at the ruffled carpet in the closet. Her imperfect camouflage would be covered up with a swipe of the vacuum. "Our bedroom."

"I noticed my bathroom sink looked a little grimy this morning."

Another lie. "Next on my list."

She heard him expel a breath into the receiver and knew what was coming.

"About last night. I didn't expect you to come home early."

Of course, it's my fault that I came home to find my husband with his lover.

"I'm under a lot of stress with the Blanchard account. Taren came over to help me brainstorm."

Carolyn closed her eyes. "Brainstorming wasn't what I walked in on."

"You have no idea the pressure I'm under at work, the stress I endure to provide you with a home and pretty clothes!"

"I work, too, Robert."

"I'm trying to say I'm sorry that things got out of hand," he said, his tone softening.

Again.

"Carolyn, you know it didn't mean anything. You are the only woman in the world for me."

Until your next brainstorming session.

"Look, it wouldn't hurt you to be a little more understanding."

There was so much she wanted to say, and this would be the perfect moment. There would be no repercussions. Thoughts scrambled to the forefront of her mind, but the words would fall on deaf ears. Anything she said would only make him mad, and possibly raise suspicion, since she'd been meticulously taught not to speak out. Besides, they were beyond words, and had been for a long time.

"You know I love you."

You have no idea what love means, and never will.

"Did you hear me?"

"Yes...me, too."

"*You too, what?*"

Carolyn put a hand to her throat to ease the building pressure. Maybe Rob was right. Maybe his making love with Taren meant as nothing as the words he was forcing her to say. "I love you, too."

"How about we go somewhere nice next weekend? We'll take a few days off and just get away."

"That's not necessary, Rob."

"Honey, how many times have I told you to call me Robert?" His voice had taken on the hard edge she was so familiar with. "Shortening my name is unprofessional."

"I don't do it in front of your coworkers." *Even last night when I opened the bedroom door and found you and Taren tangled in our sheets—the sheets you made me sleep on as punishment for coming home early—I called you Robert!*

"Don't do it at all."

A female voice murmured in the background, and Robert cleared this throat. "I have to go. I have a meeting. I'll call you at the restaurant."

He always did. Three o'clock on the dot to make sure she'd arrived. Five o'clock to make sure she was still there. Nine o'clock to check once again before he went to bed. Only tonight someone would be covering for her. "Okay."

"I'll make something special for breakfast, baby."

"Breakfast sounds nice."

"I'll see you in the morning. Oh, and be real quiet when you come home. We didn't get much sleep last night."

He was right. She was berated for coming home early in front of her husband's lover. After Taren left, the berating became violent.

Unfortunately, her compliance to his request for quiet was never reciprocated. Robert making breakfast entailed a gigantic pot-banging mess. After only three hours of sleep, she'd be expected to eat with him, clean the kitchen afterward, and complete a list of chores. Only then would she be able to fall into bed for a quick nap before work.

Except tomorrow morning Robert would wake up to an empty bed. "I'll be very quiet."

"Thanks, doll. See you in the morning."

"Have a nice day, Robert."

As soon as he disconnected the call, she ran for the vacuum. Following through would eat into her valuable time, but not doing the job would raise suspicion before she was far enough away. She vacuumed the bedroom and closet, covering all traces of the ladder.

She lugged the suitcase down the stairs with both hands, careful not to leave scuffmarks on the wooden risers. She wasted precious minutes fumbling with the latch on the car's trunk, wishing she had more time to familiarize herself with the older, nondescript rental. While stowing the suitcase, she raced over her mental checklist, ticking off each item.

Back inside, she ran up the stairs, stumbled, and fell with a *thud*, smacking her shin on the hard wood. *Another bruise.* Backpack over her shoulder and box in her arms, she rushed back down, committing the sound of her heels clacking to a memory entitled *Escape*. She stopped at the door of each room. Everything was mopped, shined, and in its proper place.

No reason for Robert to suspect anything was amiss.

From the kitchen window, her reflection stared back at her. The old glass distorted her features in a weird, Picasso sort of way. The image fit. She pulled her sunglasses from the backpack to cover her black eye and bruised cheek—a gift for coming home early last night—and stepped outside. The fog was thick this morning, which helped conceal her from neighbors' prying eyes. She knew they suspected, yet they never said a word. Better to stay out of others' affairs. She also knew if anyone saw her leaving with a suitcase, they wouldn't say anything to Robert. He'd never win a popularity contest in this neighborhood.

The smell of decaying leaves in the corner of the back-yard wafted past. Mold. Rot. More memories filed under *Escape.*

Mist from the fog settled on her face as she looked at the house she'd called home since graduating from culinary school. The roof needed replacing and the old windows allowed cold air to seep in, but the house had been good to her, and she would miss it.

Turning away, she opened the car door, and slid behind the wheel. Inserting the key in the ignition proved almost impossible, her hands were shaking so hard.

Leaving would only provide temporary security. Rob would find her.

She pulled out of the driveway without a backward glance.

MEMORIAL DAY

Carolyn climbed out of her SUV and shed her sweater. Late May weather was warmer in central Washington than in San Francisco.

The smell of popcorn and hot dogs permeated the air around the ballpark, overriding the ever-present scent of evergreens. Smells she associated with childhood, along with swimming, hiking the trails near Eden Falls, and watermelon after it had been sitting in the river to chill. Memories of the carefree days of youth lifted her spirits with a dizzy exhilaration she hadn't felt in a very long time.

If only there were such a thing as a do-over, a moment you could change from your past that would alter the place where you now lived. A chance to erase the life you'd chosen, but retain the valuable knowledge you'd gained. Of course it wasn't possible, but how many people wished the same? How many regretted that one minute, that one decision, that one day or night or event that shifted the universe?

Truth be told, she had two such moments.

Given the ability, would she do anything differently or would she make the same choices for the same reasons she made them the first time? Would she be able to detect the warning signs and avoid the mistakes, or would she be exactly where she was now?

Regret was a bitter pill and not worth choking down on this beautiful day.

She walked to the high chain-link fence and laid her hands flat against it. The warm metal gave her a sense of security, something unfamiliar yet welcome. Tilting her face to the sun, she closed her eyes and granted herself permission to be happy, even lighthearted, for one afternoon.

The bleachers in the distance were packed for the annual Eden Falls Memorial Day baseball game—Gunslingers vs. Smoke Eaters. The scoreboard showed the Smoke Eaters up by a run. The pitcher wound up and released the ball. A crack resounded as the bat connected. Cheers rose from the crowd.

She took a deep breath, filling her lungs with sweet air, and held it as long as possible.

Her last trip to Eden Falls had been three and a half months earlier. A quick, one-night stay for a friend's wedding. A critical decision that changed the course of her life and led her here, to this moment. Being able to witness her friend's joy had been worth the bruises. The beating finally opened her eyes to possibilities she'd contemplated, even planned for, but had never been brave enough to pursue. Two days later, she left Robert for good.

Another cheer rose over the baseball diamond and she opened her eyes. How hard would it be to re-enter this world she left eleven years earlier? As much as she loved San Francisco, it never fit comfortably. After all these years, she still thought of Eden Falls as home.

It was impossible to know where the winds of life might blow and scatter a life. When she left here, she thought she'd never be back to stay, yet here she was, hoping her gale would settle into a calm breeze and then die completely.

Her attention was drawn back to the field as the two teams exchanged places. Even from here, she could pick out JT Garrett, her adolescent crush, walking to the pitcher's mound. He threw a ball to the first baseman as his sister, Alex, jogged past him to take the shortstop position. The two exchanged a few words, then they laughed.

JT glanced toward the fence. His eyes locked on Carolyn. He tipped up the brim of his hat and stared. He was still as handsome as she remembered him. Her stomach flip-flopped, and not in a good way. Until she secured a job, she'd rather remain anonymous. Without a job, she'd be forced to move on, which would raise questions she didn't want to answer. Better to fly under the radar of Police Chief JT Garrett.

She turned her back to the field and hurried to her SUV. Once inside, she waited, head lowered, until he turned back to the game before she started the car and drove away.

Since it was a holiday, almost everyone in town was at the ballpark. Carolyn had Town Square to herself. Not much had changed in eleven years, which was oddly comforting. The giant ice cream cone in front of One Scoop or Two still spun next door to The Fly Shop. She passed Renaldo's Italian Kitchen with hopes he still served the best pizza in the county. Eden Falls Cinema had survived the economy. The old restaurant next to Pages Bookstore, which had been boarded-up since she was little, was now Noelle's Café. She had breakfast there with friends the morning after Alex's wedding. The exteriors of Eden Falls Emporium and Jiffy Drugs had been updated to the twenty-first century.

The red, white, and blue stripes on Fred's Barbershop pole turned lazily in the mid-morning sun. The empty lot next door caught her eye and she pulled to a stop in front of what used to be Douglas Hardware and Lumber. All that remained of the store were the charred sidewalk and cement slab. The sight left a hole in her heart and she wondered what had happened.

She circled around Town Square again and continued down Main Street. Just before The Dew Drop Inn, she made a snap decision and a quick left turn, drove two blocks, and took another left.

Her car rolled to a stop in front of the three-bedroom ranch that had been her childhood home. Instead of mashed-pea green, the house was painted dove gray with crisp white trim, which made it appear larger. From the street, she could tell the backyard was still bordered by the pines her father planted. Of course, they were much taller now. She remembered lying under a blanket of stars, the cool grass tickling the backs of her bare legs. Sometimes she'd been with girlfriends, Alex or Stella. Most times she was alone.

She turned the engine off and slid from behind the wheel.

The large shade tree in the front yard was gone, replaced by a much smaller one. Grass filled the flowerbeds that used to run along both sides of the driveway, which actually looked much nicer. The lawn was well-manicured and the bushes along the front neatly trimmed.

A red and white sign in the living room window caught her attention. For Rent. And she needed a place to live.

She leaned against the used SUV she'd picked up in some small town in New Mexico. Could she live in the house that held so few happy memories for her?

Worry about a place to live after you secure a job.

She pulled her cell phone from her jeans pocket and stored the phone number on the sign. Just in case things went well tomorrow.

Her stomach growled, reminding her she hadn't eaten since the bagel at breakfast.

In fact, she felt truly hungry for the first time in as long as she could remember.

She decided to grab lunch, browse the furniture store she spotted when leaving Harrisville this morning, and get back to the hotel before dark. Once there, she would close the door on a world that had grown smaller in her three months of travel. She'd fall into a fitful sleep for three or four hours then jolt awake, her heart racing, because that was her routine. In the morning, she'd cover the dark circles under her eyes with concealer and begin her job hunt.

~

JT Garrett surveyed the sea of people on blankets and lawn chairs spread over the lush grass of Town Square. A temporary stage stretched along the north side of the park, with the mountain peaks as the backdrop. Rays from the setting sun reached through the sky like fingers of gold trying to hold onto the last bit of daylight.

A morning person, he loved to watch a new day dawn bright and glorious with promise, but right this second, while the sun lowered over his town, he couldn't remember seeing a more beautiful sight.

Tantalizing smells tickled his senses. He glanced toward the food tents on the opposite side of the park. Benny's Barbecue was selling pork sandwiches and East Winds, bowls of chow mein or fried rice. Renaldo served pizza by the slice and Patsy's Pastries always had an array of tempting sweets for dessert.

Band members took their places on the stage and struck their first chord to cheers and applause. Other than tourists enjoying their Memorial Day weekend here in Eden Falls, almost every face was familiar.

He keyed his radio and asked the other three officers on duty to report their positions. Then he waved to each in turn.

They were a small force. In addition to him, there were five officers and two office staff.

He felt a tug on his shirt. "Hi, Uncle JT!"

"Hey, Charlie." He squatted down eye to eye with his six-year-old nephew. "Are you excited for the fireworks to start?"

"Yeah, but Grandpa said we have to wait until it gets dark."

He ruffled Charlie's black hair. "Not too much longer."

Alex came up behind her son. "If you want a piece of Mom's apple pie, you'd better hurry. Colton's got his eye on it."

JT straightened and glanced over the top of his petite sister's head. His mom and dad sat in the same spot they'd shared with his aunt and uncle since time began. Aunt Glenda always packed a picnic basket of fried chicken and potato salad, and his mom brought her famous apple pie. Their family traditions ran deep and strong.

"Tell your husband to keep his paws off my pie."

"I'll tell him," Charlie said with a snicker, and ran off.

"I thought Brittany was coming to watch you play baseball today," Alex said.

"Yeah." JT tried to ignore his sister's inquisitive stare. "We're not dating anymore."

"Good."

He raised a brow. "Good?"

"Brittany wasn't right for you, and you knew it, or you wouldn't have broken up with her."

"How do you know she didn't break up with me?"

"Because she was already in love with you. You really should break up with them before they reach that point."

"We only went out three times."

"Doesn't matter." Alex slipped her arm through his. "I met a really nice woman at—"

"No."

A frown knit her brows together. "What do you mean, no?"

"I mean I'm tired of people setting me up. In fact, I'm tired of dating." He unhooked her hand from the crook of his arm. "As of tonight, I'm on a dating hiatus."

Alex cocked a hip and crossed her arms. She looked about as threatening as forest pixie. "You'll never meet anyone if you're on hiatus. Don't you trust my judgment?"

"I've decided I don't trust anyone's judgment but my own. I'm tired of being set up with women who have nothing in common with me."

"You're the one who found Brittany."

"No. Brittany's mom and Maude Stapleton are friends. Maude gave Brittany my phone number with the usual *you'll be perfect for each other*. We weren't."

Alex laughed. "You do a great Maude impersonation."

"I don't think she'd appreciate hearing that."

"Will you at least think about meeting this woman? She's a couple of years older than you and has two sweet kids. I really think you'd like her."

"I'll think about it"—JT shook his head—"but I doubt I'll change my mind."

"You're so stubborn."

"No more than you are."

Alex glanced at her son and husband. "I better get back before the fireworks start."

The memory of a beautiful woman flitted through his mind. JT caught his sister's arm before she walked away. "Hey, what make of car does Carolyn drive?"

"Carolyn who?"

"Your friend from high school—Carolyn West—I can't remember her married name."

"Richmond," Alex said wrinkling her nose. "I have no idea what she drives. Why?"

"I swear I saw her at the baseball game."

"No. She would have told me if she was coming into town. I seriously doubt her husband would *allow* her to come again so soon after my wedding. He seems pretty—"

JT's radio crackled. "JT, I need some help. I have a couple of rowdy tourists in the southeast corner of the park, near Patsy's tent."

He keyed the radio. "On my way, Phoebe."

~

Tuesday afternoon, Carolyn parked in front of One Scoop or Two. School was out for the summer and kids were lined up out the door. Two little girls holding hands and chattering away calmed her jittery stomach slightly.

She climbed out of her car and took in her surroundings. Most of the benches around Town Square were occupied with people enjoying the sunshine. Flowers cascaded from the baskets hanging on each light post. Since her friend Alex owned the only flower shop in town, the handiwork was probably hers.

Carolyn pushed her sunglasses up her nose. The frames were big and hid most of her face, although there wasn't much she could do to hide her red hair.

She took a deep breath, squared her shoulders, and turned toward her destination. Patsy's Pastries sat kitty-corner across the square.

She'd only been back to Eden Falls a couple of times since high school graduation, opting to build her now non-existent career instead. What took a lot of sweat, tears, and extremely long hours, had vanished overnight. But the knowledge she gained, both in business and in her personal life, would always be hers.

She stopped in front of the pastry shop. Patsy had hung

a new sign since she was here last, flower pots on each side of the door held clusters of spring blooms, and five of the six bistro tables along the sidewalk, also new, were occupied.

Patsy's Pastries seemed to be doing well.

Carolyn could smell the sticky sweetness from the sidewalk. Once inside, the unseen confections settled on her skin, in her hair—powdered sugar, butter, cinnamon, chocolate—all separate, yet mingling in such a lovely way. The pristine pastry cases were filled with a plethora of color and texture, reminding her she hadn't eaten since her small salad last night. She rested a hand on her growling stomach to silence it and walked to the counter.

The two girls working were too young to be familiar. At one time she'd known almost everyone in town, if not by name, at least by face. Melancholy squirmed under the edge of the defenses she'd built up, but she pushed it back into place. She'd been right to leave Eden Falls and take full advantage of the scholarship to culinary school in San Francisco. As scary as it was to leave everything familiar behind, she had been determined to set her sister free of feeling obligated.

"Hi. Can I help you?" one of the girls asked, breaking into her thoughts.

Carolyn pushed her sunglasses to the top of her head. "Is Patsy here?"

"Sure. Can I tell her—?"

"Carolyn West, is that you?"

Carolyn turned as a vivacious blonde pushed through the swinging kitchen doors carrying a platter of pastel-frosted cupcakes. Her attempted smile was shaky around the edges. She hoped it went unnoticed. "Hi, Patsy."

"I absolutely love that shorter haircut on you, hon. Wish I had natural curl like that." She set the platter down and came around the counter to hug Carolyn. "I wanted to tell you at Alex's wedding, but never got the chance."

Carolyn reached up and gave her short curls a tug. The cut, an impulsive decision, had earned her the small scar under her left eye. Robert hated short hair. "Thank you."

"You in town for a visit?"

Carolyn glanced at the girls behind the counter. Both were flirting with a couple of boys and paying no attention to their conversation. "Actually, I'm hoping you have a moment to talk."

Patsy's smile remained in place. "Let me grab a couple bottles of water. We can sit outside." She turned, hands on hips. "Boys, are you going to buy something, or spend the afternoon gawking at my cute employees? If the answer is gawking, I'll start charging by the minute instead of the muffin. Believe me, I will come out ahead."

Outside, three tables were now vacant. Carolyn lowered her sunglasses and took the one farthest away from people. Her knee bounced in rhythm to her heartbeat—a nervous habit she'd picked up over the years. She was wound so tight, she felt like she might pop out of her skin if touched. *Calm down. The worst she can say is no. You have other options.*

In the past three months, life had become a series of baby steps. One foot carefully placed in front of the other. She tried to make sure one good thing happened each day, one thing she could be grateful for. If things didn't work out here, she'd be thankful for the sunshine. She had a plan and a solid work ethic. She was good at what she did and confident in her skills. Still, she said a silent prayer that Patsy would say yes. *Please, let this be the good thing that happens today.*

Patsy walked into the sunshine carrying two bottles of water in one hand and a small plate in the other. "I heard dessert was your specialty in culinary school."

Carolyn nodded, surprised anyone knew that tidbit.

She set one of the bottles and the plate in front of Carolyn. "Try this, tell me what you think."

Even though she was hungry, her stomach felt too much like a pile of soggy noodles to eat. Yet, if this would get her a job… She picked up what looked like a cranberry scone and nibbled the corner. Before she could say anything, Patsy held up her hand. "I know it's awful. I just can't get the recipe right. I make the most sought-after turnovers in this state, but can't make an edible scone to save my life."

Carolyn swallowed the dry dough, grateful she was spared from comment.

Patsy unscrewed the lid from her water bottle, took a sip, and then relaxed back in her chair. SMART AND BLONDE was emblazoned across the front of her T-shirt. "I always knew you'd grow up to be a gorgeous woman." Patsy laughed. "I can tell you disagree by your frown."

Carolyn wasn't stupid. Gorgeous was beyond her reach, and always had been, but she wouldn't jeopardize her chance at a job by contradicting Patsy.

Patsy crossed one leg over the other and swung her foot back and forth. "By your serious expression, I gather this isn't a social visit, sweetie. What can I do for you?"

Clutching her water bottle like a life preserver, Carolyn took a deep breath. She was a wimp by nature, a card-carrying namby-pamby. To ask for anything was out of her comfort zone, but she was desperate.

With the exception of a small inheritance when her parents were killed in an auto accident, she'd been given nothing in life. Out of necessity, she and her older sister had to grow up quickly. Life wasn't always fair, but she wasn't one to dwell on the injustices. She'd been handed a raw deal and prevailed despite many obstacles. She'd worked hard, graduated culinary school with honors, and clawed her way up the ranks, going above and beyond to earn every promotion.

Her personal problems were of her own making and she would handle them as they occurred. But for now… "I need a job, Patsy."

Patsy's perfectly arched eyebrows rose as the breeze lifted a clump of her stiffly over-sprayed, platinum-colored hair. Carolyn, who had never really looked at her until this moment, realized Patsy was a beautiful woman. A few fine lines ran from the corners of her eyes, and she wore parentheses around her mouth, but she had them for good reason. Patsy was a happy person and smiled more often than not.

She was also blunt and wasn't afraid to say exactly what she thought, which Carolyn was nervous about at the moment. If Patsy said no, Carolyn had other options. But Patsy's Pastries was her first choice.

She had fond memories of the bakery, which had been the go-to place after school. Patsy's donuts were melt-in-your-mouth delicious and she sold a wide variety of cupcakes even before they became a fad.

"I heard you were a sous chef at a fancy restaurant in San Francisco."

"I was." Carolyn hoped she'd only have to share the bare basics.

Patsy's eyebrows rose higher.

"I wasn't fired or anything. I will give you the manager's number." She didn't want to involve Trish. The less the restaurant manager knew, the better, just in case Robert called, again. He already suspected Trish knew more than she let on. He'd visited her at her home to try intimidation, but Trish had stood her ground. "I left in good standing. After coming home for Alex's wedding, I realized how much I miss Eden Falls. I decided it was time to come home."

Patsy's gaze dropped to Carolyn's left hand, to her bare

ring finger. Carolyn struggled not to lower her hand to her lap.

"Things didn't work out?"

She shook her head, hoping it would be answer enough.

Patsy's expression turned empathetic. "Is that a good thing or a bad thing?"

Carolyn bit into her bottom lip. "A little of both, I guess. It's hard to admit to a failed—" She stopped and her chest heated with embarrassment. Patsy had been married and divorced several times. She glanced away.

Patsy reached across the table and put a hand on Carolyn's arm. "Don't I know it, sister. I'm up to four of those failures."

"I'm sorry. I shouldn't have—"

"What? Said to my face what everyone else in this town says behind my back?" Patsy waved a hand. "I don't care what the gossips say. I did my best to make my marriages work. If you did too, you have nothing to be ashamed of."

"I tried." *To the point of being afraid for my life.* Still, the thought didn't lessen her feeling of failure.

Patsy slapped the table, startling her. "Fate. Do you believe in it?"

Would a "yes" get her a job? "I haven't really thought about it much, but…I do believe things happen for a reason."

"Well, I believe we are led to places we're supposed to be, and you just might be the answer I've been searching for." She didn't explain further, just picked up the scone and pointed it at Carolyn. "Can you make these things?"

"Yes."

"Better than this?"

Carolyn's knee began to bounce, shaking the table. This was more nerve-wracking than middle school truth or dare. She opted for truth. "Yes."

"When can you start?"

"Now?" she squeaked out around the lump in her throat.

Patsy's laugh was as authentic as it had been when Carolyn was a teen. Like comfort food for the soul. "How about Friday morning at four? Meet me at the back door."

She wanted to fall down on her knees in both thanksgiving and tears. Her one good thing had happened. "Thank you, Patsy."

Patsy's eyes narrowed. "You're not in any kind of trouble, are you, hon?"

"No." Her quick, clipped answer sounded as guilty as she felt saying the word.

Patsy's mouth twisted to the side for a split second and Carolyn held her breath until Patsy nodded. "I'll see you Friday morning."

Patsy stood, dumped the scone in a nearby trashcan, and opened the shop door. "Okay, boys, you've loitered long enough. Either buy something or you're outta here."

When the door swung shut, Carolyn wilted in her chair, relief washing over her in waves. She had a job. They hadn't discussed hours, or pay, or if benefits were available, but she didn't care. She had a job.

Next on her To Do List: Find a place to live.

Carolyn pulled out her cell phone and scrolled to the number she entered when she was in front of her childhood home. She had no idea what the rental market was like around here, but it couldn't be worse than San Francisco.

Glancing down the street toward Pretty Posies, she pushed up from her chair. She had a job, so she should probably tell Alex she was back in town. And because Alex was the mayor, she would know about rentals and rates.

She passed several storefronts until she stood in front of the flower shop. Alex's grandmother had built Pretty Posies years ago, in an abandoned Green Stamp store. As a young girl, Carolyn spent many hours here with Alex. They'd stop by after school and visit with Grandma Garrett while she assembled breathtaking arrangements. Along with inheriting the shop after her grandmother's death, Alex was also gifted with Grandma Garrett's talent for creating uniquely gorgeous bouquets.

The door was propped open and Carolyn stepped inside. The interior was different, but still very much the same. Alex would never change it enough that she'd erase her grandmother's presence. Carolyn took in the colorful displays and the pungent smell, as aromas mixed one with another, some tangy and bitter, some sweet and heady.

Alex was behind the counter with a girl Carolyn met at Alex's wedding. The girl's name eluded her, but her black Goth outfit was memorable. Today she had pink and green streaks running through her dark hair. An off-the-shoulder T-shirt covered in neon purple skulls topped her black tutu skirt.

"Hi, Alex."

Alex turned and released an ear-splitting screech as she dashed around the counter. "Carolyn! JT said he saw you yesterday. I told him that you wouldn't come to town and not tell me. What are you doing here?"

"It was a spur-of-the-moment decision." Carolyn wrapped her arms around Alex's tiny frame, the sting of tears threatening. Alex had been her first friend when she moved to Eden Falls in the third grade, and one of her best friends until she left for college. Just standing here felt so completely right. She'd been lost a long time, taken a few wrong turns on her journey, been stopped by a couple of dead ends, but she'd finally chosen a one-way road in the right direction. She had a job.

"How long can you stay? Please tell me longer than your last trip."

"Yes."

Alex's eyes widened along with her smile. "Really? Long enough we can have a girls' night out?"

"Even longer."

Alex's smile faltered. "What?"

Carolyn held her arms out at her sides, then let them drop. "I'm moving back. I start at Patsy's this Friday."

"Patsy's?" Confusion clouded Alex's expression. "But you're a chef. You graduated from culinary school. You've been featured in food magazines."

Carolyn shrugged while trying to keep her expression neutral. "The hours were crazy."

With narrowed eyes, Alex took Carolyn's hand. "Let's go in the back and have a talk. Tatum, Carolyn. Carolyn, Tatum," she said as they passed her Goth-y assistant.

Right, Tatum.

Tatum wrinkled her nose, the left nostril pierced. "Good luck."

In the back room, Alex pulled a stool from under her worktable and pointed. "Sit."

Carolyn did as she was told while admiring her beautiful friend. Marriage certainly agreed with her. "You look happy."

Alex's smile returned, her mossy green eyes sparkling with an inner joy Carolyn envied. "This will sound stupid, but I feel like I'm floating on the sunny side of the rainbow. It doesn't seem fair to be this happy."

"It doesn't sound stupid. You deserve a place on the sunny side. How's Charlie?"

Alex slid onto a stool next to her. "He's excited to be out of school for the summer. Baseball starts in a week, and he'll drive me nuts until it does."

"And Colton?"

"Fabulous. Loving small town life, busy doing things he never thought he'd do. When he's not writing his next best-selling murder mystery, he's bowling or fishing or kicking a soccer ball with Charlie."

"I'm happy everything worked out for you all."

"We had a rough start, but things did work out." Alex nodded toward her. "Now you. What's going on? And don't tell me you're moving back because of crazy hours."

Carolyn shrugged. "Things didn't work out."

"At the restaurant?"

Carolyn lifted her left hand and Alex's eyes dropped to her ring finger. "Oh, Care, here I am going on and on about how happy I am, and you—"

Carolyn waved her ring-free hand. "Don't you dare apologize for being happy."

"I'm sorry."

"Don't be sorry, either. It's for the best."

Alex's expression shifted as concern puckered her eyebrows. "Do you want to talk about it?"

Carolyn felt her façade slip. What she wanted was to erect a sign that read *Restricted Area. Keep Out!* "Maybe someday. Not now."

"From sous chef to a job with Patsy. Are you sure you'll be happy?"

Her feelings of worthlessness surfaced like floating garbage in a polluted lake. Robert had whittled her already fragile self-esteem to nothing. *How you ever made sous chef is beyond me. This chicken tastes like you dredged it in dirt. Maybe next time you could try leaving some moisture in the cake instead of baking it all out. Please, explain how you graduated culinary school with honors. Were you sleeping with the chefs?*

She was tired of questioning herself, of living with regrets and feeling bad about her choices. And she was tired of running. She wanted to settle down in a place and feel safe.

Carolyn looked down to hide the threatening tears. She

was tired of crying, too, of feeling insignificant, alone, and unloved. Above all, she was tired of being afraid.

Alex leaned closer and hugged her. "I'm sorry. I shouldn't have said that. It's just such a huge shift in your universe."

Carolyn straightened her spine and met Alex's gaze. "It's a shift I'm looking forward to. I'm ready for a change. I love to make desserts and what better place to bake than at Patsy's?"

"Patsy will welcome the help. She's run that shop by herself since we were little." Alex leaned an elbow on the worktable. "Where are you staying?"

"I'm in a hotel until I find a place." She ran her thumbnail along a gouge in the table. "I noticed the house my family lived in before my parents' accident is up for rent. Do you know who owns it?"

"Leo Sawyer bought it. Remember the Sawyers?"

"The name sounds familiar."

"They own the organic farm out by Jillian's house. Leo was a few years ahead of us in school. He wore black-framed glasses and worked at the library."

"Oh, I do remember him, kind of geeky, but really nice. He helped me with that horrible science project I barely passed our freshman year."

"He started a software company right out of college, moved it to Silicon Valley, and then sold it for millions two years ago. Since moving back, he's been funding a lot of improvements around town. He helped revitalize Riverside Park and has bought several bankrupt and foreclosed properties. He fixes them up and either rents or sells them. Volunteers at the animal shelter, donates to charities, lives in a gorgeous house he built overlooking the river."

"Sounds like he's still a nice guy."

"A very nice guy. I know I'm asking a lot of questions, but are you sure you want to move back into that house?

You didn't exactly come away with many happy memories."

Alex was well aware of how ignored she'd been as a child, but Carolyn didn't hold a grudge against her parents for loving Catherine better, or for the way her sister treated her after her parents' death. She understood where the anger came from. Catherine had been standing on the cusp of freedom with a college degree in hand when their parents died. She could have placed Carolyn in foster care rather than put her life on hold until her little sister graduated from high school. Carolyn would be forever grateful for Catherine's choice.

"It isn't the house that holds bad memories, it's me. And it's long past time I let them go."

Alex pulled her cell phone from the back pocket of her jeans. "Want me to call Leo for you?"

"Would you?"

While Alex set up an appointment to see the house, Carolyn looked around the workroom. She'd spent so many hours here with Alex, finishing homework while Grandma Garrett arranged flowers, eating homemade cookies, hoping to catch a glimpse of Alex's older brother, JT.

Alex disconnected the call. "It's all set. He'll meet you at the house in an hour."

"Thank you."

"Anything, anytime, my friend." Alex stood. "Hand me that fluted pink vase on the shelf behind you, will ya?"

Carolyn easily reached the vase Alex would have had to use a stool to get.

Alex moved around the table, gathering flowers from their individual buckets. Grandma Garrett had taught Alex and her friends the Victorian language of flowers. Carolyn wasn't sure she remembered much, but Alex took those meanings to heart and used them in her arrangements.

She placed bunches of lilacs—first emotions of love, daffodils—new beginnings, and sprigs of fern—sincerity, together. She always made it look so easy, but Carolyn knew it wasn't. She'd never been able to create the beauty Alex could pull together in moments.

"I don't remember their meaning," Carolyn said when Alex added white hyacinths.

"Beauty."

"You still create bouquets like I've never seen anywhere else."

Alex raised her eyebrows. "Guess who this is for?"

"Obviously someone I know."

"Misty."

Carolyn smiled. The gesture felt so good she almost cried.

"Misty had a rocky start to her year. She found her mom in Sacramento, only to have Arleen abandon her a second time, taking everything Misty owned."

Their friend Misty always thought finding her mother would change her life for the better. She believed that once her mom saw her, she'd be filled with regret, and spend the rest of her life making up for leaving Misty behind. "Poor Misty."

"Actually, it was the best thing that could have happened. The experience finally opened her eyes to the kind of person she was becoming. She came home, apologized to a lot of people, and got her job at Dahlia's Salon back. She's turned over a domestic leaf, too. She changes diapers and cooks."

As hard as she tried, Carolyn couldn't imagine the mean girl of their group of six cooking or changing diapers.

Alex pinched a brown-at-the-edge petal and added another twist to the bow. "Occasionally, she slips into her old self, but she's pretty quick to catch it. She, Beam, and Sophia are a darling, mostly well-adjusted little family."

"I'm happy for her. For them. Beam deserves wonderful and, I guess after what Misty went through, she does too."

The bell over the front door tinkled merrily and, like a light switch had been flipped, Alex's expression melted into serene. "That's my husband."

Carolyn glanced at the door leading to the front of the shop. "How do you know?"

"Because the door was propped open and he always jingles the bell." A moment later a male voice carried into the back room. Colton didn't take long to find his way to his wife's side, taking Alex in his arms and kissing her passionately. Carolyn tried to look away, but there was something so magnetic about the pair, it was impossible not to watch.

Alex finally pulled back and pointed to her. "McCreed, you remember Carolyn."

Colton turned and flashed a grin. "Hey, Carolyn. Sorry about that. I didn't know Alex had company."

Carolyn held up a hand. "Don't be sorry. I love to see my friend so happy." It was obvious she was extremely so. Alex's first husband was killed in Iraq. Alex was notified the same day she took a positive pregnancy test. Based on what Carolyn saw at the wedding, Alex chose a very good stepdad for her six-year-old son, Charlie.

Alex unwrapped herself from her husband's arms. "Guess what, McCreed? Carolyn is moving back to Eden Falls."

"That's great."

"She's meeting Leo Sawyer in an hour about one of his rentals." Alex glanced at her. "Why don't we have a barbecue tonight to celebrate you coming home? I'll invite the gang over."

"Sounds good," Colton said. "Make a grocery list. I'm on my way to the pool to pick Charlie up. He can come with me."

Carolyn stopped Alex before she could grab a pen and

paper. Her pulse had shifted into overdrive at the suggestion of "the gang". "I appreciate dinner, Alex, but I'm not sure I'm ready to face everyone yet. Maybe once I find a place to live…"

"Sorry. Insensitivity seems to be my middle name today," Alex said. "New plan. Dinner at six-thirty, but just the three of us and Charlie."

Carolyn nodded. *That I can handle.*

CHAPTER 3

Patsy Yarberry's thoughts remained on Carolyn throughout the afternoon. She'd pursued a dream, graduated culinary school with honors, and worked long, hard hours to become a chef at a five-star San Francisco restaurant. She was an Eden Falls success story. She was young, gorgeous, and accomplished.

So why was she asking for a job in a small town bakery?

Patsy pulled out a chair and scrubbed at sticky fingerprints, one of the drawbacks of serving frosting and glazes to pint-sized patrons.

She remembered Carolyn's parents. They'd been older when Carolyn's mom finally conceived and gave birth to Catherine. They'd doted on that girl, built their lives around her. She was their pride and joy, and half grown when Carolyn surprised them. Their routine as a family had been set and the new baby caused a rift in their Catherine-centered world.

Divorce was hard, but Patsy believed Carolyn was too strong a person to give up on her dreams and come back because of a broken marriage. She knew how to go after what she wanted. Something else must have happened.

Straightening, she put a hand to the small of her back. Having someone so capable—a culinary school graduate, no less—a body she could count on in her kitchen, would be a dream come true. The high school kids weren't always dependable. If she woke up with the flu, she had no choice but to close the shop for a couple of days. Juanita Mezo helped occasionally, but the woman was in her seventies, so Patsy only called her when she was truly in a bind.

Carolyn could be trusted to open the shop and start the ovens, which would allow Patsy the luxury of sleeping past three a.m. one or two mornings a week.

Sticky fingerprints on the door stood out like black on white when the sun hit them, so Patsy went into the kitchen to get glass cleaner and paper towels. She squatted, her knees popping, and hoped she could get back up when she finished. The girls who worked today were supposed to do this before they left. She wondered how good Carolyn was at policing teens.

Patsy also wondered if Carolyn could possibly rev up some of the worn-out recipes, add some fresh ones of her own, and take over some of the daily responsibilities. The thought of having a life outside the shop, to take a few days off, possibly travel to another state, was euphoric. She'd always wanted to take a cruise.

She loved her bakery, loved seeing smiles on the faces of her customers, but she was tired. Carolyn's name would spread through town faster than a juicy piece of gossip. The locals who frequented her shop would come in to compare Patsy's pastries to a real master. The ones who didn't come in regularly wouldn't be able to resist the temptation of seeing Patsy fall to that master. She'd have the last laugh, because she wasn't too proud to welcome new recipes and the revenue they would generate.

Since she had the glass cleaner out, she turned to polish the pastry cases, her knees protesting loudly, again.

The door opened, and her reason for wanting more of a life stepped inside. He stopped dead when he spotted her, a little kid caught with the last cookie expression on his face. Patsy enjoyed the nervous tingle that ran through her at the sight of him.

The straight line of his posture and sharp angle of his jaw gave him the air of an English gentleman from the historical novels she read. She could imagine him in eighteenth century attire, nervously removing his top hat and bowing. The gray running through his dark hair and the wrinkles at the corners of his eyes made him look even more distinguished.

She'd noticed Mason Douglas for years. He was sweet, in a slightly awkward way, and handsome. His wife had abandoned him and their daughter more than twenty years ago, and he'd been alone ever since. She knew part of the reason was his daughter. Misty was not the sharing type. The poor girl had naively believed her mother would return one day and wanted her father unattached and waiting with open arms. Sadly, that scenario never played out.

He held out his hand to help her up.

They sure don't make 'em like you anymore. She put her hand in his and stood.

She loved the touch of color that moved up his neck. For a man who was almost sixty, he was unusually shy and old-fashioned, but she loved that, too—not that she was *in* love. The most they'd ever done was sit next to each other at the Memorial Day baseball game yesterday, and that was at her invitation, or it wouldn't have happened. Other than him holding her elbow to steady her steps up the bleachers, they hadn't touched. Well, he hadn't touched her. She'd put her hand on his arm several times while they talked. She was a people person and liked human contact, even if it was only verbal.

Still, yesterday was one of the best days she'd had in a long time. "Hi there, handsome."

"Hello, Patsy." He pushed his glasses into place on his nose. "How are you?"

Another thing she loved about him. He asked and then listened. The habit probably came from years of living with his selfish, self-centered daughter. "Fabulous now that you're here. I was afraid you might decide I was a little more than you can handle."

Frown lines appeared between his brows in the cutest way. "No, Patsy. I wouldn't—you're not—" He cleared his throat. "Beam and I met with our insurance agent and the construction company today."

She probably shouldn't have said that. The poor guy was nervous enough without her making it worse. "Sounds like you had an interesting day."

He nodded.

"I did, too."

"Would you..." He swallowed and his Adam apple bobbed. She'd like to kiss that spot on his throat. "I would like to take you to dinner—if you're free." His ears turned the same shade of red as his neck. "I mean, if you don't already have plans. I...I know this is short notice." He shook his head as if trying to clear his thoughts. "I should have called first. I'm sorry."

She smiled. He'd probably been practicing that invitation all day, which she found endearing. Mason wasn't a spur-of-the-moment type. He studied things in his mind, worked out all the angles. She was more of a fly-by-the-seat-of-her-pants type.

Perhaps that was why she'd made so many bad choices in

men. Four times married—yes, she was the talk of the town. And had been for as long as she could remember. Luckily, being the brunt of jokes didn't bother her. Let them talk. Actually, she liked to shake the residents up once in a while. Otherwise, life got kinda stale.

Mason, on the other hand, was the soul of discretion. He led a very quiet life. Being seen with her might change that. She sure didn't want to tarnish his reputation as a solid, upstanding pillar of the community.

"Are you sure that's a good idea?"

A look of confusion passed over his face. "I don't understand."

Of course you don't, you sweet man. "I would love to join you for dinner."

"I could…would six o'clock give you enough time? I'll pick you up."

"I can meet you at Noelle's Café if that would be easier."

He nodded. "We could go to Noelle's or…I was thinking we could go somewhere a little nicer. Beam recommended a place in Harrisville."

Pride raised its ugly head. *Does he really want to take me somewhere nicer, or somewhere we won't be recognized?*

"I don't mean Noelle's isn't nice." His face was beet-red now. "I just thought…for our first date…"

She had to remember who she was speaking to—a man completely without guile. She got on tiptoe and kissed his cheek. "You are the sweetest man I've ever met. I'll be ready at six."

One side of his mouth lifted—another place she'd like to kiss. "I'll see you then."

She watched him disappear down the street. Six would give her enough time to get home and shower. Smelling like spun sugar would be enticing to a six-year-old, but a man might like something a little more feminine.

Anticipation shimmied through her system, but she tamped it down firmly. *It's just a dinner invitation, old girl. Don't get all worked up over a Meatloaf Special.*

~

Carolyn was lucky Leo Sawyer could meet her before she was due at Alex's house for dinner. More memories of Leo were coming back to her. He'd been a loner through school, always sitting by himself, or with Phoebe Adams. Carolyn had always puzzled over their odd boy-girl friendship, because most people who didn't know them thought they were a couple.

Leo's parents, longhaired hippies wearing fringe, tie-dyed clothing, and piles of beads, had been arrested more than once for marijuana possession. They owned an organic farm just outside of town where they sold vegetables from a psychedelic VW van-turned-roadside-stand during the summer. When she was old enough, she used to ride her bike past the farm on the way to her friend Jillian's house.

She stopped in the driveway of her childhood home and a truck pulled in right behind her. She wasn't sure what she expected, but it wasn't the handsome man who climbed out and approached. Gone were the thick glasses, ankle pants, and acne. He wore aviators—that he raised to the top of his head—with jeans and a T-shirt that clung enough to show off some nicely defined muscles.

He laughed, and she liked the sound—deep and honest. "Carolyn West? I never would have guessed."

"Leo Sawyer, neither would I." She held out her hand, but he pulled her into a hug. Her body tensed on contact and she jerked away. Surprise flashed across his face, but he masked it quickly. A man hadn't touched her since she left Robert.

She regretted her hasty reaction, but couldn't have stopped it if she tried.

"I guess we've both changed. Your braids are gone."

She smiled. "So are your glasses."

He looked her over from head to toe and smiled. Even as a geeky teenager, he had a wonderful smile. That hadn't changed. "You look great."

"So do you." She flushed at the compliment and turned toward the house so he wouldn't notice. She'd always been a blusher, but the sight wasn't pretty. The burning started on her chest and surged over her face until she was scarlet and her brown freckles even more pronounced. White blotches followed, making her look like she should be rushed to the hospital.

"What do you think?"

"It feels strange to be standing here after all these years." Catherine had refused to live in the house after their parents' accident. She sold it and put Carolyn's share into a college fund, which she hadn't used, thanks to her full-ride scholarship. Catherine moved them into a dreary one-bedroom apartment, where Carolyn slept on a sleeper sofa in the living room until she left for California.

She used to ride her bike past after the new family moved in and wonder who slept in her tiny front bedroom.

"I hope you won't be disappointed with the interior. I made major changes so it would be more rentable—and marketable, if I decide to sell."

Poor Leo thought she had an attachment to the place where she grew up feeling like an outsider. "I like the exterior paint. The color's great."

He pushed his hands into the front pockets of his jeans. "I have to credit Benjamin Moore."

"Can I see the inside?"

She followed Leo onto the just-large-enough-for-two-chairs porch. While he unlocked the door, she glanced toward the mountains, remembering how many sunsets she'd watched from these steps. He pushed the door wide and she stepped inside, expecting emotions to assault her. Instead, she felt nothing.

Once-yellow walls were now a soft gray. Harwood floors replaced the putrid green carpet. The doorway between the living room and kitchen had been widened, making both rooms seem much larger.

When Leo appeared beside her, she jumped slightly.

Concern etched his brow. "Are you okay? That's the second time I've startled you."

She waved a hand, embarrassed by her reaction. Robert used to love to sneak up on her, try to catch her in a vulnerable moment. "I'm fine, just jumpy from the move, I guess."

"Are you sure you're not upset by the changes I've made?"

She glanced around at the enlarged living room, the beautiful flooring, and patterns the sunlight made coming through the blinds on the front window. "I'm positive."

He pointed to the back of the house. "Want to see the kitchen?"

She walked ahead of him so he wouldn't see her second blush. Beautiful wood cupboards replaced the old metal ones, and a walk-in pantry had been added. The space must have come from the master bedroom's closet. A bay window, which overlooked a new patio, enlarged the eating area. The laundry room, just inside the carport door, was the same. "Wow."

He moved around to face her. "Is that a good wow?"

"Everything is beautiful. I love the bay window and the pantry is a wonderful addition."

His shoulders visibly relaxed.

"The changes don't bother me, Leo. You didn't erase any fond memories."

He leaned a hip against the wall separating the kitchen from the living room. "Everyone has fond memories of their childhood home. Even me, and I grew up with throwback hippies."

She smiled. "How are your parents? Do they still have their organic farm?"

"Yep, still growing vegetables"—he sighed—"among other things."

She looked out at the backyard. "That's where my fond memories took place. Changes to the interior won't bother me."

He nodded toward the opposite end of the house.

She walked down the short hall, into a bedroom that had once been two, glad to see the wall between was gone. There were more lonely hours than happy memories of the room that once had been hers. Hours spent wishing she'd been born before Catherine.

The enlarged hall bathroom was a dream. The avocado sink, tub, and toilet had been replaced and some of the space from her small bedroom was now a beautifully tiled shower.

The back wall of her parents' room had been bumped out and a bathroom added. The closet was moved to the other inside wall, explaining the extra space for the kitchen pantry.

She turned to Leo. "This is gorgeous."

"You like it?" he asked as if he didn't quite believe her.

"Who wouldn't? It's beautiful, Leo."

"I never thought I'd be showing this house to previous owners who might have a personal attachment."

"I was too young to form any personal attachments."

"I read an article about you in a food magazine. I even came into your restaurant when I lived near San Francisco."

"You did? Why didn't you say hi?"

He shrugged. "It was a busy night. I figured you'd be too slammed to come out of the kitchen."

"You should have sent word back with your waiter. I would have made time."

"The food was excellent."

"Ah"—she smiled—"you caught us on a good night."

He politely laughed at her sad attempt at humor. She wasn't a funny person.

"Are you going to work at a restaurant around the area?"

"I start at Patsy's on Friday."

She braced herself for questions, but he simply nodded.

They discussed rent. Utilities were included and everything was within the budget she set for herself.

"Most of the neighbors are elderly. They won't appreciate loud music or all-night parties."

She had to smile at that. There would be no loud music or all-night parties. She'd be up way before the sun. The elderly neighbors would probably be keeping her up. "I'll be a very low-key, quiet neighbor."

A bit more of the weight on her shoulders lifted. Three happy things happened today. She had a job, a place to live, and she was having dinner with a friend.

After signing the lease, she waved to Leo as he drove away. Key in hand, Carolyn wanted to do a happy dance and shout for joy.

Maybe a do-over is possible after all.

~

*M*idafternoon, JT walked the perimeter of Eden Falls Town Square, as was his habit when he was on duty. He liked the business owners to know he was close by if they needed him. Maude Stapleton stepped out to meet him in front of Pages Bookstore, as was *her* habit. "It's a beautiful afternoon, JT."

"It sure is."

"Any leads on the lumberyard fire?"

He wished people would quit asking. He'd be the first to tell everyone when there was a break in the case. It really soured his gut that the perpetrator remained free. "Not yet."

"Sorry about the Gunslingers' loss yesterday."

He lifted a shoulder. "The Smoke Eaters played a great game."

"That they did."

He pulled the shop's door open for two young girls as they approached. They broke out in a fit of giggles when he winked.

Maude raised a brow.

"I can't help being irresistible."

"If you're so irresistible, why did Brittany break up with you after only three dates?"

Since Maude was the one who'd given Brittany his phone number, he'd spare her the truth of who broke up with whom. "We had nothing in common."

"I told her she should have given it more time."

"I think we both knew after one date."

Maude put her hands on her hips and stood toe-to-toe with him. "How are the two of you so different?"

"The biggest difference was I want kids. She doesn't."

"She doesn't want them right away."

He smiled down at the redheaded fireball. "That's not what she told me."

"You should both stop being so picky."

"You sound like Alex."

"I always said that sister of yours was a smart cookie."

"Really? 'Cause when I told her Brittany and I weren't

dating anymore, her exact words were, 'Good, Brittany wasn't right for you.'"

"Oh"—Maude flapped a hand—"what does Alex know?"

JT laughed and opened the door for two more bookstore customers.

"When are you going to find a nice girl and settle down?"

Good question. "I guess when a nice girl finds me." He was tired of the back-and-forth game they were playing. Time to change the subject. "Business looks like it's good."

Maude grinned. "It's been one of the best springs ever for the bookstore."

A police cruiser pulled to a stop at the curb. Mac Johnson lowered the window on the passenger side. "JT, Mr. Polanski is missing some chickens. He swears Sasquatch is up in the trees behind his place. I'm going to drive out that way and take a look. I suspect kids cut the wire on the back of his coop. Again."

"Thanks, Mac. Hey, since you'll be near Ms. Kennedy's place, will you stop to pick up her grocery list? Tell her I'll be by on Friday."

"Will do." Mac raised the window and drove away.

Maude looked at him over the top rim of her glasses. "I don't care what anyone else says about you, JT, you're a good man."

"Yeah, well, let's keep that between us."

Her bawdy laugh hung in the air as she walked into her shop.

JT turned to the square where two parks and recreation workers were taking down the Memorial Day Concert on the Square banner. The holiday celebration was a success, with only minor scuffles and altercations, which wasn't unusual for their sleepy town. Even when their population almost doubled with summer tourists, Eden Falls remained fairly quiet.

Their biggest happenstance of the year, which he considered major, was the fire at the lumberyard. Eden Falls Hardware and Lumber burned to the ground two months earlier. The fire was ruled arson, but there still were no leads. People had been questioned. No one had seen anything out of the ordinary. JT had walked the area with the state fire marshal several times. They found evidence the fire was deliberately set, but with no witnesses, the case had ground to a standstill.

He'd been with the police department since college graduation and moved into the position of police chief three years earlier with confidence. That arson had happened in his town, that he still, after three months, didn't have a handle on the situation didn't sit well. Irrationally, he felt as if he was letting the owners, Mason Douglas and his own cousin Beam, along with the residents of Eden Falls down.

JT walked past the library and took the stone steps two at a time up to the front door of the police station. He waved to Gianna at the front desk and turned toward his office. Helen, his energetic and efficient assistant, put a hand over the receiver of her own phone and rolled her eyes dramatically. He didn't want to know, but was sure he'd hear sooner or later.

He wrote a note on a Post-it that he wanted a staff meeting Friday morning and stuck it to her hand. She nodded.

Entering his office, he shut the door and walked to the window, ignoring the stack of paperwork he'd been putting off. Helen was good about weeding out the unimportant stuff but he still spent too much time at his desk, a definite drawback of being chief.

When he heard Helen tapping on his door, he glanced over his shoulder. "Yeah."

She stuck her head in. "Mac needs you at the Polanski farm. Apparently Mr. Polanski has Bigfoot on the run."

~

*P*atsy opened her front door and enjoyed the look of appreciation on Mason's face clear down to her toes. He'd seen her in a dress at Alex and Colton's wedding, but before that, it had probably been years. She lived in jeans and tees.

He swallowed and she pressed her lips together at the sight of his Adam's apple bobbing.

"You look…lovely," he said, in a hushed voice.

Lovely. Patsy smiled. "I don't think I've ever been called lovely. I like that word."

She picked up her purse and shawl lying on a nearby chair, flipped the lock on her front door, and stepped outside, pulling it shut behind her.

"I didn't know where you lived. I had to look up your address." He glanced at the surrounding houses. "I've always liked this neighborhood."

She knew where he lived. In a beautiful house he'd built soon after buying the lumberyard more than twenty years ago. "My house is probably small by your standards."

Another look of confusion passed over Mason's expression. "I don't have any standards."

She raised a brow. Kinda mean on her part, but she couldn't resist making him blush again.

Color moved up his neck. "I mean…I guess I don't understand what you mean by my standards."

"You live in a big house, mine is tiny, only two bedrooms."

"Mine is only big because that's what my wife—" He stopped suddenly and his ears turned as red as his neck. "Sorry, I didn't mean to mention Arleen on our date, but she wanted the big house."

"Don't be sorry. Those exes are part of our lives, whether we like 'em or not."

Mason tentatively took her elbow and guided her down the porch steps. "Your house matches your personality. It's painted a sunny color, the lawn is well-manicured, and it's situated in a nice neighborhood."

He was too cute for words. "So, you think I'm sunny, well-manicured, and nice?"

"I… Well, yes… I do think those things." The skin over his nose puckered. "My words didn't come out in a very complimentary way."

She laid a hand on the lapel of his jacket. "Thank you, Mason. You are a sweet man."

He escorted her to his car, opened the passenger door, and she slipped inside. When he walked around to the driver's side, she could see his lips moving slightly. Possibly giving himself a pep talk to relax.

Part of his nervousness might be due to his daughter, Misty. Even though she was married and no longer under his roof, Patsy imagined she still frowned on him dating. Most kids from broken marriages probably hoped their parents would one day get back together, but after twenty years, Mason getting back with Arleen was highly unlikely, and Misty was old enough to get over it.

If asked, Patsy would have to admit she hadn't felt this nervous since a high school date with the football quarter-back, many, many, *many* years ago. Mindless babble might ease their tension. As soon as he got in the car, she started talking. They discussed the weather and rehashed the baseball game during the fifteen-minute drive to Harrisville. She would save contemplating how much higher the river would rise with the spring runoff until they reached the restaurant.

When he pulled into the parking lot of Portelli's, he glanced her way. "I should have asked if you like Italian. I just assumed…since I've seen you at Renaldo's. We can go somewhere else if you prefer."

"I love Italian."

Relief washed over his face.

A hostess showed them to a table. Mason pulled out her chair and her heart thumped as if he'd given her their first kiss. When was the last time a man held her chair for her? She glanced over her menu while Mason took his seat. She heard Portelli's was good and looked forward to trying something new. She knew Mason didn't date often. Had he already brought a woman here?

She glanced over the top of her menu "Everything looks good. What do you recommend?"

Mason picked up his own menu. "I've never eaten here, but Beam said the food is wonderful. He brought Misty here a few weeks ago."

Had Mason told his son-in-law who he was bringing here tonight? If so, Misty probably knew by now. Would he get a call that his daughter had a terrible stomachache? Patsy heard that was a stunt she pulled when she was little. She smiled at the thought. She wouldn't put anything past Misty.

A waitress brought glasses of water and a basket of bread to their table. Once they placed their orders, Mason picked up the basket and held it out to her.

"You said you had an interesting day. Would you like to tell me about it?"

Patsy selected a roll and placed it on a small plate by her water glass. "You first. I drove past the hardware store. All the debris is gone and the lot is empty."

"Yes, a construction crew cleared it away before Memorial Day. The lot looks eerie, but construction starts next Monday, so it won't be bare for long."

He removed his glasses and cleaned them on his napkin, revealing the bridge of his nose—one more place she'd like to kiss. "If this is too personal a question, you don't have to answer, but as a business owner, I'm curious. Will your insurance cover the cost of the new building?"

He flashed a rare and beautiful smile. "Not too personal. I have very good insurance, even before Beam bought into the business. So, yes, they will cover most of the cost. Since Beam and I are starting from the ground up, so to speak, we'll expand a little. He has some great ideas. Did you know his brother Rowdy has some architectural training from college? He drew up plans for an expansion."

"I didn't know." Patsy smoothed her napkin over her lap. "I'm happy for you. I'm sure both you and Beam are anxious to get the store up and running again."

"Beam more than me. I'm embarrassed to admit the offer for my son-in-law to buy into the business was selfish on my part. I knew if he accepted, it would provide him a good living, but it would also keep my beautiful granddaughter in Eden Falls."

Patsy rested her forearms on the table. "Not selfish."

"A little selfish. Once we get the building up, I plan to semi-retire."

"Just semi?"

"I'll fill in when Beam takes a vacation or someone calls in sick, but I won't be working full-time anymore." Mason settled his glasses back into place. "Now you. Please, tell me about your interesting day."

"I have a little selfish in me, too. Guess who came in and asked for a job today?" She waved her hand. "I'll tell you 'cause you'll never guess. Carolyn West."

His face showed the surprise she expected. "Really?"

Their waitress placed salads in front of them. Mason waited until Patsy picked up her fork and took a bite before doing the same. One of many wonderful little things she noticed about this man with impeccable manners.

"I always liked Carolyn," Mason said. "She was a nice girl living under difficult circumstances. Actually, I liked all of Misty's friends. They were all good girls."

"I liked those girls, too. Still like 'em as grownups. They're a good group. I always had a special spot for Carolyn, though. Once she won that cooking competition, I felt we had a common thread."

"A happy event turned tragic. That was the same night her parents were killed."

"Yes, it was." She leaned back as the waitress set her plate in front of her. "Thank you." The mushroom ravioli smelled divine.

She glanced at Mason. "Things were hard for Carolyn before the accident. They got worse after."

"I imagine it was hard for Catherine, too. She'd just graduated from college and her parents were killed a week later. She had to put her dreams on hold to raise her little sister."

"Catherine took the situation out on that little sister though. It wasn't Carolyn's fault their parents were killed, or that Catherine was her only living relative."

"No, it wasn't." He waited until she'd taken the first bite of her dinner. "Now that Carolyn's an accomplished chef, I'm surprised she's coming back to Eden Falls," Mason said, seemingly mulling over the same thing she'd been wondering all afternoon.

Patsy remembered the little redheaded girl at her parents' funeral, her big brown eyes swollen from tears. "I was surprised when she asked for a job, but,"—she smiled—"here's the selfish part, I'm thrilled, too. I've never had anyone I could rely on to open the shop in the morning so I can sleep past three am, or close so I can take an afternoon off." She sat back in her chair and looked up at the ceiling. "I'm not sure I'll know what to do with an afternoon off."

"You probably don't get many days to sleep in."

"Only Sunday, the one day the shop is closed, and a few holidays."

The waitress cleared their plates. "How about dessert?"

Patsy lifted her eyebrows and Mason blushed in the most adorable way.

CHAPTER 4

Carolyn had time to drive to her hotel in Harrisville to change clothes before heading back to Alex's house. As she turned onto her friend's street, she almost ran into the curb. Patsy was coming down the porch steps of her house with Mason Douglas. She wore a flowing summer dress, a simple shawl around her shoulders, and her happy smile.

Carolyn wondered how long they'd been dating. She couldn't think of a couple more opposite, yet so perfect for each other. She loved the idea. As far as she knew, Mason Douglas hadn't dated anyone more than twice since his wife left him twenty years earlier. Mean girl Misty had gloated at school every time she sabotaged one of his dates. How did she feel about Mason and Patsy together?

She parked at the curb in front of Alex's house and gave herself a moment to relax. Things were falling into place faster than she'd anticipated—almost too fast, which worried her. She'd grown cynical enough to worry when things were good.

She had a job and a lawn to mow. With an address, she could begin to establish herself as a resident. She still had her old driver's license, the one with her maiden name on it. Would it be against the law to just change the address and use it as a valid ID? The thought of being arrested for fraud scared her—a lot, but not as much as being found by her husband. He was just arrogant enough to believe she'd continue to use her married name.

She never told Robert about Eden Falls, just that she was from Washington State, and he never asked. When she came for Alex's wedding, she flew into Seattle. Robert didn't know about the rental car or the five-hour round trip drive into her hometown.

She believed he was still looking for her and hoped the trail she left through southern states heading east had led him far from here.

She climbed out of her SUV. Three cars in the driveway meant Colton and Alex weren't the only ones here. In a matter of days, everyone would know she was home anyway. She inhaled deeply. *I can do this.*

Charlie opened the door at her knock. He'd inherited his smooth, bronzed skin, dark eyes, and shiny, coal black hair from his late Native American father, but his bright smile was all Alex.

She bent at the waist. "Hi, Charlie. Do you remember me?"

His grin revealed two missing front teeth. "I walked you down the aisle at my mom and Colton's wedding."

"That's right. Before that night, I hadn't seen you since you were a baby."

A dog came to investigate and sat beside Charlie. "My mom says you've been friends since you were little."

"Your mom was the first friend I made when I moved to Eden Falls."

"I made some new friends this year in first grade."

"It's nice to have a lot of friends."

"Tyson is still my best friend. He lives over there." Charlie pointed down the street.

"It's even better to have friends who live close." Carolyn turned her attention to the golden lab. "Is this your dog?"

A thick tail thumped the floor.

"His name is Barney. Colton gave him to me."

She straightened as Colton walked up behind Charlie. "With or without mom's permission?"

Colton laughed. "Without, and it wasn't a pretty situation."

"But she likes Barney now, huh, Colton?"

"She always liked Barney, she just didn't like me giving him to you without asking her first, hotrod." Colton ruffled Charlie's hair. "Let's move out of the doorway so Carolyn can come in."

As soon as she stepped over the threshold, Stella Adams, the second friend she'd made in Eden Falls, ran into the room and threw her arms around Carolyn's neck. "Ohmygosh! I'm so happy to see you."

Alex followed, hands held up in surrender. "I didn't tell her you were in town. Rita Reynolds saw you driving past the post office."

Stella stepped back. "I can't believe I had to hear you were in Eden Falls from the town gossip."

"I'm sorry. I made a quick decision and packed my car."

"Alex said you got a job at Patsy's," Colton said.

"Wait." Stella narrowed her emerald eyes. "You got a job at Patsy's?"

"Colton," Alex said on a groan at the same time.

Colton glanced from Carolyn to Alex. "You didn't tell me it was a secret."

"It's okay." Carolyn raised her shoulders, then let them drop. "By Friday afternoon, everyone in town will know I'm back."

Stella turned to Alex. "You didn't tell me she was *back* back."

Alex slipped a hand through Carolyn's arm. "Let's go out to the patio. Appetizers are on the table, so we can snack while we catch up."

As soon as they sat at the picnic table, Stella started asking questions. Colton kept Charlie busy, so they were free to talk. Carolyn gave what would become her standard answers. Because of their opposite work hours, she and Rob never saw each other and had grown apart. She was tired of working until two in the morning and sleeping through the day. She missed small town life. She missed them…

Alex scooped hummus onto a cracker. "Did you get the house?"

"I did."

"What house?" Stella asked. "How am I so in the dark here?"

Carolyn smiled at Stella. "I rented my childhood house from Leo Sawyer."

Stella looked longingly at a cracker, but picked up a celery stick instead. "What do you think of Leo? He's gone from geek to oh-my-goodness hot. Right? If I wasn't dating Len, I'd seriously ask him out."

Len hadn't been able to make it to Alex's Valentine's Day wedding. At the reception, Misty's cutting question had been, *"On Valentine's Day, Len can't make it? Doesn't that seem a bit odd to you?"* Carolyn also remembered the doubt she'd seen around Stella's eyes. Knowing what it felt like to hold on to something not worth holding onto any longer, she wondered if Stella was doing the same.

"Leo has definitely changed, but he said the same thing about me," Carolyn said.

"I heard he made some changes to the house." Alex bit into a carrot stick.

"He did and I love them. He opened up the rooms, making the whole house seem more spacious. I'll be close enough to Patsy's that I can walk to work."

"I'm so excited you're moving back." Stella slapped the table with the palms of her hands. "This is going to be the best summer we've had since high school!"

~

IT could hear laughter coming from the backyard of his sister's house, but went through the front of the house to drop off a wrench Colton had asked to borrow.

"Hello," Alex yelled from the kitchen when he closed the door.

"Smells good. You have any left?"

She turned from the sink when he entered the kitchen. "As a matter of fact, we do. Grab a plate."

He glanced through the kitchen window. "You're having a party and I wasn't invited?"

"I heard you were busy chasing Sasquatch through the woods," his sister said with a smirk.

"No, Mr. Polanski was chasing two kids with their mother's bear rug over their heads. It's a good thing Mac caught them first. Mr. Polanski had a gun that—Hey, who is…that's Carolyn West." He glanced at his sister. "I told you I saw her."

"You were right. Good cops are supposed to be observant."

"Hold on," he said pulling his cell phone from his back pocket. "I need to record this."

She laughed. "I always tell you when you're right. It just happens so seldom."

He wrapped his arm around her neck and squeezed. "I'm right way more often than you admit."

"Whatever."

He pointed out the window with the index finger of the arm around her neck. "Carolyn didn't call to say she was coming?"

"She said it was a spur-of-the-moment decision."

He released his hold and picked up an open bag of chips from the counter. "How long is she staying?"

Alex turned to face him. "She rented her family's place from Leo."

He stopped with a chip halfway to his mouth. "What?"

"She starts work at Patsy's on Friday."

"I thought she was a chef at a fancy restaurant in San Francisco."

Alex blew out a breath. "She was. She said she's tired of working nights."

Carolyn leaned over and hugged Charlie close. JT felt a stirring from somewhere deep and long-forgotten. "Where's her husband?"

Alex snagged the chip from his fingers. "She's divorced."

"She was married at your wedding three months ago. Can you get a divorce that fast?"

"She said she was divorced then, but wore her wedding ring to avoid questions."

JT pulled another chip from the bag and popped it in his mouth before Alex could steal it. "You never liked her husband."

"I never met him. I just know every time I called, he wouldn't let me talk to her. He always had an excuse for why she couldn't come to the phone. She was sleeping or at work or in the shower. Even her cell phone seemed to be monitored."

"You didn't believe him?"

"Maybe the first, second, and third time I called. After that? No."

JT popped another chip in his mouth while studying his sister's facial features. "You think there's more to her moving here, don't you?"

Alex glanced out the window and nodded. "Yep, I do."

~

Carolyn threw away the last of the paper plates and wiped off the plastic tablecloth. Once Alex's backyard was straightened, she pulled her sweater tighter and sat on the covered back stoop. Her friend's green thumb was as evident here in her yard as it was at the flower shop. The flowerbeds along the fence would be a riot of colors and textures by midsummer.

The evening had waned to the moments before night. The soft, diffused light of dusk hung suspended, reluctant to give way to full darkness. She loved this time of day, when everything was winding down. Of course in the restaurant business, things would have been in full swing. She missed the rush and bustle of a busy kitchen. She missed the people she'd worked with, but not the egos, tempers, or tension when things weren't running smoothly. She had enough of that at home.

A sudden shower had chased them all inside tonight. Now the rain was gone and the air smelled of wet cedar and grass. Fresh. Everything was quiet except for the drip, drip, drip from the leaves and Stella's voice rising and falling from the front yard as she talked to her boyfriend on her cell phone. From what Carolyn gathered, he was breaking another date and Stella wasn't happy.

Carolyn wondered about Len and Stella's relationship. A small worry niggled at her that he might be a little like

Rob, though Rob had never broken a date in their early days. He'd been attentive and charming…and a complete fraud.

Alex and Colton were inside tucking Charlie into bed. JT had followed them in. She hoped he'd gone home. He made her a nervous wreck when he was around—not only because of her girlhood crush, but because he was the law. Had Robert reported her as a missing person? Was her picture on every police station bulletin board across the country, or had Rob kept her disappearance quiet?

She'd turned a hundred shades of red when JT unexpectedly stepped out of the house tonight. He hugged her from behind as he said hi, and her muscles had tensed so tight they still hurt. Would she ever be able to relax under a man's touch again? She wanted to jump up from the picnic bench and run. Instead she blushed like a silly schoolgirl. Just hearing his deep voice set her heart hammering.

She breathed in the sweet air knowing she should leave. Tomorrow was move-in day and she wanted to get an early start. Instead, she sat quietly reflecting, committing to memory the evening she just spent with old and dear friends. She hadn't been reprimanded once. She'd analyzed every word in her head before she said them aloud, but from habit, rather than fear of repercussion or argument. Tonight had been about friends enjoying good conversation and each other's company. When was the last time she'd been able to do that?

The door behind her opened and JT stepped out. "Mind if I join you?"

Yes! "Of course not."

When he sat, their shoulders touched, and she flinched. Instant, automatic reflex. Looking over her shoulder at the door gave her the opportunity to scoot further away. "I thought you were Alex."

"She'll be out in a minute. She and Colton are still tucking Charlie into bed."

He was close enough she could smell his cologne and starched uniform shirt. "I thought"—*hoped*—"you'd gone home."

He glanced at her and smiled, as if he knew what he did to her insides. "I was tightening a loose bathroom faucet. Colton can write a great novel, but he's hopeless with tools."

"It's nice that Alex has you and your dad so close by." The thought of having no family scratched at her heart a little. If JT or Denny weren't around, Alex still had her Uncle Dawson or her cousins, Rowdy and Beam. What would it be like to have that much family support? She could only imagine.

She tried to put a little more distance between them without being too obvious. "How are your parents?"

"They're great. Dad's still at the post office. Mom helps with Charlie or at the flower shop. She also babysits for Misty and Beam whenever she can. She can't wait for Alex to have another baby."

"Or you." She covered her mouth, shocked the words had escaped.

He laughed. "Or me, though I think she's given up hope that I'll ever have kids."

"You have a great family."

Out of the corner of her eye, she saw him nod. "Yes, I do. I'm very lucky that way. How's your sister?"

"Oh…uh, I guess she's okay. She's married. They have two kids, a boy and a girl. She seems happy."

"You don't talk to her much?" He bumped her shoulder with his. She jerked away so quickly she almost toppled off the step. He wrapped his arm around her waist to steady her and she flinched from his touch. He held up his hands. "I didn't mean to scare you."

Grateful darkness had fallen so he wouldn't see the heat rush up her neck, she took a settling breath, mortified by her reaction. "No, I'm sorry. I'm just a little jumpy from the move," she said repeating her words to Leo.

"A little?" JT's chuckle was soft on the night air.

She tried to laugh, but it came out more like a frog croaking.

"So…you don't talk to Catherine?"

"No." *She doesn't have time for a sister she considered a burden and a murderer.* Carolyn gave herself a mental shake. *No pity parties tonight.* "She's busy with work and the kids, and doesn't like talking on the phone."

"Doesn't she live in Seattle?"

"Tacoma."

JT leaned forward, rested his elbows on his knees, and laced his fingers together. Settling in like he had all night. "Alex told me you've rented your parents' place from Leo."

She nodded to the same beat her bouncing knee was keeping. Aware he was looking at her, she kept her gaze on the shadows beyond the yard, searching for a new topic— anything to turn the conversation away from her. "Alex told me about the fire at the lumberyard. Stella said it was ruled arson, but no one has been apprehended yet."

JT hung his head and exhaled loudly. "That fire has me stumped."

The clouds parted, allowing just enough moonlight to filter through that Carolyn saw JT clearly. She could almost feel the frustration radiating from him and regretted mentioning the fire.

"I hate that I can't find the person responsible."

"You will. I'm sure Mr. Douglas and Beam know you're doing everything you can."

"I can't believe there's someone in this town capable of setting the fire. Whoever is responsible had to be small enough to fit through a tiny break in the fence at the back of the lumberyard. That break was the only way someone could have gotten in without setting off an alarm."

Her knee stopped bouncing. "Small as in child-size?"

"Beam said the hole was too small for Alex to fit through, but there is no way a child could have set this fire without some adult help, which bothers me even more. The whole thing was very well planned out."

"I can't imagine an adult putting a child in that much danger."

"Exactly. At least, no adult I know. Like I said, I'm stumped." They were quiet for a moment, both lost in their own thoughts, then he slapped his hands on his thighs. "Enough on that subject. Tell me about yourself."

This was the part she'd been afraid was coming since he came outside. She covered her mouth and faked a yawn that turned into the real thing before standing. Maybe once she was finally settled she'd be able to sleep more than a few hours a night. "It's been a long day. I better get back to the hotel."

He pushed to his feet. "Are you moving into the house tomorrow?"

"Yes."

"What time? I'll gather a couple of lowlife cousins to help."

She knew he meant hardworking Beam and Rowdy. "Thank you, but I can do it alone. I didn't bring much with me."

"Is the rest coming on a moving truck?"

Please don't make me lie. She looked at her watch. "I really have to go. Tell Alex and Colton thank you again for dinner. I had a great time."

He opened his mouth to say something, but she cut him

off with, "It was good to see you, JT." *Even though you make me a jittery mess.*

She walked to the gate and let herself out before he could respond. Stella put her phone to her chest. "Where are you going?"

Carolyn gave her a wave. "I'm exhausted. I'll talk to you tomorrow."

~

*C*arolyn woke before dawn and repacked her suitcase. After she attached the small trailer she'd been dragging around the country to the back of her SUV, she drove to her old-new home. She scrubbed out already clean kitchen cupboards, then dust-mopped all the floors. Scouring the two bathrooms to her satisfaction came next.

She glanced at her watch when the doorbell rang. Ten minutes to ten. She'd been cleaning for over three hours, and every minute showed when she peered at her cringe-worthy reflection in the mirror. The buff holding her crazy red hair back from her flushed, makeup-free face only made it worse.

Great.

She considered not answering, but the backed-in trailer attached to her SUV was a dead giveaway that she was home.

Home, that sounds so nice.

The doorbell chimed again. *Please, let it be Alex or Stella.*

No such luck. When she opened the door, JT and Colton stood on the front porch.

"Looks like you started without us," Colton said grinning at the rubber gloves she still wore.

She pulled them off and straightened her T-shirt. "I really don't need—"

"We can have that trailer unloaded in less than thirty minutes," JT said.

She'd taken very few things from her house in San Francisco when she left three and a half months earlier. Other than the suitcase and box of clothes, she'd filled a couple of boxes with pots, pans, and mixing bowls that Robert would never miss. She'd also taken her collection of books, a set of china she'd bought but never unpacked, afraid Robert would break it as a way of hurting her, and her good set of knives. She'd stored these boxes in the restaurant manager's office until she left San Francisco. In reality, she'd been preparing for flight, packing belongings and storing money, long before she actually left.

She dyed her hair brown, ditched the rental car, and purchased a beat-up Subaru in Nevada. In New Mexico, she bought the little trailer when she came across a farm table at a Flea Market. From there, she unearthed an old trunk in northern Texas, four mismatched chairs in Oklahoma, and a beautiful side table in Louisiana.

She'd worked odd jobs, waiting tables or washing dishes, leaving her married name at hotels along the way. She intentionally used her credit card in hopes of leading Robert astray. She picked up the used SUV in Mississippi. In Georgia, she left Carolyn Richmond behind, and began using cash on her trek northwest as Carolyn West.

By their determined expressions, she knew Colton and JT weren't going to leave until the trailer was empty, so she led them outside. The sky was a cloudless, brilliant blue. Birds twittered happily in a huge pine across the street. She looked heavenward, allowing the sun to warm her face. *Fresh start. Yes, second chances just might be possible.*

"This is all you brought with you?" Colton asked when she unlocked the back of the trailer and JT lifted the door.

The only thing she'd carried inside besides cleaning supplies was the money filled backpack, stowed under the master bathroom's sink until she could open a bank account.

"I'll buy what I need as I need it."

JT looked from the contents of the trailer to her. "You don't have a moving truck coming?"

"Fresh start." She said aloud, making it sound more possible, if only to her ears.

Colton picked up a box labeled books and flipped the top open. "I don't see any of my books in here."

"I did read one of your books," she happily admitted.

"One?" he asked, only half teasing.

"Yes! After reading it, I had to sleep with the light on for a week. I'll be living alone, so one is enough."

JT laughed. "Alex said the same thing. Her husband's books give her nightmares."

Colton grinned. "Your sister didn't marry me for my ability to write."

Carolyn could tell by their banter that the brothers-in-law, who were raised in two very different worlds, were great friends. Exactly the way they should be. Alex was lucky to have them in her life.

The two men made quick work of unloading her trailer, placing the boxes and the few pieces of furniture in their designated rooms. When they were finished, she pulled a couple of sodas from a cooler she'd been traveling with and held them out. "I'm sorry I can't offer more. Until I make a trip to the grocery store, this is all I have."

Both men popped the tabs.

JT took a sip and glanced around her bare living room. "What are you going to do for a sofa?"

She'd already bought one at a Harrisville furniture store. Until she opened a bank account, she could only purchase with cash. It wouldn't be a good idea to make the employees suspicious by pulling out a wad of money to buy more. She'd collect one piece at a time, as she needed them. "A sofa is being delivered later this afternoon."

"And a bed?" Colton asked.

"I'll sleep on the sofa until I get one."

JT nodded toward boxes that held the television and a DVD player she picked up at a Memorial Day sale in Idaho, her last stop before coming to Eden Falls. "Would you like me to set those up for you?"

"I can do it after I get a TV stand."

"I have an extra one in my garage," JT said. "You're welcome to use it until you find one you like."

She waved a hand, wishing he'd stop offering his help. "I'll find something soon."

JT kept a steady eye on her. "Can we help unpack boxes?"

She imagined he, as a police officer, had noticed she didn't have any pictures or tchotchkes. Would that small detail make him suspicious? "I know it looks like I don't have much. When I decided to start, I got rid of a lot of stuff. It won't take me long to unpack." Ready for them to leave, she walked to the front door. "I really appreciate your help."

"I'll get out of here, then." Colton joined her. "I have a fishing date with a six-year-old."

Carolyn turned, hoping JT would follow, but he stayed near the kitchen door. "Thanks for your help, Colton. You and Charlie have fun and be safe."

"Always. If you need anything, we're only a phone call away."

He strode out to his expensive SUV.

She turned toward JT, who was looking out the bay window.

"You have a great backyard," he said.

"My dad planted the pine trees along the back when we first moved here."

"I remember. The Yancys live in the house right behind

yours. Layne and I used to shoot BBs at targets we hung in those trees."

A laugh bubbled up and she put fingers to her mouth. "One of you broke the window over the sink."

"It was never proven which one of us did that," he said with a chuckle. "We both mowed lawns for the rest of the summer to pay for that window."

He glanced at her mouth when she lowered her fingers. "You start at Patsy's on Friday morning?"

Feeling self-conscious, she looked away. "Yes."

"Working in a small-town bakery will be quite a change from a five-star restaurant in San Francisco."

She didn't want him to call San Francisco or to check up on her in any way. She'd called Trish yesterday to let her know she was okay, but never mentioned where she was, which was how it had to stay for Trish's safety. "It is, but it will be a good change. Most of my days, actually nights, at the restaurant were twelve hours long."

He crossed his arms. "I don't think working for Patsy will alleviate the long hours."

She felt like she was being interrogated and didn't like it. "They'll be daylight hours, though. I didn't get out of the restaurant until two, sometimes three, in the morning. I never got used to sleeping through the day."

JT nodded like he was taking mental notes of everything she said. "You didn't bring much with you."

"I told you, I got rid of a lot. Most of it was worn and old, not worth dragging"—she barely stopped short of saying around the country—"here from California."

Carolyn took a moment to study him as he studied her. He and Alex looked nothing alike. JT was tall, with his mom's brown hair and eyes, while Alex had her dad's blond hair and the Garrett mossy-green eyes. He had inherited his dad's height, though. All the Garrett men were tall and handsome.

"I don't mind helping you unpack your kitchen boxes."

"No." She almost shouted the word, wanting him out of her house. "I still have to clean the cupboards out."

"Right," JT said as his glance settled on the cleaning supplies and wet rag she'd hung over the faucet. He walked to where she stood near the door to the living room. He stopped close enough that she noticed a small crescent scar above his left eyebrow. What would it feel like under the tip of her finger?

"Tell me a truth, Carolyn."

Her breath caught. "What do you mean?"

"Tell me something I don't know about you. Something no one knows."

My husband beat me and I pathetically defended him for years. I'm terrified of my own shadow. Her mind scrambled for an answer that wouldn't reveal her darkest secrets. "I…I like glazed carrots."

He stared at her for a long moment and then smiled. "I do, too."

~

*A*fter leaving Carolyn's house, JT was restless. He parked in town and walked the square, not sure what he was looking for, then walked it a second time before wandering into Noelle's Café for a burger. He took a seat at the counter and glanced over the menu he knew by heart. The only thing that changed since the day Noelle opened the doors of the café two years earlier was the daily special.

Noelle stopped in front of him, order pad in hand. "Hey, JT. What can I get you?"

"Why did you move to Eden Falls?"

She pulled a pencil from behind her ear. "You know why. I inherited this place."

He did know the story. An estranged uncle died and left Noelle the run-down, rodent-infested restaurant that she'd transformed into one of the busiest eateries in Eden Falls. But why would she leave her family, a Wall Street job, and everything familiar, to come here?

What he really wanted to know was why Carolyn, after graduating from culinary school and working her way into a prestigious kitchen, would want to make pastries in a small, unknown town. Alex was right. There had to be more to her story. She'd acted nervous last night, and again today. She'd also been anxious to get him out of her house. But why? "I'll have the Cascade burger and a chocolate shake."

Noelle studied him a moment. "You okay?"

"Yeah, I just have some things on my mind." He should be thinking about who started that fire rather than why a high school friend of Alex's was so jumpy.

"I'm a pretty good listener."

"You leave here late at night." JT tapped the menu on the counter to the rhythm playing on Noelle's jukebox. "Have you seen anyone hanging around town? Anyone suspicious, who looked out of place?"

Noelle snatched the menu he was beating against the counter. "You're talking about the night of the fire."

"Not just that night. Any time. You drive past the hardware store on your way home every night. Have you ever seen anyone hanging around that you didn't recognize?"

She tucked the menu in a menu stand out of his reach. "If I had, I would have told you."

"Right." JT picked up a saltshaker, set it on the counter, and started scooting it back and forth between his palms.

Noelle picked the shaker up and set it back in its holder. "You want me to get you one of the coloring pages I give kids? It might occupy your hands until your burger is ready."

"Sorry," he said, pulling his cell phone from his jeans pocket.

"I'll get your order in."

JT scrolled through the notes in his phone. The arsonist was small...smaller than his sister, who was tiny. There were plenty of kids in town small enough, but he just couldn't believe someone from Eden Falls, someone he knew, would set that fire.

"Hey, JT." Russell Walsh slid onto the stool next to him.

"Hi, Russ."

Russ had joined their small police force two years earlier when he moved from somewhere in Oregon. He was quiet and kept to himself, and other than his exemplary work record, JT didn't know much about him. "What made you pick Eden Falls? Out of all the places you could have moved, why here?"

Russ lifted a shoulder. "Eden Falls was hiring, and I needed a job."

"But you came from Oregon, right? Why wouldn't you pick somewhere closer to family?" Carolyn said her sister lived in Tacoma, so why hadn't she moved there, or Seattle? Both cities had five-star restaurants.

"I was a Navy brat. My family is scattered around the country. I went to college in Oregon and liked the area, so I stayed. My first job with a police force was in Portland, but I wanted something in a smaller town." He rested his forearms on the counter. "It feels good to put down roots after moving around all my life, you know?"

JT didn't know. Except for his four years of college in Montana, he'd lived in Eden Falls, and couldn't imagine living anywhere else. Maybe that was why Carolyn came back—she craved a sense of home.

Noelle set JT's milkshake in front of him. "Hi, Russell. You ready to order?"

"I'll take a turkey club and a chocolate shake."

"Coming right up. JT, your burger should be out any minute."

"Thanks, Noelle."

He heard a familiar belly laugh, and turned to see Charlie and Colton coming through the door. Charlie caught sight of him and waved. "Hi, Uncle JT!"

"Hi, buddy. Did you catch anything?"

"Nah, the fish weren't biting, huh, Colton?"

"Nope," Colton said with a grin. "The fish weren't biting. Want to eat at the counter or get a table, hotrod?"

"Table. Come eat with us, Uncle JT."

JT turned to Russ. "Want to join us?"

"I'm good here. Thanks."

JT followed the kid he loved more than life itself to a booth. Since the moment Charlie was born, his head of black hair sticking up in every direction, he'd found a home in JT's heart.

Charlie's dad was his best friend all through school. A roadside bomb had killed Peyton seven years earlier. JT still missed him. They shared many important firsts. They smoked their first cigars behind Mr. Polanski's chicken coop. They also vomited together afterward. They double-dated their first time out—*courage in numbers*—and shared their first bottle of whiskey, again vomiting together afterward. They both played high school baseball and football. They applied to the same college and were accepted.

JT was also the first to find out his best friend had enlisted in the Marines. And the second to learn he'd been killed.

CHAPTER 5

Carolyn spent an hour lining kitchen shelves while her mind whirled with sickening speed. She could tell by the look in JT's eyes that he suspected something. She didn't like that he didn't trust her, but how could she—

The doorbell echoing through the quiet house made her jump. She peeked around the corner of the kitchen wall, praying it wasn't JT again. She didn't think her heart could take answering any more questions.

Stella had her face pressed against the front window, just like she used to do when they were kids. Her mom used to say, "Look at the mess that girl made on my front window. Was she raised in a barn?"

Carolyn unlocked the door and pushed the screen open.

"You've lived in the big city too long. Locking your door in broad daylight?"

I'll be locking the door twenty-four hours a day for the rest of my life. "I thought you were helping Alex with flower arrangements for a wedding."

"We finished early, so I came to help you."

"Were the arrangements pretty?"

Stella rolled her eyes, a signature expression she'd used forever. "More like gorgeous. This bride's daddy is loaded. Alex and I are delivering the flowers to the Seattle venue in the morning. Hey, you should come with us."

Probably not a good idea. "I have to be at Patsy's at four a.m. the next day."

"We'll ask Alex what time she plans to get back here." Stella glanced through the front window. "She should be here any minute with one of Renaldo's pepperoni pizzas."

"Mmm…I haven't had Renaldo's since I left Eden Falls."

Stella clapped her hands together. "So, what can I do to help? Should I start unloading the trailer in your driveway?"

"Colton and JT unloaded it earlier."

Stella spun in a three-sixty. "Where's all your stuff?"

The incredulous look on Stella's face would have made Carolyn laugh under different circumstances. "This is it."

"This is everything you own? I could have filled six trailers that size with all my crap."

I could have filled two dozen. But I had to leave it all behind or Rob would have suspected before I could get far enough away. She wanted to scream the words. She wanted people to understand something she didn't understand herself. Instead, she took a deep, calming breath.

"Why did you leave everything with your ex?"

The question pushed Carolyn into defense mode. "What I had wasn't worth bringing with me!" It was all the explanation she could give without opening up about the nightmare she'd lived through. Every day.

Stella opened her eyes wide. "Okaaay, you don't have to wig out."

Carolyn blew out a breath of frustration. "Sorry. I'm just tired."

"So, are you going to show me around?" Stella glanced toward the bedrooms. "Or do I have to guess at the changes Leo made?"

Carolyn led her down the hall.

"Leo did a great job." Stella stuck her head in the bathroom. "I love this."

Carolyn loved it too.

The front door, which Carolyn had forgotten to lock, opened. "I have pizza from Renaldo's," Alex called out. "Hey! I thought Colton and JT were going to unload your furniture this morning,"

Stella rolled her eyes. "Don't get Carolyn started again. I just got her settled down."

Carolyn sighed.

After pizza, Stella and Alex made quick work of unpacking boxes and helping Carolyn arrange the kitchen to her liking. The sofa was delivered. Later she would visit stores in surrounding towns to pick up filler pieces of furniture, things small enough to fit in the back of her SUV or on the trailer. She decided building her home piece by piece would be fun.

As they worked, Alex and Stella filled her in on the town and its residents. Most names she knew, some were new to her, but it felt good to be with friends again. She hadn't been permitted that luxury in San Francisco.

"Tell me about you and Colton, Alex. We really didn't have much time to talk before the wedding. I know how you met, but not what happened after."

Alex and Stella laughed together. Carolyn felt a little pang of regret. She was out of the loop, a non-participant in their inside jokes. She'd been gone a long time and missed the joint secrets they used to share.

"You know most of the story. Colton flew in to research small-town life for his next novel." Alex shook her head. "He was an arrogant, self-centered pig who insulted me every time he opened his mouth."

"You should have seen his face when he found out she was the mayor. It was priceless," Stella said.

"That was nothing compared to the morning he found out I was a mother. Until then, I think he thought I was some teenage fan of his." Alex shrugged as a faraway look came into her eyes. "I don't know when I fell in love, but was shocked when I realized..." She shook her head. "No, shocked isn't a strong enough word. I was appalled when I realized it. I knew he was planning to leave at the end of summer and never look back, so I wasn't about to get involved with him."

"And he tried," Stella interjected. "He took her for a romantic overnighter in Seattle."

Alex waved Stella's comment away. "I was most concerned for Charlie. He loved Colton. He'd never lost anyone before. He didn't understand why Colton had to leave once his book was written, or why he wasn't coming back. Colton went back to LA at the end of summer, but called about once a month and talked to Charlie."

"And you," Stella said.

"And me," Alex admitted.

"Then, four months later, he came back."

Alex smiled at Stella, who couldn't stop interrupting. She glanced at Carolyn. "Colton showed up at Pretty Posies with an engagement ring and a proposal. He said he had to make sure he could give up his life in LA, but after he went back, realized it was Charlie, me, and Eden Falls he'd be giving up."

Carolyn wasn't sure why but Alex's narrative made her

heart thump unevenly. "That story belongs in a romance novel."

"Too bad Colton writes gory slasher-murder mysteries instead." Stella stood. "I've got to go, I have a date in a little while."

"I thought Len broke your date last night."

Carolyn noted the tone of disapproval in Alex's voice.

"That was for this weekend. Something came up that he can't get out of, but he said he'd take me to dinner tonight to make up for it."

"I have to go, too. Tatum took an early lunch so I could come over. I'll pick you both up tomorrow morning at seven."

Still uncertain whether going to Seattle to help with wedding flowers was wise, Carolyn said, "Maybe I should stay here."

Alex waved her concern away. "Nonsense. I'll have you home by six p.m. at the latest."

Carolyn hugged both friends. "Thank you for the pizza and the help unpacking my kitchen. You guys are the best. Tell Colton thanks again, too. I appreciate his and JT's help."

Alex looked around at the nearly empty room. "It doesn't look like they did much."

"Not true. You saw how many boxes of kitchenware I had. They also brought in my boxes of clothes, books, and my kitchen table and chairs." She didn't miss the look Alex and Stella exchanged.

"Are you going back to the hotel tonight?" Alex asked.

"No, I'll sleep on the sofa."

Alex shook her head. "Come stay with us until you get a bed."

"I'll be fine. You tried the sofa. It's comfortable."

She stood on the porch, watching both friends drive away.

She'd anticipated spending an afternoon unpacking, but there was very little left to do, so she got in her car and headed back to Harrisville to shop for a bed and mattress.

~

*P*atsy hadn't heard from Mason since their date on Tuesday night. She was fighting conflicting feelings about whether it was a good thing or bad.

On one hand, she had a wonderful time. The conversation was perfect, the food wonderful. Visibly nervous at first, Mason had relaxed and opened up by the time their dinners were served. In between raving about bites of each other's food, they discussed favorite books and movies. A history buff, but not in a boring way, he told stories that captured her interest. And he was a rapt listener when she talked, which was a refreshing change.

On the other hand, he took her to Harrisville rather than Eden Falls for dinner. Though he said he wanted to take her somewhere nice, had he subconsciously tried to keep their date off everyone's radar? Was he embarrassed to be seen with her? Even though it would make perfect sense, the thought still hurt. He had a stellar reputation around town. She did not. The town gossips could be vicious. Dating her would shine a spotlight on him, which he didn't deserve and seemed naïve enough not to understand.

She shuffled through some invoices on her desk, but her mind returned to the first hand. Mason was kind, engaging, and extremely sweet in his old-fashioned way. He held her shawl, opened her door, and pulled out her chair. Not all men performed simple courtesies anymore. The blush that touched his cheeks when he was flustered was so endearing—and he was easily flustered.

Dating would fill the gaping chasm of loneliness that threatened to swallow her at times, but the thought of dating again scared her to death. She'd already been married four times. Did she really want to wade through that quagmire of heartache again?

The phone rang, breaking into her thoughts. She set the invoices down and reached across her desk for the receiver. "Hello?"

"Patsy? It's… Hi, it's Mason."

The second she heard his voice her heart fluttered and she pressed a palm to her chest. Maybe her heart couldn't handle another romance. "Hi, handsome," she said, trying for a light tone of voice.

"I'm sorry I haven't called. Beam and I have been busy ordering building materials for the new hardware store. I don't know if you've driven by, but we've started framing the building."

"I haven't seen it."

"I'd like to show you, then. We could go to dinner afterwards."

A "no" would let him know he couldn't just call at the last minute and expect her to be free—even if she was. But who was she fooling. She couldn't wait to see him again.

He was a big boy and could handle a little scandal.

"That is, if you're free."

She could imagine the blush moving up his neck to his cheeks as he spoke. Which hand should she choose? Selfish or selfless? "A tour and dinner sounds wonderful."

~

Summer tourist season and drunk and disorderly went hand in hand. JT had an arrest report sitting in front of him that was typical for the season.

The guy busted up a couple of Cascade Club barstools in a fight over a woman before officers Phoebe Adams and Russ Walsh could get to him. After he spent the night in one of Eden Falls' two jail cells and paid for damages the next morning, his buddies bailed him out. He was probably standing thigh-deep in the river by now, casting his line, telling tales of the fish—or woman—that got away.

The sound of tennis shoes slapping the wood floor and a happy voice hollering "Hi, Helen" made him smile. A moment later Charlie burst into his office wearing a baseball uniform. "Hi, Uncle JT!"

JT pushed back from his desk, making room for Charlie to squirm in close. "How is my favorite nephew in the whole wide world?"

Charlie let loose his six-year-old belly laugh. "I'm your only nephew."

"Oh, that's right." He tugged Charlie's baseball cap down over his eyes. "Looks like you have a baseball game this morning."

"Yeah! The first one!"

"Where's you mom?"

"She's at Pretty Posies. Colton had to go to the Fly Shop for a new reel and said I could visit you." Charlie pushed his hat back into place and shoved his hands in the back pockets of his uniform pants. "Do I have enough for a donut?" He pulled out a couple of rocks, a Matchbox car, a squashed dandelion, a small action figure, three LEGOs, five dimes, two nickels, and a penny.

"That's some haul." JT separated the money from the treasures. "I think you might just have enough. Especially if Patsy takes dandelions."

Big, dark eyes looked up at him. "You think she will?"

JT scooped Charlie's riches into his palm. "Let's go over and ask."

Charlie skipped, hopped, and talked nonstop across the square. He was explaining why the Hulk was green when they entered Patsy's Pastries. The shop was busy as usual for a summer Saturday morning. If scents could be seen, cinnamon, chocolate, and maple would be swirling through the air, with a hint of citrus and powdered sugar.

A line wound past the front of the pastry case. Two high school girls plus Carolyn were busy at the counter filling orders. JT hadn't seen her since unloading the trailer three days earlier, and, to be perfectly honest, she'd been on his mind a lot since then. She glanced up and smiled when Charlie called her name and waved, but the smile didn't reach her caramel-colored eyes. There was a sadness there, huddled deep down, trying hard to stay hidden. He noticed it across the picnic table at Alex's, and again at her house while they talked. What had put the sadness there, and how deep did it run?

His little sister's friend had changed from the gangly teenager of twelve years earlier, but the familiar pink coloring her cheeks was exactly the same. When she was young, she had a crush on him, taking advantage of every opportunity to be at their house. She never approached him. Just stared. He wondered if she remembered how he used to tease a blush out of her. She would turn so red it nearly concealed her freckles. She was just a cute little girl, one of his sister's many friends who inflated his teenage ego with her attention, but much too young to notice.

Now? Now was a different story.

He'd cornered her at Alex's wedding. While he did most of the talking, she twisted her wedding band around on her finger compulsively, evading personal questions and circling the conversation back to him, or the town and the people they knew. She turned down his offer to dance before he even finished asking.

When he and Charlie reached the front of the line, she turned her pretty smile on his nephew. "Good morning."

"Uncle JT said I might have enough for a donut if Patsy will take a dandelion."

Carolyn laughed. The sound was sweet, yet hesitant, as if she might not be allowed. "Well, Patsy isn't here this morning, or she just might."

"Charlie has sixty-one cents burning a hole in his pocket."

Charlie looked from him to Carolyn before he twisted and pulled the material of his back pocket away to peer inside.

JT rubbed a hand across Charlie's shoulders. "Burning a hole in your pocket is just an expression."

Charlie grinned and rolled his eyes. "Ohhh, like it's not real."

"Right," JT said. "It means you have money you want to spend."

"Well, I don't want to spend it, but I want a donut." Charlie scrunched his nose, looking so much like his mother. "Will sixty-one cents be enough for two?"

"You have enough for two if Carolyn will accept your dandelion"—JT winked at her—"and you'll have eleven cents left."

Charlie took the weed from JT's palm as if it was a precious jewel and handed it to Carolyn. There was just enough stem to tuck behind her ear, which, to Charlie's delight, she did.

"Pick out two donuts. I'll keep the nickels and penny, along with your other treasures, so you don't lose them. You can have them back after your game."

He glanced at Carolyn. "Word around the station this morning is those cranberry scones are fabulous. I'll take that last one."

JT sent Charlie to the bathroom to wash his hands while Carolyn bagged their order. He paid, pulled his scone from the paper bag, and took a bite. Scones weren't something he normally ordered, but Layne and Gianna both said Carolyn's were too good to pass up. The tartness of the cranberry and the sweet orange glaze settled on his tongue. Firm, moist, tart, and sweet. "Rumor is right. This is really good."

"Thank you." She turned away so he wouldn't see her blush.

Charlie ran out of the bathroom and JT handed him the paper bag. "You need to get to the park. You don't want to be late for your first game. I'll be there in a few minutes."

"Okay." Charlie pulled a glazed donut free of the bag. "'Bye, Carolyn!"

"'Bye, Charlie. Good luck with your game." Carolyn's eyes met JT's for a brief moment before she busied herself filling a napkin holder.

He leaned against the counter, glad the line had diminished enough that they could talk. "Are you settled in?"

"Getting there."

"One of your neighbors informed me your sofa delivery came."

Carolyn's head jerked up and her eyes narrowed.

He was surprised by her unsettled reaction. "They don't mean any harm."

She drew in a deep breath and the tension around her mouth relaxed.

"You should know most of your neighbors. They've lived in those same houses forever. They keep an eye out for each other. Sort of an unorganized neighborhood watch."

"Oh. That's…good then."

He wished he could read what was going on behind those unhappy eyes. Why would elderly neighbors watching out for each other raise such an alarm? "It is good. Makes my job easier and helps keep the neighborhood you live in safe."

She nodded.

"How is the job going?"

Her smile reached her eyes this time. "It's only my second day, but I think I'll like it."

"I'm sure Patsy is glad to have you."

"I hope so."

Her smile added a pretty sparkle to her eyes. A sparkle he wouldn't mind looking at for a while longer, but he had places to be. He pushed away from the counter. "I better make sure Charlie got to the ballpark. He likes to stop along the way. I'll see you around, Carolyn."

"Bye, JT."

JT sauntered out of the shop into the sunshine and the tension in Carolyn's jaw relaxed. At twelve, Carolyn had been so jealous of the gaggle of girls who hung out at the Garrett house, girls JT's age, girls who didn't have red hair and a face full of freckles. Girls who had boobs. Back then, she would have given just about anything for him to pay attention to her. Now, she wished he wouldn't. When she'd devised this bright plan to come to Eden Falls, she hadn't added Police Chief JT Garrett into the equation.

She waved when Rance Johnson from The Fly Shop walked in. Word that she was baking for Patsy had spread, so Eden Falls' natives were coming in to try her treats and to reintroduce themselves. She could tell some still felt lingering pity for the girl who lost her parents when she was very young. She was tempted to tell them not to feel sorry for her losing something she never had.

She wiped a countertop thinking life at the bakery should prove very different from the life she'd been living. Still, she loved it so far. She was a morning person until she started working for the San Francisco restaurant, and she never got used to sleeping through what she considered the best part of the day. Now she had to get up way before dawn, but she was off by one. She took a quick shower as soon as she got home yesterday and had revived enough to enjoy an afternoon of weeding a bare flowerbed.

She adored the house she was slowly turning into a home. She lived close enough to walk to work and enjoyed the quiet before dawn when the echo of her footsteps was the only sound. Unlocking the back door of Patsy's this morning had been her favorite moment of the day. She switched on the lights and lit the ovens, all the while inhaling the sugar and cinnamon still infusing the air. Patsy was there by five, the doors opened to the public at six, and lines formed by eight.

She appreciated being near friends again. She'd missed them more than she realized. She considered the freedom of picking up the phone, knowing one or the other would answer. She considered that a precious gift. Tonight she was meeting the whole gang at Rowdy's Bar and Grill for a girls' night out. Anticipation zinged through her, as well as trepidation. She knew they'd have questions. She just hoped her answers would appease them until they got tired of asking.

Even though JT's comment about neighbors noticing a delivery initially alarmed her, the knowledge that they watched out for each other was comforting. She had to be careful, though. She couldn't let her guard down just because some elderly neighbors organized an unofficial neighborhood watch.

"Morning, Carolyn."

She glanced at the industrial clock on the wall behind her. Patsy said Colton came in almost every morning. He thought his wife didn't know, but Alex was well aware of Colton's sweet tooth and how he satisfied it. "I was beginning to think you weren't going to make it in this morning, Colton."

"Who knew sugar could be a muse?"

She smiled. "Are you headed to Charlie's game?"

"Sweets first."

A man she didn't recognize walked through the door behind Colton.

"Hey, Russ. You here to check out the sweet pleasures Carolyn offers?" Colton asked.

The man's cheeks turned the same color she imagined her own did. He stepped to the counter and offered his hand. "We haven't met, yet. I'm Russell Walsh. Everyone calls me Russ."

Carolyn shook the man's hand. "Hi, Russ, I'm Carolyn West. It's nice to meet you."

"Everyone at the station is talking about your scones this morning."

"At the station?"

"Russ works for the police department," Colton said while studying the selections in the pastry case. "I hear you ladies are meeting at Rowdy's tonight."

"We are. I'm excited to see everyone." She backed away from the counter, ready to escape to the quiet sanctuary of the kitchen. "I've got some baking to do, so I'll let one of these ladies help you. It was nice to meet you, Russ."

~

*A*fter JT finished lunch at his desk, he stepped outside to walk the square. He spotted Rance Johnson who was on the sidewalk in front of The Fly Shop.

"Howdy, JT."

"Hey, Rance. How's business?"

Rance lifted his baseball cap and scratched the crown of his head with its fringe of snow-white hair. "Couldn't be better. One of the best starts to the summer season I've ever had."

"Maude was saying the same thing about the bookstore."

When Rance didn't respond, JT glanced at him. His words didn't match his worried expression. JT followed Rance's gaze. Three kids were crossing the street from Patsy's Pastries to the square.

"They were in here"—Rance thumbed over his shoulder —"about fifteen minutes ago. I'm pretty sure that short one stuffed something in his pocket—not because I saw him, but because of the smart-aleck smirk he threw my way."

Without taking his eyes from the kids, JT said, "I can't do a whole lot about it if you didn't actually see him take anything."

"Not asking you to, I just came out to keep an eye on 'em."

JT nodded. "I'll take over so you can get back to your shop."

After Rance went inside, JT moved to the corner. All three kids, two boys and a girl, were dressed in black Goth garb. Both males wore long trench coats, too warm for the day. The tallest had skin so pale it appeared translucent. His jet-black hair emphasized his sickly pallor. The other boy's hair was spiked and orange. The female wore heavy black makeup on her eyes and lips, with stick-straight dark hair hanging down to her waist.

His cousin Beam and fireman Brandt Smith had been questioned after the hardware store fire, and both gave a description that fit the two boys. They'd been in front of the fire station talking when the boys walked past them on Main Street a couple of days before the fire. The kids happened to be the only strangers noticed around town. That fact didn't make them guilty, but it did make JT suspicious.

JT didn't recognize them as locals. He watched as they

entered the park and sat under a tree. The girl and the orange-haired kid lounged and laughed, doing what kids their age did. The taller male was somber, and looked older by a couple of years. When either of the other two made a comment, he simply nodded in reply.

JT walked to the middle of the block until he stood opposite them. The tall kid seemed to feel JT's eyes on him. He turned his head and stared back, showing no emotion. Then he stood and walked away. The other two jumped up and followed. So, Kid Dracula was the leader. JT pulled out his cell phone and snapped a couple of pictures of the retreating trio, catching them in profile, then called Harrisville Police Chief. After trading greetings, he brought up the kids.

"Yeah," Chief Brody said. "They sound like mine—well, not mine personally, but they belong to Harrisville."

"They've been in trouble if you know them."

"Sadly, yes, they keep me busy."

"What are they into?"

"Trying to be tough. They're minors, except for the tall one—Anthony Harris aka Thorn. He's been in juvie a couple of times and spent a night or two in lock-up for petty stuff. He's twenty and too old to be hanging with high school kids, but he has a whole group of followers."

JT watched them climb into a 1980s blue Ford Bronco. "Drugs?"

"Marijuana. Buying, not distributing."

"Hold on." JT snapped a picture of the Bronco. "Any of Thorn's *followers* in trouble?"

"Minor stuff. Mostly underage drinking, speeding tickets."

"Shoplifting?"

"Yeah, a couple of them."

He lifted his sunglasses and noted the Bronco's license

plate as the kids drove past, Thorn behind the wheel. "Setting fires?"

"Not to my knowledge." Chief Brody blew out a breath. "At least not yet. Why?"

"Kids matching Thorn and the orange-haired kid's description were seen in Eden Falls a few days before our big fire." *And the little one is probably the right size to fit through the gap in the fence.*

"The orange-haired kid's name is Aaron Meeks, aka Blaze."

Great.

~

*A*lex and Jillian were already saving a table when Carolyn arrived at Rowdy's Bar and Grill for their girls' night out. She hadn't seen Jillian or Misty since arriving in Eden Falls, and Jolie only in passing, when she stopped in to buy donuts at Patsy's for the law office where she worked.

When she approached, Rowdy held out his arms for a hug. "Your *sweet pleasures*, as Colton has dubbed them, are the talk of Eden Falls, Carolyn. I'm sorry I haven't had a chance to partake."

She tried to remain calm under the physical contact of a man, but her muscles didn't relax until Rowdy released her.

"Aww, there's that cute little blush I remember. You and Jillian used to turn red as fire engines when I teased. I'm glad to see that hasn't changed, especially since I don't have those red braids to tug on anymore."

"We blushing sisters have to stick together." Jillian stood and hugged her tight. "I'm so glad you're back. Now I have someone to commiserate with."

Carolyn laughed as she held her palms to her hot cheeks. "Glad to be of help."

"So do you." Carolyn felt as if her heart might burst with happiness. To be here with her childhood friends at this moment was a dream she thought she'd never get to experience. Until now, she hadn't realized just how lonely an existence she'd lived in San Francisco.

After Rowdy walked off with their drink order, Stella and Jolie joined them. Misty was the last one to arrive, late as usual. She had always kept them waiting. Obviously, arriving on time wasn't a part of her dramatic change. She wore what looked suspiciously like a smear of mashed peas—or poop—along her jawline.

"Sorry I'm late. Sophia is teething and fussy."

Carolyn couldn't stop her smile. Misty had always been the diva of their group, or thought she was. Those words coming from her mouth were probably the most unnatural Carolyn had ever heard.

Stella patted Carolyn's arm. "You're not alone in your amazement. We're all still completely boggled by Misty and motherhood in the same sentence."

"Shut up, Stella."

Stella pointed. "Now *that's* the Misty we remember."

"Misty has turned over a new leaf. She's nice now…most of the time. We always knew she had a sweet side."

Misty glared at Alex. "You can shut up, too."

"She still reverts back to the old Misty occasionally, so be prepared," Stella warned with a laugh.

"How is Sophia?" Carolyn asked. Sophia had been a month-old, black-haired, blue-eyed, beauty at Alex's wedding.

"I told you she's cutting teeth, keeping us awake half the night." Misty's voice was hard. If Carolyn hadn't seen the softness of love around her eyes, she wouldn't believe Misty had changed at all. Those vivid blue eyes darted around the group, and then her face eased into a gentle smile, one

Carolyn had rarely witnessed while growing up. "She's funny and beautiful and the light of my life. Our life."

Carolyn chest tightened unexpectedly to see this side of Misty, to witness her joy at being a mother. Carolyn had always wanted to be a mother, but Rob didn't want children, something they should have discussed before marriage—not that he would have told the truth.

If second chances are possible for mean girls, they're possible for you.

She was glad to see Misty so happy. "Things are going well for you and Beam?"

"Yes." Misty's expression changed once again as she pressed her lips together in a silly smile. "Things are good."

Misty's transformation was amazing, something Carolyn wouldn't have believed possible. Peas—*please, let it be peas*—looked beautiful on her.

Carolyn glanced around the table at her five friends. They'd grown up together. Jillian's mom called them the stair-step friends. Petite Alex was the bottom step. She was now a mother, business owner, and the mayor. Stella, who was a second-grade teacher, came next. Jolie was the third in height. Now married and expecting her first child, she worked for the only attorney in town. Misty was fourth, a hair tech at Dahlia's Salon. Carolyn came fifth. The tallest of their group had always been Jillian Saunders, now a personal trainer at Get Fit, Misty's in-laws' gym.

Their slumber parties, birthdays, fun times and crazy, along with their sad moments and disappointments, were all etched into Carolyn's memory.

They laughed through a platter of nachos and ordered more appetizers to share while they caught up with one another's lives. She gave her standard, pre-prepared answers to their questions. She'd loved her job in San Francisco, but her hours and the demands of the job left very little time for life. Her days were over-the-counter-pill-induced sleep, her nights long. She loved the city, but missed Eden Falls, and had missed them. All true.

"You'll never guess who my dad is dating," Misty blurted out, finally tired of Carolyn being the center of their conversation.

"Patsy Yarberry," was the collective answer from everyone but Carolyn, who decided to stay quiet about seeing Patsy and Mason emerge from Patsy's house.

"Can you believe it?" Misty threw her hands in the air. "The whole town knows Patsy is notorious for her multiple marriages."

Stella's eyebrows rose. "Patsy isn't the only one in town with a notorious reputation."

Misty shot a glare Stella's way.

"Just because they sat together at the Memorial Day baseball game doesn't mean they're dating," Jolie said.

Except I saw them together the next night.

"I think they make a cute couple," Jillian said.

"You would," Misty fired back.

"Don't you think it's past time your dad started dating? He's been alone since your mom left, and stayed alone to take care of you."

"I know that, Alex, but he could date *anyone*. Why does it have to be Patsy?"

"What do you have against Patsy?" Jolie asked. "She's always been nice to all of us."

"We don't know the reasons for her divorces."

"And why is that?" Misty asked, jabbing a finger at Jillian.

"She let her stepson Jack stay with her until he got a job with the fire department." Alex set a calming hand on one of Misty's flailing arms. "If she'd been an awful stepmother, or had mistreated his dad, Jack wouldn't have stayed in town after his dad left."

Not appeased by Alex's answer, Misty turned to Carolyn. "Has she said anything to you?"

"No." Another truth. Since she'd spent the past two days training on Patsy's cash register and baking, they hadn't had any time to discuss personal matters.

"What has she said about her divorces?"

"I've only worked there for two days. She hasn't told me anything, and I certainly wouldn't ask."

"Exactly!" Misty jabbed her finger, again. "Why does she keep everything so quiet? If the divorces weren't her fault, why wouldn't she tell people?"

"Maybe because she doesn't have anyone to tell." They all glanced at Alex, who was frowning. "Patsy isn't exactly popular because of her divorces. People have made assumptions, and because of that, she doesn't have many friends. Not being a finger-pointer says a lot about her character."

"So do multiple divorces." Misty rubbed at her jaw and felt the dried green on her face. She wet a napkin in her drink and scrubbed at the spot. "Patsy has never liked me."

"You do realize there are reasons for that," Stella said. "Remember the time you soaped her windows? And got caught. Or how about the time you—"

"Okay, I got it. I have another person to apologize to." Misty glanced at Carolyn. "I forgot you, Carolyn. Sorry for everything I've ever done to hurt your feelings."

Stella rolled her eyes. "That sounded sincere and heartfelt."

Carolyn waved Stella's comment aside. "Apology accepted."

"I'll apologize to Patsy"—Misty shook her head—"but I still don't want her dating my dad."

"You may not have a choice, and that's as it should be,"

Alex said. "It's none of your business, Misty. Your dad has lived his life in support of you for a long time. It's his turn. Try being supportive instead of selfish. Be happy for him for a change."

Carolyn couldn't believe Misty wasn't exploding with anger. She could tell it was just under the surface, vibrating through her system, but she said nothing. Carolyn half-expected to see blood dripping from the corner of her mouth where she must be biting her tongue.

She liked the new Misty.

Carolyn's gaze wandered to the door when JT entered and took a seat at the end of the bar. His eyes roamed the interior of Rowdy's and came to rest on her. He winked and her heart flopped like a grounded fish as heat moved up her chest to her cheeks.

~

JT smiled. Even from across the room he could see the blush move across Carolyn's cheeks. She'd popped into his mind several times during his day, her sad smile, her cute freckles, how sweet she was with his nephew.

He caught his sister's eye and she grinned because she'd gotten her way. His dating hiatus had lasted less than a week. Alex had bugged, texted, and whined about meeting the woman she wanted to fix him up with until he caved.

He blew out a frustrated breath. He was tired of the dating scene. Tired of meeting women, hoping this one might be *the one*, making small talk through dinner, then discovering before dessert that it was pointless to set up a second date. He was ready to find someone and settle down. He always thought that after he got his career started the rest of his life would fall into place, but it hadn't. He never thought it would be so hard to find a woman he felt compatible with, who shared the same values, enjoyed the same things. Wanted kids.

Sometimes he was envious of his sister and his cousin. Alex and Beam had found their other halves. They were both living their happily-ever-afters.

Rowdy came over and planted his palms on the bar. Maybe he should take a page from Rowdy's love 'em and leave 'em manual. Beam's brother seemed in no hurry to settle down. "What brings you in tonight?"

"Meeting a date. Who's the new bartender?"

"Hey, Mike," Rowdy called. "Come meet my cousin, JT."

The dark-haired man walked over. "Mike Stettler."

JT shook the hand he offered. "Nice to meet you, Mike. Are you new in town?"

"I drove in about a week ago to crash with my cousin for a while," Mike said.

"Who's your cousin?"

"Noelle Treloar."

JT could see the resemblance. "Massachusetts to Washington is a big change."

"Yeah, it has been. Excuse me." Mike moved off to help another customer, but added over his shoulder, "Good to meet you."

JT glanced at Rowdy. "We have a lot of move-ins lately. What would bring someone clear across the country to little Eden Falls?"

"Don't know, don't care. I needed the help with tourist season and Mike's the most reliable bartender I've hired in years."

"Why isn't he working for Noelle?"

Rowdy lifted his left brow. "You're kidding, right? Bartend here or wait tables at Noelle's Café? He can make four times more money here. It's a no-brainer."

Rowdy was right. Bartending over the summer would bring Mike more tips than he'd make in six months at Noelle's.

While waiting, JT noticed the new bartender's attention kept turning to the table holding his sister and her friends. He glanced that way and wondered which woman had snagged his attention. *Better not be Carolyn.*

He shook his head. *Where did that come from?*

CHAPTER 6

He stood in the shadows of a big evergreen waiting, not sure how long he'd been staring at the dark house across the street. As his feet stirred the pine needles, the air smelled of Christmas, even though it was early summer, a contradiction to the fragrant flowers blooming just behind him.

The night had turned chilly and he was glad he'd thought to grab a ski hat. He pulled his gloved hand from the depths of his jacket pocket and squinted to read his watch in the darkness. Lighting the face was too dangerous, even at this late hour. He was well hidden from the street, but he wasn't positive he couldn't be seen through a house window.

He rubbed his hands over his arms, but stopped when he realized the movement would be too easy to spot. He couldn't risk being seen. Turning to look at the closest house, he searched the windows, but saw nothing. He'd driven down the street several times today. The only neighbors he noticed were elderly. Single woman, living alone, the neighbors might feel the need to keep an eye out for her.

At the sound of a car's engine, he stepped farther back

into the dense green branches. He pulled his hat lower over his forehead when a set of headlights turned the corner. His heart thumped uncomfortably at the same time the back of his neck tingled with anticipation.

Tires on the asphalt echoed through the still night air. The car turned into the driveway opposite where he stood, then stopped under the protection of the carport. She opened the door, illuminating the interior of the car. He'd considered hiding next to the small trailer she had backed into the second spot of the carport. But there was a chance she'd spot him. Studying the area now, he noted the light didn't quite reach the other side of the trailer. The position would be suitable next time, and he wouldn't have to cross the street.

She swung a foot out, then another. His gaze traveled the length of her long, lean legs when she stood. He pulled his hands out of his pockets and tried to slide his wet palms down the thighs of his dark pants. *You're wearing gloves, stupid!*

She walked to the back of the car, then stopped and glanced around. Common sense told him she couldn't see him, but when she looked straight at his hiding spot, he held his breath. He'd made no sound, yet she seemed to be staring straight at him. His neck felt like it would snap from the tension before she turned toward the back door.

She'd left the outdoor lights on, which was wise for a woman coming home after dark. She pulled her key from her jeans pocket, stopped, and scanned her surroundings again, as if sensing someone beyond her view.

She inserted the key into the knob. He'd already scouted out the doors and windows. No deadbolt, and the back door had a window. Easy access.

The door closed behind her and the light in her kitchen came on. He studied the dark windows of the surrounding houses for any movement. When he saw none, he eased from the shadows and crossed the street, glad for the cloudy sky tonight. He ducked around the side of the carport and ran for cover behind another evergreen along her back fence. A dog barked in the distance and he froze.

She wasn't clearly visible through the lace curtain above what he suspected was the kitchen sink, but her outline moved into view and then disappeared, again. The light went out.

He slipped from pine to pine along the back fence line. Standing among the boughs, he was nearly invisible. Another light flicked on. Her pretty face and red hair came into view as she walked to the window, then vanished after she twisted the handle on the blinds. A gap between the two bottom slats allowed light to show through, providing a glimpse into her new life.

He glanced at the houses on either side of hers. Both were quiet and the houses behind were hidden from view by pines. He left the shadows of the tree and crossed the lawn. Stepping gingerly over the junipers against the house, he peered inside. She peeled out of her jeans and sweater, and tossed both into a hamper. Pink bra and panties were all that hid her naked beauty from him. Her skin was silky smooth, luminescent under the soft light. He imagined it under his fingertips as he removed those pieces of lingerie. He could hear her sigh of pleasure…

Movement brought him back to the present. She removed something from a dresser drawer and disappeared. Another light came on, illuminating his face, and he squatted down so fast he almost lost his balance. He quickly shifted his weight and planted one hand in the dirt, the other against the house to keep himself upright.

When the light went out, he slowly straightened and peered through the slats again. She'd curled up on the right side of the bed with a book in hand. Just as he turned to leave, her phone rang. Without thinking, he pushed the light on his watch—eleven-twenty. Realizing his mistake, he quickly released the button.

He heard the hesitancy in her "Hello?" Then she said, "I made it home just fine." Her soft laugh wafted through the closed window, like music to his ears. He loved her voice.

"I had a great time, too. It was fun catching up. Thanks for inviting me."

He squinted through the slats. She paused, apparently listening to the person on the other end of the line as she absently smoothed a hand over her bedding.

He knew who she was with tonight, because he followed her to Rowdy's Bar and Grill, but he hadn't done more than glance inside. He couldn't risk being seen. Who was she talking to now?

Tapping her phone wouldn't be impossible, but did he need to go to those lengths? Her voice stopped his wandering mind. "No, I won't be in church tomorrow, but tell your parents thanks for the invite. Since I have the day off, I'm going to Tacoma to visit my sister. I haven't seen her since I've been back in the area." Another pause. "I will. Thanks for calling."

She replaced the phone in the charger on the bedside table, followed by her book, then turned out the light.

He waited several minutes before sliding away. Keeping to the deepest dark, he walked down the quiet streets of Eden Falls.

CHAPTER 7

"**Y**ou what?"

Carolyn was surprised by her sister's outburst. Her niece and nephew looked up from the presents they were unwrapping like she might have stabbed their mother.

"Tell me I heard you wrong."

Carolyn opened her mouth, but Catherine held up a hand to stop her as she paced to the opposite side of the huge kitchen. She spun around, her perfect haircut swinging in a way Carolyn's curly mop never would. "How could you?"

"I…I needed a place to live and it was for rent."

Catherine's husband, Don, stepped into the room. His glance bounced from Catherine to the kids, who were eyeing Carolyn suspiciously. "What's going on, honey?"

Catherine jabbed a finger at Carolyn. "She rented our childhood home in Eden Falls." She slapped her hands on the island countertop. "How could you?"

Don's expression showed confusion. "What does it matter?"

Catherine scowled at her husband. "That was the house I

lived in with my parents. It was the last place I saw them before she…" Catherine burst into tears.

Carolyn was very aware she hadn't been included as a resident in that house. In Catherine's eyes, she hadn't mattered then, and she didn't matter now.

Her niece jumped off her chair at the table and ran over to cling to her mom with a mixture of apprehension and fear.

"Maybe you two should talk about this in the other room," Don suggested.

When Carolyn called three days earlier and asked if she could come for a visit, Catherine had hemmed and hawed while Carolyn sat in awkward silence. Finally, her only living family member said, "I guess."

Her two-and-a-half-hour drive to Tacoma this morning turned into three because of a pouring rainstorm, which didn't let up until she reached the city limits. Her niece and nephew only warmed to her when she pulled gifts from her overnight bag, which her sister eyed like she might be carrying something illegal. True, she hadn't asked if she could spend the night, but had naively assumed she'd be asked. At this point, it was abundantly clear she'd packed for nothing.

"I'm sorry, Catherine, I didn't think it would bother you." Thanks goodness she hadn't mentioned the changes Leo made. Catherine would have imploded in hysterics.

"Of course, you didn't think about anyone but yourself as usual. You're as insensitive an adult as you were a child."

"Catherine," Don said.

"Insensitive? I was ignored, Catherine. You were like an only child." *Certainly the only child they cared about. I was invisible to them.*

"Mommy, why are you crying?"

Catherine swiped the tears from her face and snorted. "You were such a drama queen. You were always doing something to grab their attention. Jealous. That's what you were, always jealous."

"You're right. I was jealous. I felt like I had to do back-flips just to get a nod from them. Everything was always about you."

"About me?" Catherine pointed a damning finger again. "If you hadn't insisted they go to that stupid cooking contest, they wouldn't have been killed in that accident!"

"Dad," said Carolyn's nephew, now becoming concerned as well. "What's wrong with Mom?"

"Honey, I really think you and Carolyn should—"

Catherine burst into tears again. "They would still be alive if it wasn't for you! You—"

Carolyn didn't wait around to hear the rest of Catherine's sentence. She scooped up her bag and ran out the back door on shaky legs.

Catherine still blamed her for her parents' death, and she had every right. The guilt from that tragic day hung as heavy as the storm clouds before a tornado.

Carolyn threw her bag in the back seat, climbed behind the wheel, and backed out of the driveway, the memory of that tragic night as fresh as if it had just happened.

At eleven-years-old, she'd entered a kids' baking contest in Harrisville and had begged them to attend the awards cere-mony. Even if she didn't win, she wanted them to care enough to be there for her, to care about this one thing as much as she did. When she was awarded first place for her pineapple upside down cake, she held her blue ribbon up proudly and stored her parents' smiles deep in her heart. She'd finally done something grand enough to get their atten-tion. Maybe they did care.

On the way home, a drunk driver crossed the center lane and crashed head-on, flipping their car several times. Carolyn was the only survivor. How many times had she wished she'd been the one to die? She was trapped in the car with her parents' lifeless eyes staring in her direction, accusing her. She'd closed her own eyes and cried until firemen worked the seat off her legs to free her. Her blue ribbon was hauled away with the mangled car.

Many had told her repeatedly that the accident wasn't her fault, but Catherine still blamed her for her parents' death, and always would.

Making matters worse, Catherine ended up putting her life on hold to raise Carolyn, so she wouldn't be placed in foster care. A fact Catherine would never let her forget, no matter how many times Carolyn thanked her. She owed her teenage years in Eden Falls to Catherine, and she'd never forget that either, even though her thanks always fell on deaf and resentful ears.

Over the years, they spoke when Carolyn called. She always sent her niece and nephew Christmas and birthday presents, but could only assume they were received, since she never got a thank-you note or call. Catherine was the only family Carolyn had left. Losing that connection frightened her. But Carolyn knew there was nothing she could do to fix things. Catherine believed what she believed and always would.

It was time to let go, which made her feel extremely sad. And lonely. No doubt the prospect of never seeing Carolyn again wouldn't bother Catherine a bit.

Her planned overnight stay had ended in less than thirty minutes and she was back in Eden Falls by early afternoon. She should have just accepted Alex's invitation to sit with them at church and have Sunday dinner at the Garretts' house afterward.

She pulled into the carport, got out of her car, and stopped to look around just as the sun broke through the clouds. The feeling of being watched she experienced the night before was gone. Still, she took in her surroundings, slowly scanning the neighborhood houses, trees, and bushes.

She'd planned to take Catherine and her family to dinner somewhere nice in Tacoma. Instead, she dropped her overnight bag by the kitchen door and walked into the back-yard. There was a long, narrow flowerbed behind the carport. When her mother lived here, this bed was full of roses. Now, it grew weeds. The thought of Charlie giving her a dandelion for a donut—such a sweet, innocent gesture—popped into her mind. With the help of her parents and her brother, Alex had done a great job raising her son.

Of course, from there her thoughts turned to JT, as they always did. She wondered why he wasn't married yet. The woman who met him at Rowdy's last night was gorgeous. JT stood when she walked in. She kissed him on the mouth in a familiar way, as if they'd been together for a while. Carolyn had to concentrate to keep her eyes off them, but her gaze wandered back when the woman smiled and flipped her hair or when JT leaned in close to listen to something she said.

Just thinking about it made her short of breath.

She got down on her knees, wrapped her fingers around the stem of a weed, slowly pulling it free of the dirt, and sat back on her heels. The white of the root, with its many lateral feelers, had lain hidden from the sun, growing in the dark. So much of her life lay hidden in the dark, away from where the truth could be discovered, away from the humiliation of her own stupidity.

Pulling roots was like cleaning a cellar, stripping windows of their dirt and cobwebs to allow light in. Feather-like rays of sun were beginning to clear the dust and debris from around her heart. The beat was strengthening. Her frayed self-confidence was attempting to mend itself, strand by strand. All because people bought and savored her sweet creations.

This is for you, Robert Richmond. You're exposed to the light, even if it's only my own.

~

The afternoon was gorgeous. Birds twittered in the treetops, and the mist from the waterfall glistened in the sunshine. Patsy lay on her back watching white clouds drift overhead while Mason read one of Colton McCreed's murder mysteries aloud. She was enchanted by Mason's voice, so full of inflection as he impersonated the different characters. He was handsome in a way that made her insides tingle with anticipation. His rare smile caused her heart to pound. *So silly for a woman your age.*

Mason had put a lot of thought into their afternoon. The picnic basket he picked up from Noelle's Café was packed with BLTs, potato salad, cheese, grapes, and apple slices. Patsy added two of her own mixed berry turnovers. Mason spread a quilt in the shade of an evergreen at the base of Eden Falls. After lunch they waded through the shallows while sharing information about their younger days and long-forgotten hopes and dreams.

"You seem happier today than you were last night." Mason had set the book on his thigh and was looking down at her.

"I wasn't unhappy last night. You took me to another restaurant I've wanted to try. Dinner was wonderful."

"You were quieter than normal."

She smiled up at him. "Are you saying I talk too much?"

He moved the book aside and scooted down until he was lying on his side next to her, his head propped on his palm. "You know that's not what I'm saying. I like that you talk. I'm not very good at conversation. You fill in what would be a lot of silence."

She cocked an eyebrow. "I think that was a compliment."

"In my own awkward way, I meant it as a compliment. You talk, I like to listen. Last night you were quiet. Was it something I said?"

"No, Mason." *It was nothing you said. It was the fact that you took me out of town for another dinner. We saw no one we knew. Wise on your part, but it still hurts.* "Today was wonderful. Thank you for this."

"You're welcome." He sat up and started packing things away. Once the sun disappeared over the mountain, the temperature would drop quickly. She stood, shook out the quilt, and folded it over her arm.

The drive home was a comfortable silence. Patsy, lost in thoughts of self-preservation, was glad for Mason's quiet nature. She'd been through four hurtful divorces and wasn't sure she wanted to risk her heart again. She was wise enough to know, after just three dates, that she could easily fall in love with Mason. Before he asked her out, she thought she wanted this. Now she wondered if she was stepping off into the deep end of the pool. Her record with men was proof she didn't swim well.

At her door, Mason tipped her head up with a finger under her chin. "Is it okay if I kiss you, Patsy?"

That was a question she'd never been asked before. She'd hoped for this moment for a week. Imagined it would happen just as it was. Now that it was here, she wasn't sure. She looked at his eyes, then his mouth. He had very kissable lips.

He took her gaze as consent and those lips touched hers in a sweet blending of souls.

～

*J*T finished setting his mom's dining room table just as Alex, Colton, and Charlie came through the front door.

Alex set a salad in the middle of the table and punched him in the arm. "How was the date?"

His date, the woman Alex was so sure would be perfect for him, was beautiful. She'd greeted him with a kiss, and her lips, full and soft, tasted like cherries. She had long, dark hair that curled softly over her shoulders, blue eyes, and a cute dimple when she smiled. They talked for a few minutes Then she said something softly and he'd leaned closer to hear. What she suggested, within minutes of their meeting, was so lewd he was shocked. His face must have registered astonishment, because she laughed and asked if he was as stuffy as her ex-husband. Obviously he was.

"It didn't."

"What? Why? She's so nice."

"What do you know about her?"

Alex lifted a shoulder. "Not much. I met her at the vet when I took Barney to get his shots. She talked about her kids and her job. She was so sweet with her dog. I thought she'd be perfect."

He leaned over and whispered what his date had suggested so Charlie wouldn't overhear.

Alex's eyes grew wide. "Really? Boy, I should have lined her up with Rowdy."

He blew out a breath. "I'm done, Alex. No more blind dates. No more setups."

"Carolyn's single."

Carolyn was single and attractive and... "I'm done dating for awhile."

"I invited her today, but she was going to Tacoma to see her sister."

Two hours later, here he was driving down Carolyn's street with a glimmer of hope that she might be outside so he could pull over and talk to her. He felt like he was back in middle school, riding his bike past Susan Jensen's house. She'd been an older woman—by six years—a lifeguard at the city pool and so beautiful. He went swimming every day that summer, rode his bike past her house every night. He thought his heart would break when her family moved away.

Carolyn's car was in the carport, but the house was dark. He wondered how her trip to Tacoma went. When he asked about her sister, it hadn't sounded like they were very close. He didn't remember much about Catherine, but knew Alex had never liked her, which was unusual, because Alex liked everyone.

If lights had been on, he would have stopped to check on her. See if she needed any help hooking up her television. It was probably best the house was dark.

He drove by two more times during his shift that night.

~

*C*arolyn wiped the outside tables off and straightened the chairs while birds flitted down around her to pick up leftover crumbs from the ground. The morning was sunshiny, the temperature perfect. Since there was a slight lull in business, she decided to enjoy the fresh air for a moment before heading back inside. She pulled her sweater around her and sat in one of the chairs facing Town Square. Eden Falls was just waking up for a new day. People were unlocking the doors of their shops, coming out of The Roasted Bean with cups of coffee. She liked being part of that wakefulness.

She glanced toward Town Hall when movement caught her eye. JT walked down the steps. He looked skyward and adjusted his hat against the sun, then glanced left and right, as if surveying his domain. The skin along her arms and the back of her neck tingled when his eyes met hers. She was anxious to make a quick escape, but was too late when he started across the street in her direction.

Her mind flitted to the woman who joined him at Rowdy's on Saturday night, a gorgeous brunette who made Carolyn feel like the wart on a toad in comparison—not that JT was likely to make any comparisons between them. And not that she could date. She was still legally Carolyn Richmond, and would be staying that way for a very long time.

"Morning, Carolyn."

She shaded her eyes against the sun when she glanced up. "Hi," she replied, afraid to say more for fear her voice would come out breathless and embarrass her.

"Nice day, isn't it?"

Carolyn looked around her. The birds were happy, the flowers were blooming, and the sun was shining. She nodded.

"Mind if I sit?"

She held her palm out toward the chair she'd just tucked under the table in an invitation she didn't feel.

He pulled out the chair and lowered his tall frame into it. "I thought I might see you in church yesterday."

Why was he looking for me in church? She felt a blush start and spoke to stop it before it became a full-blown blotch attack. "I drove to Tacoma to see my sister."

He leaned back and stretched out his legs. Her hope for a quick hello and good-bye diminished. "How is she?"

Her knee begin to bounce. "She's okay."

"You just took a day trip over and back?"

She didn't want to explain that her sister didn't want to see her, or have anything to do with her, or to admit Catherine considered her a murderer. "She had something to do today, so I didn't spend the night. It worked out well because I didn't want to ask Patsy for a late start day already. I just came home after a short visit and did a little yard work." *Ohmygosh! Stop blabbering. He doesn't care about your day off or your yard work.*

"Do you need any help?"

The question stopped her internal yammering. "With what?"

He smiled and her heart kicked her in the ribs. "With your yard work."

"Oh! No, thanks. I actually like working outdoors. It's very…therapeutic." *Ripping out weeds, exposing their roots to the light.*

"How do you like being back in Eden Falls so far?"

"I love it." She loved everything about it. The freedom from tension and the worry of saying the wrong thing was exhilarating. Over the past four months all her external bruises had healed. Now, she just had to work on the internal wounds. She still looked over her shoulder occasionally, expecting Rob to be there, but even that was becoming less frequent. "The fact that I can pick up a phone and call a friend is wonderful."

A frown appeared. "You couldn't before?"

Had she just said that aloud? "Oh…with my crazy hours…" The skin on her chest began to burn.

JT leaned forward, resting his forearms on his knees. His eyes, the color of the rich earth she had her hands in yesterday, watched her intently. The burning moved up her neck. "I guess they were asleep while you worked and vice versa."

"Yes," she almost shouted, relieved he'd provided a valid answer.

He smiled, and her heart kicked her again. "I now know you like glazed carrots"—he leaned toward her and she noticed the crescent scar again—"which was quite thought-provoking. Tell me something else, Carolyn."

Why did he keep asking her question about herself? Had her empty house raised suspicion? "There's nothing to tell. I'm a boring person."

"I doubt that."

"Seriously, there's nothing to tell."

"Come on, Carolyn. Everyone has something no one knows."

She had a lot of somethings that no one knew, but nothing she could say aloud. While she searched her mind for something trivial, he placed his flattened palm on her bouncing knee. She twisted from his reach and he retracted his hand. "You're jumpy again."

"Sorry."

His smile was slow, as his eyebrows came together in confusion. "Why are you apologizing? You did nothing wrong."

According to my husband, I can't do anything right. She almost apologized for saying sorry, but stopped herself.

"Just one thing," he said, reminding her that he hadn't forgotten the question hanging in the cool morning air.

"I don't have any secrets." *Except I'm almost as big a liar as my husband.*

Another frown appeared. "I didn't say anything about revealing secrets."

Her heart thumped hard once. Twice. She had to be more careful about blurting her thoughts out. "I love the sound of rain."

"Two for two."

She looked at him in question.

"Things we have in common"—he lifted an eyebrow—"carrots and the sound of rain."

"I have to go back to work." She stood, knocking her thigh against the small table. She didn't look around to see his expression in her flight to get to the safety of the sugar-spun shop.

Once inside, she came to an abrupt halt.

Patsy, her arms resting on the tall pastry case, wore a Cheshire cat grin. "That JT sure is a good-looking man."

Carolyn's skin prickled with heat. If JT wasn't suspicious before her rush to get away, he would be now. She took a breath to steady her words. "Yes, he is."

"Why would a guy that good-looking be single?"

Because he asks too many questions. "Maybe he isn't. I mean, I saw him with a woman in Rowdy's on Saturday night. She kissed him like they were a couple." Her mind flashed to that moment. Her reaction felt suspiciously like jealousy, which was ridiculous. *You're married.*

"Really? Too bad. I was going to suggest you ask him out."

Carolyn sucked in a huff of air at the completely unexpected comment. "Me? No. No, I'm not interested in dating." Between JT's questions and Patsy's comments, she was on the verge of hysterical laughter—and not the funny ha-ha sort.

"I'd like to talk to you in the office about something. Cory and Jess just came in, so they can watch the front for us."

As if Carolyn's knees weren't trembling enough, Patsy's request almost made them collapse. Had she done something to upset Patsy? Maybe sitting outside with a handsome man was against the rules.

Cory came into the front of the shop, tying an apron around her waist. Jess followed close behind.

"Carolyn and I will be in the office for a few minutes. Cory, it's your turn to check the bathrooms. Yell if you need anything. And no flirting with the customers," Patsy said over her shoulder as she disappeared through the kitchen door.

Carolyn had no choice but to follow.

Patsy's office was a separate room off to the right of the kitchen. She took a seat behind her desk and nodded at a vacant chair. "Have a seat, hon."

Carolyn sat and laced her fingers together in dread. *I need this job, Patsy.*

"How are things going?"

Another unexpected question. Carolyn pointed at the floor like a dunce. "You mean here?"

Patsy nodded.

"Fine. Great. Everything is great." She waited a moment then added, "I'm sorry I was sitting outside. I shouldn't—"

"Oh, my goodness! Do you think I'm upset?" She laughed. "Heavens, I'm all for sitting with a handsome man whenever opportunity permits. Don't ever apologize for that. I'm asking how you feel about the job."

Carolyn straightened in her chair as relief washed through her. "I…love it."

Patsy nodded again. A smile tipped her fuchsia mouth up at the corners. "You feel comfortable when I'm away from the shop?"

"Sure. Yes, I do."

"If I took a couple of days off, you'd be okay running this joint?"

"Of course."

"I've decided to make you manager." She waved a hand. "I know you already manage when I'm not here, but I've never really taken any time off. If I do, I have to close up shop. I'd like to change that. Of course, I'll up your pay. I'm not sure how good you are with bookkeeping, but it's not hard. If you're willing, I'll show you over the next couple of days."

Carolyn tried to wrap her mind around what Patsy was saying. "You want me…"

"…to take over some of my responsibilities. I've been running this shop alone since I opened and, to tell you the truth, I'm tired." She fell back against her chair, as if to demonstrate. "I want to be able to take some time off. I want to travel a little. I want to sleep late a couple of mornings a week, enjoy life a little. You seem more than capable of taking over. And I'll only be a phone call away if you need help."

"I'd be happy to help more. You don't have to make me a manager to do that. I know bookkeeping. I use to help at the restaurant in San Francisco."

The lines on Patsy's forehead relaxed. "That's music to my ears."

Carolyn opened her mouth, then pressed her lips together. *Oh, what the heck.* Everyone was asking *her* questions. She would ask one of her own. "Does wanting time off have anything to do with Mason Douglas?"

Patsy pink mouth quirked into a grin. "How do you know about Mason?"

"I saw you two coming out of your house last week when I was going to Alex's."

"Did you tell Misty?"

"No, but she knows. I was out with the girls on Saturday night and she brought your name up." Carolyn wanted to show her support. "I think it's wonderful that you're dating. Mr. Douglas is such a nice man."

"He is nice, sweet, kind, considerate, and adorably old-fashioned, but in a good way. His blush gets me every time. We went on a picnic yesterday, and he actually asked if he could kiss me. It was the sweetest moment, and the kiss…" Patsy raised her eyebrows as she fanned her face. "Wow. Yep, he's one of the good guys, which always seem to belong to another." She met Carolyn's gaze. "Don't ask me what he sees in me, but I'm glad he finally opened his eyes."

"You are a wonderful person, Patsy. I'm happy for you."

"What about you, hon? The divorce still too fresh to talk about?"

So fresh as to be nonexistent. Carolyn nodded.

"It might help to talk things out." Patsy tapped the eraser end of the pencil on her desk a few times.

"There really isn't anything to talk about. We got married too quickly and grew apart...probably"—*but not really*—"because of the opposite hours we worked."

She was too humiliated to talk about the real reasons she was in Eden Falls. She wished she could file for divorce without running the risk of Rob finding her, but it was impossible. Carolyn flattened her expression to neutral. Until she married Rob, she'd always worn her emotions on her sleeve. Then, necessity taught her to keep them hidden, only showing the ones Rob wanted or expected to see.

"Did he cheat on you?"

Carolyn glanced away.

"Oh, honey, I'm sorry. That's none of my business. Sometimes my mouth says things before my head catches up." Patsy studied her for a long, uncomfortable moment before she picked up a piece of paper, and jotted something down. "You're okay with me taking a day off now and then?"

"Anytime."

Patsy handed the piece of paper to Carolyn. "Are you okay with this amount?"

Carolyn stared at the number Patsy had written on the paper, sure that if her lap hadn't stopped it, her jaw would have hit the floor. She'd made good money at the five-star restaurant, but this was a small pastry shop in Eden Falls, Washington. "This is too much."

Patsy waved a hand. "I've been working in this place since I opened the doors, and I've spent none of the profits. I've taken a total of eight weeks off in all those years. Three times I was sick, three were for honeymoons, and the other two were to attend funerals. If I don't start getting away from here, the next funeral will be mine."

"But Patsy—"

"It's only money, hon, and I got plenty." Patsy leaned forward. "That's something no one knows about me. I was born rich. My great granddaddy was a railroad man in the early days."

Patsy had many layers no one knew about. Would Misty be so against a match between her dad and Patsy if she knew that bit of information? Not that Mason needed money. Misty had never wanted for anything, except her mom, the one thing her dad couldn't give her.

Patsy pushed up from her desk. "Now that's settled, let's get some cream puffs made. The senior center has a luncheon tomorrow and there's nothing they like better than cream puffs."

~

While Patsy worked side by side with her new manager, the only manager she ever had, her mind wandered to Mason more times than she liked. What was he doing today while she filled her light-as-a-feather pastry with cream? Was he at the building site with Beam, or meeting with contractors? He gave her a tour of the framed hardware store, showing her where everything would be once the walls were up. She hadn't visited the hardware store often before the fire, so she didn't understand much of what he was talking about, but she loved watching his face light with enthusiasm.

After her last divorce, she decided she was through with men, but loneliness wore down her defenses, made her vulnerable. Loneliness always won the battle. That's when she began noticing Mason, who never seemed lonely.

The kitchen door swung open and in walked Alex carrying a pink pot with a single white hyacinth. "Special delivery for you, Patsy."

"Oh," Patsy said on a sigh. "Is that from Mason?"

Alex pulled the card from the little plastic pitchfork inserted in the dirt and handed it her. Patsy ripped the envelope open, pulled the card out, and smiled. "It says, 'Thanks for being you.'" She glanced at Alex. "What does it mean?"

Alex grinned. "I think it means you have an admirer."

"No, I mean, what does the flower say?"

Alex set the pot on the worktable where she and Carolyn were lining up creampuffs. "White hyacinths mean beauty."

Beauty. Patsy pressed a hand to her heart as it thumped two beats too hard. "Do you think Mason knows what it means?"

Alex's mouth quirked to the side. "Sadly, past a red rose, most men have no idea flowers have meanings."

"Mason's different."

Alex nodded. "Yes, he is. Misty knows the meaning of flowers. She might have told him."

Patsy laughed. "If she helped him, she would have picked flowers that said stay away from my dad…or drop dead."

"Possibly." Alex's smile faded. "Be patient. She'll come around. She's never liked sharing."

"She's had her dad all to herself for a long time," Carolyn added.

Patsy shouldn't be talking to the girls about their friend, but she was also one to call a spade a spade. "She never appreciated what she had."

Alex laughed. "You're right, but she's trying to change. One day she'll realize everything her dad gave up to make her happy and she'll regret her selfishness."

Patsy snorted. "You're optimistic."

"That's the pot calling the kettle. You're one of the happiest, most optimistic people around," Carolyn said.

Alex ran a comforting hand down Patsy's arm. Silly as it was at that moment, Patsy realized how long it had been since she had any kind of physical contact. It was a wonder she hadn't attacked Mason Sunday afternoon.

"I promise, Misty will come around. Meanwhile, you and Mason have fun, and enjoy your beautiful hyacinth." Alex gave a quick wave as she left the kitchen.

Patsy set the flowerpot on her desk just as the phone rang. "Patsy's Pastries."

"Hi. It's me."

Her heart fluttered happily. "Hi, me. Thank you for the beautiful hyacinth."

She imagined his cheeks flushing and wished she was with him to see it. Had he gone into Pretty Posies knowing exactly what he wanted, or had he looked around, trying to pick out the one he thought she'd like the best?

"You're welcome. I have a beautiful woman on my arm. Would you like to join us for lunch?"

Patsy laughed. "On one condition. That beautiful woman better not be more than five months old."

He chuckled. "Can you come to my house about twelve-thirty-ish?"

"I'll see you then."

CHAPTER 8

Lunch with Mason and his granddaughter, Sophia, was enlightening. Patsy had never been able to have children, other than a few grown stepchildren, and she was still close with only one of them.

Mason handled the five-month-old with ease. The repressed knowledge that she'd never have grandchildren because she had no children of her own pinged around the hollow place in her chest.

All her hopes of cuddling grandkids landed on her stepson Jack. He had a job with the Eden Falls Fire Department, and she knew he'd stay if he found a local girl to settle down with. Her mind ran over the single women of Eden Falls. The idea swirled around and around as she thought about the possibilities. She'd have to work on it later, when she didn't have a handsome man in front of her preparing lunch. A man had never prepared a meal for her before and tuna had never tasted so good.

He put Sophia down in a swing where she was content as long as Grandpa talked to her every other sentence.

As they ate, Mason talked about ways he planned to

simplify his life. "This house is too big for a single man. Now that Misty and Beam have Sophia, they need more room. This place would be perfect, if they're interested. It's far enough out of town to be quiet and the lot is big enough to build a play area for Sophia." He picked up a potato chip. "They could even add a pool if they wanted."

The way he talked, this idea had been brewing for some time, which worried her. Where would he go? Did he plan to move away?

"I would have to talk to Beam first. He and Misty seem to work better that way. No one has ever been able to tell Misty what might be best for her except Beam, and he does it in a way that makes her think it's her idea." He smiled. "I never learned to do that."

She didn't dare ask him what his plans were if he did sell to his daughter and her husband, so she decided to change the subject. "I read the article about rebuilding the hardware and lumber store in the Eden Falls Chronicle this morning." He'd told her Jace Dickson interviewed him and Beam for the town's weekly paper. The story centered on Beam buying into the business and becoming partners with Mason four months earlier. "It was a good interview."

"I stuttered and stammered my way through, but Beam did a good job." He pushed his plate back and lifted Sophia from her swing. "Once we're up and running again, I'll cut back to part time, so I can watch this sweetheart a little more often." He glanced at Patsy. "I'll eventually sell my remaining half to Beam and Misty, or another partner, if they chose to take one on. And I'll give the house to them as a gift of thanks. Misty never has to know how grateful I am to Beam for turning my wayward, self-centered daughter around. She's done an about-face since Sophia's birth, but only because of Beam."

That remains to be seen.

He chuckled. "Misty laughed at me this morning. She said she couldn't believe her always-serious father was making silly faces to get Sophia to laugh. I'm not always serious, am I?" he asked stealing another glance at her.

She raised an eyebrow in answer.

"Misty is right." He flashed a rare smile as he cuddled Sophia close. Patsy loved this lighthearted side of him that he didn't show often. "This little *cricket*, as her Uncle Rowdy calls her, has changed me in ways I never thought possible. She made me realize I was getting old before my time. I guess I have spent way too much of my life being serious."

He buried his nose in Sophia's hair and his ears turned red. Then he glanced at Patsy. "You helped to change that."

Mason seldom strung more than a couple of sentences together, yet here he was carrying the conversation. She hated to interrupt him with a question, but she wanted to know how she'd helped without being aware. "How?"

"By being you. I like spending time with you."

"What about Misty? She can't be happy that you're spending time with me."

His brow crinkled in an expression of frustration. "My days of trying to please my daughter are over." He leaned forward and took her breath away with a simple kiss.

*A*fter lunch, Mason changed Sophia's wet diaper and then held her out to Patsy.

The thought of holding the baby terrified her. "I haven't held an infant in years."

"There's nothing to it." He set Sophia in her lap, and Patsy held her close while he mixed a concoction of blueberries and rice cereal together. She really was a gorgeous baby. Probably the prettiest Patsy had ever seen.

Once he had Sophia's lunch together, Mason took her

from Patsy and undressed her. "She'll ruin her clothes otherwise," he said at Patsy's questioning look.

He set the baby in a little seat on the countertop, buckled her in, and spooned the mixture into her mouth. Half came back when Sophia blew a raspberry. Patsy laughed.

Sophia grinned and reached into the bowl for a handful of the mixture. Some made it to her mouth, the rest was smeared on her pudgy belly

"I think I'm in love," Patsy said. "She's adorable."

"She's a witch. She wraps everyone around her finger before they realize what's happening."

After a messy twenty minutes, Mason filled the kitchen sink and lowered the cereal-and blueberry-covered baby into the water. She splashed around while Mason washed her clean, only fussing when he got to her hair.

"You're having the time of your life."

Mason smiled when he realized she was talking to him. "I am. I love my days with Sophia."

"I can see why. You have a gorgeous granddaughter. I'm jealous."

"Don't be." Mason glanced at her and smiled. "I'll share."

~

Carolyn left Patsy's Pastries at one-thirty Wednesday afternoon. The advantage of being at work by 4 a.m. was getting off while there was still plenty of daylight. Working in a bakery wasn't the future she pictured while in culinary school, but she had to admit, she liked where she'd ended up. Patsy allowed her more freedom to experiment than she ever had at the restaurant.

She'd received a wedding cake order today, something she didn't have time for in California. Every once in a while, she had requests for cakes or specific pastries for special events at the restaurant, but nothing like she was getting now. She specialized in desserts in school, but her employment path veered off in other directions. Now she was doing what she truly enjoyed.

Usually by lunchtime she was feeling the effects of waking so early, but the walk home always invigorated her. She changed clothes, threw a load of laundry in the wash, then decided to plant the rose bushes she'd bought, with Leo's permission, to spruce up the back side of the carport. Once she changed into denim shorts and slathered her pale skin with a liberal dose of sunscreen, she went out to the backyard to get dirty.

When she was little, her mom had roses in this same bed. They loved the sun in this patch of earth and had bloomed beautifully.

After the roses were in and mulch spread, Carolyn moved along the back of the house, pulling a few weeds that had sprouted between the junipers and evergreens. If she owned this house, she'd pull the bushes out and put something more aesthetic, more—

She stopped. There was a single footprint in the dirt, right below her bedroom window. A large footprint, and by the indention of the heel and the size, probably made by a man's boot.

"No." She closed her eyes as that one word wheezed from her throat.

Lifting a branch, she spotted a hand print close by. She measured her hand against it. The fingers were wider than hers, and about an inch longer.

Rob's size.

Don't jump to conclusions, she thought, even as she remembered the feeling of being watched. Maybe Leo made the footprint unhooking a hose. She searched the wall, but there wasn't a water spigot anywhere near.

A hand grabbed her shoulder and she screamed.

Stella stumbled back and fell onto the grass. "You scared me to death! What are you screaming for?"

"You scared me just as bad," Carolyn said, closing her eyes in relief. "What are you doing here?"

"I came to see how you were doing." Stella pulled on a flip-flop that she'd lost in her fall. "What are you doing back here?"

"I was weeding." She pointed at the dirt. "Look."

Stella squinted her eyes. "Uh, huh…what am I looking at?"

"The footprint."

Crawling closer on hands and knees, Stella touched the edge of the imprint, then glanced at the window directly above. She slowly turned her head to Carolyn. "Looking at the size, I'd say you didn't make this."

"No, I didn't make it."

Stella raised her brows. "You don't have to be snarky about it. I was just making an observation."

"Sorry," Carolyn said, glancing around her yard, looking for places Robert might conceal himself.

"Is this the first time you've been back here?"

Carolyn nodded.

"So maybe it was made before you moved in."

Or maybe Rob found me.

Stella glanced up at the window again. "It's kind of creepy, though, isn't it? Go inside and close the blinds. Turn on the light you use at night."

Carolyn hurried inside and twirled the wand to shut the blinds, turned on the bedside light, and went back outdoors. Stella was standing on tiptoes, trying to peek over the window ledge. She moved back so Carolyn, who was taller, could look inside. There was a small gap between two of the bottom slats. When she leaned to the left, she could see clear to the closet. A chill wiggled up her spine as the hairs on the back of her neck stood on end. Rob was watching her, but why just watching? Was he trying to discover her most vulnerable moments, or was he making sure she was alone? Thoughts tumbled through her mind faster than she could process them. Waiting was so unlike Rob. He usually struck first and stopped to think afterwards.

"Maybe you should call the police."

"What if it was made before I moved in, like you said? Maybe Leo has been back here for some reason."

"Leo wouldn't be stupid enough to look through the window of the house he was renting to you."

"I'm not saying he was looking in the window, but maybe he was back here to check the sprinklers or something." Carolyn didn't know Leo anymore, but if what everyone said about him was true, she knew Stella was right. Besides, deep down, she knew Leo hadn't made the footprint.

"You should call JT."

If she called him, she might slip and give JT reason to believe she suspected someone specific, which would mean more questions and maybe an investigation. As scared as she was, she wasn't ready for that. "I'm not going to call JT."

"Why not?"

"I've only lived here a week. The footprint could have been made before I moved in. I don't want to make a big deal out of something that might be completely innocent." She started for the back door. "Want to go to Harrisville with me?"

"For what?"

"Curtains. What if that isn't an old footprint?"

"I think we both know it's not an old footprint," Stella said, adding her signature eye-roll.

"Do you want to go with me or not?"

.   .   .

*H*e found me. *He found me.* The words echoed through Carolyn's mind long past her shopping trip with Stella, past hanging curtain rods and heavy drapes, past going into the backyard to make sure the new curtains covered the window completely.

They were still clamoring through her consciousness when she waved to Stella as she pulled away from the curb. Carolyn stood on the porch for a long time after, searching the shadows as night fell.

She'd been so careful to leave a trail headed in the wrong direction, so careful to cover her tracks while she traveled. He knew she was from Washington State, but she'd never mentioned Eden Falls. How had he found her so quickly?

An owl hooted, and she searched for the birds hiding spot. She thought about screaming into the darkness. *Come and get me! Get this over with!* At the same time, she wanted to cower in the corner with her head covered.

She checked the locks on the doors and windows twice before she finally crawled into bed. She left a light burning in the kitchen and the living room. Her bedroom light would stay on all night, too.

~

*P*atsy pulled the door of the oven open and leaned over to take in the fragrant smell. She should have asked Mason if he liked roast beef. She shook her head. *What man doesn't like beef?*

A knock sounded on the front door. She put a hand to her quaking stomach—sixty percent excited and forty percent nervous…or maybe it was the other way around. She wasn't sure, but she still rushed to answer. Mason stood on the other side with a bunch of yellow daffodils in hand. "You're early."

Mason glanced at his watch. "Did I get the time wrong? I thought you said six."

"I did, but I'm trying to impress you and I'm not ready. Can you go home and come back in an hour?"

Mason laughed. "I can if you really want me to, but I'd rather come in and help."

Her eyebrows rose. "Help me? You cook?"

He bent to kiss her cheek. "Patsy, how do you think I've survived all my life? I don't eat out every night."

"Right." She released a huff of air with a smile. "I'd love the help."

"I like your house." He glanced around her living room. "You've made it very homey."

"Thank you." Her furnishings were pretty old, but still comfortable. She never thought of her house as homey, but she liked the word. In fact, she liked a lot of the words Mason used. Her gaze drifted to the daffodils. "Are those for me?"

"I thought a handful of new beginnings were in order," he said holding them out.

She took the bouquet. "Is that what they mean?"

"What they mean?" he asked with a puzzled look.

"You know, the language of flowers?"

He shook his head. "I just thought they were pretty like you."

Oh, well. "Thank you. They're lovely," she said, using one of Mason's words.

"*Y*ou're a million miles away."

Patsy looked across the table at Mason. She'd been thinking about the daffodils since he gave them to her. If Mason did know the language of flowers, she was more touched than she'd ever been by a man. The idea that he might be sending her messages through flowers was romantic and thrilling…and unheard of in this century. "Not a million miles, just a few steps. I drove past the hardware store today. It's really starting to take shape."

"Seeing a new building going up is strange for me. It's almost as if the original hardware and lumber store never existed."

Patsy reached across the table and patted his hand. "It did exist, and it will again, bigger and better than ever."

He gave her one of his elusive smiles. One of his bottom teeth crossed, slightly, in front of the other, proving not everything about him was perfect after all. Good to know, because she was far from flawless.

He pushed his plate back and leaned his forearms on the table. "This was an excellent dinner, Patsy. Thank you for inviting me. It's been a long time since I've had a home-cooked meal that I didn't prepare myself."

"Are you a good cook?"

"I'm not bad."

Patsy set her napkin on the table. "Do you like to cook?"

"I enjoy creating something tasty, though sometimes I find it hard cooking for just one."

She nodded.

He stood and gathered the dishes on the table.

"You don't have to do that."

"You cooked, I'll clean." He set the dirty dishes in the sink and started the water. Patsy stood in awe. None of the men she'd dated or been married to had ever helped with the dishes.

"How was your day?" he asked

She opened the dishwasher and began loading the dishes he rinsed. "Perfect. Carolyn is like an answer to a prayer I never spoke aloud. She moved right in and took over every task, as if she's been doing it for years. She's made my life easy for the first time since I opened Patsy's Pastries."

"Congratulations on finding her."

"She found me." Patsy loaded another dish. "She's sad, though. I see it in her eyes. I've tried to get her to talk about her divorce, but all she'll say is that she and her husband grew apart."

"Maybe she's sad her marriage didn't work. Maybe she still loves him."

"Maybe."

After dishes, they snuggled on the sofa. A cop show was on television, but Patsy didn't pay much mind to the plot unfolding on the screen. Mason's arm around her shoulders felt too good. His thumb moving up and down her bare arm felt even better.

He'd helped her put the finishing touches on dinner and then they cleaned the kitchen together. She knew he wasn't just trying to make new relationship impressions. Mason was the real deal. He was a true-to-life Horton. He meant what he said, and he said what he meant. Mason would be faithful, kind, and true one-hundred percent.

"Would you like dessert?" she asked.

"Can we wait? I'm completely comfortable."

She smiled up at him. "So am I."

He gave her shoulder a light squeeze. "You make my heart happy, Patsy."

More words she liked. Her own heart sighed in contentment. "You make my heart happy, too."

He was selfish with his kisses, though, and she ached with anticipation before he finally leaned down to touch his lips to hers. She was more aware of him than she'd ever been of anyone or anything. His cologne was light, the perfect mix of male and woodsy outdoors. Her fingers skimmed his smooth jaw, and she knew he'd shaved just for her.

The kiss was so sweet and tender, she was carried out to sea on a tide of emotion. Her heartbeat didn't match the lazy movement of his lips as he explored her mouth. Warmth spread through her. The sensations that held her aloft in the swells of waves were too much. She came to the slow realization tears trickled down her cheeks.

Mason pulled back, concern etched over his features, while his thumb moved across her cheek softly. "What is it, Patsy? Why are you crying?"

"They're happy tears." She touched the slight dip in the center of his bottom lip with the tip of her finger. "I'm happy."

~

Patsy let herself in through the back door of the shop the next morning. The kitchen smelled like sugar and lemon. She breathed deeply, filling her lungs with the goodness of someone else cooking. She'd been able to sleep in until eight o'clock this morning and felt well rested and completely blissful. So much so, she was tempted to shed more happy tears.

Carolyn looked up from the worktable and smiled. "Good morning."

Patsy waved as she dropped her purse on her desk and grabbed a clean apron from the shelf next to the door. She plopped down on a stool next to Carolyn and glanced at the loaf cakes cooling on racks near the oven. "Those cakes smell divine."

"Lemon-raspberry. I hope they taste as good as they smell. How did your dinner turn out last night?"

"Wonderful." She waved a hand. "Oh, not the dinner so much, though my pot roast turned out perfect, but the whole night was so...I don't even have the words."

Carolyn smiled.

Patsy blew out a heavy breath. "I'm drowning in conflicting emotions and I don't know what to do."

"Conflicting emotions about what?"

Patsy hated telling Carolyn her problems, but she desperately needed someone to just listen, someone who could tell her if she was making sense or was completely insane.

She grabbed a teaspoon and dipped it in the glaze Carolyn was mixing. *Mmm, orange. Perfect.* "Dinner with Mason was wonderful. Every date we've been on has been wonderful. He is so easy to talk to, but the silence is comfortable, too. We talk about books and music, and we like the same kinds of movies. He talks about interesting stuff…and then he listens, which is a refreshing change from most of the men I've known. When he asks a question, I can tell he really wants to know the answer. He's interested in what I have to say."

"It sounds like he's very interested in you," Carolyn said.

Patsy held up a finger. "Yet on the two dates where we've gone out to dinner, he's taken me to Harrisville rather than Eden Falls."

"Is that a bad thing?"

"You tell me. Deep down, is he trying to keep anyone from finding out we're seeing each other? Is he embarrassed to be seen with me? He's respected in this community, I'm not."

Carolyn frowned. "That's not true, Patsy."

"Sure it is. I don't want his reputation to be tarnished by being with me, but the anticipation of seeing him fills the empty hole of loneliness that threatens to drown me at times. I'm a people person, you know? My nights are lonely."

Color rose over Carolyn's cheeks and Patsy laughed. "I don't mean my nights in bed, though they're lonely, too. I just mean from the time I close the shop until I go to bed, those long hours before sleep, when other people are eating dinner together or watching TV, sharing a bowl of popcorn. Those hours."

Carolyn nodded as if she completely understood.

Patsy grabbed butter from the fridge. "The thought of dating again scares me. I've been through four husbands. Do I really want to start all over?" She glanced at Carolyn. "I'm sorry to dump all this on you. I thought I just needed someone to listen, but now…well, what do you think?"

Carolyn turned from what she was doing. "Mr. Douglas wouldn't ask you out if he didn't want to be seen with you. He's been single for a long time, so I believe dating you wasn't a sudden decision for him." She balanced the spatula she was using on the rim of a bowl. "As far as reputation is concerned, people in town respect you more than you know. Mr. Douglas wouldn't care either way. He took you to Harrisville to show you a nice time, not to hide the fact that he asked you out."

Patsy put her hands on her hips. "I'm overthinking this, aren't I?"

Carolyn smiled. "If it's any comfort, I would do the same."

Patsy came around the worktable and hugged Carolyn. "Thank you for listening. I feel better."

~

Carolyn was exhausted when she left Patsy's Pastries thirty minutes later, but she wanted to go to the library and get a card before heading home.

After finding the footprint, she'd driven to work this morning, too afraid to be alone on the deserted streets of Eden Falls so early. She glanced toward Town Hall and noticed JT on the steps talking to his cousin Beam.

"Hi."

Carolyn whirled around, nearly jumping out of her skin. "Would you stop popping out of nowhere, Stella? This is the second time in two days that you've scared me to death."

"You scared me back yesterday, so that one doesn't count. Besides"—Stella glanced across the street—"you might have noticed me if you weren't staring at JT."

"I wasn't star—"

"Save it." Stella waved a hand. "Every single female in town, and some of the married ones, stare at JT."

No use denying it. She was staring, and she'd been caught. She would need to be more careful in the future. "What are you doing here?"

"Craving something sweet to eat. Come over to Noelle's Café with me. We can share a piece of pie."

Carolyn laughed. The reaction was becoming familiar again, after so many years of living without it. She'd missed laughing and crazy friends and spontaneity. Suddenly the hair on the back of her neck rose. The feeling of being watched was back. She glanced around the square, sure she would spot Robert peeking from behind a tree, or sitting in a car. Everything was as it should be.

"Why are you laughing?"

She turned her attention back to Stella. "I work around sweets all day."

"Then you can watch while I eat a piece of pie." Stella grabbed her arm and pulled her in the direction of the café.

"Okay, you win. Besides, I've missed doing spur-of-the-moment things like this."

"You didn't do this kind of thing in San Francisco?"

TMI. She had to start thinking before blurting out her thoughts. "I didn't really have time."

"What did you and your friends do for fun?"

I wasn't allowed friends. "I worked with most of my friends. We never had the same days off."

"What about your husband? Did you guys go out often?"

Carolyn stopped and pulled her arm from Stella's grasp. "Why does everyone want to know about my husband? Every time I'm around you guys, you're asking questions about him. He's not a part of my life anymore!"

She cringed at her outburst as heat prickled over the skin on her chest and rose up her neck. The dreaded blotches were soon to follow. She dropped her head and glanced at Stella through a veil of lashes. "Sorry."

"No, I'm sorry. You've said you don't want to talk about him, and I should have respected that." Stella hugged her. "I wasn't fishing for information, just curious about your life in California."

"I know. I just…didn't have much of a life in California. I worked. A lot." *To be away from home, I spent every hour I could at the restaurant. I was safe there.*

"I won't bring him up again."

Stella pulled the café's door open, and Carolyn followed her inside. She'd only eaten here once, for breakfast, but had enjoyed the homemade goodness of the meal. A young girl greeted Stella and showed them to a booth by the front window.

Carolyn looked out, the feeling of being watched not completely gone.

After Stella ordered, Carolyn decided to give her friend a few facts. Not only did she feel bad for snapping at her, but if Stella had a glimpse into her San Francisco life, she might quit asking questions. "Robert and I shouldn't have gotten married so quickly. We didn't know each other very long before he proposed. He swept me off my feet and I…" She closed her eyes in humiliation. "I was so starved for attention, I let him."

Tears burned the back of her eyes. She blinked them away, looking everywhere but at Stella. "After years of my sister blaming me for our parents' death, reminding me what a burden I was to her, how Mom and Dad never planned to have me, I craved validation, and Robert gave it to me." *At first.* "He won me over with smiles and compliments. He praised my cooking, said I was the most beautiful woman he'd ever met. I'd never been in love before and I fell hard. For the first time in my life, I felt loved and cherished. I felt like I'd finally found where I belonged."

She looked down at her hands, clutched in her lap so tight, her knuckles were white. "I should have waited until I knew him better, but when he said we should get married, I didn't see any reason to wait." She shook her head as she looked across the table to meet Stella's gaze. "I was so happy to discover someone out there who could love me."

"Carolyn," Stella said. Her expression of compassion wasn't deserved. "Then what happened?"

Carolyn rubbed her naked ring finger, free of the symbol that bound her, but not of the bonds themselves. "He changed."

"How?"

"After we got married, nothing was good enough. The mashed potatoes he liked lumpy were suddenly too lumpy, the gravy wasn't thick enough, the chicken was too dry." *Stop talking.* "He became impossible to please."

"I'm sorry it didn't work out, Care." Stella's compassionate expression turned sad. "Guys suck."

"Yes, sometimes they do."

The waitress delivered Stella's pie and Carolyn's diet soda.

"Your turn," Carolyn said. "Tell me about Len."

Stella shoved a huge bite of pie into her mouth and rolled her eyes. "He's the most confusing guy I've ever dated. One day he's romantic and seems completely into me, the next he's so distant I don't recognize him. He breaks dates at the last minute with excuses that sound legit, but… I don't know…" She shook her head. "It's his voice, you know? There's something in his voice."

Carolyn did know. She used to judge Rob's mood by his tone of voice or the look in his eyes. Sincere or condescending, she usually knew within a few words if it was a good day or if she had to tread lightly.

"One day everything is going great, the next it's as if I don't know him at all."

For a second time, Carolyn wondered if Len was like Robert.

"He's not mean or anything," Stella said, as if reading her mind. "He's just…I don't know any other way to describe it. He's just not there."

"Do you love him, Stella?"

"Yes. No. I don't know." She blew out a breath on a sigh. "This subject is depressing. Did you get any sleep last night?"

"Not much." Carolyn knew Stella was questioning whether she was nervous about the footprint, but she'd lived with Rob. Nothing was scarier than that. She'd looked out the front window of Patsy's more times than she could count. She would continue to be extra-careful, stay alert and aware of her surroundings.

Before Carolyn knew it, an hour had flown by. Luckily, once they got the downer part of their conversation over, Stella made her laugh so hard she had to wipe away tears. Her friend was gifted that way.

As she drove home, Carolyn was glad she'd opened up to Stella's questions. Her explanation seemed to satisfy Stella's curiosity without completely revealing her shame at staying with a man who beat her for so many years.

~

*H*ere he was again, turning down her street, but this time, he actually stopped in front of the house where Carolyn lived. He had no other explanation than she'd been on his mind all day. He saw her in front of the pastry shop twice. He watched her cross the street and enter Noelle's Café with Stella, had contemplated joining them. Unfortunately, a call pulled him in another direction.

She walked around the side of the house as he climbed from his patrol car. She was searching the ground but turned toward the street when she heard the car door shut. Her face registered alarm. Was she threatened by him? He remembered bumping shoulders with her at Alex's and her jumping away so fast, she almost tumbled off the back stoop.

"Hello, JT."

He glanced toward Carolyn's neighbor, who was waving from her rose garden. "Hi, Mrs. Bingham. How are you this afternoon?"

"As right as rain. I wonder if I could bother you for some assistance."

JT crossed Carolyn's yard and took the stool Mrs. Bingham was folding up. "What can I help with?"

"My son attached the sprayer nozzle on my hose when he was here last weekend and he put the darn thing on so tight, I can't get it off." She pointed to the house across the street. "Duffy tried to help this morning, but he couldn't budge it, either."

He followed her to the side of the house and loosened the sprayer head from the hose, all the while keeping an eye on Carolyn, who was squatting under the front picture window, lifting juniper branches.

"There you go. Is there anything else I can help you with?"

"That will do it." She glanced toward Carolyn and nudged his arm. "Is this a business call, or a social one?"

He caught the teasing twinkle in her pale blue eyes and decided the truth wouldn't hurt. "A little of both."

Mrs. Bingham pulled off her gardening gloves and winked. "You'd get a good one there."

"No matchmaking, Mrs. Bingham. I simply stopped by to check on our newest resident."

Her smile said she thought differently. "Have a nice time checking."

Carolyn had disappeared around the opposite side of the house. He jogged to catch up and found her squatted down, scanning the dirt on the side of the carport. "Did you lose something?"

"Nope." She straightened and brushed her hands together. "Just looking…at the soil."

He grinned and she blushed. She was so cute when flustered. He folded his arms and surveyed her nice-sized yard. The back fence was lined with pines and shrubs. "This yard will require some maintenance."

"I don't mind."

"I remember. You said you like yard work."

I do. I didn't get to do much in San Francisco…because of the hours I worked."

"Well, you'll get to make up for it here." He took off his uniform cap and ran his fingers through his hair, feeling unexpectedly nervous. "The pastry shop looked busy today."

"Patsy's is busy every day." She smiled. "Your brother-in-law alone could keep the place in business."

"Colton thinks Alex doesn't know how often he visits, but she knows."

"She knows," Carolyn said at the same time.

They both laughed, and this time it reached her pretty eyes.

He ran fingers through his hair again. "I stopped by to invite you to my Father's Day barbecue. It's become an annual tradition."

"Alex mentioned it to me."

"Oh, good. She and I will be happy to share our dad. He'd claim you as his own in a heartbeat." *Say you'll come.*

"I always adored your dad when we were kids—still do."

"Then he'll expect you to be there to celebrate the day."

She glanced around backyard, her eyes landing everywhere but on him. "I work until one."

"The party doesn't usually get hopping until then."

Her gaze finally met his. "What can I bring?"

"Just a side dish, whatever you want."

She touched her ring finger like she was going to twist the wedding band she no longer wore. "Alex said you live in your grandparents' house."

"Right. Do you remember where it is?"

She smiled. "Yes."

He performed a mental high five. "I'll see you then."

Pink touched her cheeks. "See you then."

He turned to leave, but stopped and looked back at her. "You have a beautiful smile, Carolyn."

CHAPTER 9

Mason Douglas entered Patsy's Pastries and Carolyn watched joy light his face when he spotted Patsy behind the counter. She was helping a customer, but stopped long enough to flash a smile meant just for him. A blush moved up his neck and spread across his cheeks in the adorable way Patsy talked about.

Patsy said her last marriage ended because her husband accused her of being too happy. How was that possible? And why would being too happy be a problem? Patsy was a glass-half-full-kind of person. What a wonderful way to look at life.

In Carolyn's opinion, the world was too short of happiness these days.

She moved around the counter. "Hi, Mr. Douglas."

He opened his arms, hugged her tight, and she let him without any tension on her part, which was a nice change. "Carolyn, it's so good to see you. How are you doing?"

"Wonderful. How is the rebuilding of the hardware store coming? I drove past the other day and saw they have the frame up."

He released her. "It's coming along fine—though a little too slowly, in Beam's opinion."

She could imagine Beam was ready to get the business up and running again. "I'm sorry about the fire."

"Thanks, sweetheart."

"How's your gorgeous granddaughter?"

"Perfect." He pulled his glasses off and polished them with a piece of cloth he pulled from his shirt pocket. "I love every minute I get to spend with her."

"I'll bet. She's growing so fast."

"Too fast." He smiled at her. "Patsy told me you are a tremendous help. She's very glad you came back to town."

All her life, from childhood through her marriage, she felt more like a hindrance. His words helped confirm that she'd finally found her niche. Her work was appreciated at the restaurant, but that's all it had been—work. Here, she felt the pleasure of being able to create and the freedom to choose what she created. She loved to see the smiles on customer's faces as they chose the perfect sweet to start their day.

"Hi, handsome," Patsy said when she joined them. She had a way of making people feel special.

Mason blushed as he placed his glasses back on his nose. "Hello."

Carolyn slipped behind the counter to bow out of their conversation.

"What brings you in?"

"I was on my way to the building site and thought I'd pick up donuts for the construction crew."

She smiled. "Are you using donuts as an excuse to see me?"

His ears turned red. Carolyn wondered how many times in a visit Patsy made him blush. He took her hand. "I did want to see you, to ask you something."

Patsy's smile brightened. "Ask away."

"I would like to take you to JT's Father's Day barbecue on Saturday."

Patsy's smile faltered. No doubt she was worried about being seen with him in front of the town. Even Misty would be there.

Still holding her hand, Mason pulled her a step closer. "Please, come with me if you can get away from the shop."

She glanced at Carolyn who hoped her smile of encouragement worked. "I can probably get away for a couple of hours."

Patsy looked as terrified as Carolyn felt when JT showed up at her house last night with the same invitation. Of course, he wasn't asking her as a date, like Mr. Douglas was asking Patsy.

"We can iron out the details later." He still held her hand, which touched Carolyn's heart. Then he smiled. "Now, about those donuts."

Ten minutes after Mason left, Carolyn found Patsy slumped behind her desk with tears on her cheeks, which she couldn't stand to see. Patsy was the superstar she looked up to. She was courageous and self-confident. She wasn't afraid of anything…except selflessly worrying about Mason's standing in the community. "Are you okay?"

"I've heard about JT's barbecue, but I've never been. I know half the town goes." She glanced up at Carolyn. "I'm not sure I'll be welcome."

"JT would want everyone to feel welcome."

Patsy nodded as she moved some papers aside so Carolyn could perch on the corner of the desk. "I told you I felt a little hurt when Mason took me to Harrisville for our dates, but really, for Mason's sake, going out of town was for the best. Now he's asking me to a party, an Eden Falls tradition, where we'll be seen by many. People will know we're dating. They'll be judging not only me, but Mason. I don't think he realizes how awkward this might be for him, especially since he's so low-key." She shook her head. "His reputation's spotless. He's a good man and doesn't deserve what people will say."

"You're overthinking this again. Mr. Douglas asked you to go with him because he *wants* to be seen with you."

Patsy pushed to her feet, took Carolyn's arm, and led her to the back door. They stepped outside into the sunshine. The sky was heartbreakingly blue, a beautiful contrast to the white clouds chasing each other across the sky.

They crossed the small parking lot to a narrow patch of dirt where a riot of wild flowers bloomed.

"Alex tilled this dirt and scattered seeds a few years ago. I love to come out here and check on them, give them a drink. Sometimes I just come here to think. The sight gives me hope, such beauty in a back parking lot. Not many people know these flowers exist."

Carolyn reached down to cup a wildflower blossom between her fingers. Alex had a magic touch with anything that grew…from flowers to kids to love.

"I'll have to bring Mason back here to show him. He'd appreciate the profusion of colors and heights. Funny, I already know that about him."

Carolyn turned to Patsy. "What are you going to do about Mason's invitation?"

"These flowers growing in such a crazy place make me believe anything is possible."

Carolyn hoped that was true. For both of them.

Patsy nodded. "I'll go the barbecue and watch peoples' reactions. If Mason is shunned because of me, I'll break things off. Losing him will hurt my heart, but it will hurt worse to watch him being rejected because of me."

Carolyn hated that Patsy was going through such turmoil at a time when she should be joyous. Carolyn wasn't so damaged that she couldn't remember what new love felt like. The shortness of breath or the smile that popped up at unexpected moments.

She was head-over-heels in love with Rob in the beginning, and even later, after the beatings started. When had her feelings changed? She wasn't sure she knew the answer.

～

He watched her shadow move back and forth past the living room window from his hiding spot among the evergreen boughs. He kept as still as possible, careful not to disturb the branches that concealed him. He'd been here a long time. Why was she still up? She had to be at the pastry shop way before dawn. He knew, because he followed her to work. She used to walk, but had suddenly started taking her car. Why?

A light appeared in the windows behind him. He fell backwards into the pine tree, sending a shower of dried needles on his head and down the back of his neck. He waited, with held breath, until the light went off. Then he waited another eternity before he dared crawl out of the pine. When he did, he noticed Carolyn's light was off. Anger churned through him at the thought that he'd missed seeing her undress.

He watched the windows behind him for a several minutes. All was quiet.

Slipping from his veiled shelter, he crossed the street and ducked behind the carport. Here, the hedge that ran between the houses hid him from the neighbors next door. He slithered around the corner into the backyard. In his haste to see her, he tripped and landed full-body into a short bush that hadn't been there on his last visit. A thousand needles jabbed him, piercing his flesh. He bit his tongue. Nearly yelping aloud in pain, he twisted as branches snapped beneath him. He tried to roll free, but his jacket tangled in the serrated ruins of the bushes he'd fallen into. The rip of fabric sounded loud in the quiet night as he tried to yank from the stinging, razor-sharp hold.

He reached down and something sharp stabbed his thumb. He stuck it to his mouth and grimaced at the metallic tang of blood, not sure if it was from his thumb or his tongue. Putting his hand against the wall of the carport he pushed hard and rolled free, smacking his hip on the concrete patio. At least he was untangled. He sat up and tried to assess the damage to himself and the bushes, but it was too dark.

Great! Just great. Now she'll know someone was here.

He stood, brushing dirt from his jacket, and backed into a patio chair that tipped over before he could swing around and catch it. Metal hitting concrete exploded through the quiet night air, loud as a gunshot. He turned and ran full speed in the opposite direction, keeping to the shadows as much as possible.

~

*C*arolyn awakened with a start, her heart racing, as she was yanked from deep sleep to consciousness. She stared at the dark ceiling, trying to recall…oh, yes, she'd been dreaming, and wished she could have had five more minutes to see what happened next.

Her eyes drifted shut again, but an alarm was ringing in her subconscious. She glanced at the clock next to the bed. She'd only been asleep for about twenty minutes. Generally she slept for at least three hours before nightmares woke her.

Rolling over, she lay quiet, listening to the night sounds, searching her mind for whatever it was that had awakened her. Deciding it was only her imagination, she closed her eyes once more.

A scraping sound sat her upright in a second. Something or someone was outside. She knew there were raccoons and an occasional fox. Deer, bear, moose, and mountain lions lived in the surrounding forests, but she knew deep down that the sound she heard was man-made. A loud crash echoed through the window, and, without thought, she rolled to the floor, grabbed the phone from the nightstand, and punched the numbers 911.

"Nine-one-one, what's your emergency?"

"I think someone's in my backyard." Carolyn tried to sound coherent around the trembling of her voice. *Why can't he just leave me alone?*

"Are your doors and windows locked?"

"Yes." A sob worked its way up her throat, but she swallowed it down.

"Can you confirm your address?"

"1020 Cedar Drive."

"Carolyn?"

The operator saying her name startled her. "Y…yes."

"This is Phoebe Adams. Stella's sister. Stay on the line with me, while I give the guys on duty a call. Do not open the door until the police arrive."

Her whole body was quaking. She stayed on the floor, waiting for Phoebe to return, straining to hear more sounds, but the pulse pounding in her ears was too loud.

"Carolyn? Russ and JT are on their way. Stay on the phone with me until they arrive."

What is he waiting for? Why doesn't he just come for me?

"Carolyn?"

"Yes, I will."

"Where are you in the house?"

"I'm in my bedroom. The back bedroom."

"Will you feel safe there until the police arrive?"

I don't feel safe anywhere.

"If not, go into a bathroom and lock the door."

A locked door never stopped him before. She wanted to push the window open and try to reason with him. She'd give him everything she had, if he'd just leave her alone. But she knew he wouldn't listen. Hadn't she tried before? Hadn't she begged and pleaded? *Everything I said only made him angrier.*

A knock on the front door nearly catapulted her to the ceiling.

"Carolyn? JT just radioed. He's out front. If you have a peephole or chain, use it before you open the door. I'll stay on the line until you let him in."

"Okay."

She crawled across the floor until she was out of the bedroom. She recognized the voice calling through the door. "Carolyn? It's JT."

"Thanks, Phoebe," she said, before disconnecting the call and unlocking the front door. JT stepped inside. Another patrol car stopped at the curb.

"Are you okay?" he asked.

"I think someone is in the backyard."

"Stay here," he said, then addressed the officer who'd just stepped onto the porch. "Sit with her while I look around outside."

The officer stepped inside and shut the door. She recognized him, remembered Colton introducing them, but couldn't remember his name.

"Are you okay, Carolyn?"

"Yes. I'm sorry to call you out."

"That's what we're here for. Phoebe said you heard something. Can you describe the noise?"

She sank down on the sofa. Then, realizing she hadn't put

anything on over her flimsy camisole, she excused herself. In the bedroom, she grabbed a sweater from the back of the door and wrapped it tightly around her shaking body. When she returned to the living room, the officer was looking at her shelf of books. "I know we've met, but my mind is so muddled I've forgotten your name."

"Russell Walsh, but everyone calls me Russ."

She closed her eyes and nodded. "Right. Please, have a seat, Russ. Can I get you anything? Water?"

He smiled as he took the chair she'd indicated. "No, thank you."

As soon as she sat, her knee started bouncing. Remembering JT's touch, she stopped. "Sorry, I...I can't think straight."

"Perfectly understandable. Why don't you tell me what you heard?"

"I don't...I'm not sure what woke me up...some sound that I can't identify. Then there was a loud crash. The only thing I can think of was maybe something"—*someone*—"knocked over one of my patio chairs." Which had to be an accident, because Robert wouldn't do anything that would cause her to call the police.

JT knocked on the door before stepping inside. "Are you okay, Carolyn?"

She stood. "Did you see anything?"

"There's no one out there." He closed the distance between them.

"But there was," Carolyn said under her breath. She met his gaze. "Wasn't there?"

He nodded. "One of your patio chairs is on its side and branches on the bushes behind the carport are broken."

He touched her elbow and she flinched away. A frown appeared, but was gone just as quickly. He pointed toward the sofa. "Let's sit down." He sat beside her, leaving little space between them. "Is this the first time you've heard anything?"

She pressed her lips together and knew he noticed her hesitancy.

He glanced at the other officer. "Russ, I only checked the patio area. Will you take a look along the back fence and side yard?"

"Sure."

After Russ left the house, JT rested his forearms on his knees, leaning closer. "Carolyn, talk to me."

Time to tell another truth. "I found a footprint in the back-yard a week ago."

Both his eyebrows rose. "Why didn't you call me?"

"I wasn't sure it was anything. Leo could have left it before I moved in. There was no way to tell how old it was."

His gaze was direct and intimidating. "Is that why you were walking around the house yesterday?"

She looked down at her hands. Her fingers ached from being clutched so tight. "Yes."

"Did you find any more?"

"No."

"Where was the footprint?"

She waited a beat. "Under the bedroom window."

His features hardened. "The bedroom in the back?"

She nodded.

He blew out a forced breath. "I'll talk to Leo tomorrow and see if he's been in the yard for any reason."

Russ came back inside, slipping his flashlight into his utility belt. "I don't see anything."

JT nodded and glanced at Carolyn again. "I haven't had any complaints from your neighbors, but I'll talk to them tomorrow. Have you seen any cars you don't recognize, seen anyone hanging around the neighborhood?"

Carolyn shook her head. "No."

"I'll be back in the morning to have another look around. Why don't you pack a few things? I'll take you to Alex's?"

"I'm not going to put"—she stopped short of saying, Alex's family in danger—"Alex out at this time of night." Her leaving would have enraged Robert. She believed he was capable of almost anything to win, whether he truly wanted her back or not. "I'll be okay."

JT's mouth twisted in indecision, then he nodded. "Okay. Russ and I will take turns driving by the rest of the night. Although, I don't believe whoever it was will be back. I'm sure they took off as soon as that chair tipped over."

Carolyn shook her head. "I don't want you to go out of your way. I'll be fine.

JT glanced at Russ. "Drive by every thirty minutes."

"Will do. 'Night, Carolyn."

"Goodnight, Russ. Thank you for coming."

"I'm going to check all your window and door locks before I leave," JT said after Russ left the house.

She waited in the living room while he checked the house. She'd finally stopped quaking, and was present enough in the moment to wonder how she looked. Was her hair squashed flat on one side? Did she have a pillow crease down her face?

JT entered the living room. "I'll talk to Leo about installing dead bolts on both your doors. You should also have a peephole in this one," he said pointing at the front door.

Carolyn had never had a man concerned for her safety and wasn't sure how she felt about it. She'd been taking care of herself for so long...

"Are you sure I can't drive you to Alex's house?"

"I'll be fine."

"I'm going to look around outside once more before I leave."

Even though he was doing his job, she saw the worry

around his eyes. She wasn't sure how she felt about that either. "Okay."

She watched JT circle the outside of her house several times from the front window, widening his search with each pass. She knew Robert wouldn't be back tonight. He'd want her nervous and insecure. Scared out of her wits would come later.

She woke up on the sofa with a stiff neck when her alarm sounded at three a.m.

~

JT pulled to a stop in Carolyn's driveway just as the sun crested the eastern horizon. The carport was empty, so he knew she'd already left for Patsy's. He was glad she drove rather than walked, which he'd seen her do a couple of times while patrolling before dawn.

He started at the footprint in the dirt below her bedroom window. While examining it, he moved a branch of the evergreen shrub aside and spotted a handprint she'd neglected to tell him about, or hadn't noticed. He put his hand near the print, smaller than his.

He straightened and stared at the bedroom window directly above. There was a place where the blinds didn't quite meet, but he couldn't see in because of the drapes she'd hung.

Next, he studied the fallen patio chair and the tromped-on rose bushes. Broken stems were scattered near the bed and one bush was completely uprooted. He squatted to take a closer look. An animal didn't do this—at least not a four-legged one. Might be the work of kids out to vandalize, but kids didn't live in this neighborhood. He tried to prop up the uprooted bush and pricked his thumb on a thorn. He noticed a piece of fabric tangled in the mess. Someone had fallen into the bushes rather than tromping through. He pulled his cell phone from his pocket and snapped a few pictures before pulling the fabric free—black, heavy, possibly from a jacket. *Bet whoever fell in the middle of those thorns has some major wounds.* He'd have to keep an eye out.

Straightening, he made slow circles around the perimeter, just as he'd done last night, but found nothing further. He stood in several spots around the yard, trying to imagine where someone would hide if they was watching Carolyn. The best bet was among the pines along the back.

He rounded the house to the front yard and glanced from house to house. There wasn't a fence between Mrs. Bingham house and Carolyn's. The fence on the left was hidden under shrubs that blocked any view of Carolyn's backyard. He stood on her front porch and studied the surroundings. The huge pine on the side yard of the house across the street caught his eye. He crossed the road, still looking for signs. At the tree, he squatted down. Someone had been standing almost against the trunk when a shower of needles fell. He pulled his cell out again and took more pictures of the visible footprints, then moved some needles aside. Some were pressed into the soft soil below.

He glanced up when a car stopped at the curb. Russ climbed out.

"Find anything?"

JT stood and brushed his hands together. "Yep. I think I found where our guy might be watching from."

"Kids?"

"I don't think so." *Wish I was wrong.* Kids out causing a little harmless trouble would be easier to deal with than an adult spying on a woman. The idea that some guy was watching Carolyn through the slats of her blinds raised his blood pressure.

"Unless you need me for anything, I'm headed home."

"Nope. Get some sleep, Russ. I'll see you tonight. Let's take the same shift around this neighborhood. Every thirty minutes."

"I'll take the top of each hour." Russ climbed back in his car and drove away.

On the way to his patrol car, JT scrolled through phone numbers on his cell. He hated to call so early, but felt this couldn't wait.

"Hello." Leo's greeting came out polite but groggy.

"Hey, Leo, it's JT. Sorry to call so early."

"Not a problem," came out more clear. "What's up?"

"Carolyn West had to call 911 last night. Someone was hanging around her place after dark."

"Is she okay?"

"She wasn't hurt, but after looking around a bit, I found a footprint under the bedroom window."

"Which bedroom?"

"The one she's using in the back of the house. Have you been back there for any reason?"

"No. I haven't been to the house since I rented it out. I did have a landscape company keeping the lawn maintained, but Carolyn said she wanted to do the work herself after she moved in."

"Can I get the number of that company?"

"Sure. Hold on a minute."

"I suggested deadbolts for both doors and possibly a peephole in the front," JT said when Leo came back with the number.

"I'll take care of it today."

"I'll let Carolyn know."

"No, I'll stop by Patsy's and set up a time that'll be convenient for her."

I'd rather stop by myself. "Okay. Thanks, Leo."

JT had one more stop to make before he went home to bed. He found a parking place in front of Noelle's Café and went inside, glad to see Noelle Treloar working the counter. He slid onto a stool at the end, away from everyone.

The memory of her cousin watching a table of women in Rowdy's the weekend before had flashed through his mind when he was searching the exterior of Carolyn's house. She'd been one of the women at that table.

Noelle came over with her usual smile. "Morning. Just coming on or just getting off?"

"Just getting off."

"What can I get you?"

The sweater Carolyn wore last night had smelled of maple. "I'll take a short stack, a side of bacon, and a large milk."

"Coming right up."

Before she could turn away, he said, "Can I ask about your cousin, Noelle?"

"Sure."

"What brought him from Boston to Eden Falls?"

Her eyebrows furrowed in question. "Why?"

"Curious. Rowdy says he's doing a great job at the bar and grill."

She reached for a pitcher of milk in a cooler behind her. "His fiancée broke their engagement six weeks ago. I offered him a place to stay, so he could get away for a while. He accepted."

Mike was a dead end. He wouldn't be watching Carolyn if his fiancée had just broken his heart. "I bet it's nice having him close with the rest of your family so far away."

"We were close as kids, so I'm glad he's here." She grinned. "I'm also glad the rest of my family is far away."

He took a sip of the milk Noelle set in front of him as he pondered Carolyn's reactions last night. She'd acted nervous, which was understandable under the circumstances. But she'd also acted guilty. Was it from not reporting the footprint, or was there something else?

~

He unbuttoned his shirt and pulled his arms out, then carefully lifted his T-shirt over his head with a hiss. Scrapes and dried blood covered his chest, side, and arms. Luckily, he hadn't fallen face-first. Explaining those kinds of marks would be impossible. As it was, he'd be wearing a long-sleeved shirt for the rest of the week.

He unzipped his pants and flipped the right side down. The spot where his hip smacked the concrete patio was already black and blue.

He finished stripping and climbed into the shower, wincing as hot water hit the scratches. Where had those rose bushes come from? They weren't there the last time he was in the backyard.

Had he left remnants of his jacket on those bushes? Not good if they were discovered, though they could never be traced back to him. That jacket was years old, bought in another state, and now at the bottom of the river, weighed down with rocks, ten miles out of town.

~

The unique fragrance of yeast floated through the air when Carolyn punched the dough in the stainless steel bowl, her mind on Robert. He'd intruded on her thoughts all morning. She covered the dough with a towel and turned to the oven to check her apple spice cupcakes. Her outside world might be topsy-turvy, but all was well in Patsy's Pastries kitchen.

While JT searched the perimeter of her house last night, she'd been tempted to call the San Francisco house. If Rob didn't pick up the phone, she'd have her answer. He was here. She kept wondering why he hadn't made a move to show himself, but she knew the answer to that, too. He'd draw things out, make her insane with fear, then revel in her anxiety. He enjoyed terrorizing her.

Patsy came into the kitchen carrying an empty tray. "Your blueberry scones were a hit. A tourist bought every last—"

The kitchen door thumped against the wall and Carolyn jumped, her heart in her throat. She relaxed when she saw it was only Alex who'd stormed into her quiet haven.

"Why didn't you call me last night?"

Patsy's eyebrows rose, her look bouncing from Alex to Carolyn.

Carolyn picked up hot pads and opened the oven door. "Everything is fine, Alex."

"Everything is *not* fine. Why didn't you call JT earlier about the footprints you found?"

Patsy set the empty tray on the counter. "What footprints?"

Carolyn pulled the cupcakes from the oven, filling the kitchen with the scent of apples and cinnamon. She set the hot pan on the stovetop and turned to her friend. "There was only one footprint. I didn't tell JT because I wasn't sure when it was made."

"Seeing a footprint below your bedroom window is grounds for calling the police."

"You found footprints under your bedroom window and you didn't call the police?" Patsy paled and sank onto a stool. "Tell me what's going on."

"Carolyn had to call the police last night because there was someone in her backyard."

"Or something. There's no proof it wasn't a raccoon."

Alex crossed her arms and cocked a hip. "Raccoons do not make human prints. You should have reported it the day you found it."

"Yes, you should have reported it." Patsy shook her finger as if scolding a child, panic raising her voice an octave.

"Okay." Carolyn held up her hands up in surrender. "Leo probably made it weeks before I moved in, but you're right. I should have called the police."

"I think you should stay with me until we find out for sure."

"Don't be ridiculous, Alex. It was one footprint, and I'd —" she almost said, I'd never put your family in danger, but Leo came through the kitchen door and stopped her just in time.

"Are you okay, Carolyn? JT called me about your intruder." His pale blue eyes with their navy rims around the irises revealed his concern. The same concern her manager at the San Francisco restaurant showed every time Carolyn came into work with a fresh bruise or a new bandage.

To avoid meeting his gaze, Carolyn tipped her head back and stared at the ceiling. "I'm fine."

"I've got a locksmith on call to install deadbolts. Is this afternoon convenient?"

"Yes," Alex said. "I'll be there if she can't."

"I'll be there," Carolyn said at the same time. "If you'll tell me how much—"

Leo slashed a hand through the air. "Absolutely not. I should have done this before I rented out the house."

"Leo…"

He shook his head. "I'll come over at the same time as the locksmith and install a peephole in the front door."

"That's good," Patsy said, pointing her at finger Leo. "A female living alone should have a peephole." She stood and took Carolyn by the shoulders, giving her a little shake. "Number one, you always call the police when you find footprints, especially when they're under your bedroom window. Number two, you don't ever open the door if you can't see who it is."

"And number three," Alex joined in, "you tell JT immediately if something like this happens again."

Carolyn was close to tears over the concern her friends were showing. She crossed her heart with an index finger.

*A*fter another stern lecture from Patsy, Carolyn left the shop for the day. She'd promised to help Mrs. Bingham move furniture around in her living room. Once home, she showered, changed clothes quickly, and ran next door. When Mrs. Bingham greeted her at the door with a hug, she realized she'd made a new friend, and it felt wonderful. Rob hadn't allowed friends.

She vaguely remembered Mrs. Bingham and her rose garden from when she lived here as a little girl, but just barely. Back then, Mrs. Bingham's white hair was brown, and there'd been a Mr. Bingham, who loved to laugh.

While they were situating a chair in front of the picture window, Mrs. Bingham pointed outside. "A locksmith just pulled up in front of your house. Is he here because of the ruckus last night?"

Carolyn moved to the other side of the window and saw Leo's truck pull up behind the locksmith. Both men climbed from their vehicles and shook hands. She walked outside and called to Leo. "You can let yourself in."

He waved.

"Did the noise wake you?" she asked Mrs. Bingham when she reentered the house.

"No. I saw JT out early this morning circling your house and—busybody that I am—I went to ask why. He said someone was in your backyard, and asked if I'd seen anything. I haven't, but I called the neighbors and alerted them. We'll all be on the lookout."

Be on the lookout echoed through Carolyn's mind. Her eyes filled with unexpected tears as a memory popped into her mind. Once, when she was little, Mrs. Bingham invited Carolyn into her home and let her help make chocolate chip cookies. The first time she'd ever been allowed to cook was here in this house. She remembered sifting the dry ingredients together, cracking the eggs, creaming the sugar with the butter, adding the sweet scent of vanilla.

She walked to the kitchen door. "I'd forgotten that we baked cookies together in your kitchen." She turned to Mrs. Bingham. "But the memory is suddenly so vivid. The countertops used to be blue Formica and you had white curtains with blueberries on them."

Mrs. Bingham laughed and the wrinkles around her eyes and mouth deepened. "That's right, I did."

"I'd forgotten all about that day."

Mrs. Bingham lifted her shoulders. "We can't remember everything or everyone who passes through our lives."

"But that was a happy day in my life. You were so patient with me. I remember getting eggshell in the dough, and you said it didn't matter. You just picked it out. My mom wouldn't have been…" She tried to swallow around the lump in her throat. Mrs. Bingham had somehow known how unhappy Carolyn was. "Mr. Bingham came in from work that afternoon and told me they were the best cookies he'd ever eaten."

"And Mr. Bingham always told the truth," Mrs. Bingham said, a knowing twinkle in her eye.

Carolyn hugged the woman standing next to her. "He also said you'd been looking out for me."

"Did he? Well, what would this world be like if we didn't look out for each other?"

The words, simple as they were, warmed Carolyn's heart.

Mrs. Bingham was exactly as she'd always imagined a grandmother would be. What Alex's grandmother had been like. Carolyn never knew her grandparents. They were gone before she was born, so she'd lived vicariously through her friends.

Carolyn glanced out the window into the backyard. Seeing more roses along the back fence reminded her of her own sad rosebushes. "Could I borrow a rose pruner? Whoever was in my backyard did a number on the rose bushes I planted the other day."

"I already took care of them. JT said they were a mess. I went over later to look. They're a little lopsided, and the one on the left might not make it since the roots were exposed all night, but with a little tender care, the others will be fine."

Mrs. Bingham's thoughtfulness touched her heart again. "Thank you. You didn't need to do that."

"Sure I did. That's what neighbors do. You help me move furniture, I trim your rosebushes."

At the sound of the doorbell, Mrs. Bingham put a hand to her heart. "Oh, I bet it's that cute Leo."

"Do you need anything else moved before I go?"

"No, dear," she said as they walked to the front door. "I like this change. I get so tired of the furniture sitting in the same old spots. Thank you for helping me."

"I didn't mean to interrupt," Leo said when she joined him on the porch. "I just want to let you know the locksmith has finished installing the deadbolts. Here are the new keys for both locks. The peephole is in. I didn't want to go through your closets looking for a broom or vacuum, so there's a mess of sawdust around both doors."

"Not a problem. Thanks for doing this, Leo. It's probably

unnecessary, but I appreciate it." *Robert will find a way to get to me despite the best locks.*

Leo nodded. "The door and doorframe are solid wood, so you should be safe. Let me know if you have any more problems."

After Leo drove away, Carolyn went to check on her roses. This morning before dawn, she'd been afraid they weren't salvageable, but Mrs. Bingham had trimmed them nicely. The one of the left did look a little wilted, but with some love and tender care, maybe she could persuade it to live. As she circled to the front yard, a patrol car pulled to a stop at the curb.

Russell lowered the window and raised his sunglasses to the top of his head. "Hey, Carolyn, everything okay?"

She walked out to the car. "Everything's fine. Thanks for the drive-bys."

"It's trite to say, but our job is to keep the citizens of Eden Falls safe. I'm not sure if JT asked last night, and I didn't think to until this morning. Have you noticed anyone hanging around Patsy's?"

She shook her head. "Not anyone in particular."

He nodded, as if in thought. "Well, keep your doors locked. People tend to let their guard down after a little time goes by."

"I will. Leo had deadbolts installed this afternoon."

"Good." He lowered his glasses into place. "Let us know if you have any more problems."

"I will. Thanks for stopping by, Russ."

"My pleasure."

As he drove away, she glanced at the darkening sky. She'd planned to mow the lawn today, but it would have to wait until tomorrow. She ate a light dinner, then sat on the front porch, listening to the thunder echo off the surrounding mountains.

Memories of sitting on the steps in the evenings of her childhood flooded her mind. That was before life got complicated, before her parents' accident. Before Catherine had to take over parental duties. Before Carolyn began to feel even worse about herself.

She realized with a start that darkness had fallen while she was sitting in another day and time. She went inside and twisted the deadbolt, which gave her a sense of safety, but not peace. Sometimes she wondered if she'd ever feel at peace.

The only time her world had ever made complete sense was during her years at culinary school. The years between Catherine and Robert. Everything was in order. She got up, went to class, and came back to her tiny apartment to cook. When neighbors were drawn by the smells coming through the thin walls, she gave out samples, happy to make friends. That's how she met Robert. He was a buddy of one of her neighbors and the scent of fresh bread had drawn them to her door.

It wasn't healthy to live in the past, but her thoughts drifted there more often than not.

CHAPTER 10

He stood back, past the edge of the lawn, amid the pines and brush, well hidden unless an errant volleyball or Frisbee was thrown in his direction. Carolyn had just arrived. She looked over the crowded backyard, seemingly unsure of herself. Seeing her there, alone and vulnerable, made him wish he was by her side. *Be patient.*

Carolyn turned, smiled, and his heart thumped hard against his ribs. He followed her gaze to where several kids were playing a game. The temptation to come out into the open was so strong, he had to hold onto one of the tree trunks to keep from joining her. *Too soon. It's too soon.* She needed to realize she was his, needed to be ready to give herself over to him completely. She needed to understand and accept that there was no one else who would love her and take care of her as only he could.

He shouldn't have followed her here. It was impetuous. He couldn't risk being seen until the time was right. Being here made him impatient to have her now. He watched until she carried her covered dish to the tables laden with food. Then, ducking into the trees, he made his way down the hill.

*L*ike an anxious teenager, JT kept an eye toward the path leading around his house from the driveway. He glanced at his watch for the umpteenth time. Carolyn had to work, but she should be off by now. As soon as the thought ran through his mind, she appeared, the sunlight dancing in her red hair. He felt short of breath at the sight of her. The sudden emotion took him by surprise.

She stopped to watch a few of the kids playing a game off to the side before she continued to the food tent and set a big bowl of something that he knew would be good on one of the many tables. Charlie ran up to show her some treasure. She cupped her hands around his as they discussed whatever he had found. Her animated expression matched Charlie's enthusiasm.

After Charlie ran off, Carolyn greeted his mom and dad. His dad gave her one of his bear hugs and his mom fluttered around her for several minutes. Clearly they were thrilled she came. At their urging, Carolyn turned to the tables and perused the fare. She dressed a hamburger, added a scoop of his mom's macaroni salad, and a scoop of the fruit salad his aunt contributed. When she finished, Stella called her name and waved her over to a vacant chair where she and Rowdy sat in the shade of a pine.

JT hadn't eaten, and realized, again to his surprise, that he'd hoped he could eat with Carolyn. The reality was there in the open for him to ponder, which he'd do when he didn't have a backyard full of guests.

He quickly fixed a plate, adding a scoop of the seafood salad Carolyn brought, grabbed a vacant lawn chair, and flipped it open next to her. She glanced up and her face flushed a pretty pink.

"Great party as usual, JT," Stella said. "I think this is the biggest crowd I've ever seen."

What started as a small Father's Day barbecue had turned into a huge annual event. He provided hamburgers and hot dogs. Everyone else brought a dish to share. "I think you're right."

"Thanks for inviting me," Carolyn said.

"I'm glad you could make it." *Very glad.* He held up his fork. "And thanks for bringing this. It's great."

She flashed her sweet smile.

"I finally got to Patsy's yesterday and had a couple of your sweet pleasures," Rowdy said, bouncing his eyebrows. "Colton is right, you create some truly mouthwatering treats."

When Carolyn's blush deepened, Stella punched Rowdy on the shoulder. "Would you leave her alone? You've been a bully since you were little."

Rowdy frowned "What are you talking about? I was never a bully."

"A teasing bully. You said that just to make Carolyn blush, and that's being a bully."

"Sorry, Carolyn. I don't mean to be a teasing bully." Rowdy grinned. "Though your treats are mouthwatering, I did phrase it that way to see you blush."

Carolyn set her plate in her lap and covered her face with her hands. "Stop. The more you talk about it, the worse it gets."

Stella laughed. "I don't want to make you feel bad, but I don't think you could blush any harder than you are at the moment."

Rowdy glanced at Stella. "Why don't you blush?"

"Because I don't get embarrassed."

His mouth quirked up at the corners. "I bet I could get a blush out of you."

Stella rolled her eyes. "Eat your hamburger."

While they ate, JT watched Rowdy and Stella bicker back and forth like an old married couple, which had him wondering what was up. He and his cousins had always been careful not to date local girls, because residents of small towns tended to take sides in a breakup. Was Rowdy flirting with Stella out of interest or because there was no one else who grabbed his attention?

Unlike him, Rowdy didn't seem to be in a hurry to change his solo status. He enjoyed single life and the parade of women crowding his bar and grill every night.

"I thought you were bringing your boyfriend today, Stella," JT said.

"He had plans with his own father."

JT knew Alex was concerned about Stella's relationship with Len. She'd hinted that he look into Len's background, but a few broken dates didn't justify what he considered interference and breach of privacy. Alex could dig into the guy's background on her own with an internet connection and a few dollars.

"I remember coming to this house with Alex when we were little," Carolyn said to him. "Your grandparents were always so much fun to be around."

"They were fun," JT replied.

Rowdy looked up at the house. "We had some great times with them, didn't we, JT? Thanksgiving, Christmas, we always came here to celebrate. Grandma Garrett was a good cook."

"Yeah, we did." JT had many memories of this house, which had played a big part in his childhood. He still remembered the day he told his grandfather, "I want to live in this house when I'm big," never believing he'd be doing it without his grandparents.

"Have you made any changes?" Carolyn asked.

"A few." Suddenly, he wanted to show those changes to

her. He stood and took her empty plate. "Come in and tell me what you think." When she didn't move, he took her hand, pulling her to her feet. "Seriously, I'd like your opinion."

"I want to see," Stella said.

Rowdy grabbed Stella's arm before she could stand. "First, you promised me a game of horseshoes."

JT nodded at Rowdy over Carolyn's head. *Thanks for running interference, cuz.*

~

Carolyn glanced at Stella with a silent plea, but she was too busy glaring at Rowdy.

"We can play horseshoes after I get back."

"You said after lunch, and it's after lunch. Unless you're chicken."

Stella raised a brow. "Excuse me?"

Rowdy had thrown out a challenge and Stella wasn't one to back down. Carolyn felt herself being pulled along as JT threw their plates in the nearest trashcan. She glanced around for anyone else who might join them, but the barbecue was in full swing. People were either busy playing games or eating. She was glad he at least dropped her hand when they climbed the stairs to the large deck that ran along the back of the house.

He had inherited the contemporary house from the same grandparents who left Alex the flower shop. Rowdy got enough money to buy the bar and grill and Beam bought a plane with his share. The sharp lines and angles of this contemporary home would look silly in town, but here on the side of a hill, surrounded by pines, all those edges and angles were softened. The stream running through the backyard made the setting even more enchanting.

They entered the kitchen through a sliding glass door,

which looked exactly as Carolyn remembered. She and Alex used to climb onto stools and watch Grandma Garrett arrange beautiful bouquets on the butcher-block counter or mix up a batch of brownies she could actually smell as the memory flitted through her mind.

"I started the renovations upstairs. Obviously, I haven't done much down here yet."

She ran a hand across the old kitchen table, recalling the times she'd eaten homemade bread, still warm from the oven, butter melting over the sides. She'd lived an idyllic childhood when she was with Alex, Stella, or Jillian. Their homes had always been open to friends. Her girlfriends weren't welcome in the home where she'd grown up—too messy, too loud, too giggly, even though Catherine's friends had been allowed to mess, yell, and giggle anytime.

"When I start renovating the kitchen, I'd appreciate your input."

The comment surprised her. "Why?"

He smiled and her heart thumped erratically. "Because you cook. You'd know what a woman wants in her kitchen."

Your wife will be able to tell you exactly what she wants.

He led her down the hall to the den, which still wore its wood-paneled walls. The living room and Grandpa Garrett's office were the same, except for a few new furniture pieces.

"Come see the changes I've made upstairs."

"I'm not sure I'd recognize any changes. I can't remember ever going upstairs."

"Come see anyway." He led the way up the curving stair-case she'd always loved. When they reached the landing at the top, he picked up a stack of photos from a table. "This is what the master bedroom used to look like."

She thumbed through the pictures and did remember. The floor to ceiling windows had created a tree house effect on the top floor. The master bedroom jutted out over the stream, and she remembered hearing the water through the open windows in the summertime. Alex's grandparents had a king-size bed before they were a norm. It faced a huge stone fireplace.

Earth tones colored the first bedroom, obviously used for guests. The window overlooked the backyard. Noise from his guests floated through the house.

The bathroom next door was tiled in beautiful shades of brown and fitted with bronzed faucets. The vanity was an old sideboard with shutter doors, the slats in variegated shades of muted colors.

"This is beautiful."

"Thanks. I can't take complete credit. Alex and Mom helped pick out a few things."

The colors and fixtures looked wonderful together.

"I've been renovating a room at a time." He nodded across the hall. "That room is Charlie's. He stays over occasionally."

The room overlooked the front yard and was decorated in blues and greens. She could imagine Charlie flopped on the bed, reading a book pulled from the built-in shelves, or playing with the model airplane on the dresser. It was sweet of JT to set up a room especially for his nephew. Charlie probably loved staying here.

"There used to be a small guest room next to the master bedroom. Alex stayed there when she slept over."

"Oh, right. I remember." She ran her hand along the wall where the room's door used to be.

"I closed it up and made a second bathroom."

"I bet Alex was sad. She always loved staying with your grandparents."

"She wasn't too heartbroken," JT said, leading her into the renovated master bedroom.

When she stepped over the threshold, she gasped. The

room was painted a beautiful blue-gray. The new king-size bed still faced the fireplace, where a wood mantel had been added. Two gray leather chairs sat in front of the raised hearth. The bed was covered with a simple gray spread with pure white pillows stacked on top. Two lamps with bright white shades sat on bedside tables of aged gray wood that matched the headboard, and the deep-pile gray carpet beckoned one to stretch out in front of a warm fire on a cold night.

She walked to the window and looked out at the treetops, down at the stream, then turned. "This is gorgeous."

His mouth quirked on one side in a grimace. "Gorgeous isn't exactly the look I was going for."

She smiled. "I mean in a…manly way." The room was stunning. Inviting. Peaceful. Handsome, yet beautiful at the same time. "Who chose the colors?"

"You don't think I could do this?"

She tipped her head and looked at him from the corner of her eye.

"Mom and Alex did the decorating."

"You all did a truly wonderful job." She meandered to the fireplace and peeked at the framed pictures on the mantel. Most were of Charlie, a few of the whole Garrett family, JT and Alex, or JT with his parents. She had very few pictures from her childhood.

When she turned, she noticed the additional bathroom. "Do you mind?" She asked gesturing in that direction.

"I brought you up here to look around."

JT had installed a freestanding tub. A granite countertop held two sinks. *In preparation for that wife.* The vanity was aged gray wood. The shower was huge, with a seat, and all kinds of spray heads. He'd turned the small closet in the old bedroom into a separate room for the toilet, and the colors matched those of the bedroom. She turned in amazement.

"You've done a marvelous job. This bathroom is bigger than my bedroom in San Francisco."

"I imagine real estate in California is expensive."

"Outrageous is a better word."

He stood in the bathroom door, filling the space with his tall, broad-shouldered frame. She couldn't believe she was standing here having an everyday conversation with JT Garrett. He'd always been larger than life to her little-girl eyes. He'd patted her head more than once in an older brother fashion, sending a shimmer of delight through her skinny girl's body.

He stepped closer, peered down into her eyes. His woodsy cologne made her head spin in a deliciously crazy fashion. "Will you have dinner with me Friday night?"

By JT's puzzled expression, she guessed his offer was as big a surprise to him as it was to her. "No."

He frowned.

"I mean…I can't. I…I'm not ready to date so soon after my divorce." She fanned her face. "It's hot. We should go outside."

JT backed out of the room so Carolyn could scramble past. "How long have you been divorced?"

She turned away so he couldn't see her eyes. "Not very long." *Please, don't ask any more questions. Don't make me lie.*

"Six months? Eight?"

She didn't reply.

"Alex said you were divorced before her wedding."

She nodded without giving a direct answer, because she had none, and left the bedroom. Rushing down the stairs, she knew he was right behind her. At the back door, she reached for the knob, but his hand shot past hers, holding it closed.

"Carolyn, I didn't mean to upset you. I don't know from

experience, but I'm sure getting over a divorce is difficult. I'm sorry if I brought up bad memories."

Concern etched his brow, which touched a tender spot in her hollow chest.

His gaze moved over her face. "Tell me one true thing, Carolyn. Another something I don't know about you."

His face was close, too close, the crescent scar taunting her fingertip. "Why do you keep asking me the same question?"

"I just asked you out to dinner, so it should be obvious. I want to get to know you better."

Why me when you could have any woman? "I don't understand. Why?"

"Why?" He moved so he was between her and the door. "Because you're sweet and kind and beautiful."

You're okay looking, Carolyn, but you'll never be beautiful. How many times had Robert told her that? Enough that she believed. How many times had he tried to get her to wear more makeup to hide her freckles, to color her hair to cover the red?

"I'm attracted to you."

Impossible. "Well… Don't be." *Rob will never let me go.* She looked up to meet his direct gaze. "I'm not interested."

As he studied her for a long moment, she felt heat built on her chest. He glanced down at her neck. "Your blush says different."

She covered the exposed skin with her hand.

"So does the pulse at the base of your throat."

She moved her hand higher. "I'm not interested."

He looked at her lips, his gaze lingering until she pressed them together to suppress the silly smile that threatened. How ironic that he finally noticed her, and she was tied to someone else. Someone she'd never be free of.

He smiled. "When do you think you might be interested?"

"I won't. I…can't ever…"

A small line appeared between his brows. "You can't ever date?"

"Yes. No. I mean I don't want to." *Stop asking.*

"Tell me one true thing, Carolyn."

One true thing. She studied his face, his brown eyes with their long, feathery lashes, his perfect nose, and strong jawline. She'd pictured his face in her mind a thousand times, but now there was something new. The crescent scar. Her heart was beating so hard her chest hurt. This would be the boldest thing she'd ever say aloud.

"I want to touch your scar."

His eyes held an unspoken question, but he leaned closer.

She glanced around afraid someone might catch her, but there was no one else in the house. Raising the tip of her finger, she ran it over the lighter skin while he stared down at her. The indent cut into his eyebrow slightly. "How did it happen?"

"I was rock climbing with a friend and slipped."

She was close enough she felt his warm breath on her cheek. Never would she have imagined herself here with JT. Her own breathing was hurried and irregular, making her lightheaded. "Did it hurt?"

"Not much. Can I touch yours?"

Before she could protest or step back, he put his hand to her cheek and ran the pad of his thumb just under her eye. His skin was warm and she fought the urge to close her eyes. Instead, she took a step back.

"What did you do?"

"I…tripped, fell against a cupboard in the kitchen."

"Did it hurt?" he asked, repeating her questions.

She nodded, while swallowing around the lump growing in her throat.

"I have a truth to tell."

She was afraid to hear. At the same time, she'd never been so curious in her life.

"I think the freckles on your lips are sexy."

"I…" She put fingers to her mouth. "I want to go outside now."

He reached back, twisted the knob, and opened the door. She hurried past, but knew he watched her escape.

~

*P*atsy and Mason sat next to each other at a picnic table in the shade. They'd collected a few stares, which never bothered her in the past. She'd taught herself not to care what Eden Falls thought of her. Let the naysayers and busy-bodies have their fun. She was a good person, always volunteered for the fall festival, cooked for the shelter on holidays, and donated baked goods to the little league teams for their bake sales and fundraisers. She was kind to kids and animals.

Mason, on the other hand, didn't deserve the kind of stares aimed in their direction. He looked completely at ease, waving to a friend, or exchanging a few words with another.

He leaned toward her. "I hope you aren't feeling uncomfortable about being seen in public with me."

And that's why she was falling in love with him. He cared more for her feelings than his own reputation. "Mason, people have been staring at me and whispering behind their hands since my second divorce. Their twitter doesn't bother me a bit. It's you I'm worried about. You've never had scandal follow you down the street."

His expression turned a bit sad. "*Au contraire.* After Arleen left, I had a battalion of single women lined up at my door with casseroles. Of course, when I didn't reciprocate, rumor had it I was gay. Which explained why my wife left me."

She laughed and several heads turned in their direction. "That's a bit of gossip I never heard. I always assumed it was Misty who chased any interested woman away."

"She chased away dates, not the women with casseroles. My cooking skills weren't great in the beginning. I guess that's common with most kids." He shook his head. "There I go, making excuses for my daughter, again. I have to stop, let her take the blame when she's guilty. Old habits…"

Patsy laid her hand over his. "You're the one who has to let the guilt go. She's a married woman with a family now. Time for you to quit worrying about things you can't change."

"You're right. And I'm trying." He flipped his hand over and laced their fingers together. "Let's get something to eat."

They walked hand in hand to the tables, which were over-flowing with food.

After she loaded her plate, she started toward the table they'd vacated with Mason following. Alice Garrett stopped her with a hand on her arm. "Join us. We have plenty of room at our table."

Alice, her husband, Denny, Denny's brother, Dawson, and his wife, Glenda, welcomed them with smiles. The Garretts had never been ones to shun, no matter what the circum-stances. They were good, down-to-earth people, who'd raised good kids.

She and Mason sat and were included in the conversation about JT's house renovations. She looked toward the back door just as Carolyn slipped out, followed by JT. He watched Carolyn cross the yard, a look of disappointment on his face. She sat down among girlfriends, facing away from the house, not looking back the way she'd come. *Interesting.*

Patsy was a successful business owner and she'd become

even more successful since hiring Carolyn West. That girl could bake up a storm and not even break a sweat. The single men in town liked to come in just to look at her, which was fine with Patsy, because they always bought something while there. Carolyn showed no interest in their attention, usually disappearing into the kitchen. When questioned, Carolyn was always careful to skirt around the details of her marriage and divorce. Patsy didn't push, since she didn't like to discuss her own divorces.

But wouldn't a romance between Carolyn and JT be—to use one of Mason's words—lovely?

Mason wrapped an arm around her shoulder. "What do you think, Patsy?"

She turned her attention back to the conversation at the table. "Sorry my mind was wandering. What did you say?"

~

arolyn pulled into the carport in the waning daylight. She slid from behind the wheel and surveyed her surroundings before she started her usual walk around the house to check for footprints. A sweet floral scent floated through the summer air and she closed her eyes to enjoy. Russian olive trees. She looked around for the source and spotted the silvery, sage-green leaves two doors down.

The smell reminded her of golden summer afternoons spent with the friends of her childhood. Alex's backyard had been lined with Russian olives. Thinking of Alex turned her thoughts to JT. *"Will you have dinner with me Friday night?"* His simple, direct question made her heart sing and shatter at the same time. Shatter, because, of course, she could never go. She was married and always would be. To file for divorce would alert her husband to where she was.

She'd started to believe the footprint was old, but like

Russell said, after a time, people let their guard down. She wouldn't make that mistake.

Robert was a patient man when he needed to be, but he wouldn't wait this long to show himself. At least he would have done something by now to make sure she knew he was watching. Even though she was still looking for footprints, it wouldn't be enough for him. He'd want her to be terrified all the time.

"Hello, dear." Mrs. Bingham waved from her front porch when Carolyn rounded the corner of the house.

Carolyn walked over to join her. She enjoyed Mrs. Bingham's company and appreciated that she didn't ask questions about Carolyn's San Francisco life.

Mrs. Bingham patted the empty chair next to hers. "Isn't the weather gorgeous?"

Stars were just beginning to show their shiny faces in the darkening sky. A breeze swayed the branches of the willow tree in Mrs. Bingham's front yard. She sat. "It is gorgeous."

"Did you have fun at JT's barbecue?"

"I had a wonderful time." *I ate a slice of watermelon without a fork. Robert would have been appalled to see juice dripping off my chin.* The thought made her giddy with happiness.

Mrs. Bingham patted her hand. "Good. You deserve some fun. A friend of mine called to tell me Mason Douglas took Patsy as his date."

"He did."

"That's also good. It has been way too long since Mason dated and Patsy's a good choice. I think they'd balance each other out nicely, don't you?" She smiled with a slight shake of her head. "Though I imagine the gossips will have a heyday with that information. I'm surprised I've only had one phone call."

"Misty isn't excited about her dad dating Patsy. She glared at her all afternoon."

Mrs. Bingham fluttered a hand. "Misty will need to get over it. Patsy is a good woman. Mason would be lucky to have her."

"I hope the gossip doesn't discourage them. They really seem happy when they're together."

Carolyn was glad Mrs. Bingham was on Patsy and Mason's side. Patsy had been uncomfortable at the picnic. But when Alice and Glenda Garrett included her at their table, the baker soon returned to her carefree self.

Noticing the darkening shadows of the neighborhood, Carolyn felt a sudden urgency to be inside. She scooted out of her chair. "I better get home."

Mrs. Bingham pushed to her feet. "Thanks for coming to visit. Will I see you tomorrow in church?"

"I'll be there."

Carolyn ran across the lawn and let herself in the front door, locking it tight behind her. She pulled the drapes closed, making sure there were no gaps. In the dark kitchen, she ran cold water and filled a glass. Lifting the curtain over the sink, she peered into the darkness.

Her insides were still jittery from her house tour with JT. She'd always treasure his invitation to dinner, but it was too late. She'd never be free.

She made her way down the dark hall to her bedroom. After setting the glass of water on the nightstand, she pulled the drapes and switched on the lamp.

Today had been like old times. Her heart pinched at the thought of everything she'd missed while living in San Francisco. But she graduated culinary school with honors, and that was nothing to regret.

Then she met Robert... She pushed the thought away,

tired of dwelling on the past. What was done was done. There was no going back.

Eden Falls was giving her a second chance, the do-over she'd believed impossible, and she'd hang on to it with both hands.

She turned to get a hanger out of her closet.

One of the doors was slightly ajar.

The hair on the back of her neck stood on end. A tingle of dread skittered down her back.

Her habit after living with an anally retentive husband was to firmly shut all doors and drawers, and double-check them—not a habit she'd broken yet. She slowly studied the room, taking in every detail. A framed photo on the dresser was off kilter, as was the book on the opposite nightstand.

She reached under the curtains to assure herself the window was locked. Breathing became impossible as her throat closed up.

She turned toward the closet. Was he in there, watching her through the crack? Enjoying the look of terror splashed across her face? To get out of the room, she had to pass the closet door. Would he grab her? She sank to the floor, grabbing the phone from the nightstand as she did so. Her hands shook hard, making it almost impossible to punch in 911.

"Nine-one-one. What is your emergency?"

Not Phoebe's voice this time. "Someone's been in my house." She tried to calm her panic enough to make sense.

"Is he still there?"

No. If he was still here, he would have grabbed me before I picked up the phone. "I—I don't think so."

"What's your address?"

As Carolyn recited her address, she glanced at her dresser. The top drawer—her underwear drawer—was ajar. She fought the shudder of disgust that rattled through her.

"Hold on a moment while I make a call. Stay on the line."

A moment seemed an eternity as Carolyn tried to breathe. How had Robert gotten in? All the doors and windows were locked. She'd checked before she left for the barbecue.

"My name is Gianna Yancy. What's yours?"

"Carolyn West."

"Carolyn, we met today at JT's barbecue," the woman on the other end said in too calm a tone. "I'm married to Layne Yancy. You went to school with him."

Carolyn tried to engage her brain in the conversation. Layne was JT's age, but she remembered him, and also remembered meeting his wife today. "Right, yes."

"Do you know Phoebe Adams? She's Stella's sister?"

"Yes, I know Phoebe."

"Phoebe is on her way. Where are you in the house?"

Emotion was beginning to win out as tears stung her eyes. "I…I'm in the bedroom."

"Hang on, Carolyn. Phoebe should be there any minute. Do you feel safe enough to get to the front door? That's where Phoebe will go."

Robert wouldn't have given her the chance to call the police, if he was still here. "Yes. I think so." She felt silly crawling on hands and knees, but she didn't think her shaking legs would carry her. Headlight beams flashed through the curtains as a car pulled into her driveway. "Someone's here."

"Phoebe is still a few minutes out."

Even though she was expecting it, the knock on the front door almost stopped her heart.

"Police."

"Carolyn, it's Mac Johnson," Gianna said. "Do you remember him? He's Rance and Lily Johnson's son. He's been with the police—"

She stopped listening when she heard Mac say, "Carolyn, can you open the door? It's Mac Johnson."

She stood and looked through the peephole. *Thank you,*

Leo. "I see Mac. Thank you…" The dispatcher's name had slipped her splintered thoughts. She disconnected the call and unlocked the door.

Mac eased inside. "Are you okay, Carolyn?"

No. Tears flooded her eyes and ran down her cheeks.

He reached for her arm and she flinched away. "Sorry," he said, holding up his hands. "I think you should sit down."

She flipped on a lamp and moved to the edge of the sofa. As soon as she sat, she began to tremble, hard enough to rattle her brain. *Why can't he leave me alone?*

"Gianna said someone broke into your house. Are they gone?"

"I don't—Yes, I believe so."

Phoebe came through the front door. "Hey, sweetie." She sat next to Carolyn and pulled her into a hug. "Are you okay?"

Carolyn covered her face as sobs shook her body and soul.

"I'm going to take a look around," Mac said, and left the room.

"Do you know who's doing this, Carolyn?"

Carolyn shook her head. An inner voice whispered, *Liar.* "I don't…know for sure."

"But you suspect someone."

One true thing. Carolyn swiped at the tears on her cheeks. "My husband and I didn't separate amicably."

"You mean your ex? Stella said you're divorced."

Carolyn pressed her lips together. Lying wouldn't help her, and she needed help. If Robert got to her, he'd either drag her home in the trunk of his car, or kill her trying. "I left."

"You're still married?"

Carolyn nodded as heat spread across her chest. Why was she embarrassed? There was no reason, except she'd lied to everyone she knew. She'd been lying for so many years, she didn't know what the truth was anymore.

"Does he know where you are?"

Tears began to fall, again. "I don't know. I didn't tell him."

"Someone broke out the window in the back door," Mac said coming back into the living room.

"After the barbecue, I went next door to Mrs. Bingham's. I came in through the front door. I locked the back before I left, but I didn't check it when I came home."

"How did you know someone had been in the house?" Mac asked.

Carolyn pointed to the hall. "He was in my bedroom. The closet door is ajar. A dresser drawer is open. A picture frame is out of place."

"Why do you suspect your husband, Carolyn?" Phoebe asked.

Carolyn took a shuddering breath. *Second truth.* "He... didn't want me to leave, always threatened that if I did, he'd find me. I never told him I was from Eden Falls, just Washington state."

She caught the looks exchanged between Phoebe and Mac before Mac squatted down in front of her. "Are you still in touch with him?"

Carolyn shook her head. She'd always thought Mac had kind eyes, inherited from his father Rance.

Mac pulled a notebook from his breast pocket. "What's his name?"

"Robert Richmond, but unless he's found—" She pressed her lips together.

Another look was exchanged between the two police officers. Phoebe took her hand. "Carolyn, look at me. Are you afraid he might have found you?"

Carolyn closed her eyes.

"Are you running?"

Carolyn nodded slowly, humiliated to the core. The burning on her chest had moved up her neck to her cheeks.

"Since when?"

Carolyn pulled her hand from Phoebe's. She rested her elbows on her knees and her head in her hands, unable to look either police officer in the eye. "I left in February, right after Alex's wedding. I rented a car, traveled east through southern states, leaving just enough of a trail to lead him away from the West Coast. I colored my hair brown, changed cars twice, and used my married name. When I reached Alabama, I became Carolyn West, colored my hair back to red, and began to use cash, so he couldn't follow a paper trail northwest."

"Didn't he know you'd come to Eden Falls for Alex's wedding?" Mac asked.

"I booked a flight to Seattle. He didn't know I rented a car and drove from there."

Phoebe stirred beside her. Carolyn could only imagine what she was thinking. "Does he still live in San Francisco?"

"As far as I know." She recited the address of their house.

"Could it be anyone else, Carolyn?" Mac asked. "Has there been anyone hanging around Patsy's? Has anyone asked you out?"

The chief of police. "No."

"There hasn't been anyone who's made you feel uncomfortable?"

The chief of police, but not in the sense you mean. "No."

Mac stood and put the notebook back in his pocket. "I'm going to check the rest of the house, and then have a look outside. Why don't you take Phoebe to your room and show her what's been moved."

He put a hand under Carolyn's elbow and she recoiled. Phoebe and Mac exchanged another look. A moment earlier, she'd thought her face couldn't burn more. She was wrong.

Carolyn led Phoebe into the bedroom, showed her the open drawer and the out-of-place picture and book. "It might not seem like anything to you, but that drawer and the closet door were closed. My husband was very…*particular* about things being perfect." She closed her eyes at the memory of a chokehold over an open kitchen cupboard and a bruised cheek because of an off-center vase. "Out of habit, I would never have left them open…even slightly."

"Do you have a plastic storage bag?"

On her way to the kitchen, Carolyn noticed the broken glass on the laundry room floor. A stack of mail sitting on the table had been shuffled around. Insignificant to anyone else, but a huge, flashing sign to her. She wondered what Robert was searching for. She pulled a gallon bag from the pantry and took it to Phoebe who slid the picture frame inside.

"We'll try to lift fingerprints from this."

Carolyn nodded.

Phoebe pulled the drawer open. "Of course, it's your underwear drawer. Can you tell if anything is missing?"

Another shudder of disgust ran through Carolyn as she lifted a few things. "I'm not sure. I don't think so. I've never cataloged my bras and panties."

Phoebe smiled. "Me either, but if you notice anything, call me."

Carolyn nodded.

"Anything else?"

"Whoever was here went through my mail."

Phoebe followed her into the kitchen. "You can't stay here tonight, not with the window broken. Stella and I have a pull-out couch and—"

"No. Can you give me a minute to pack a few things and then follow me to The Dew Drop Inn?"

"I'd feel better if—"

"I'm not going to put you or Stella in danger." At

Phoebe's arched brow, Carolyn realized she'd raised her voice. "I'm sorry, Phoebe. I'll be fine at the Inn." Which was another truth. If Rob were still in town, he'd want her to wonder and worry. He'd want her scared. He wouldn't come back tonight. He'd make her wait.

By leaving a drawer ajar and moving things slightly, he'd already let her know he was watching.

JT sat stiff at his desk, struggling to keep his emotions in check while Mac gave his report. Someone had been in Carolyn's house, and that someone was bold. Carolyn left his place before dark, so whoever broke the back window had done so during daylight hours. "Who is this guy?"

Phoebe turned from the window. "She thinks it's her husband."

He glanced sideways at her. "You mean her ex. Carolyn's divorced."

"I told you that part would get his attention," Phoebe said to Mac. She winked at JT. "I saw you disappear inside with her yesterday."

"I was showing her the house renovations."

"No need to explain. We understand completely. Don't we, Mac?"

Mac waved a hand. "Leave me out of this."

JT picked up a pencil from his desk, then threw it back down. "You're both fired."

"Did you notice him watching her at the barbecue?"

"I leave the noticing to women," Mac responded wisely, but added a not-so discreet thumbs-up.

"Sorry, JT. I had to have a little fun before the serious," Phoebe said, patting his shoulder. She came around the desk and plopped into the chair next to Mac. "Carolyn is running from her husband. My guess is he's abusive."

That would explain her flinching every time I'm close. It also explained her vague answers to his questions. He leaned back and twisted his chair so he faced the window. "What makes you think she's running, or that her husband's abusive?"

"Phoebe asked her straight-out if she was running and she indicated she was."

JT's anger escalated. Not only was her house being broken into, but she was on the run. "Why did she come here? Eden Falls would be the first place her husband would look."

"She never told him she was from Eden Falls, just Washington," Mac said.

"She left San Francisco two days after Alex's wedding, headed east before backtracking," Phoebe added. "She's been on the run ever since."

"And she thinks her husband's found her."

"Yes," Mac said.

JT rubbed a hand over his jaw. "Did she say he'd been abusive?"

"No, but she did say he was very particular about things being perfect, and out of habit, she would never leave a drawer or closet door open. She also said she didn't want to put me and Stella in danger when I offered her our couch."

She refused to stay with Alex when someone was in her backyard. Why didn't I pick up on that?

"She was terrified, JT," Mac added.

"Did she ever file a formal complaint against her

husband?"

Mac shook his head. "No. I checked."

"Of course not. They never do." He understood why abuse victims were reluctant to seek help. That didn't stop him from wishing Carolyn had told him the truth. JT turned his chair to face his computer and punched a few keys. He wanted to get a look at Carolyn's husband. "Is there anyone else we should be looking at? Anyone she might suspect?" *Anyone asking her out besides me?*

"She said there wasn't," Phoebe replied.

JT turned the computer screen so Phoebe and Mac could see the photo on Robert Richmond's driver's license.

"Handsome."

JT was sure Mac's frown mirrored his own.

Phoebe lifted a shoulder. "What? It's not my fault Carolyn married a hot lunatic."

"Phoebe bagged a picture frame, moved by the perpetrator. We might be able to lift a print."

JT clicked a few more keys on his keyboard. "I just printed out Richmond's driver's license, Mac. Will you make sure everyone gets a copy, including Gianna and Helen? I want as many eyes as possible on the lookout for this guy. Phoebe, will you take a copy by The Dew Drop Inn on your way home? Ask Karen if she's seen him. Carolyn spent the night there and, if Richmond's in town, he may have, too. Check to make sure she's okay."

Phoebe slapped her forehead with the palm of her hand. "Stupid! I didn't even think of that."

"Just make sure she's okay. I need Robert Richmond's address. I'll call San Francisco's PD, ask them to swing by Richmond's house to see if he's there, see if they can verify his whereabouts yesterday."

Mac stood. "I'll see you tonight."

"Yeah, get some sleep. Tonight, continue with your drive-bys of Carolyn's house, but up it to every twenty minutes instead of thirty. I'll call Leo and see if he can get the back door replaced ASAP."

Mac left, but Phoebe stayed in her chair, a smile on her face. "So, do you have a personal interest?"

He pointed to the door. "Get out. Make sure Carolyn's okay."

She left his office laughing.

JT turned to his computer again. He entered Robert Richmond's name in a search and found a few priors. Simple assault charges from a bar fight, a domestic assault, not filed by Carolyn. He added Carolyn's name, looking for any information about a divorce. There was none.

He picked up the phone and called the PD in San Francisco. He was lucky enough to be transferred to a detective, and explained that he needed to know where Robert Richmond was last night. He said that it was likely an abuse situation and the information had to remain confidential. The detective said he'd have someone check it out and promised to call back.

After JT hung up, he called Leo about the broken window.

"You've got to be kidding. Who's doing this?"

"I'm not sure yet, but can you take care of the door? I'll foot the bill."

"I'll take care of it. I should have changed the door out for her when I had the deadbolts installed."

"Thanks, Leo."

He stood and looked out the window toward Patsy's Pastries. The shop was closed on Sundays, which would give Carolyn a break.

He wondered if Alex knew about the abusive husband. No. If she had, she would have told him.

Why hadn't Carolyn told him the truth? Even as he asked

the question, he knew the answer.

Many victims of abuse blame themselves. They're too ashamed to admit they are being abused. They feel responsible for the abuse, or believe the abusive partner will change. The abuser often threatens to kill their victim if they report the crime or try to leave. Victims are made to feel guilty about the failed relationship and responsible for their beatings, or believe if they did something different, the abuse would stop. It wasn't unheard of for victims to stay because they didn't have the means to leave or were afraid of major life changes. That wasn't the case with Carolyn. She'd made a major change in both her career and surroundings.

He should have picked up on the abuse when Carolyn jerked away from him. He'd been too busy noticing everything else about her.

A powerful surge of protectiveness coursed through him when he imagined Carolyn being beaten by someone who thought himself a man. While he was listening to Mac and Phoebe's report, he'd thought her coming to Eden Falls was a mistake, but she'd been right to come here. She would get the emotional support she needed to heal. Her friends would surround her, circle their wagons, and his tiny sister would be right out front to fight for and defend Carolyn. He'd be standing next to her.

~

*A*fter a long, mostly sleepless night, Carolyn woke groggy, and much later than usual. As she made her way to her room last night, she realized Robert might be in the same hotel, since it was the only one in Eden Falls. Though she knew deep down he'd never stay so close and risk being seen, she still checked and rechecked the lock on her door and kept the lights on all night.

Once the sun was up and the cover of darkness gone, she checked out and drove to her house to clean up the broken glass, hoping it would be okay to do so. Neither Mac nor Phoebe told her she shouldn't. She'd also check for missing underwear.

Her cell played a happy tune and she pulled it out of her pocket. "Hello?"

"Okay, spill it. What is going on with you and psycho stalker? Phoebe said she spent time at your house last night. And why didn't you come here instead of The Dew Drop?"

"Good morning, Stella. How are you?"

"The question is, how are you? Did you get any sleep?"

"A little."

"I just got home from church. I'll change and be over in a few. Hope you haven't eaten. I'm bringing lunch."

Carolyn did a quick check around the house to see if anything was missing. In her bedroom, she opened her underwear drawer, wondering what Robert was looking for. Did he think she'd bought all new bras and panties since leaving San Francisco? Did he think she was living some crazy, wild life now? Did he expect to find hidden notes from secret lovers, like she had? Though she knew Robert wanted her to find the notes, had planted them so she would.

Was he searching for something when he went through her mail? If so, what?

The doorbell rang. When she looked through the peephole, she expected to see Stella pulling funny faces, but it was JT. Her heart performed its usual hip-hop dance, making her short of breath. He knew she was here because her car was parked in the driveway. There was no use hiding. She'd have to face him eventually, might as well get it out of the way.

She opened the door and wanted to shrink into a puddle of shame at his look of compassion.

"Are you okay, Carolyn?"

Looking at the floor, she nodded, not trusting her voice.

He held up a small black case. "I came to take your fingerprints. I thought you'd be more comfortable doing this at home."

"My fingerprints?"

"I lifted two off the picture frame Phoebe picked up last night. They're probably yours, but I want to be sure."

She opened the door wider and he stepped inside. "We can go in the kitchen."

While he set things up on the kitchen table, she watched from a safe distance. His unspoken words hung heavy in the air. *He knows I'm still married, he knows I lied. Does he know I'm hiding? Yes. Of course, he does.* Phoebe and Mac would have told him everything she said last night.

He motioned her over and then moved close behind her. "First roll your finger in the ink and then again on the card."

She knew he was right behind her and willed her body to relax.

"Let me help you for the first one. He reached around her and she put her hand in his. His palm was cool and callused, a contrast to Robert's soft hands.

JT turned her thumb forty-five degrees. "Like this." He rolled it across the inkpad and then the paper. He took her index finger and did the same.

After the first two fingers, her muscles, taut as a piano strings, began to relax. JT would never hurt her. His breath on the back of her neck relaxed her even more.

He took her middle finger. "I wish you'd told me you were still married."

"I said no to your dinner invitation."

"I still wish you had told—"

"Why?" She turned to face him. Heat burned her chest, and for once she didn't care. Normally the cowardice in her won out, but she was tired of being taken advantage of by men—her husband. She had to learn to stand up for herself, learn to fight back, and she might as well start now. "Just because you're the Chief of Police doesn't mean you're entitled to know my personal business."

"Unless you're in danger, at which time it definitely becomes my business."

The heat moved up her neck and flooded her cheeks. She hung her head, embarrassed by her outburst. He was right. He'd sworn an oath to keep the citizens of Eden Falls safe.

The tip of his finger touched the underside of her chin. She stepped back and bumped into the table.

"I would never hurt you, Carolyn. Ever. I just want you to look at me."

"I know you wouldn't," she said shaking her head. "It's… just a reflex."

"Because your husband used to beat you," he said. Tears burned her eyes as she allowed him to lift her chin. "You have nothing to be ashamed of, Carolyn."

He held her gaze for a long moment. Something shimmered between them, something golden and warm around the edges. Did he feel it, too?

"I'm sorry I asked you out." She started to lower her head, but his finger held her chin in place. "Not because I wouldn't like to take you to dinner, but because I would never do anything to add to your already-stressful life."

The look in his eyes was intense, sincere, his smile easy. He was telling her without words that she could trust him with her heart.

He turned her around by the shoulders, lifted her pinky finger, and rolled it in the ink. This time she closed her eyes when his breath whispered across her cheek.

When he finished both hands, she went to the sink to wash.

"Mac and Phoebe said you left San Francisco in February."

"Two days after Alex's wedding."

"They said you didn't leave with your husband's blessing."

"He didn't know." She turned her back to him as she dried her hands on a paper towel. "I caught him cheating with an associate…in our bed. The next day I left while he was at work."

"Sorry."

Carolyn lifted a shoulder in a what-you-gonna-do? gesture, because there was nothing she could do but what she'd done. "I'd been planning to leave for a long time, just waiting for the right moment or the perfect circumstance. For some reason…that day was *the day*.

"You think he's the one doing this?"

"Robert was very specific about things being in their place. By moving things slightly, he's letting me know he's watching."

Someone knocked on the back door and she gladly turned from the conversation. Would she ever be free of the humiliation? Would she ever enjoy a normal life?

As if she had a clue what a normal life was. The thought would be funny if it weren't so pathetic.

Leo stood on the other side of the broken window. "Morning, Carolyn. JT called to tell me you had another break-in. I brought a replacement door."

JT appeared next to her like he lived here, which felt surreal and crazy, sending a silly tremble through her stomach. "Hey, Leo. I can help get that new door installed."

Carolyn needed air. She walked through the living room and stepped out onto the front porch. The day was warm and should be an ordinary, carefree summer day. Instead, her back door was being replaced because Robert found her.

She sank onto one of the two chairs just as Stella pulled to a stop at the curb. She got out of her car and pointed at the patrol car parked in front of her car. "What's going on?"

"JT stopped by to take my fingerprints."

"Why is he taking your fingerprints?" Stella climbed the stairs with a brown paper bag and sat in the other chair.

"Whoever was in my house yesterday moved a picture frame and they want to rule out my fingerprints."

"Why is Leo's truck in your driveway?" She opened a bag and handed Carolyn a Chinese takeout box and a set of chopsticks.

"He's installing a new back door."

"That's how the psycho got in?"

"He broke the glass out." She opened the flaps on the white box and took a deep, appreciative breath. "Why are you bringing me Chinese at eleven in the morning?"

"East Winds was the only place open this early on a Sunday, and I eat when I get stressed."

Carolyn turned to Stella. "What are you stressed about?"

Stella looked at her as if she'd said something completely moronic. "*I'm* not stressed. You are!"

Was she stressed? Both JT and Stella thought she was. She was terrified, overwhelmed, and humiliated. Maybe when she added all those things together, she was stressed. "Thanks." She lifted a piece of broccoli with her chopsticks and popped it in her mouth. "This is good. I haven't been to East Winds since I moved back."

"It's my guilty indulgence. Along with everything else edible." They both laughed as Stella pulled an eggroll from the bag. "So, did psycho take anything?"

"Like I told Phoebe last night, I don't keep inventory of my bras and panties."

"Ewww, he went through your undies drawer?" Stella's face scrunched comically.

"Yup."

Leo came through the front door, followed by JT. He spotted Stella and performed a Marlon Brando impression. "Hey, Stella."

"Ha ha." Stella slapped her thigh in fake amusement, and then rolled her eyes. "I haven't heard that one a thousand times—most of them from you. I'd call you a dork if you weren't so cute."

Leo snatched Stella's eggroll and took a bite. "You think I'm cute?"

"Yeah, in a St. Bernard sort of way—friendly, even if you have high drool potential and are a little hard to train."

JT laughed as he snatched the last of Stella's eggroll away from Leo and popped it in his mouth.

Leo grabbed the bag of Chinese takeout from Stella's lap, pulled out another eggroll, and tossed it to JT. Stella stretched to get the bag of food, but he held it out of her reach. "The door's installed and secure, Carolyn."

"Thank you." She glanced from Leo to JT. "Both. I appreciate what you've done for me."

JT nodded. Their gazes held for a long moment. *Will you have dinner with me Friday night?* She'd remember that moment forever.

"Not a problem." Leo followed JT down the steps.

"Hey!" Stella hollered at the same time Leo held up the takeout bag. "I'm taking this."

"You're a cop," she called in JT's direction. "He's stealing my Chinese food!"

JT slid behind the wheel of the patrol car and pulled away from the curb. Leo backed out of the driveway, honked, and drove away.

Carolyn handed Stella her box of Chinese. "Have mine. I'm not very hungry."

Stella pinned her with a look. "Do you have any idea who broke into your house?"

Time for another truth. "My husband."

"Your ex? Why would he—"

"He's not my ex."

"—break…" Stella frowned. "What?"

"We aren't divorced." Carolyn slouched down in her chair and put her feet on the porch railing. "I caught him cheating and left."

"Oh, Care."

"It wasn't the first time. He's cheated before. He's a sociopath. I did some research." Carolyn laughed without humor, because she remembered the day vividly. "He has all the symptoms."

"Oh, brother. Being a teacher, I've had some training on the subject."

"He's a regular prince charming on the outside. Manipulative, but he does it in a way that makes you think you're in the wrong. Domineering, uses humiliation like a pro. Believes he's entitled. His cheating is my fault. He's a pathological liar, and extremely convincing at it, never shows signs of remorse or guilt, an expert in turning any situation around to be the other person's fault. When he shows love, there's always an ulterior motive, something expected in return. He becomes uncontrollably furious when there's a spot in the sink or a piece of lint on the carpet, even when he's the one who put it there. He's a con artist, can't keep friends, doesn't accept blame—"

"I hate him already, and I don't even know him."

Carolyn had shared the cheating part. The beating part she kept to herself. "Don't hate. It doesn't become you. Besides, I'm the enabler. I allowed it to happen, and then permitted it to continue. I've been closing my eyes or looking the other way for years, hoping it would all go away or correct itself."

Stella leaned forward and set the carton of forgotten Chinese on the railing. She turned to look at Carolyn. "By hiding out in Eden Falls, you allow him to win."

Carolyn shook her head. "No. If Robert won, I'd still be in San Francisco. If he hadn't done what he did, I wouldn't be here right now, sitting on the front porch, enjoying a Sunday morning chat with one of my best friends."

Stella sat back and laughed. "Only you and Alex—and possibly Jillian—could put such a positive spin on something so awful."

Without a positive spin, life would be unbearable.

~

A few days had passed since the break-in at Carolyn's and JT had as many leads as he had in the arson case. Nada. San Francisco PD said Robert Richmond was home when they finally knocked on his door twenty-six hours after JT put in the request, which would have given Carolyn's husband plenty of time to get back to California if he had been in Eden Falls, so the information wasn't much help.

Carolyn told him her husband had cheated, but he suspected Robert had done far more than that, based on the way Carolyn flinched away when touched. She hadn't confirmed or denied anything when he made the comment in her kitchen. Why else would she be running?

He hadn't paid much attention to her reactions at first, but over the course of four weeks, he had plenty of time and opportunity to notice Carolyn's aversion to being touched. Robert Richmond had left scars. Were they permanent?

Alex walked into his office. "Hi, big brother."

"Hey, there. What brings you by?"

She sat in one of two chairs in front of his desk. "Just wondering if you have any leads on Carolyn's stalker?"

"Nope. Do you?"

"You're the cop."

He sat back in his chair. "Yeah, well, I seem to be striking out. When San Francisco police finally got around to checking on Carolyn's ex—on her *husband*—he was home, and said he'd been there all weekend."

"Well, of course he did. What's he going to say? Sure, I was in Eden Falls going through my wife's undie drawer."

"What would be wrong with that? They're married."

Alex lifted a shoulder. "For now."

He rested his ankle on the opposite knee and looked into his sister's eyes. "Did you know?"

"What? That she was still married?"

"Yeah. Did she say anything to you?"

"No. I knew something wasn't right, but I thought she was divorced, because that's what she told me." Her smile was sympathetic. "Carolyn isn't a liar."

"Except she's been lying since she got here."

"There's a reason." She sat forward. "The guys in San Fran didn't mention Carolyn's name or whereabouts, did they?"

"I told the detective I talked to not to mention Eden Falls or Washington."

"If her husband was home, who else could it be?"

He'd already run through a list of men. He ruled out Noelle's cousin, the only newbie in town. Other than him, JT had no idea.

"Have you seen anyone hanging around or watching the pastry shop when Carolyn is working?"

"No one but Colton."

JT snorted a laugh. "And he doesn't think you know."

"I know exactly how often he visits Patsy's, and how many pastries he eats a day." His sister narrowed her eyes. "I have spies everywhere."

"Except at Carolyn's."

She shrugged. "I can't do everything."

"Ouch."

"You know I'm kidding. I know you have your guys driving by day and night. I just can't believe no one has noticed anything."

"Carolyn told Mac and Phoebe that no one has asked her out. Do you believe her?"

"Yes. She's still married, so she wouldn't go, even if she was asked."

Yep.

His sister's green eyes grew wide. "Do you think it could be the same person who set the fire?"

"I don't think so, but I haven't ruled it out." He uncrossed his ankle and leaned forward, resting his elbows on his desk. "Whoever set the fire wanted to destroy something. I think if it was the same person, they would have torn Carolyn's place apart rather than go through a drawer and move a picture frame."

"What about the demolished rose bushes?"

"I don't think that was deliberate. Someone fell onto the bushes. Someone who'd been at the house before and didn't expect those bushes to be there."

Alex shivered. "You're scaring me, JT. You make it sound like this guy has been watching for some time."

"I think he has."

The office grew dark. He pushed to his feet and moved to the window. Billowy black clouds covered the sun, and the trees in the square were whipping wildly in the sudden wind.

Carolyn was in front of Patsy's, chasing down a paper cup blown from one of the tables. She pushed her red curls back from her face, and his heartbeat stuttered. *Not good.*

Alex came to his side. "Why did you just groan?"

"Looks like rain."

Alex studied him a moment. "Yeah, but you weren't looking at the sky. You were looking across the square. At Carolyn."

He cut a look at his sister. "Don't go there, Alex. She's married."

"For now." She pulled his face down and kissed his cheek. "See ya around, big brother."

People scurried for cover as fat raindrops began to fall from the black clouds overhead. Carolyn grabbed a napkin that skittered along the sidewalk and hurried inside the pastry shop.

She looked out the window when thunder rumbled and saw JT standing on the steps of City Hall staring at the Pastry Shop. He glanced up at the threatening sky, as if trying to decide what to do about something. She held her breath, wishing he would come over, praying he wouldn't.

She turned from the window and busied herself straightening chairs and wiping tables, but whirled around in anticipation when the door opened.

"Hi, Carolyn.

Her smile wobbled. "Hi, Mr. Douglas."

His eyebrow quirked. "Don't you think it's about time you called me Mason?"

"I'm not sure I can. You've been Mr. Douglas my whole life, just like Mrs Bingham is Mrs. Bingham. I don't think I could ever call her Edna."

"Has she asked you to?"

She shook her head.

"There's the difference. I'd like you to call me Mason. Mr. Douglas makes me feel old."

"Okay, Mason, what brings you…?" She glanced at the

pot of purple petunias he carried. "Never mind. Silly question."

He smiled shyly and pushed his glasses into place on his nose. "Is Patsy here?"

"She's in her office. I'm sure she won't mind if you go back."

Carolyn was happy for Patsy, and happy for Mason. She glanced back out the window. JT was gone.

While thunder vibrated the window glass, she searched every car parked around the square, wondering if Rob was out there. Was he watching? Once he saw her back door had been replaced, he would be more wary. He'd suspect the police were watching. He'd wait until she was occupied. Try to catch her off guard. She needed to remain mindful of her surroundings.

∽

*P*atsy looked up from her computer and smiled when Mason knocked on her open door with a pot of flowers in hand. Their day together at JT's had been perfect. She hadn't felt shunned by anyone but Misty, who still shot her the stink eye every chance she got. Despite Patsy's growing feelings for Mason, she didn't want to come between father and daughter.

"Hi, handsome."

"Hi, Patsy." He set the petunias on the corner of her desk. "I know I've said it, but I want to thank you again for going to the barbecue. I usually go alone, so it was nice having someone with me."

She raised an eyebrow. "Someone?"

She loved, loved, LOVED the blush that crept up his neck. He was just too adorable for words. "You. It was extra nice to have *you* there with me."

"I had a great time, too. Do you have time to sit?"

"No, I have to get back to the hardware store. I was just thinking of you and…" He gestured toward the pot of flowers.

"Thank you. They brighten my office perfectly on this dark afternoon."

"Would you like to have dinner tomorrow night?"

"I'd love to, but I'm a little worried about Misty's reaction to us seeing each other. She was not happy with me—or you—at the barbecue."

Mason came around her desk and pulled her up into his arms. "Misty doesn't have any say in our relationship, Patsy. Either she accepts it or she doesn't. The choice is hers, but it won't make a difference in how I feel about you. Let's go to a movie before dinner." He kissed her, setting her heart galloping in happiness. "I'll pick you up at six."

She waited a long, excruciating three minutes after he left before grabbing the pot of petunias and heading for the front door. "Hold down the fort. I'll be right back," she said to Carolyn.

"Patsy, it's pouring out there!"

Patsy waved Carolyn's concern away and ran all the way to Pretty Posies. She pushed through the door, dripping wet. "Alex!"

Alex stuck her head around the corner from the backroom. "Hi, Patsy. What can I do for you?"

Patsy walked toward her, holding the pot out. "Did you sell these to Mason?"

"Tatum did, about twenty minutes ago," Alex replied with her beautifully contagious smile.

"What do they mean?"

"Your presence soothes me. Tatum will you grab a towel?" she called over her shoulder.

Patsy felt the sting of tears at the backs of her eyes. "He's so adorable."

Tatum appeared from the backroom in her Goth glory, black lips and all. "They're pretty, aren't they?"

Patsy set the pot of flowers on the counter and dried the rain droplets from her face with the towel Tatum handed her. "Did he ask you what they mean?"

Tatum grinned and two cute dimples appeared in her cheeks. "No, but he said they reminded him of you."

"Aww." Both Patsy and Alex sighed at the same time.

"I know, right?" Tatum straightened the hem of her *Be Afraid* T-shirt. "I had the same response."

Patsy eyes filled with stupid tears. She wasn't a crier and hated for anyone to see her susceptibility. "I like Mason more than I should already. He just called what we have a relationship, and it makes my heart hurt, because Misty is like a storm cloud hanging over my head, threatening more thunder and lightning than we're getting outside right now." She tried to smile, though the lump in her throat threatened to choke her. "It's not like she has the shiniest reputation."

"Your relationship with Mason is none of Misty's business," Alex said. "She'll come around."

"But what if she doesn't? I don't want to cause a rift between Mason and his daughter. I also don't want to mess with Mason's reputation."

The bell over the door jingled, and they all turned to see Misty walk in, shaking out an umbrella. Patsy picked up the pot of petunias and clutched them close to her chest.

"Hi, Misty," Alex said.

Misty looked up. Her bright blue eyes changed to ice cold when she spotted Patsy. Her gaze dropped to the flowers, then raised to meet Patsy's. "I want you to stop seeing my dad."

"Misty—"

"Stay out of this, Alex." She said the words without taking her eyes from Patsy. "You've got everyone in town talking about my dad. Every client that comes into Dahlia's Salon wants to discuss what's going on between you two. I want it to stop."

Patsy raised a brow. "Don't you think you should talk to your dad about this?"

"I'm talking to you, because he has lost all sense of reason."

"Misty, your dad deserves some happiness," Tatum said, not looking as brave as her statement.

Misty's sneer was as well known around town as Patsy's cream puffs. "Maybe, but not with her. He's not going to be her number five husband." She glanced at Patsy. "Or have you already hit that number?"

"Misty! Don't listen to her, Patsy," Alex shouted as Patsy darted out of Pretty Posies.

Patsy ran all the way back to her shop, straight to her office, and closed the door. She grabbed her cell phone and scrolled to Mason's number, tears and raindrops mixing on her face. Her thumb quivered over the little phone icon. She had a speech all worked out in her mind. *Mason, I just remembered I have something tomorrow night. I'm sorry.* That would be for the best—a clean break.

But then Misty wins. She gets her way once again. She didn't press the button as Misty's face loomed before her. *Are you going to let a bully chase you away? Or are you going to stand firm?* The ball was in her court. She'd never been afraid of a bully before. That's all Misty was—had always been. Maybe it was time for Miss Misty to realize life didn't always bow to her demands.

Mason said his daughter didn't have any say in their relationship. Either Misty accepted it, or she didn't.

What if she didn't? How miserable could she make life?

Patsy dropped her phone on the desk and sank into her chair.

CHAPTER 12

Carolyn had changed into shorts and a flowered T-shirt after work, her red hair held back by a bandana, Lucille Ball style. She looked sexy and girl-next-door-sweet at the same time. He imagined her in a flowered negligee. He'd unwrap her like a present. Slowly, allowing the anticipation to grow until they were both frenzied.

He could tell she was nervous about the weather. She kept glancing at the darkening sky while pushing the mower across the front lawn. With the motor running, he was certain she couldn't hear the distant rumbling of thunder. The black clouds would open soon and chase her indoors.

He itched to pay the house another nighttime visit, but couldn't risk it with patrol cars passing by so often. He had to remain patient and play it safe. When rushed, people got careless, made mistakes, and he couldn't afford to be caught before his plan was secure. Besides, there was no hurry. From the little bit he overheard, she wasn't dating anyone.

She finished the last swipe along the driveway just as the first raindrops hit his windshield. Pushing the lawn mower under the protection of the carport, she ran into the house.

He started the car and drove past.

~

*P*atsy stepped over a puddle left by last night's rain and stopped in front of what would be the new hardware and lumber store. Once the frame had been erected, the rest of the building took shape quickly. Exterior walls were in place, along with the plywood roof.

She shifted the boxes of donuts as she walked inside. Beam turned from a table holding blueprints.

"Hi, Patsy." His arm moved in a sweeping motion. "What do you think?"

She glanced at the stud walls and concrete floor. "It looks like the beginnings of a hardware store."

He took the boxes from her arms. "Thanks for bringing the donuts. The guys on the construction crew look forward to them at break time."

Patsy leaned close with a smile. "Guys look forward to anything that has to do with food or women."

Beam grinned, his mossy green Garrett eyes flashing happily. "You're right. As Alex would say, we're all dogs."

"Most, but not all," Patsy said when approaching footsteps echoed through the building.

Mason appeared from behind a pile of lumber. Before she could step back, he lowered his head and kissed her—long and lingering—right there in front of Beam. "Thanks for the delivery."

All Patsy could think was *Misty will not be happy when word gets back to her.*

His gaze held hers for a long moment. "Did I embarrass you?"

She glanced at Beam, who was looking the other way. "No, I'm just wary about Misty's reaction."

Beam raised a brow, grin back in place. "Misty has her own love life. And a pretty good one at that, thank you very much. She doesn't have time to interfere in her father's."

"I told you yesterday, Misty has no say-so in our relationship. She has her life, I have mine." Mason cupped her face between his palms, his expression more serious than usual. "And I want you in my life. I hope you want the same."

Patsy was surprised that Mason was talking about this in front of his son-in-law. "I do."

"As much as I'd like to help, I try to steer clear of any conflicting opinions with my wife."

"There's no need to drag you into this, Beam." Mason slipped his arm around Patsy's waist. "Misty will have to accept our decision. Are we still on for tonight?"

"Yes." The word sounded more convincing than she felt.

"I'll pick you up at your place in a little while," he said, giving her another quick kiss.

Patsy made her exit, telling herself she did want this. She liked Mason and he liked her. She enjoyed every minute they spent together.

DÉJÀ VU.

Her last husband and stepson had a slight falling out over her. Jack wanted to stay in Eden Falls after she and his dad divorced. Their father-son relationship was still strained and she felt responsible.

Of course, Jack and Misty were two very different people. Jack was a sweetheart, where Misty was self-centered. If she and Mason continued to date, would Misty ever be able to accept her? And what did Misty have against her in the first place? Until recently, it was a tossup who was the most gossiped about, although Patsy was sure she was winning now. Dating Mason had put her back in the spotlight.

Walking two blocks back to the pastry shop sent her thoughts into high gear. Was she doing right by Mason? What if their *relationship* evolved into more? Would he become known as the man who'd been seduced by the divorcee? That's what the residents would probably think—she'd somehow tricked him.

She'd always been closed-mouthed about her divorces. She'd simply deemed herself a bad judge of character.

Her first marriage was to a bad boy, who, unbeknownst to her, knew her family had money. He liked to hit and the abuse started soon after the wedding. After her dad offered him a chunk of money, he signed the divorce papers, loaded up his shiny new truck, and drove away, never to be seen again. Number two was an addict she thought she could reform with lots of love and attention. Of course she'd been wrong. Her third marriage was to a man who was verbally abusive on top of being a cheater. The most puzzling was number four, who couldn't deal with her positive attitude and sunny outlook on life.

He stormed out the door with bags in hand. "You're too happy!"

Out of all her divorces, that one hurt the most.

Luckily, she'd gained a wonderful stepson from that marriage. Jack fell in love with Eden Falls when he came to visit. He earned his fire science degree and applied when the local department was hiring.

"Patsy!"

Misty barreled across the square toward her. *Oh, goody.* She pasted on a smile. "Hello, Misty. Nice to see you again so soon."

Misty's glare assured Patsy she hadn't crossed the square for a friendly chat. She stopped a foot away, arms crossed over her chest. "I told you to stop seeing my dad."

Stay calm. She smiled as sweetly as possible. "We don't

always get what we want." She could practically hear Misty's unspoken "*I* do," though she didn't say it aloud.

"You are making my dad the talk of this town, and I'm going to put a stop to it."

Patsy crossed her arms, too, determined to hold her ground. "Why do you keep coming to me about this, Misty? I'm not the one asking your dad out. He's asking me."

"Stop saying yes!"

"Raising your voice is going to cause more of a scene than your dad and I do by going to dinner." She tipped her head. "Maybe I can make him happy."

"Or miserable."

"We have a nice time together. We enjoy each other's company. Look, I'm not going to fight with you, Misty."

"Then stop seeing him, or I'll ruin you." Misty narrowed her eyes. "And don't think I can't." She turned and marched back across the square.

Patsy snorted in disgust. She'd survived four husbands, she could ride out Misty.

But, as she entered her shop through the kitchen door, her thoughts turned to Mason. She wouldn't be the cause of friction between him and his daughter. She went into her office, picked up her cell phone, and scrolled to his name.

If everyone at Dahlia's Salon was discussing her and Mason, it could ruin his business once it was up and running again. She couldn't do that to him. She pressed the phone icon, relieved when the call when directly to his voicemail.

She listened to the message, to his voice, and said a silent goodbye. "Mason, I just remembered I have something I have to do tonight. I'm sorry I have to break our date."

Disconnecting the call, she tried to convince herself breaking up with Mason was for the best. He might not agree in the beginning, but in the end, he'd see she was right.

She had to make this final. The next day or two would be

crucial. Leaving town would be the best way, because Mason wouldn't give up that easily. And she was afraid she would give in.

Patsy went into the front of the shop. Carolyn was helping a customer, and she waited impatiently until her new manager finished and then waved her into the kitchen.

"I didn't expect you back from the hardware store so soon."

"Mason was busy. I should have talked to you about this before now, even though the shop is closed on the Fourth of July, I always set out a table for the parade and do a booming business. I also set up a booth in Town Square for the fireworks. Would you be able to help me?"

"Of course, anything you need."

Carolyn deserved another raise. "I know you have tomorrow off, but I was wondering if you could work for me. I need to go to Spokane. Family emergency."

"Sure. I haven't made any plans. Is it something serious?"

"No. You're a lifesaver, hon. I hate to ask, but can you also close this afternoon? I'd like to leave immediately."

Carolyn touched her arm. "Patsy, are you all right?"

"Yes, I am. I'm fine. I just need a day or two off. I'll be home by Saturday so we can start baking for the Fourth of July."

"Any special instructions?"

"No, hon, but thanks. I know I'm leaving the place in good hands. I'll be back before you know it. I'll have my cell handy if you run into any problems, but I have complete confidence in you."

~

*C*arolyn stood at the window of the pastry shop after locking up for the day. She looked at the surrounding cars, examined the faces in the square, searching for her husband's face.

Rob was not patient enough to let this go on much longer. There'd been no sign of footprints since the break-in, no more tipped over chairs. She'd been on alert since she married Rob, so checking her surroundings and taking note of the interior of her home was nothing new. She drove to work now instead of walking and always checked the neighborhood for unfamiliar cars when she pulled onto her street. Seeing a patrol car drive by was an everyday, almost every hour, occurrence.

Still, she was on constant lookout for her husband.

When she got home, she wandered around the house, then decided to clear away some of the undergrowth along the back fence. The work was hard, but it occupied her mind and she enjoyed the exertion, hoping it might give her a full night of exhausted sleep.

She filled six garbage bags before the feeling of being watched shimmied up her spine. Her head snapped up and she glanced around the backyard, realizing darkness was fast approaching.

In her imagination, shadows moved past the front of the house and danced behind a tree. A dog barked, and she turned in that direction, but saw nothing. Straining her eyes, she was afraid of what she might see, yet tired of playing this waiting game. Everything was still, not even a stir of a breeze, but the feeling remained, lifting the hair on the back of her neck.

She dropped the rake at her feet and hurried to the back door. She fumbled for the keys in her pocket, furious that she couldn't even work in the yard without locking the door. Once inside, she checked the locks on the windows, pulled the curtains, and walked around the house making sure everything was in its place. In her bedroom, she lowered the blinds, closed the curtains, and checked for gaps. Satisfied no one outside could see in, she took a quick shower and changed for bed.

Back in the bedroom, she climbed into bed and turned out the light, but her senses were too alert to allow her eyes to close. As tired as she was, her blood felt as if it was bubbling through her veins.

After living in the city, she appreciated her space. She also valued her independence since leaving her husband. Rob hadn't allowed much freedom, and very little solitude. Naïve mistakes had cost her a sense of security and the ability to choose for herself. She would be paying for those mistakes for a long time, but she hoped she'd learned from them.

The next morning, Carolyn was frosting cupcakes for a birthday party when Mason stuck his head into the kitchen. "Good morning, Carolyn."

"Morning, Mr. Doug"—she stuck her tongue out and pantomimed biting it—"Mason." His smile lit his dark eyes. She knew Patsy had put that light there. "How are you?"

"A little frustrated, actually." He stepped into the kitchen and let the door swing shut. "I've been trying to reach Patsy with no luck. The girls out front said she didn't come in today."

"She told me yesterday she had a family emergency."

A slight frown pulled his eyebrows together. "Did she say what happened or where she was going?"

"She went to Spokane." Why hadn't Patsy told Mason she was leaving?

"I hope everything's okay." Mason looked at the floor. "She hasn't answered any of my calls. If you happen to talk to her, will you ask her to call me?"

"I will."

He turned to leave just as Stella bounced into the kitchen.

"Hi, Mr. D. How's your granddaughter?"

"Gorgeous. Have a nice day, girls." His comment didn't match his concerned expression.

Stella turned to Carolyn after he left. "What's up with him?"

"Patsy had a family emergency and isn't answering her phone. He's worried."

"Uh-oh. I bet this has more to do with Misty than a family emergency. I saw her and Patsy on the sidewalk yesterday. Steam was coming out of Misty's ears before her head did a 360 on her shoulders."

"Patsy told me Misty confronted her in Pretty Posies the day before that." Carolyn hated to see Misty causing trouble between Patsy and Mason.

"You know Misty. She's never been able to share her dad." Stella plopped onto a stool she pulled from under the worktable. "If there's a fight, my money's on Patsy."

"There isn't going to be a fight. Maybe I can talk to Misty." The thought terrified Carolyn, but it was time for Misty to grow up. She glanced at Stella. "What are you doing here? I thought you were helping Alex with an anniversary party today."

"We finished early so Alex could spend some time with Charlie." Stella held out her finger for a taste of frosting. Carolyn picked up a spare spatula, swiped it against the side of the bowl, and then over Stella's finger. "Do you have plans for tomorrow night?"

Carolyn held back a laugh. She didn't have plans for *any* night. "Nope. Free as a bird."

"Good." Stella stuck the finger in her mouth and rolled her eyes in exaggerated ecstasy. "Girls' night out at Rowdy's."

"Mmm, I'm not sure I should—"

Stella held out another finger and Carolyn swiped it with more frosting. "I'll pick you up and drop you off afterwards. I'll even walk through the house with you to make sure it's safe."

Carolyn felt like a child needing a babysitter. "I don't want you to have to do that."

"It's not up for discussion."

A night out without worry—well, only partial worry— sounded too good to pass up. "Okay."

"I'll see you tomorrow then."

As soon as Stella walked out, Carolyn pulled her cell phone from her apron pocket and called Patsy, who answered on the first ring.

"Hello, hon. Everything okay?"

"I was wondering the same thing. Mason said he's tried to get in touch with you and you're not returning his calls. Are you okay?"

"I am. Just dealing with a few things."

"He wants you to call him."

Patsy released a breath into the phone and Carolyn wondered, again, what was going on. "Thanks for the message, hon. Are things okay there?"

"Everything is fine. Patsy? You're not letting Misty ruin things between you and Mr. Douglas are you?"

"I'll see you Saturday." Patsy hung up, ignoring her question.

~

JT looked up from his computer when Mac Johnson walked into his office. "Hey, what's up?"

Mac pointed toward the window facing Town Square. "I

thought you might like to know those two kids from Harrisville, the ones you had us watching for, are hanging out in the park."

JT followed Mac to the window. Four kids dressed in Goth black sat on the grass under a tree. The orange-haired kid stood in the middle, waving his hands wildly while three of the others laughed. The fourth—their leader, Thorn—watched impassively.

They weren't doing anything wrong, but something about them made JT uneasy. It wasn't a matter of profiling. It was more an inner-gut, down-to-the-marrow-of-his-bones feeling. "Thanks, Mac."

"I'll watch them while you take lunch."

"You won't have to. I'm going across the square to see if Alex has time to join me."

He guessed right. When the kids saw him coming, they scattered like leaves in the wind. They climbed into two cars and drove away from the square. He stopped in front of Pretty Posies and watched Alex rearranging a new display in the window. He knocked and she turned and waved him inside.

"Looks great."

"Desmond brought in these driftwood pieces and they're too beautiful not to display. What do you think?"

JT picked up a driftwood bird about the size of a blender. "Pretty cool."

"I know. Look at that fish."

He examined several one-of-a-kind pieces. Desmond was a local artist who combed West Coast beaches for driftwood, then transformed them into works of art. Alex was happy to display his work. "I came to see if you're free for lunch."

She flashed a smile. "I'd love to go to lunch with you."

They both turned when the bell over the door jingled, disappointed when Carolyn's smile fell away when she spotted him. She quickly glanced at Alex. "Stella said you were working on a new display and I thought I'd stop by on my lunch hour to see."

"What perfect timing. JT and I were just going over to Noelle's. You can join us."

Carolyn's cheeks flushed a pretty shade of pink, making her freckles stand out. "I don't want to interrupt."

"You aren't interrupting. JT just stopped by to take me to lunch. Tatum, I'll be back shortly," Alex called over her shoulder as she ushered him and Carolyn out the door.

JT let Alex lead the way with Carolyn in tow on her other side. He wondered if his sister had hatched this plan beforehand or if she was working by the seat of her pants. Once inside Noelle's, Alex asked for a booth. She nudged him to sit next to Carolyn. "I'm going to call Colton and see if he can join us."

Carolyn scooted over as far as the wall would allow and JT slid in next to her. Alex took the other side of the booth and pulled her cell phone from a pocket.

Noelle stopped next to him, notepad and pen in hand. "Hi, gang. What can I get you to drink?"

"Just water, please," Carolyn said.

"I'll have a chocolate shake."

Noelle moved over when Alex scooted off the bench and thumped her forehead with the palm of her hand. "Dumb. I forgot all about a flower order that has to be done in an hour. Sorry. You guys enjoy lunch without me." She almost ran out of the café.

JT shook his head. His tiny munchkin of a sister was going all out to push them together. A plan he'd be okay with if Carolyn wasn't married. JT turned to Carolyn, whose wide eyes looked like a deer caught in headlights. "You game?"

She opened her mouth, then closed it before she nodded.

"Okay," Noelle said. "I'll get your milkshake while you

look over the menu. We have an open-faced turkey sandwich on special today."

After Noelle walked away, Carolyn tried to put more space between them as she glanced around. "You should sit on the other side so people don't talk."

He chuckled. "People are going to talk anyway. That's what they do in a small town."

Her look of horror grew. "Well, we don't have to give them more fuel."

Afraid she'd panic and leave, he moved to the other side of the table. "We can eat lunch like we planned, or one of us can leave. If we both stay, we can plot how we'll get back at Alex."

She smiled. "At the moment, the thought of getting back at Alex sounds pretty appealing."

He raised a brow. "Being stuck with me as a lunch partner is that bad?"

A blush bloomed across her cheeks. "You know that's not what I meant."

Noelle set Carolyn's water and JT's milkshake on the table. "Ready to order?"

JT waited until Noelle left with their order before he sat back. Maybe if he relaxed, Carolyn would, too. "Tell me one true—"

Carolyn held up her hand. "I'll eat lunch with you, but I'm not playing that game."

"This time, I'll reciprocate—a truth for a truth."

Carolyn stared at him a long moment before she nodded. "Okay. You start."

He spooned chocolate shake into his mouth. Her eyes followed the spoon, so he pushed the shake toward her. She hesitated a moment before she picked up her own spoon and dipped it into the chocolaty goodness.

"One truth I hate to admit, but everyone in town knows, though you may not. I dated Misty for three months."

"Really?" Carolyn asked, her brown eyes wide again. "Why?"

"She asked me out, and for some incomprehensible reason, I said yes." He pointed his spoon toward her. "Now you."

She laughed, and he enjoyed the sound. She hadn't done much laughing since she'd arrived in Eden Falls. "Wait. You can't leave me hanging without an explanation of why it only lasted three months."

"You'll owe me two truths."

"No, this is a…" she rolled her hand "…continuation of your first truth."

He nodded. "Since this is the first time I've reciprocated, I'll give you a part two. I wasn't ambitious enough for her. She wanted me to apply for jobs in bigger cities."

"Because she wanted to leave Eden Falls." He watched her lick the underside of her spoon. "I love Drumsticks."

It was his turn to laugh. "As in chicken, wooden sticks, or the ice cream ones?"

"The ice cream ones. They are an incredibly yummy weakness."

He pushed the chocolate shake across the table again and she dipped her spoon in. He liked that she felt comfortable enough to share with him. They'd broken through a tiny barrier that she might not even realize existed. "My truth was a little more revealing than yours."

"You didn't say there were rules to this game." She popped the spoon into her mouth and his eyes stayed on her lips.

"Rule one, no more food-related truths"—he looked up and grinned—"unless they're kinky."

More than likely, she'd be wearing pink cheeks all

through lunch. "Okay, no more food-related truths. It's your turn."

He tapped his fingers on the table. "I've always wanted a motorcycle."

Noelle set Carolyn's shrimp tacos in front of her, his open-faced sandwich and fries in front of him. "You need anything else?"

"Nope, this looks good," JT said. "Thanks, Noelle."

"Thank you," Carolyn echoed.

~

"**Y**our turn."

Carolyn forked a shrimp from her taco with a sigh. She'd hoped he would forgo the game in favor of eating. No such luck. "Okay, I let Jolie's husband, Nate, kiss me."

He sat forward. "When?"

"In the fifth grade."

He fell back against the bench seat. "That's another dumb truth."

"And you always wanting a motorcycle is newsworthy?" she asked, laughing.

He grinned and her heart slammed into her ribs, hard. "It is to me."

Carolyn shook her head. She couldn't believe she was sitting here with JT Garrett, having an everyday, fun conversation. Her nervousness at being around JT had melted away with their laughter. She was relaxed with her girlhood crush for the first time in her life.

Glancing out the window, she realized she hadn't thought of Rob since she entered the café, and almost wished he were out there watching her having a good time with a friend. Almost.

She turned her attention back to JT. "Your turn."

"I always wanted to be a policeman." He forked a bite of turkey into his mouth.

"I always wanted to be a chef." She popped a slice of carrot into her mouth.

"I love fishing."

"I love cooking."

"I hate lifting weights."

"I hate exercise, period," she said, laughing again.

The longer they ate lunch and revealed frivolous truths, the more comfortable she became. Robert had stolen precious moments like this from her. Maybe it wasn't too late to get some back.

JT tapped his spoon against his lips. "I want to visit Scotland."

"My dream vacation would be Venice."

He glanced at the ceiling, as if trying to think of something. Then he looked into her eyes, all playfulness gone. "I'm ready to find *the one*."

That truth stopped her and set her heart pounding at the same time. He'd taken off the gloves. *But I can beat it. A truth for a truth.* "You asking me out seems surreal, because I used to have a huge crush on you."

"Errr." He made the sound of a buzzer on a game show. "I already knew that, so your truth doesn't count."

Her mouth fell open as the skin on her chest began to prickle with heat. "How did you know?"

"You used to stare at me whenever you thought I wasn't looking."

Carolyn buried her face in a hand. "I just told my most embarrassing truth, and you already knew."

He sucked in air through his teeth. "I don't think that's your most embarrassing truth."

She opened her mouth to object, but knew there was

nothing to oppose. His statement, true as it was, had crossed an invisible line. Humiliation burned up her neck and blossomed across her cheeks as she grabbed her purse. She pulled money from her wallet and set it on the table. "I have to go."

"Wait, Carolyn."

"Patsy's off today and I've been gone too long. I have to get back." She stood and he reached for her arm, but she pulled away.

"Don't go. I shouldn't have said that."

Shaking her head, she wanted to scream, *Why? It's the truth!* Instead, she walked out into the sunshine.

Carolyn had been looking forward to girls' night out ever since Stella asked. She loved meeting up with her friends and listening to what was going on in their lives. They all took turns putting their palms on Jolie's pregnant belly. They shared a huge plate of nachos and she laughed until her cheeks hurt. The night was perfect until JT walked in. Then her laughter died.

He glanced her way. Their gazes clashed and held for two heartbeats, then she looked away. She was careful not to look his direction again.

~

Rowdy's Bar and Grill was hopping tonight. He was lucky to get a stool at the end of the bar. Hidden by the crowd, he could observe Carolyn without anyone noticing. She talked animatedly and laughed until she wiped tears from her eyes. He wished he knew what made her laugh so hard.

She looked pretty tonight, in a soft green sweater and jeans. The lights were low, casting soft shadows across her face. Every once in a while, she turned just right and the red in her hair glowed.

He noticed the chief of police come in, noticed him and Carolyn look at each other for a long moment. She grew subdued afterward, her smile still there, but her laughter was gone.

Why?

CHAPTER 13

Patsy unlocked the kitchen door before dawn Saturday morning. Carolyn was at the oven, pulling out pans of blueberry muffins that smelled divine. Heavens above, she'd missed this place. She'd only been gone three days, but it felt like twelve.

"Welcome back," Carolyn said with a smile. Just as quickly, worry etched her features. "You are back, right?"

"I'm back." Patsy set her purse on her desk and grabbed an apron from the back of the office door. "Was being in charge so bad?"

"No, but I've never worked a bake sale on the Fourth of July. I'm not quite sure what needs to be done."

Patsy pulled a piece of paper out of her jeans pocket. "I have a handy-dandy checklist."

She held it so Carolyn could see. "This is pretty specific."

"If I stick to this checklist, everything runs as smooth as silk." Patsy slipped her apron over her head and tied it around her waist. "Is the coffee started?"

Carolyn nodded as she opened the oven door and pushed two more trays of muffins inside.

Patsy went into the front of the shop, poured herself a cup of coffee, and looked around. The place was just as she'd left it, just as she'd expected it to look with Carolyn in charge. She strolled over to the front windows and looked across quiet town square. The only other lights showing this early in the morning were in Noelle's Café. She'd be in the back, heating the ovens and grills, getting ready for her breakfast crowd.

Preparing for the bake sale she held over this holiday would keep her hands busy and her mind off Mason, along with the eight messages he'd left on her cell phone over the past three days.

*H*ours later, she had just glazed her sixth batch of turnover when someone knocked on the back door. She knew it was Mason before she looked through the peephole. Unlocking the door, she pushed it open, allowing him room to enter. She flashed a smile that she hoped showed self-confidence, but felt it wobble at the corners. Inside, she was a quivering mess who longed to be held and loved. "Hello, Mason."

His expression fell at her formal greeting. "You made it back. Carolyn said you had a family emergency. I got worried when you didn't return my calls."

Time to come clean. "There wasn't a family emergency. I just...I had to get out of town for a couple of days."

Several emotions passed over his handsome face. He pushed his glasses into place on his nose. "Because of me?"

"I don't think we should see each other anymore, Mason." She closed her eyes and took a fortifying breath. "Cliché as it sounds, it's not you. It's me. People are talking. They'll start to shun—"

"I don't care if people talk." He took her by the shoulders.

"And if they shun me, they weren't true friends in the first place."

"I don't like to feel uncomfortable, and I do with you. I'm always worrying and…this just isn't working for me."

"We were working fine. What happened to change your mind? Was something said? Was it Misty? Did she say something to you, Patsy?"

She shook her head. "This is for the best. We both know it."

A blush turned his ears red. He took a step back, stuffed his hands in his front pockets, and looked down at the floor. "Okay. I won't push."

"Please understand, it's not you, Mason. I had a lovely time with you."

He nodded slowly, acceptingly, then turned to the door. He stopped for a moment with his hand on the knob. "I'll miss you, Patsy."

Then he was gone.

Patsy blinked several times to keep the burning tears at bay. She had hurt him, but better now than later. She didn't know how to keep ahold of love. She'd tried. Four times, she struggled to hold on when she saw it slipping, but never could manage to keep a grip.

~

*I*t was wrong to eavesdrop, but Carolyn couldn't pull herself away from the kitchen door. She was angry Patsy had caved to Misty. People had been giving in to Misty's whims for as long as Carolyn could remember. Patsy should have stood her ground against Misty.

She could go after Mason, tell him not to give up, but then he'd know she'd been listening. She could also stalk over to Dahlia's and tell Misty, "Enough!" But Misty wouldn't listen, and talking to her might even make matters worse. Patsy and Mason had to work this out on their own.

When she heard the back door close, she walked into the kitchen. Patsy was crimping the edges of a new batch of turnovers that lay on parchment paper. "I hired a couple of high school boys to set up our booth for the Concert on the Square and fireworks. Are you sure you don't mind working there with me? I hate to ask the girls to help. They always want to spend the evening with their friends." She glanced up at Carolyn.

"I have no plans. I can help set up and tear down. I can be in the booth all night. It's not a problem."

"Here you are, new in town, and I have you working the Fourth." Patsy slumped against the worktable. She looked tired and sad. "I imagine you'd like to spend the night with your friends, too. What kind of a boss am I?"

"A fabulous one. You gave me a job when I was desperate." *You believe in me enough to hand me the keys to your business. You trust me.* "I'll never forget what you've done to help me."

"You're the best thing that's happened for this shop, but you really should—"

"I'll be able to hear the concert and see the fireworks from the booth." Carolyn leaned a hip against the worktable. "Remember what you told me about destiny? This is why you hired me, to help with these situations. Just tell me what to do, Patsy. I'm here for you."

Patsy's attempt at a smile was heartbreaking. "For the first time since opening Patsy's Pastries, my heart isn't in it. In fact, it feels very fragile at the moment." She untied her apron as she walked toward her office. "I have some paperwork to do. Can you finish the turnovers for me?"

Helplessness washed over Carolyn. If only there was something she could do.

Cory pushed the kitchen door open, a smile on her face. "Stella is out here asking for you."

Carolyn went out front, where she found Stella with her face smashed against the pastry case glass like a little kid.

"Do you know how many kids"—Colton flitted through her mind—"and adults put their hands all over that case?"

"I looked for a clean spot."

Carolyn handed glass cleaner and several paper towels over the counter. "You made the mess, you can clean it."

Stella stepped back with a grin. "I'll clean it while you tell me about your lunch with JT a couple of days ago."

Carolyn walked around the counter and took the glass cleaner from Stella. "Alex was supposed to be with us, but took off as soon as we sat down." She sprayed the case.

"So it wasn't a date?"

"No, it wasn't a date. I'm still married, remember?" Carolyn glanced at the girls working the counter. Both had stopped what they were doing to listen. She raised her eyebrows at them. "The tables out front need to be cleaned off and the coffee cups need to be refilled."

The girls grabbed rags and headed for the door, glad to be in the sun for a few minutes.

"You shouldn't send them outside with that gang of boys in the square."

Carolyn shrugged. "That's where you'd want to be."

Stella smiled. "You're right. I loved my summer working for Patsy. There were always boys close by."

"I remember." Carolyn took the paper towels from Stella and cleaned the spot she'd sprayed.

"Want to grab some Chinese tonight?"

"I better not. I have to be here extra early to bake for the fourth."

"I'll get takeout and bring it over. I won't stay late."

The dejection in Stella's tone made Carolyn look her way. "What's wrong?"

Stella swallowed so hard, Carolyn heard it. "Len broke another date."

She sent her friend a commiserating smile and wondered, again, if this Len was worth what Stella invested in him. But who was she to pass judgment? Rob had never broken a date. He was the quintessential gentleman before they married. "Chinese sounds great."

She glanced out the window to see if the girls were cleaning the tables as instructed and spotted JT walking through the square. Her silly heart sped up at a ridiculous rate. Stella leaned against the front glass.

"Stella would you stop leaving your fingerprints all over the place?"

"Sorry, just wanted to get a closer look at a handsome man."

Carolyn smiled. "A handsome man in uniform."

"A tall, dark, handsome, well-built man in uniform."

Stella was very good at making Carolyn laugh and she loved her friend for it. Laughing was something she'd gotten out of the habit of doing, and every time one bubbled out, it was kind of a wonderful surprise.

~

JT watched the stage come together for the July Fourth activities. Town workers were setting up chairs in rows along the side of the park, and turning benches to face the stage. Rowdy and Manny were stringing a banner for the Concert on the Square.

"A little to the left," Rance said from below, lifting his ever-present baseball cap and scratching at his bald pate. "Your side's crooked, Manny. It needs to be higher."

"I can't get it any higher, Rance."

Rowdy laughed. "He's vertically challenged."

"Ha ha. That joke hasn't been told a hundred times before. Lower your side, Rowdy," Manny said. "It doesn't have to be that high."

JT glanced toward Patsy's Pastries. He'd been tempted to go in several times since his lunch with Carolyn to apologize for his remark. Even though he knew it to be true, he regretted saying it aloud. Abuse was a delicate subject and he hadn't meant to hurt Carolyn's feelings or make her distrustful of him.

Stella walked out of Patsy's and headed his way, stopping next to him. "Hey there, head gunslinger."

"Hey, yourself."

She looked up at Rowdy's backside. "Nice view, Garrett."

Rowdy grinned down at her. "I aim to please."

She laughed. "That's not what your last girlfriend said."

He lifted a shoulder in nonchalance. "I didn't say I could please everyone."

"Could we please finish up here?" Manny grumbled, directing a look at Stella.

Stella turned to JT. "I heard you and Carolyn had lunch together."

He held up his hand. "Leave it alone, Stella."

"Why? Carolyn is gorgeous and fun and—"

"Married."

Stella scrunched her nose. "Yeah, to a cheating scumbag."

"Doesn't change the fact."

"Would you ask her out if she was single?" she asked, a mischievous twinkle in her brown eyes.

I already did.

"JT?"

"She isn't."

"But if she was?"

"JT," Rance called. He angled his head toward a group of kids dressed in black. "Our friends are back."

JT turned to watch the group walk into One Scoop or Two, all but the tall, vampiric one, who leaned against the outside wall. He had dark sunglasses on and seemed to be staring straight at JT.

JT stared back.

The small kid with orange hair came out carrying a cone. He glanced at the tall one and then followed his line of sight to JT.

"Who are they?" Stella asked.

"Kids from Harrisville." More of their friends came out of the ice cream shop, five more in all.

"I can't even imagine what my mom would say if I came home with hair that orange. She'd have me in Dahlia's Salon so fast."

Thorn pushed off the wall with the heel of his boot, said something to his followers, and they all climbed into two cars parked at the curb.

JT watched them drive around the square on their way out of town.

~

Carolyn sat in a chair on her porch. Stella plopped in the chair next to her and held out a box of Chinese.

"What did you bring?"

"The special, Beijing Chicken."

The neighborhood was quiet, as usual, the scent of roses heady in the warm summer air. Mrs. Bingham's garden was in full and glorious bloom.

"What's your favorite time of day?"

Carolyn glanced at her friend, who had her feet propped on the porch railing. "Morning. I love when the birds are just waking up and the sun is peeking over the horizon. I like the promise of a new day."

"Mine is right now." Stella gazed out over Carolyn's front yard. "Twilight, when the day is hanging suspended by waning light."

Carolyn smiled at the schoolteacher side of Stella. "I missed this kind of thing in San Francisco. Sitting with you or Alex or Jillian, talking about silly girl things like fingernail polish or which mascara is best."

"What do you mean silly girl things? Fingernail polish and mascara are still hot topics." Stella turned her way. "Remember when we dyed Jolie's hair black and her parents went ballistic?"

"Yes. How about the time Misty tried to pierce Jillian's ears with ice and a potato and she fainted? She scared us all half to death."

Stella laughed. "Oh, man, I'd forgotten about that. Remember the time we took that trail past Eden Falls and got lost? Jolie was sure we'd have to eat each other to survive."

Carolyn choked on a piece of chicken, she was laughing so hard. Stella pounded her on the back.

When Carolyn could breathe again, she added, "That's right. Alex found the right trail, but it was way after dark. Catherine was so mad, she didn't speak to me for a week."

"How is the Wicked Witch of the West Coast?"

"The same."

They both looked at the street as a patrol car passed. Carolyn waved to Mac who was behind the wheel.

"The police are still driving by?"

"Yeah. Though I don't think it's as often since Leo installed the new back door."

Stella set her box of Chinese on the table between them. "Why haven't you filed for divorce?"

Carolyn lifted a shoulder. "I will…eventually. I guess."

"Why would you want to stay married to a cheating pig?"

She sat a little straighter. Maybe she could file now. Robert knew where she was, so there was no reason not to.

She wished she could tell Stella everything, but the shame of living with Rob for so long kept her quiet. *How did you tell a friend that your husband beat you and you continued to stay, continued to believe that one day he would change, continued to lie for him, even though everyone who worked at the restaurant knew your black eye and bruised face came from your husband, and not another fall down the stairs.* "I'm not in any rush."

"I bet JT would ask you out if you were single."

He already has.

Crickets started tuning up for their evening serenade as the sun dipped below the horizon. The temperature cooled. Night closed in around them. The familiar feeling of being watched lifted the hair on Carolyn's arms, causing an involuntary shiver. It was that moment between day and night when the eyes played tricks and shadows moved in and out of places they shouldn't be.

Carolyn stood. "Let's go inside."

~

Carolyn carried another tray of turnovers to the worktable to be boxed up for transportation. According to Patsy, they were ahead of schedule, so she joined her employer on the sidewalk to watch the high school band march past. Cheerleaders threw candy from the back of the pickup truck following the band around the square.

She hadn't been to a Fourth of July parade since the summer before her senior year. She committed the scene—the sun shining, flags flapping in the breeze, smiling faces—to memory.

Patsy looped her arm through Carolyn's and pulled her close. "I was a cheerleader."

Carolyn glanced at her, but not in surprise. Patsy was vivacious and joyful, the perfect person to cheer a team to victory. "I bet the teamed loved your spirit."

"They did." She grinned. "I looked great in those cute uniforms, too. Of course, they covered up much more than they do now."

"Did you live here?"

"No, hon. I grew up in Spokane. I was also the home-coming Queen."

"I'm impressed."

"I was impressive back then."

"You still are, Patsy. Inspirational. I want to be just like you when I finally grow up."

Patsy threw her head back and laughed until tears appeared. "Oh, honey, you are gorgeous and talented and have so much potential. Promise me you'll aim higher."

The mounted posse rounded the corner with JT in the lead. He turned his head their way, but with his sunglasses on, Carolyn couldn't tell if he was looking at her or someone else. Yet, the longer he looked in their direction, the hotter her cheeks grew.

Patsy patted her arm. "Breathe, girl, or you'll pass out."

Carolyn hadn't realized she was holding her breath and sucked air into her oxygen-deprived lungs. Just as she was about to look away, a smile broke across JT's face, and he touched the brim of his hat.

Patsy leaned close. "He likes you."

"He likes everyone."

Patsy bumped her with an elbow. "I mean he *liiikes* you."

Carolyn smiled. "Does it mean something different when you stretch the word out that way?"

"Don't play coy with me, sweet Carolyn. You know

exactly what I mean, and if that blush is any indication, I think you like him, too."

You'd be right.

As JT's horse disappeared around the corner, Carolyn spotted Mason watching the parade on the opposite side of the street. He should be here by Patsy's side.

"Oh, look. Here comes Rance," Patsy said, waving.

The float moving past them was so ridiculous, it was funny. When Carolyn was about ten, Rance Johnson had somehow constructed a massive fish out of paper mâché and attached it to a Volkswagen Beetle with a big sign advertising The Fly Shop. The fish's mouth had been at windshield level, with Rance behind the wheel. Halfway around the square, the fish started falling apart, piece by piece, until there was nothing left. Well, here he was again. The fish had been updated, was more colorful, and looked to be more securely attached. Rance waved through the windshield. She waved back.

Suddenly, the prickly feeling she was being watched skittered through her. She slowly scanned the area around them and the spectators across the street in the square. Most were families out enjoying the parade together. Both Mac and Russell were opposite her, standing with arms crossed over their chests, feet apart, sunglasses in place. She was safe.

Scanning further, she saw nothing out of the ordinary. Still, the feeling persisted, strongly enough that she pulled from Patsy's hold. "I'm going back inside to check the brownies I put in the oven. I don't want them to burn."

J T made his way through the crowd to where his parents and his aunt and uncle sat around a card table. His mom always made this night into a party. She had an apple pie in a warming mitt and a gallon of vanilla ice cream in the cooler near the table. They had already finished their fried chicken and potato salad dinner and were playing a game of hearts when he joined them. He bent to kiss his mom's cheek.

"Hi, sweetheart. Grab a chair."

"Can't tonight. I'm on duty."

"We'll save you a piece of your mom's pie," his dad said.

JT glanced toward Patsy's Pastries booth between Renaldo's pizza by the slice and Jerry's Gyros. Carolyn was helping tourists, a family of five. "Maybe later. Thanks."

"Have you seen Alex and Colton yet?" His mom asked.

"No, but I'll keep an eye out." He glanced over his shoulder at the sound of loud laughter and a few words inappropriate for the families with small children and blew out a breath. The Goth kids were back. "I gotta go. Enjoy the concert and fireworks if I don't make it back around."

"Be safe, honey," his mom said.

He headed in the direction of the rowdy teenagers. They were walking along the edge of the park, yelling and trying to cause trouble. Nine of them followed Thorn tonight, all dressed in black. Four wore trench coats, too warm for the summer night. The kid with the orange hair—a.k.a. Blaze— stood out, as did Thorn.

He pulled his radio from his utility belt. "Mac, Russ, where are you?"

"I'm near the stage," Russ replied.

"I'm perusing the sweet pleasures at Patsy's booth. Whatcha need?" Mac radioed back.

"There are a group of teenagers looking for attention near the middle of the food tents. Russ, head over to Benny's Barbecue stand. Let the kids see you. Mac, you circle around the back of the food tents and I'll come at them through the middle of the crowd. Just seeing us might be enough to settle them down."

Keeping his eye on the gang, JT made his way through the square. One of the kids noticed Russ and tapped vampire boy on the shoulder. Thorn turned in the opposite direction and the group followed, moving toward Mac.

JT pulled out his cell and called Harrisville Police Chief. "I've got those kids here again. This time they brought a whole gang with them."

"I know a few of the parents. Let me make some calls."

His hope that they'd stay out of trouble until Tom Brody called some parents was short-lived. Three Eden Falls' teenagers walked past the rowdy group. Insults were exchanged. An argument ensued. Mac moved forward, so did JT. Russ stepped into the middle of the scuffle, holding a couple of the boys apart, and Mac was now close enough to help. JT reached the kids and pulled the tall one aside, while Mac moved the three locals along.

A cell phone chirped as the tall kid tried to pull from JT's grip.

"Hey, back off, dude!" yelled the orange-haired kid when Russ took his arm.

Mac stepped between JT and the rest of the gang.

The tall Goth narrowed his eyes at JT, trying to look dangerous. The black liner under his eyes, smudged to his cheekbones, made his sockets look eerily hollow.

Another kid pulled a beeping cell phone from a pocket.

"Thorn, right?" JT appreciated the moment of surprise on Thorn's face. "We won't have a problem if you all want to stay and enjoy the concert, but I won't tolerate trouble."

"Man, you can't come down on us! We weren't doin' nothin' wrong, Five-O," the orange-haired kid hollered.

JT was good at pulling out his calm authority when needed. "I don't want any mouth out of you. I'm talking to your buddy, here."

"We're just postin'," Thorn said.

"That right?" JT resisted the temptation to laugh. *What the heck is postin'?*

"C'mon, Badge. Let us go," the boy holding his beeping cell phone said. "We weren't gonna cause no trouble. Let's go, Thorn."

Thorn never took his eyes off JT. "We have every right to be here."

"It says so in the Constitution," said orange hair. He pulled out a cell phone with a metal skull case and looked at the screen.

Mac chuckled. "Do you even know what the Constitution is, kid?"

"The name's Blaze, and, yeah, it says we got rights."

A girl pulled a ringing cell phone from her pocket. "Thorn, let's go."

"Yeah, let's get outta this podunk town, man," another kid said.

Thorn finally turned to look at his gang. The kids had all started to back away, all but Blaze. Thorn turned with a flare of his trench coat. "Let's bounce."

JT jerked his chin in the gang's direction. Mac and Russell followed them out of the square.

~

Carolyn watched the kids leave the square. She didn't realize JT had stopped in front of Patsy's booth until he spoke. "They're kids from Harrisville, out to cause a little trouble. Remember being young and invincible?"

Carolyn remembered the young, but not the invincible part. She'd been quiet, unsure, and painfully shy. Her height had always made her feel gangly and awkward around curvy Stella, petite Alex, tempting Misty, poised Jillian, and self-assured Jolie. She suspected her low self-esteem was the reason she'd fallen under her husband's spell so easily. He'd come on strong and suave, making her feel desirable for the first time in her life. Trusting and inexperienced, she'd been gullible enough to believe everything he said.

JT's radio crackled. "Yeah, Mac?"

"The kids cleared out. I'm going to pick up Beck and enjoy the rest of the evening, but I'll have my radio if you need me. Russ is walking the perimeter of the park."

"Thanks, Mac."

Carolyn was grateful when a customer walked up. She excused herself, hoping JT would be called away, but he slipped his radio into his utility belt and stepped to the side, scanning the park in front of him. When the first band started to play and her customer walked away with a bag of sweets, JT moved back in front of her.

Their eyes met and held for a long moment. "I've wanted to come into Patsy's and apologize for what I said at lunch."

"No need." A blush sizzled up her chest. "We both know you were right."

She could see the wheels turning, the unasked questions flashing across his face like a blinking neon sign. "What would you recommend?" he asked, instead of the obvious.

"Anything on that table," Colton replied, coming up behind JT with a hand around the back of Charlie's neck.

Carolyn smiled. "You should listen to him. He's our best customer."

JT laughed, an easy sound. One she'd heard countless times, because he laughed so often. "Patsy might have gone out of business if Colton hadn't come back to town."

"I'm investing wisely." Colton leaned over the table. "I think I'll try one of those spice cupcakes. No, a piece of that marble pound cake…or…" Colton raised his gaze to meet Carolyn's. "Why are you in this small town when you could be making a fortune in some big city?"

"I've done the big city. I like this small town better."

Patsy sauntered up and wrapped her hand around Carolyn's arm. "I'm finally able to slow down a little, and here you are trying to entice my manager away."

Colton winked. "It was a hypothetical question. We don't want Carolyn and her sweet temptations going anywhere. Right, Charlie?"

"Right! We love Carolyn's sweet temp'ations."

"Atta boy, Charlie," Patsy said, handing him a chocolate cupcake with sprinkles. "Let's keep Carolyn's sweet temp'ations where we can get to them." She winked at JT.

Instant heat blossomed across Carolyn's cheeks when JT grinned at her.

"Why don't you ask him out?" Patsy asked, after JT, Colton, and Charlie walked away.

Carolyn released a deflating breath as she glanced at Patsy. *Time for another truth.* "I'm married."

Patsy's perfectly arched eyebrows rose a fraction. "I thought you were divorced."

"The last time I caught my husband cheating, I left. I packed my bags and drove away while he was at work. He doesn't know where I am."

Carolyn watched Patsy mull the information over, then lift her shoulder. "So get a divorce."

"It's more complicated than that."

"How is it complicated?"

A confession might cost her a job, if Patsy knew what Robert was capable of. Still, it was time to get everything out in the open with her employer. She owed it to Patsy. "He doesn't just cheat, he hits."

A frown transformed Patsy's features, hardening her face. "You didn't just leave, did you? You're hiding." Her frown deepened. "And someone is breaking into your house."

Carolyn shook her head. "I don't think Robert—my husband—is the one who broke my back window. He'd take his time and make me worry, but he wouldn't wait this long. He'd be doing something daily, leaving little signs or threats, to let me know he was somewhere close by, watching."

Patsy nodded toward JT who'd been stopped by the brunette Carolyn saw him with at Rowdy's a few weeks earlier. "We need to figure out who's bothering you, then get you divorced."

"A divorce won't stop Robert. If he doesn't already know where I am, he'll find out if I file. I'm…stuck."

Patsy wrapped her arms around Carolyn and held her tight. "I wish you had told me all this sooner, Carolyn. Why did you hold it in? Never mind." She waved a hand. "I know why. First, you were afraid I wouldn't give you a job if you told me you were on the run. Second, it's embarrassing to admit you hung on to someone who beat the tar out of you. You believed he'd change with every apology. When you finally get the courage to tell him if it happens again you'll leave, he threatens to kill you."

Carolyn nodded as knowledge united them in a surprising way. She'd heard somewhere that empathy was feeling with the heart of another. At that moment, she could feel what Patsy had been through without knowing any facts. "How did you get away?"

"I told you my family has money, and, sad but true, money gets things done."

Carolyn didn't have the kind of money it would take to pay Robert off.

"That uniform sure fits JT in all the right places," she said, lightening the mood.

"Patsy!"

"What? Don't tell me you haven't noticed." Patsy laughed, the sound bawdy and head-turning. "I see by your blush that you have. Good for you, because he's noticed, too. I can tell by the way he looks at you." Patsy put her arm around Carolyn's shoulders and gave her a squeeze. "Don't you worry. We'll figure something out."

The brunette laughed, brushing against JT's arm. Jealousy gnawed at Carolyn until she turned away. Her gaze landed on Mason sitting by himself. He appeared positively miserable. Patsy stole a glance his way. He did the same. It broke Carolyn's heart that two people so perfect for each other couldn't be together because of someone else's selfishness.

"Hi, Carolyn."

She pasted a smile in place and turned to her next customer. "Hi, Russell."

"Great night, huh?"

She looked at the stars shining down on their small-town celebration. "It's beautiful out. What can I get for you?"

"I'll try one of those lemon-raspberry bars."

Russ tugged his wallet out, but Carolyn waved his money away. "On the house for your service to Eden Falls' citizens."

"I can't—"

"Sure you can," Patsy said over Carolyn's shoulder. "We appreciate you being here tonight, keeping us safe."

"Thanks." Russ accepted his lemon bar. "Have a nice night."

"You, too." Patsy waved but Carolyn's gaze had drifted to the brunette who stood, waiting impatiently while JT talked with Rance and Lily Johnson.

~

*P*atsy leaned against the side of the booth, staring at Mason, who sat by himself. He seemed to be enjoying the music. This wasn't the way she'd imagined this night when she thought of the Fourth of July celebration. Disappointment was a bitter pill, one she'd ingested before. Knowing he was here alone didn't make the swallowing easier.

At the end of a song, she clapped along with the crowd. The music was good, and the weather perfect.

"Hello." Maude Stapleton waved a hand in front of her face. "Can't say I'm surprised to see you here alone."

The remark staggered and hurt. "Why would you say that, Maude?"

Maude shook her head. "I didn't mean that the way it sounded. I saw you and Misty having it out a few days ago, in front of your shop. Personally, I'm surprised it took Mason's daughter so long to get to you."

"It wasn't our first confrontation."

"That doesn't surprise me, either." The redhead picked up

a piece of marble pound cake and took a bite. She rolled her eyes. "This is the best pound cake I've ever tasted."

"Carolyn's new recipe. How is business at the bookstore?"

"We're having a great year." Maude glanced at the stage. "I really like this band. Glad they didn't put a bunch of punk rockers up there."

"Where's Jerry?"

She pointed to the card table where the Garrett family sat. "Alice had him at homemade apple pie. I saw you watching Mason and thought I'd come over and give you some advice. Don't let Misty chase you away, Patsy. You and Mason look good together. And you made him happier than I've seen him in years."

Patsy smiled. Maude was a smart cookie who kept her eyes open. "Thanks, Maude, but I just don't see it working."

"Want me to talk to Misty?"

"No."

"I could beat her up for you." Maude waggled her eyebrows. "I got a great right hook."

Patsy smirked. "How do you know?"

"Seems I walk in my sleep. Jerry tried to wake me up one night"—she jabbed with her right fist—"and I popped him one."

"I appreciate the offer," Patsy said, laughing. She doubled up her fist. "My right ain't too shabby, either."

"I bet you can take Misty on with no problem at all." Maude threw a couple of dollars on the table with a wink. "Let me know when you do, because that's a fight I'd like to see."

Patsy watched Maude walk away. Though they weren't really friends, and had never spent much time together, they always shared a mutual respect for the other. Maude's encouragement meant there were about a dozen people in Eden Falls who wouldn't shun Mason if they were seen together.

~

He stood near the trunk of a tree, watching Carolyn. In his mind, he saw her in the pink and white bra and panties from her drawer. Her creamy skin would make the lingerie look like frosting on a cake.

He hadn't been able to get close to the house since the back door was replaced, but he knew that had been a possibility when he broke the window out. Being able to walk through the spaces she lived in had been worth it, though. Checking out the fridge, going through the bathroom cabinet and her closet, lifting her bottle of perfume to his nose—yes, being denied now was worth it. Their separation wouldn't last much longer.

Soon, Carolyn. We'll be together very soon.

He glanced at the stage where a band was playing old fifties crap. Not his thing, but he tapped his foot along with the beat just in case anyone was watching.

CHAPTER 15

T he day after the Fourth was slower than usual, which gave Carolyn time to try a new carrot cake recipe. The result was firm, moist, and fabulous. Colton—her very willing guinea pig—was inside sampling a piece. She exited the back door hauling a bag of trash to the dumpster on the way to her car.

All the years she'd struggled to be a top chef in San Francisco were becoming a distant memory—funny how you could follow the wrong dream for years, only to discover utopia in the backyard you'd been anxious to leave. She'd grown to love everything about the little bakery and its customers. Regulars like Colton, and tourists who might not ever be back, would remember the fabulous black forest cheesecake or delectable coconut brownies she prepared. She didn't mind filling in when Patsy took a day off, or working the front counter, but her heart was in the kitchen.

She lifted the dumpster's lid and hefted the bag of trash high enough to clear the edge. As she reached up to lower the lid, someone smashed into her from behind, knocking the wind out of her. Before she could drag in a breath, she was flipped around and her head slammed back against a jagged metal edge. She squeezed her eyes shut against the blinding pain hammering through her skull. Warm blood trickled down the back of her scalp.

Carolyn opened her eyes and stared into the piercing depths of her husband's fierce expression. She tried to scream, but Rob pinned her to the dumpster by closing his hand around her neck, shutting off her airway. His face was so close she could feel his hot breath against her cheek, smell the alcohol he'd consumed.

"Surprised to see me, sweetheart? You knew I'd find you, right?" His grip tightened. "You can't hide from me. You are mine."

She grabbed at his hand with both of hers and tried to pry his grip loose. "Please, Robert, I can't breathe." She choked as tears filled her eyes.

"You shouldn't have had San Francisco police question me about my whereabouts a few weeks ago. If they'd come by the firm, it could have cost me my job. I was already embarrassed trying to make excuses for your absence. Do you know that nosy neighbor, Claire, actually came over and asked where you were like I'd offed you or something. I went to the restaurant and Trish said you were a no call-no show." He sneered, baring his teeth. "Does she think I don't know you better than that?"

His features softened. "Why, Carolyn? After all I've done for you, why would you leave me? You're my wife. You are supposed to stand by your man for better or worse."

"I took time off of work to search for you." His expression hardened. "You made me look like a fool!"

She tried to shake her head, but stopped when she felt the jagged metal edge of the dumpster cut deeper into her scalp. Blood trailed down the back of her neck. Her knees quaked so hard she could hardly stay upright. Spots swirled before her eyes.

He loosened his grip and she sucked in enough air to keep from passing out. "Please," was all she managed to whisper before he tightened his grip and slammed her head back against the dumpster's edge again. Pain exploded behind her eyes. Her vision blurred around the edges.

"I have to say, you were very clever to leave a winding trail of breadcrumbs when you left. I followed right along, like a puppy chasing a bone, until I lost you in Louisiana or Alabama—one of those wasteland states. Your little plan would have worked if the police hadn't visited and told me where you were." His laugh was nasty. "I didn't even have to ask. But they wouldn't tell me what you'd accused me of."

He released his grip enough for her to gasp out, "You broke into my house."

He leaned into her, his body flush against hers, and kissed her tenderly, but she knew better than to trust anything he did. He loved to strike when her guard was down. "Sorry, baby, but until the cops visited, I didn't know where you were."

That can't be right.

"What was your plan? To disappear?" His lip curled in a familiar smirk. "Or did you want to play a game of cat-and-mouse with me? Make me chase you around the country. A little kinky foreplay."

He bit her lip hard, making her jerk back, smacking her head against the jagged edge for a third time. He licked the spot he'd just bitten. "The cat always wins, sweetheart."

They'd been playing cat and mouse since their wedding night and she didn't want to play anymore.

She scratched at his wrist as his grip on her neck tightened. The impulse to kick him or raise a knee flitted through her brain, but if she missed, the repercussions could be fatal. She *did* learn from her mistakes.

"Or did you think I'd never find you?" He rubbed his thumb along her jawline. "You will never be free, baby. You are—and will always be—mine. You will come home with me and stay put this time."

I'll never see another rainbow over Eden Falls. I'll never see my friends again. He'll never let me go…

"You ever make me look for you again—" He banged her head for emphasis sending another fierce jolt of pain through her skull. The bounce gave her just enough room to turn her head and bite down on his hand. She sank her teeth hard enough to taste blood.

He yowled just before his opposite fist connected with her mouth. Her head snapped sideways, her lip split. In that moment, she caught a glimpse of the wildflowers growing in the lone strip of soil in front of her car.

So pretty. Alex, you are a wonder.

His fist smashed into her face a second time and her world went blessedly black.

~

JT ran into Colton on the sidewalk just outside of Patsy's Pastries.

"Hey, you here for some sweet pleasures? Carolyn just had me taste-test the best carrot cake I've ever eaten."

"I'm not here to taste test." He glanced at his watch. "Is Carolyn still here?"

"Just left, but if you go around back, you might be able to catch her."

JT turned his head at the clang of metal followed by a shout. He backed up a couple of steps and looked down the alley that ran to Patsy's back parking lot in time to see a man who had Carolyn by the throat pull his fist back and punch her. She crumpled to the ground. The man kicked her so violently her body bounced backwards. JT didn't realize he was running until he saw the man glance over his shoulder and take off in the opposite direction.

"Help Carolyn," he yelled, hoping Colton had followed him. He dove over the hood of Patsy's car and tackled the man, knocking the breath out of them both. As the man rolled to escape, JT recognized him.

Carolyn's husband.

Robert Richmond grappled with him until JT flipped him on his stomach and pushed his cheek into the pavement, the stench of alcohol strong on his breath. "Do not move."

Richmond tried to turn his head, but JT anticipated the move and yanked his hand behind his back. "Stop fighting, or I'll break your arm." He pulled handcuffs from his utility belt and secured them with a satisfying click. He keyed his radio. "Mac, get an ambulance to the parking lot behind Patsy's as fast as possible!"

He tried to see over Patsy's car, but couldn't. Richmond twisted and JT planted a knee in the middle of his back. "I said don't move, but I would love an excuse to—"

"Get off me. My crazy wife attacked me."

"Shut up," he growled. "Colton, how is she?"

"She's breathing, but she's unconscious and bleeding everywhere," Colton said, his voice shaky.

"I'm telling you, she's crazy. She attacked me. I had to defend myself."

JT doubled his fist just as a patrol car screeched into the driveway and Mac jumped out. *Mac just saved you, you piece of scum.*

JT patted Richmond down, hauled him to his knees, and then to his feet. "Get him in the back of the car and read him his rights while I check on Carolyn."

He whipped his uniform shirttail out of his pants and

ripped it off, sending buttons flying as he ran around Patsy's car. He pulled his white T-shirt off, and knelt next to Colton, who had Carolyn's head cradled on his knees. His hands, as well as his jeans, were stained red. "Where's the blood coming from?"

"I think the back of her head, but I can't tell."

There's too much blood. What did he do to her? JT handed Colton his T-shirt. "Press this to the back of her head. We have to stop the bleeding."

"Colton!" Alex screamed, bursting through a small crowd forming around them. "What happened? Are you hurt? Who is that? Carolyn! What happened?"

"I'm okay," Colton said as Alex searched her husband's chest and arms for a wound. "It's Carolyn's blood, not mine."

Alex turned her attention to Carolyn. "Where is she hurt? What happened?"

"Alex, go to the street and direct the ambulance back here." JT leaned over a still unconscious Carolyn. "You're safe, Carolyn. Help is on the way." His tone was far more reassuring than he felt. He knew head wounds bled a lot, but this was more blood than he would have expected.

Patsy pushed through the crowd, her eyes bulging in terror. She fell to her knees next to Colton. "Oh, no. Carolyn, honey. Help her, JT."

Helplessness and guilt settled in the pit of his stomach. "An ambulance is on the way."

"Is she going to be okay?" Colton whispered.

This is my fault. This is all my fault. JT nodded as he wiped blood from her cheek. *I'm so sorry, Carolyn.* How had he let her husband get this close without noticing? How had he allowed this to happen?

A steady stream of positive nonsense might help if Carolyn was aware at all. He pushed bloodstained locks of hair from her face and talked until he heard a distant siren.

Relief flooded him when local paramedic, Brandt Smith, pushed through the crowd and knelt beside him.

"What we got?"

"We think the blood is coming from the back of her head."

Brandt gently ran his fingers under the now bright red T-shirt shirt.

"The guy kicked her hard enough that she bounced off the dumpster, but I couldn't see where his foot landed," Colton said.

An ambulance turned into the parking lot. Two EMTs jumped out and opened the back.

Brandt took Colton's place as Alex rushed back into the group.

Colton sat back on his heels, looking as pale as Carolyn.

"Watch him," Brandt said to Alex, thumbing toward Colton.

Russ, who was off duty, came to JT's side. "What happened?"

"We'll talk later. Help me get these people back." He stood. "Come on folks, let's give the paramedic and EMTs some room."

As he pushed the crowd back, he heard Alex's hail of questions and Colton's attempts to answer.

"Is she going to be okay?"

"I don't know."

"What happened?"

"Some guy attacked her."

"Who?"

"JT got him."

JT turned to his sister. "Mac has Carolyn's husband in his patrol car."

Alex covered her mouth with both hands. "Her husband did this to her?"

Brandt started an IV before the paramedics lifted Carolyn onto a gurney. She still wasn't moving. Her skin was so pale, her freckles stood out prominently, making her look extremely young and vulnerable.

Alex followed the gurney. "I'm going with the ambulance."

JT nodded. Someone should be with her when she woke up. "Alex, call Carolyn's sister."

"I'll tell Tatum and follow in the car," Colton said.

Patsy struggled to her feet, rivulets of mascara streaking her face. "This is my fault. I asked her to take out the trash on her way to her car."

"It's not your fault, Patsy." *It's mine.* "If he hadn't gotten to her here, it would have been at her house, where it might have been hours before we found her." He put his arm around Patsy's trembling shoulders as they all watched the ambulance pull away.

Suddenly, Mason Douglas was next to them. He pulled Patsy into his arms. "I saw the ambulance turn in here and ran all the way from the hardware store, worried you were hurt."

Mason kissed Patsy hard on the mouth, making everything seem right with the world, even if only for a moment. But reality was only a few steps behind.

After he dispersed the crowd, JT sprinted across the street to the police station, arriving just as Mac came through the back door with their prisoner. He was barely able to keep his hands off the guy while Mac escorted him into one of the two holding cells. Phoebe, who was manning the phones, must have read his expression, because she stepped in front of him, blocking the way to the cell. "Let Mac put him away, JT. You have to do this by the book. For Carolyn."

Phoebe kept him in the hall until he heard the cell door close. Then he walked into the room to stand face-to-face with the coward.

"You about broke my arm putting on these cuffs! This is police brutality. My wife attacked me."

Five minutes alone, and I'd break every bone in your body.

Mac motioned for Robert to turn around and put his wrist against the bars so he could unlock the cuffs.

"I get a phone call."

"You'll get your phone call after I find out how your wife is doing."

"I have rights."

"Your wife also has rights! She has the right to feel safe with her husband."

Mac put a hand on JT's shoulder and pulled him back from the cell.

JT's insides raged all the way to his office, where he slammed the door. His first order of business was to call SFPD. When he was connected with the detective who handled the questioning of Robert Richmond, he was sure Eden Falls' residents could hear him yelling across Main Street.

"We followed protocol," the detective said.

"It took you hours to question the guy. He had enough time to get from Washington to California four times over!" JT slammed the phone down and banged his office door against the wall when he stormed out. "I'm going to check on Carolyn. I'll let you know something as soon as I find out."

Helen nodded.

"Will you take over the phones so Phoebe can finish my shift?"

She nodded again.

"I'll drive you to Harrisville," Mac said.

"I'm fine." He was anything but fine, but he needed some time alone. He needed fresh air and distance between himself and a man who beat women. The concern on Helen's face stopped him. He sagged against the wall. "This is my fault. I should have handled it—"

"You can't blame yourself for this, JT." Phoebe leaned against the wall next to him. "There's nothing more you could have done."

"If not me, let Phoebe drive you to the hospital," Mac said.

"I'm fine." He wasn't about to be shut up in a car with Phoebe while she picked his brain apart over his feelings for Carolyn. He pushed away from the wall. "I'm frustrated, yeah, but okay to drive."

~

Mason held Patsy close. "What happened?"

Patsy glanced up at the fear still etched across his face. "Carolyn is still married to a wife-beater. She's been hiding, but he found her."

"Carolyn? Is she going to be okay?"

Patsy bit her lip as she shook her head. "There was so much blood."

She didn't realize she was crying until Mason wiped her cheeks with his handkerchief. She knew then that she loved him.

Lightning didn't strike, and she wasn't jolted by sudden awareness. Instead, like a tender vine, love wove its way around her heart, filling each empty nook and cranny. Like a new day dawning, the sun rising over the ocean, she knew she would spend the rest of her days with Mason. She looked up into his honest, trustworthy brown eyes and knew he loved her, too. As if reading her thoughts, he smiled, big and beautiful, and lowered his mouth to hers.

Patsy kissed him back. She didn't care who saw them. She didn't care about the gossips. Life was too short. She didn't want to waste another minute worrying about Misty and her silly threats.

"In the middle of the sidewalk, Dad? Really?"

Patsy tried to pull away, but Mason held her tight against him. "Yes, Misty in the middle of the sidewalk. I'm letting all my friends know that I love Patsy Yarberry."

Patsy didn't take her eyes from him as she echoed his declaration. "And I love Mason Douglas."

∼

*C*arolyn floated in and out, vaguely aware of Alex's voice at times, an irritating beeping at others. Somehow she knew the hand on her arm and the fingers pushing her hair back were her friend's. She felt every heartbeat in her right temple and every deep breath in her ribcage.

Voices moved around her, making her dizzy, then frustrated, because she couldn't make sense of the words. She finally gave up and allowed quiet blackness to overtake her consciousness, allowed a gentle touch to lead her upward, pulling her into a black sky filled with blinking stars and quiet.

*C*arolyn tried to open her eyes, but only one cooperated. Beige tiles lined the ceiling. Daylight shone through the slats of the blinds hitting drab walls she didn't recognize. And what was that irritating beeping noise? Something from chin to chest prevented her from turning her head more than a fraction to investigate. The room tilted off-balance. She tried to sit up to right things, but pain ping-ponged between her temples.

Alex's voice and snippets of conversation floated over her... *"I can't believe we didn't know she was going through this…" "This isn't her fault, Catherine…" "How did he get into her house without anyone seeing him?…" "I'll let you know when she wakes up…" "The doctor said she'll be okay…"*

The memory of Rob choking her came back full force. Panic seized as her only working eye searched for him. Where was he now? Where was she?

She tried to lift a hand, but there was resistance. When she reached over with her other hand, pain shot through her side. Had he tied her up? He'd done that once before, scaring her to death.

But that couldn't be right, because she could still hear Alex. *"Oh, Stella, you won't believe what her husband did to her."*

From the corner of her eye, she saw an I.V. stand and heart monitor. She was in a hospital.

The door opened, flooding the room with brightness. Carolyn closed her good eye against the spear of light stabbing into her temple.

"You're awake."

Even though she couldn't see Alex's face, Carolyn could hear the relief in her voice.

"Where…?" She tried to swallow past the agony in her throat.

"You're safe, Carolyn." A hand touched her arm. "You're in Harrisville Regional Hospital."

She was not safe. Even in a hospital, Robert would get to her. *"You will never be free, baby. You are—and will always be—mine."* To know he would never let her go hurt worse than the pain in her head.

The door opened again, rubber-soled shoes squeaked across the floor.

"She's awake," Alex said.

"Good," said a female voice Carolyn didn't recognize. She felt the tube on her arm pull slightly.

"How do you feel?" Alex asked.

Terrified. Desperate. Angry at myself for letting my guard down. "What…?"

"She shouldn't try to talk too much," the unknown female said.

How long had she been here? Where was Rob? Was he close? Questions burned the fog away.

The nurse touched her arm. "You've had some minor throat trauma. A doctor will be in soon."

She tried to focus on Alex. "Rob?" she mouthed.

"In jail."

The squeaky shoes moved from her right side to her left, and then grew faint until they disappeared. Alex leaned closer. "I know you're not supposed to talk, but why didn't you tell me you were in an abusive relationship?"

Carolyn's head hurt too much to think, let alone answer questions about her pathological husband. How could she explain to her friend something she didn't understand herself? "Embarrass…ment, guilt…a million…different rea…sons." She hoped Alex could understand the croaked words she had trouble forming. Her throat felt like it was on fire.

A chair scooted across the floor as Alex moved closer to the bed. "I want to be angry with you for not confiding in me, but I can't, because you're hurt, and I'm scared. I suspected something wasn't right. I should have asked more questions. I should have done more."

Carolyn tried to shake her head, but whatever was around her neck restricted her movements. Her head felt like it was being bashed with a baseball bat with every beat of her heart. *It wouldn't have mattered. I wouldn't have told you.*

"I should have pushed," Alex said in a choked voice. Carolyn was sorry she'd made her friend cry.

"I was reading about abusive spouses while the doctor stitched you up," Alex continued. "Most of the articles said the abuser isolates the victim from family and friends. That's what happened to you, isn't it? That's why you never came home or answered the phone when I called. I should have been a better friend. I should have come to San Francisco and rescued you."

Carolyn lowered her hand over the side of the bed. "Stop," came out on a croak.

Alex took her hand. Carolyn knew she was crying because her arm shook. Tears burned her own eyes before leaking down her cheeks.

A tissue dabbed at the tears on her face. "You're lucky JT and Colton were close enough to hear your husband using you for a punching bag or you might still be lying in Patsy's back parking lot. Or worse, you might be in the trunk of his car headed to San Francisco."

JT and Colton saw Rob beating me. Shame, hot as fire, scorched her face.

"He was mad because you left him, wasn't he?"

"Yes," Carolyn whispered.

"When did you leave him?"

"After…wedding."

"Stella told me you were still married, but she didn't tell me you left him in February!"

"She…didn't know."

Alex dabbed at more tears. "When did he start hitting you?"

Carolyn closed her good eye in answer while another wave of shame slapped her.

"It's all right, sweetie," Alex said quietly, continuing to wipe tears from the side of Carolyn's face. "He won't be hitting you ever again. You're safe now."

Alex's cool fingers on her forehead felt like heaven—at least compared to the hell where she now existed.

~

*J*T stood on the other side of the door, angry Carolyn hadn't told him how bad it was, berating himself for thinking that she should have, frustrated that he hadn't been able to keep her safe, and wondering what he could have done differently. They'd been driving by her house, but not checking on her at work.

Something about that niggled at the back of his brain. He tried to grasp at the impression, but whatever it was stayed just out of his reach.

He glanced down the hall at approaching footsteps. Stella and Colton were coming his way.

"How is she?" Stella asked.

"I haven't been in yet. I just got here myself," he lied.

Before Stella could push the door open, Alex emerged and went straight into Colton's arms.

"How is she? Stella repeated.

"She just fell asleep. Her husband did a job on her throat. The nurse said she shouldn't talk. The emergency room doctor stitched three cuts on the back of her head—one was really deep—and bandaged her cheek. She has bruised ribs and a mild concussion." She wiped at tears with a tissue. "She's been enduring this since she got married."

"How did we not know?" Stella covered her mouth as a sob escaped. "All she told me was he cheated on her."

"You didn't know, because she didn't want you to." JT rubbed a hand down his face in frustration, facts and statistics running through his mind. "Abuse victims cover for their abusers very carefully. They tell people they tripped. They fell down the stairs. They hit their cheek on a table or a doorknob. Their abusers threaten them to keep them quiet. Most abusers like to leave their mark, but usually in a place where it won't show. Carolyn has a small scar below her left eye. She fell against a kitchen cupboard," he said, adding quote marks with his fingers.

"But she could have told us," Stella argued. "We could have helped."

Yeah, I really helped. I knew she was running and still Richmond got to her. JT had never felt so useless. And thankful. Thankful he'd been where he was *when* he was today. Glad he'd met Colton on the sidewalk rather than inside, or he might not have heard her head hit the dumpster.

Eden Falls might still have an arsonist, but Carolyn's stalker was behind bars.

~

Carolyn blinked her eye open, grateful for the quiet. The room was dark, except for a dim light in the corner. A feeling of dread spread through her at the thought of being alone. Vaguely, she remembered her conversation with Alex. Robert was in jail…or had that been a dream? If it was true, how long would they hold him? Was he already out? Was she safe in the hospital? Could he get to her here?

The burning in her throat was unbearable. In her periphery was a cup of water. She reached for it but stopped on a groan as tentacles of agony stabbed her ribcage.

Something on the other side of her moved, and her scream came out as a raspy croak.

"You're safe, Carolyn. It's only me." Suddenly JT was leaning over her bed.

The prickle of heat moved over her chest as humiliation swamped her. She didn't want JT to see her like this, but was helpless to do anything but blush.

"Robert is locked up tight in jail. You're safe," JT repeated.

She wanted to laugh at his reassurances, because she knew better. She closed her good eye, wondering what the rest of her face looked like. As embarrassed as she was, her thirst was stronger. "Water," she croaked out.

A straw touched her lips and she sipped, wincing as the split in her lip stung. The cold water trickling down her throat felt so wonderful, it brought tears to her eyes.

"I'm sorry I couldn't keep you safe, Carolyn."

She tried to shake her head, but her neck wouldn't move. "Not…your fault. Knew…he'd found…me when things were…moved in my house."

"Still, I should have been on the lookout. How he moved around town without anyone seeing…"

Not your fault. She could tell what happened weighed heavy on JT, but she didn't have the voice or energy to tell him there was nothing he could have done. She had a hard time meeting his eyes, her shame was so acute, but had to ask. "What happens…now?"

"Your husband is locked up at the moment. Two very reliable witnesses saw what he did to you. That doesn't mean he won't get out. In fact, he probably will, but you will be staying with Alex and Colton or Mom and Dad."

"No," she whispered.

"It's not negotiable, Carolyn. Until we get a restraining order in place, you can't stay at your house."

She was too tired to argue. Her eye slid shut. A long moment…or thirty minutes…or an hour…passed before she felt a hand close over hers. She knew it was JT's without opening her eye to check. A sense of security, warm as a blanket, wrapped around her, and she let herself drift into blackness again.

~

He sat in the parking lot, looking up at the hospital window where he imagined Carolyn to be. She was here because her sleazy husband put her here.

He'd argued with himself all afternoon over what happened. He should have been the one to find her, to save her. As much as he watched over her, it should have been him, yet Colton and JT were the heroes.

She'd looked beautiful behind the counter of Patsy's this morning. She even flashed a smile meant just for him when he walked into the shop. He didn't go in often, not wanting to arouse suspicion, but this morning he needed to see her.

She drew people in with her baking skills, capturing them with her smile, especially little kids. He watched her talk to Charlie earlier, bending down to look him in the eye, giving him her undivided attention. She'd be the kind of mother who made cupcakes for her children's classroom. Their kitchen would always be filled with tantalizing scents, as would her skin. He'd always be hungry for her.

He thought he'd never find love again after Becca. The hurt of losing her to cancer so young had been paralyzing, had shriveled his heart to the size of a raisin. He moved to Eden Falls to start over, to escape all their mutual friends with their sympathetic looks, to forget all the places they'd frequented.

Then Carolyn appeared in his life and he realized he'd been handed another chance at love. He'd been given another opportunity to have the happiness that had been so elusive since Becca's death. Now he and Carolyn could get married, buy a home they both loved, and build the family he'd always dreamed of.

He wiped his eyes when tears tickled his cheeks. Becca

was gone. Carolyn was here, with the same beautiful red hair, same tall, willowy figure, and the same love of baking.

He leaned his head back on the seat, closed his eyes, and imagined her delighted surprise if he walked through the door of her hospital room. He'd hold out a dozen red roses and some of those Get Well Soon balloons. Her eyes would light up and she would beckon to him with her fingers. She would kiss him. He could see it so clearly, as if he was actually there.

He hated to think of her lying in a hospital bed, bruised and broken, but there was a small part of him that was glad her husband showed up. Everyone would believe Robert Richmond was the one who broke into her house. All suspicion would fall on her husband.

CHAPTER 16

The doctor held the door for Alex as he was leaving her room. Carolyn felt undeserving—*was* undeserving—of the beautiful vase of flowers Alex set on the windowsill. "Those are gorgeous," came out distorted because of her fat lip and sore throat.

She saw the pity in Alex's eyes when she turned toward the bed, the same pity she used to see in her neighbors' eyes, or the restaurant manager's. She didn't want anyone's pity.

"I thought the room could use some color."

Carolyn's good eye swept the room, which was actually quite nice for a hospital. "Thank you."

Alex pulled a chair close to the bed. "You sound better, but look awful."

Carolyn nodded as best she could with the brace still around her neck. The nurse had helped her into the bathroom earlier and she'd winced when she saw her face in the mirror. Her black, blue, and purple jaw matched her swollen-shut eye. Her lip was double its normal size with a scab that ran halfway to her nose. She didn't even want to know what was under the bandage on her cheek.

It could be worse. I could be dead.

"Has he ever put you in the hospital before?"

"No. He was very careful about that. I have been in the emergency room, but I've never spent the night." *One true thing.* "It wasn't because of the hitting that I left. Pathetic, huh?" She looked down as humiliation filled every crevice of her being. She was so tired of feeling this way. Ever since she was little, her parents and sister had made her feel so worthless. Rob cemented those convictions after they were married. "I came to believe I deserved the hits and insults."

"No one deserves to be beaten and insulted." Alex waved her arm around the room. "*No one* deserves this."

"Tell that to my dumb self."

Alex reached for her hand. "The important point is that you left."

"I left because I got home the day after your wedding… earlier than expected. I found him in our bed with another woman. He'd cheated before, but this time I actually walked in on them."

"How did you know this wasn't the first time?"

The rough laugh that emerged hurt her throat and sounded too loud in the quiet room. "He didn't hide his infidelity and I was punished for finding the evidence. Red panties in his car, an earring under our bed, the smell of perfume on his clothes."

"When was the first time he hit you?"

"On our honeymoon. I left a hairbrush on the counter. He said if he taught the lesson early, I wouldn't make the mistake a second time." She looked up to meet Alex's gaze. "I didn't make *that* mistake again."

"Why didn't you divorce him?"

It was so hard to explain to someone who hadn't lived through something similar. "He would never allow such a thing."

"How did you get away?"

"I never told Robert about the inheritance from Mom and Dad's death. I thought I'd surprise him with an exotic vacation for an anniversary present, but after a year of abuse, I decided I might need it someday. Trish, the manager at the restaurant where I worked, knew what was going on. She held back some of my paycheck each week in an account under her name. I added bonuses to the stash whenever I could."

Carolyn's heart hurt when she noticed the tears on Alex's cheeks.

"How did people not know?"

"I wasn't allowed to have friends, so there was no one to become suspicious. The neighbors knew, but only Trish ever talked to me about my bruises. Rob was usually careful where he put them. If they did show, he'd concoct a story for me to tell people. The only places I was allowed to go were the grocery store and work. He even came clothes shopping with me, picked out everything I wore."

"What about his family? Do they know?"

"They're estranged. He hasn't seen them in years. His parents are somewhere on the east coast and he has a sister in Florida."

"I wish you'd told me. I would have figured out a way to rescue you. I would have brought JT, Beam, and Rowdy—even Dad and Uncle Dawson. They would have gotten you out of there."

Maybe. But Rob still would have found me.

~

*J*T drove down the mountain to his parents' house. Sleep had been elusive and he thought it best if he didn't go to the station on his day off, since

Robert Richmond was locked in one of the cells, tempting JT to vent his rage.

When he walked into his parents' living room, his mom was on the floor entertaining Beam and Misty's daughter. Little Sophia had every adult she knew wrapped around her tiny finger. She looked adorable dressed in denim overalls and a pink T-shirt. Her black, wispy hair was held away from her face by some kind of band sporting a huge fabric flower. He sat down next to his mom and Sophia grinned, showing off two teeth.

"Hey, sweetheart," his mom said. "What brings you by this morning?"

"I was up early and thought I'd stop by." He held out his index finger and the five-month-old grabbed hold. "Hey, cricket, you have some major drool going on there."

His mom wiped Sophia's chin with the bib tied around her neck.

"She's cutting two more teeth. Aren't you, big girl?" His mom glanced at him. "How's Carolyn? Alex said her husband beat her pretty badly."

"He did. She was in and out of it last night."

"And what about her husband?"

"He used his call to get ahold of a lawyer, who will probably have him out of jail in a couple of days."

"Then what?"

Sophia yelped out a demand for attention, so JT picked her up. She batted at the sunglasses perched on top of his head. He set his glasses on a nearby table and picked up a toy for the baby to play with. "It all depends on whether Carolyn presses charges."

His mother looked appalled. "Certainly she will."

"She hasn't before."

"Well, Alex is at the hospital now. She'll talk some sense

into her." His mom smiled. "Your sister can be pretty persuasive. Remember what Colton was like before she got to him?"

He chuckled at the memory. "If anyone can talk Carolyn into pressing charges, it's Alex."

"You have feelings for Carolyn."

Am I that transparent? He shook his head.

"Yes, you do." His mom's eyes softened as she watched him. "I can see it."

He looked away. He'd never talked to his mom about girls or women. Ever. The subject had always been off limits, even when he was young. But why? His parents had been married for thirty-five years. His aunt and uncle were throwing them an anniversary party at The Dew Drop Inn next month. He glanced back at his mom. "Yes. I do have feelings for Carolyn."

His mom tickled Sophia under the chin. "She's always been one of the sweetest girls I've ever known. I can't believe her husband—any husband could do such a thing."

His chest tightened as emotions coursed through him unexpectedly. He was surprised at how quickly his attraction to Carolyn had grown, and angry and guilty because he hadn't been able to keep her safe. At first he pushed his feelings aside, attributing them to wanting to protect her, but he knew they'd developed into something much stronger.

He liked her shy side and sweet smile. She didn't laugh often, but when she did, it was a magical sound that made you want to join in. She was kind, soft spoken, and gentle by nature, yet fiercely independence, so much like his little sister. After living through so much adversity, she still carried herself with grace.

She was sweet with Charlie. Having a family was important to him. Anyone who loved Charlie as much as he did was mother material in his book.

He hadn't realized she held so many positive attributes until now.

How ironic it was that when he found someone—possibly *the one*—she was married.

"Colton has an attorney friend in San Francisco who's looking into Carolyn's options for divorce," his mom said as if reading his mind. She smiled and laid her hand against his cheek. "As hard as it is to witness, I'm glad my big, strong, cop son has a vulnerability. Not because I want to see you hurt, but because I was afraid you'd pick the wrong woman in a hurry to settle down."

He patted Sophia's palm against his as he contemplated the attorney news.

"You know, it may take Carolyn some time to trust another man after what she's been through."

He nodded. The thought had kept him up most of the night.

His mom took Sophia from him when she started to fuss. "Have faith, my handsome son. Things will work out the way they're supposed to."

Without saying many words, they both understood each other well. His mom had always been easy to talk to and wise with her advice. He grew up in awe of his parents' relation-ship and hoped to one day have what they shared. They'd set a wonderful example. He leaned over and kissed his mom's cheek. "Thanks for always being there, Mom."

Sophia giggled, so he kissed her, too.

JT pulled into the hospital parking lot. He had some questions for the doctor, but really he was here to see Carolyn.

He was relieved to see Alex's car still here. Hopefully, she'd talked Carolyn into pressing charges. He also preferred to have his sister present when he questioned Carolyn, believing she'd tell more truths with Alex there.

The doctor was typing away on a laptop just outside Carolyn's room when he approached. "How is she today?"

The doctor took his time examining the badge JT pulled from his back pocket. "Better."

"Were pictures taken when she was admitted?"

"Yes."

"Can I get a copy of those, if Carolyn signs a release?"

"Sure. I'll have her nurse bring the papers in."

"Thank you." He knocked on the door.

"Come in," Alex called.

He stepped into the room, his gaze going to Carolyn first. The side of her face where her husband delivered the two punches was swollen with angry shades of black and blue. She had a bruise on the other side of her face where her head hit the asphalt when she fell. The gash on her cheek was bandaged and her lip was split and swollen. The fingerprints lining her neck, marks that made his blood boil, had been hidden last night by the neck brace.

The only eye she could open met his and a blush tinted her cheeks.

"How are you feeling today?"

She winced when she tried to shrug. "Is Robert…?"

"He's still in jail. If you want to file a restraining order, I can have the papers delivered to the hospital."

Tears flooded Carolyn's eyes, but didn't spill over.

Alex was next to her with tissues immediately. "Tell him yes."

JT waited for confirmation. Carolyn finally nodded.

"I'd like to talk to your doctor about your injuries and get a copy of the pictures they took. Would that be okay?"

Carolyn nodded again.

Seeing her like this ripped his heart out. He wasn't sure he could keep the professional and personal separate.

Stella walked through the door and stopped dead in her tracks. "Holy cannoli! You look terrible."

Alex set the box of tissues on the bed and grabbed Stella's arm. "Me and Miss Subtle are going to the cafeteria to get a drink. Do you need anything?" she asked Carolyn.

"No, thank you."

"Hey! I just got here," Stella said.

"We'll be back in a few." She opened the door and hustled Stella out of the room.

"I scared her."

JT walked to the bed and took Carolyn's hand. "Your bruises will heal, Carolyn."

She squeezed his hand. "Thank you for coming to my rescue yesterday."

"Actually, it was Colton's sweet tooth that had me where I was when I was."

Her smile was so sad, his heart hurt. "I'll thank him, too."

"After a call to San Francisco police this morning, they finally admitted that the officers who questioned Robert gave away your location. I'm sorry."

She shook her head. "He would have found me anyway. That's what no one understands. This is no one's fault but my own."

"What happened is *not* your fault, Carolyn. You've got to stop believing that."

"He can't get in here."

JT shook his head. "No. I will not let him get in here."

She looked down at their clasped hands. "Thank you for staying last night until I fell asleep."

He'd stayed way past her falling asleep. "Sure." He released her hand and pulled a small notebook from his pocket. "Are you up to answering a few questions?"

*P*atsy was antsy all day, her mind on Carolyn. Once she closed the shop, she rushed to Pretty Posies and picked up the bouquet she ordered earlier in the day.

Thirty minutes later, she pushed into the hospital room. The vase of flowers slid through her fingers and hit the floor when she saw Carolyn.

Carolyn flinched, and then groaned in pain.

"Oh, Carolyn, honey, I'm so sorry. I just can't believe…"

Carolyn eased back into the pillows as a nurse hurried in.

"I'm so sorry about the mess. The vase slipped. I'll clean it—"

"No need." The nurse waved a hand. "I'll have a janitor come up." She put a hand on Carolyn's arm. "Need anything?"

Carolyn shook her head.

"I'm sorry," Patsy repeated to the nurse. Carolyn's battered face was far worse than she'd imagined, and she'd imagined some pretty awful things.

After the nurse left, Patsy pulled a chair close and took Carolyn's hand. "Oh, honey, I'm so sorry this happened to you. How long has he been doing this?"

Forever came out of Carolyn's swollen lips as "f'rev'r." Tears welled, but Patsy quickly blinked them away. Carolyn didn't need to see her crying. "I should have known. I should have seen the signs."

"Not your fault."

"No. And it's not yours either, though at this moment, you probably think it is. I know, because I've been there. Get that thought out of your mind this very minute. It's *his* fault. He's a no-good lowlife for doing this to you. You've done abso-lutely nothing to deserve it. Took me a couple of years of therapy to believe that, but I do." Patsy released a breath. "Sorry. I'm rambling. I'm just so upset this happened to you, and so worried."

She stood, gathered some of the flowers that could be salvaged, and placed them in the sink. Then she threw away the largest pieces of the vase and set paper towels down to soak up some of the water.

She glanced out the window. The day was too pretty for Carolyn to be lying in a hospital, battered so badly. Lightening should be flashing and thunder rumbling so hard it rattled the windows.

She walked back to the chair, sat, and took Carolyn's fingers in hers. Carolyn squeezed, letting her know she was still awake. "Mason kissed me in the middle of town yesterday, for all the world to see. He told me that he loves me. And I love him." She laughed. "I'm in love with a man I've barely kissed."

She slumped forward. "I don't think I can live through another rejection, Carolyn. I don't want to hurt Mason, but I just don't see how it can work."

"You are being melodramatic."

Patsy glanced up. Carolyn was looking at her, a painful smile on her lips.

"Maybe. A little."

"Please don't make me smile."

Patsy frowned. "I didn't know I'd said anything funny."

"Do you have a piece of paper and a pen?"

Patsy pulled a small notebook and pencil from her purse. Carolyn closed her eye a moment, and then opened it and started writing. When she finished, she closed the notebook and held it out. "Read this when you get home."

Patsy took the notebook and slipped it in her purse. "You look tired."

"I am. My head hurts."

Patsy covered her face. "I'm the most awful person, the worst employer, and the rottenest friend on the face of the earth. You are lying hurt in the hospital because of me. I'll never make you take the garbage out again."

"Patsy, I was the one who said I'd take the garbage out." She reached for Patsy's hand. "I'll be eternally grateful for the second chance you gave me. You are wonderful."

Patsy stood and kissed the cheek that wasn't bruised. "Go to sleep and dream about happy things, like riding across beaches on unicorns, or sliding down satin-lined rabbit holes. Don't even think about coming back to work until you're one hundred percent better. And call me day or night if you need anything."

"Thank you."

She slipped from the room and ran to her car with tears streaming down her face. She couldn't stand to see Carolyn in that bed, her skin as white as the sheets.

She should have been more alert to who was hanging around. She should have checked the back parking lot before letting Carolyn out the door.

On her way home, she pulled over next to the river just outside Eden Falls' town limits. The night was warm, so she rolled down her window and let the sweet summer breeze lift the hair on the back of her neck. She took the notebook from her purse.

Patsy,

You've been a successful businesswoman since I moved to Eden Falls in the third grade. You volunteer not only your time, but make donations to the senior center, to the food bank, the book drive, etc. You don't realize what a pillar of the community you are, because you're so selflessly worried about Mason's reputation.

Mason doesn't care what others think. He adores you. I can see it in his eyes. He would be a lucky man to get you, and he knows it, because that's the type of man he is. He's steadfast and honorable. If he is serious about you, his commitment will be lifelong. You would both have a very happy life together. Stop worrying about what other people think. If Mason doesn't care, neither should you.

Life is beautiful. Grab it with both hands and don't let go. You deserve your happily ever after.

Sincerely and with much love,

Carolyn

P.S. Don't cry.

Of course, she did.

~

Carolyn waited for Stella to show up with nervous trepidation. She was being released from the hospital, but didn't want to leave a place where she felt safe. Not yet. Not until she knew what was going to happen with Rob.

Alex came by before work and insisted she stay with her, Colton, and Charlie for as long as she needed. Carolyn didn't want to admit how relieved she was to be invited. She hated to impose, but knew if she went home, she'd shrink into a ball in the closet and not emerge for days.

Her sister called. Carolyn was sorry she answered. Catherine asked what Carolyn had done to encourage the attack. Catherine's accusations turned her self-doubt faucet on full blast. By the time Stella arrived, Carolyn was drowning in the deep end of her own self-made pool.

Unaware, Stella pushed her head under water again when she threw the small local paper onto the bed. "You made the front page."

Carolyn read the headline aloud, "Local Baker Brutally Beaten by Husband." She groaned.

Stella lifted her brows comically. "You're famous."

"I don't want to be famous. Where did they get this picture?"

"Looks like your senior yearbook picture."

"It is. Where did they get it?"

"Probably the high school yearbook archives. I don't know." Stella sat on the foot of Carolyn's bed and grinned. "Be glad they didn't come here and take a picture of you looking like that." Stella, never one to beat around the bush, added, "You are all the colors in the rainbow, and you talk funny, too."

Carolyn wished she could roll her eyes like Stella. Heck, she wished she could roll her eyes at all without sending shards of pain shooting through her head. "Yay, one thing to be glad about this morning."

"Two. Read the story. You have two knights in shining armor riding in on white horses to save Maid Carolyn. Or is it Lady Carolyn when you're married?"

Carolyn dropped the newspaper on the bed. She couldn't help but wonder where she'd be if JT and Colton hadn't come to her rescue. Would she be back in San Francisco, tied to the bed so she could never leave? Or would she be in the morgue?

Stella patted Carolyn's leg, wearing a serious expression for the first time since she walked in. "You need a bodyguard. You should hire some of the single guys in town. They could take shifts, escort you around, stay at your place—"

"I'm not hiring a bodyguard. Rob is in jail. Hopefully he stays there awhile."

"They can't stay at your place, anyway. I'm under strict orders to deliver you to the McCreed household." She stood and picked up a piece of toast still on Carolyn's breakfast tray. "Why was JT here yesterday?"

"He took pictures of the bald spots on my head and the bruises—"

"You have bald spots on your head?"

"They shaved my hair to put in stitches."

"Can I see?" Stella asked, even though she was already standing over Carolyn, lifting her hair away. "Gross, the stitches look nasty. You do have bald spots. I mean they're little, but—"

Carolyn sighed.

"What? You're not completely bald. Just a little bald."

"That makes me feel so much better."

"You don't have to get snarky. Your hair covers it up."

~

Carolyn slept fitfully, thanks to the pain in her ribs and nightmares of other beatings. Finally giving up, she rolled carefully onto her back and listened to the early morning sounds around her. The sky was growing light, but the sun wasn't up yet. The crickets' nightly song was swapped for an early morning chorus of birds.

She was a morning person. Always had been. Rob was not. Once, after a night off, and not long after they'd married, she was in the kitchen whipping up breakfast. He came stomping in, cussing and swinging. Breakfast ended up on the floor while she cowered in a corner. From then on, an energy bar had sufficed until after he was up and in the shower.

She struggled out of bed and moved down the hall silently. Charlie's bedroom door stood open, and she peeked inside. He'd thrown off all the covers and lay in a tight ball near his pillow. She tiptoed in and pulled the sheet and blanket back over his little body. His black, silky hair was standing up in every direction. Dark lashes twitched against his bronze skin as he dreamed. Once covered, he rolled to his other side, pulling the blanket with him.

In the kitchen, she poured a glass of orange juice and

meandered to the front window. The sheers muted the view of the quiet street beyond, but she could see the sun just rising over the horizon, casting a pinkish glow over the world, making everything look soft and inviting.

She had the whole day to do nothing. Her doctor said she couldn't go back to work until Monday, four days from now, and she was too sore to be of any help around here. She'd go stir crazy sitting in Alex's house all week, but she was too afraid to go home.

Was her husband out there somewhere waiting for her? JT had assured Alex that Rob was still locked up, but for how long? JT also said he'd bring the temporary restraining order over. A piece of paper with those words should give her a measure of comfort, but it didn't. She didn't trust Rob to abide by any agreement, even if it was court-ordered.

A police cruiser passed Alex's house. With the sheers, she couldn't make out who was behind the wheel, but the thought that it might be JT set her heart thumping a little too wildly for this early in the morning.

She jumped, sloshing orange juice all over the sheers when someone touched her shoulder. She groaned and grabbed her ribs with her free hand.

"Oh, Carolyn, I'm so sorry," Alex said. "I said your name twice. Didn't you hear me?"

Carolyn slowly let out a breath of air. "No. I was…I guess I was so deep in thought. I'm sorry about the drapes."

Alex flapped a hand. "They wash."

"I'll do that today."

Alex smiled. "No, you won't. You are under orders to rest."

Carolyn glanced outside, again. "I'm not very good at resting."

"Well, you'll have several days to practice. If you'll make

a list, I'll go over to your house and pick up anything you need."

Carolyn looked down. She was wearing baggy, borrowed sweats from Colton because Alex was so tiny. "Clean clothes."

Alex turned her by the shoulders. "Are you worried about your husband?"

"I…" She couldn't admit to Alex that she'd been thinking about JT. "Yes."

"We won't let him get to you again, Carolyn."

"I know. I'm okay." She smiled, hoping to reassure her friend. "I'll be okay." *I hope.*

"Colton's attorney friend will get things taken care of."

Carolyn lowered herself to the edge of the sofa. *Escape. A divorce. Safety. The end.* She had a hard time believing there would ever be an end.

"Are you sure you're okay?"

"Beyond okay, if this attorney can help me." Even though she'd escaped from her situation in San Francisco, she hadn't escaped looking over her shoulder. Would that ever happen and what would it be like?

Alex sat on an ottoman facing her. "How do you feel this morning?"

"Stiff. I haven't dared look in a mirror."

Alex grinned. "Charlie is completely impressed with your shiner. He told me last night that he thinks you're tough."

Carolyn shook her head. "If I was tough, I might have gotten a punch or a kick in. I was terrified Rob would choke me to death. I'm embarrassed I've never learned to fight back. I should be better able to protect myself."

"Hmm. Maybe for one of our girls' nights out, we should take a self-defense class. My aunt schedules them every couple of months at the gym."

Carolyn nodded. "I'd like that. I want to be prepared if Rob ever comes back."

And he will.

Carolyn showered and changed into the clothes Alex had picked up at her house. With Alex at the flower shop and Charlie at summer recreation, Colton was designated babysitter. She tried to clean up the house a little, but every move sent shards of agony through her ribcage. So she picked up a book, went into the backyard, and sat in the shade of an apple tree.

The clouds seemed unmoving in the vivid blue sky. The world was still around her, but for the twitter of a bird, or a passing butterfly. Charlie's dog, Barney, stretched out in the sunshine near her, happy with the occasional scratch behind his ear.

She closed her eyes and was close to sleep when the back door opened. JT came across the yard toward her, and he didn't look happy. She tried to hide her gasp of pain when she attempted to sit up in her lounge chair.

"Don't get up."

Grateful, she relaxed—at least, as much as she could when he was near. He wore his uniform, so she assumed he brought news of Robert.

He pulled a lawn chair close and sat. "How are you feeling?"

Tragically, she knew how she looked. "Sore."

He handed her an envelope. "Temporary restraining order."

"Thanks." She pulled the order out of the envelope and read it. A simple piece of paper forbidding Robert from contacting, molesting, attacking, striking, stalking, threatening, or harassing her did nothing to guarantee her safety. He was banned from stepping into Eden Falls' town limits. It was an order that Robert wouldn't honor.

"Robert got out this morning. His attorney swore to me he wouldn't leave your husband's side until he was on a plane headed for California."

It won't matter. If Robert wants to get to me, he will.

CHAPTER 17

He stood on the sidewalk in front of a nondescript two-story San Francisco house. The only light was dim and filtered through an upstairs window. The house Carolyn was in now suited her better. He'd heard it was her childhood home and he liked that she'd settled there. It meant family was important to her. He wondered what she'd been like as a child. Was she close to her parents? Did she have siblings? Those were all things he'd learn as they got to know each other.

He walked up the front steps and rang the bell.

Robert Richmond had been charged with second-degree assault, which carried a potential three- to twelve-month prison sentence for someone with a clean record. Ridiculously enough, his attorney worked a deal, and the guy was out on bail, living his life as if he'd done nothing wrong.

When he saw a shadow through the door's frosted glass, he pulled the ski mask over his face. As soon as the lock turned, he pushed inside and wrapped his hand around the shirtless man's neck, backing him up against a wall and kicking the door shut. Staring into the eyes of the lowlife who got his thrills from beating women, he preempted any struggle with a quick jab to Richmond's solar plexus.

He studied Richmond's face. His eyes were bulging in surprise as he gasped for air. What had attracted Carolyn to him? He wasn't much to look at, especially whimpering like a little girl. "How does it feel, struggling for air when someone hits you in the stomach or has you in a chokehold?"

"What…do you…want?"

"I came to see the weasel who'd beat up a defenseless woman in a back alley, because I bet that weasel has beat her up before. Are you that weasel?" he whispered.

"What's going…" A pretty woman in a black lace negligee rounded the corner into the living room and screamed.

"Shut up!" he demanded. He pulled a gun from his jacket pocket and pointed it at Richmond's chest. "Sit down in that chair and don't move or you'll be responsible for what happens to him."

She obeyed.

"Did you know your man here is married?"

The woman's eyes bounced to Richmond's. She nodded once.

"Did you know he beats up defenseless women?"

She glanced from him to Robert with terror in her eyes.

"Has he smacked you around yet?" He raised the gun to Richmond's temple. "Or do you save that for your wife?" He looked Richmond up and down, but addressed the woman. "What makes you stay with him? It can't be money, because he doesn't make that much, and it sure ain't his looks."

He tightened his other hand around Robert's windpipe. "You go anywhere near Carolyn again, and I'll come back and kill you. Do you understand me?"

Robert nodded slightly, but he wasn't convinced. "Any

man who beats up women is nothing but a piece of trash. An eye for an eye."

He slipped the gun back into his jacket pocket and knocked Richmond out with one punch. The woman shrieked. At his glance, she quickly covered her mouth with trembling fingers.

"Take some advice, lady," he said as Richmond crumpled to the floor. "Pack your bags and get out, before he puts you in the hospital. And he *will* eventually put you in the hospital, or worse. When he comes to, he's going to be mad, so you have about five minutes to get out of here, or he'll take this beating out on you."

He gave Robert a kick in the ribs before he slipped out the front door. As soon as he was out of sight of the house, he pulled the ski mask off and stuffed it in a pocket. Keeping to the shadows, he jogged two blocks to his rental car.

~

*H*elen came to the door of JT's office. "San Francisco PD is on line two."

JT picked up the phone. "Chief Garrett."

"Hey, Garrett, Hodges here. I thought you might like to know someone roughed up Robert Richmond pretty bad last night."

"What?" JT fell back against his chair.

"Some guy forced his way in, put him in a chokehold, and knocked him around a bit. He even pulled a gun."

JT rubbed a hand over his jaw. "Any idea who it was?"

"Nope. Do you?"

The question surprised JT, until he realized that's why Hodges called. "I have no idea. No one got a look at him?"

"He was wearing a ski mask."

JT stood and walked to the window. Today was Carolyn's

first day back at Patsy's. She was outside wiping a table. He could tell by the way she moved that her ribs were still tender. "Is he in the hospital?"

"No. Treated and released. Before the guy broke Richmond's nose and a rib, he said if Richmond went near Carolyn again—and I'm assuming Carolyn is Richmond's wife—he'd kill him. Now do you know who it might be?"

"I have no idea."

"I don't need a vigilante running around here, Garrett."

"I didn't send one." JT disconnected the call. *Now what?*

~

Carolyn had been back to work for two days. She wore enough makeup to blur the edges of her black eye, and the cut on her cheek was no longer swollen. Everyone who came in wanted to talk about what had happened, so she stayed in the kitchen as much as possible.

Patsy hovered, ordering her to sit down, or insisting she go home early. When Stella bounced in right before lunch with an invitation to the lake, Patsy pushed her toward the door. "Go get a tan. Have some fun with people your own age."

"Patsy, I've been gone almost a week."

"I don't care. You need fresh air, sunshine, and a carefree afternoon." She shook her finger at Stella. "You watch her like a hawk."

"Yes, ma'am," Stella said with a salute.

Stella came into her house while she changed and slathered sunscreen over any exposed skin. She was actually excited by the prospect of spending a day in the sun with a friend. When they arrived, the whole gang was there, including JT. She turned to Stella. "You didn't tell me everyone was coming."

Stella raised her eyebrows. "I didn't know it was going to be a problem. What's wrong?"

The T-shirt she wore over her bikini would stay on to hide the huge blue and green bruise Robert inflicted with his kick to her ribs, and—if she were truthful— hide her body. After years of being told she was inadequate… Well, it was hard to believe otherwise. "I thought it was going to be just the two of us, that's all."

To relieve her discomfort, she insisted cooking the hamburgers and hot dogs while everyone frolicked in the water, or took turns waterskiing behind Rowdy's boat. She had a sense of well-being when cooking. She felt safe.

After lunch, she finally felt brave enough to remove her shorts to enjoy the warmth of the sun on her skin. Her shirt remained on. She didn't want to hear the gasps of her friends when they saw the bruise.

Today was the first time she felt peace of mind since finding the footprint. Anxiety that Rob had found her followed on the heels of finding a job and place to live. She didn't fret about the cake she had to bake for Alice and Denny Garrett's thirty-fifth anniversary party, or the pastries that had been ordered for a baby shower in Harrisville. She didn't even think about Rob. She was having too much fun with friends during a perfect day on the lake.

From the shoreline, her eyes covered in sunglasses, she watched JT's shoulder muscles bunch as he untangled the ski rope. She tried not to stare at the ripples of his stomach, or the bulge of his thighs under his wet swim trunks—without any success.

As the day began to wane, she helped with cleanup while the guys built a fire. They all sat on downed logs and watched the sun dip behind the mountaintops, casting streamers of gold against the cotton candy-colored sky.

Carolyn consoled Stella when Len had to leave early and

helped Charlie roast the perfect marshmallows for s'mores. Several times her glance collided with JT's. He seemed to be watching her. Or was that just wishful thinking? Possibly the flickering flames were playing tricks on her. Either way, it set her heart thudding uncomfortably in her chest.

By the time they began loading cars, she'd dubbed this her best day since coming home and she was glad Patsy had shooed her out of the pastry shop.

She started to lift an empty cooler into the bed of Beam's truck. Suddenly, JT appeared, taking it from her. "You shouldn't be lifting this."

Moonlight touched his hair in places, but his facial features were shadowed. She hoped darkness hid her facial features from him as well. "If it was heavy, I wouldn't be."

He set the cooler in the back of the truck and turned to her. "Did you have a good time?"

She folded a wet beach towel, averting her eyes. "The best."

"Alex said Colton's friend is getting your divorce papers filed."

The attorney had flown in Monday night and she'd filled out all the necessary paperwork to file for divorce. The attorney said he would call in a favor to push it through as quickly as possible. "He is."

He blew out a breath. "I think you should know someone beat Robert up."

She glanced up, trying to see JT's expression. "What?"

"San Francisco PD called. Someone barged into your husband's house and beat him up."

She shook her head in amazement. "Who would…do that?"

JT didn't answer for so long she thought he wouldn't. Then he took her hand. "Do you still love him, Carolyn?"

The question surprised her. And so did her answer. She

didn't love him. In fact, she hadn't thought of Robert and love in the same sentence for a very long time.

After they were married, he stopped expressing much of anything but displeasure at her ineptness. She was clumsy, useless, and anything else negative he could think of to describe her incompetence. She'd learned to believe him.

When had she fallen out of love with Robert? "No."

He put her hand on his chest, pulling her a step closer. Her heartbeat raced and she could feel his doing the same under her palm. They were away from the fire, away from watching eyes, and JT was holding her hand to his chest. Wasn't this the sort of scenario she'd dreamed about as a silly schoolgirl?

That he was interested in her was staggering. She was plain Carolyn. A redhead covered with freckles who had a nonexistent career and zero self-esteem.

"Tell me one true thing, Carolyn."

Her breath hitched. "You first."

"Okay. I want more than one truth. I want to know every-thing about you."

She stepped back, pulling her hand from his grasp. *One true thing.* "After my divorce is final, I want the same thing."

~

*C*arolyn got out of her car and smoothed her dress over her thighs. She'd spent extra, *extra* time on her hair and makeup tonight, trying to cover the last of the bruises on her face. The pale lilac dress was both complex-ion- and figure-friendly. *Thank you, Nordstrom.* The silver sandals were flattering to her slim ankles. *Thank you, genes.*

Robert had stripped her of what little dignity, self-worth, and pride she'd possessed, but he hadn't been able to strip her of her lithe, toned body. *Thank you, yoga.*

She entered through the side doors of The Dew Drop Inn and stood in awe. The large room was draped with thousands of twinkling white lights. Tables were set with white tablecloths. Orchids in cylinders of water, a white candle floating on top were the centerpieces. A band played outside on the large deck overlooking the river. Everything was perfectly beautiful for the Garretts' wedding anniversary.

She walked across the room when she spotted Alice and Denny with their arms around each other. The Garrets had always been the epitome of the family she dreamed of having. Both had come to visit her in the hospital and extended the invitation for her to stay with them until her life was more settled. They'd been like surrogate parents during her lonely childhood years, their house always open to her.

Carolyn's heart pinched. She and Robert had never been in love like that. She told herself she was in love, and she'd believed it, but now, looking back, she wasn't so sure. Robert had provided her starving soul with affection and appreciation. She didn't know what Robert felt, but didn't believe he knew how to love.

Alex glanced her way and waved. She'd stayed with the McCreed's for a week while recuperating from Rob's beating, and Alex gifted her a small can of mace when she left, with strict orders to keep it in her pocket at all times.

She ran a hand down the slim lines of her dress. *No pockets tonight, Alex.*

Alice hugged her. "We are so glad you could come. Thank you so much for the gorgeous cake."

"You're welcome. Congratulations."

She returned Denny's hug, standing on tiptoe to do so.

"How are you feeling?"

She stepped back. "I'm okay."

"You look beautiful."

She appreciated the compliment, a boost to her fragile ego. "Thank you."

"Go eat," Denny said, indicating the tables laden with food.

Carolyn put a hand to her stomach. "I'm glad I didn't have time for lunch."

She filled a small plate with finger food and wandered around the crowd, waving and talking to acquaintances as she went. Even though she'd been careful to cover bruises, she knew people still talked about what happened a week and a half earlier.

The summer night was warm and she walked out to watch happy couples circling the dance floor. Patsy and Mason were dancing close together, smiles on their faces. Mason tucked their joined hands against his chest and kissed Patsy. They looked pretty adorable.

Good for you both.

Misty stood on the other side of the deck glaring in their direction. Carolyn hoped Mason and Patsy hadn't noticed. And if they had, she hoped they ignored Misty's obvious disdain.

At the edge of the deck, she set her plate aside and walked down the steps toward the river, deeper into the night, as thoughts of hopes and dreams crowding her mind.

She'd wanted to be a chef since she was little, as soon as she discovered food was the one way she could earn a compliment from her parents. She started out with simple desserts. When she received the proverbial pat on the back, she began to scour cookbooks for recipes she could make with ingredients they had at home. With chore money, she went to the grocery store for more elaborate ingredients, hoping for more than a pat. It never came, until she met charming Robert.

He swooped in and swept her off her feet. She was an

innocent late-bloomer. He made her feel beautiful and self-confident and…worthy of his affections. When she began cooking for him, he raved about her dishes, ate every morsel on his plate. After they were married, his palate changed. He became pickier and more critical of her cooking. There was too much pepper, not enough oregano, too bland, too hot, too cold. Altering a recipe didn't change his opinion. Or his temper.

Yet at the restaurant, she received rave reviews, and was featured in the paper as a new up-and-coming which enraged Robert rather than making him proud. The next time the paper came and asked for an interview, she declined, and no longer shared the compliments with her husband. When her name was mentioned in a magazine, he mocked her by saying, "How much did you pay the journalist for this?" If another chef was mentioned, he wondered aloud, "Why can't you be good enough to be interviewed?"

Little by little, without her even realizing it, he started controlling her life, taking calls from friends, and never giving her the messages, isolating her from anyone but him. He whispered vicious lies that she believed, breaking her fragile self-image into a thousand tiny shards.

"You're pretty, honey, but you need to accept you'll never be a beauty. It's okay, though, I love you anyway." "They aren't really your friends if they never call. You're better off without them. You'll always have me." "You'll never be a great chef, but you'll go down in history for your efforts."

Before she knew it, she was a prisoner in her own home, only allowed out for work. Hindsight was 20/20… love was blind… all those silly clichés weren't so silly when they pertained to you.

The first time Robert hit her, he'd cried and begged for her forgiveness all night, holding her close and promising it would never happen again. She couldn't remember when the beatings began to be her fault rather than his.

By the time she left, her self-confidence was nonexistent. She'd been living in a deep dark hole, too embarrassed to talk to anyone about the black eyes and bruised jaws, but someone had noticed and reported them to the police without her knowledge. Rob was questioned and was furious. The most humiliating part was when he threatened to leave and she'd begged—begged!—him not to.

Enough!

Carolyn took a deep breath of the sweet night air, following the trail by the river. The beauty around her seemed to seep under her skin, settle in her soul. The peaceful surroundings calmed the jitteriness she'd felt since leaving San Francisco. She was home.

It was time to leave the hurt behind, to start a fresh chapter of life. The idea of being free of Robert sent her heart into a giddy gallop. To know she would be free to do what-ever she wanted, to say anything that came to mind was liberating.

When she first came back to Eden Falls, she wasn't sure what true love looked like, but she had wonderful examples all around her. Alice and Denny Garrett, Alex and Colton. Even Beam and Misty were proof that love was alive. It wasn't so elusive as she thought it might be. The new love blossoming between Mason and Patsy…

"It's probably not wise for you to be out here alone."

Carolyn nearly jumped out of her skin. She was so deep in thought she hadn't noticed JT sitting on a bench near the trail.

"Sorry. I didn't mean to scare you."

"I guess I should have been paying more attention," she said, a hand to her chest to steady her pounding heart.

He patted the bench. She hesitated a moment before she

walked over and sat beside him. He gazed up into the star-studded sky. The light from the moon illuminated his nose and shadowed his cheek. He turned toward her, and she smiled.

"Your mom and dad picked a beautiful night to celebrate."

"They did." Music floated toward them as the band began another song.

He moved a lock of her hair behind her ear. The warmth of his touch ignited something deep in her belly. "Moonlight looks good on you."

"It looks good on you, too." She was grateful the darkness concealed her blush. She'd be a splotched mess in another ten seconds. How many times had Robert told her she wasn't aging well, she had bags under her eyes, she had lines around her mouth—all things she hadn't seen herself until he pointed them out.

"You've been avoiding me since the lake."

"No." *Yes.* "I didn't mean to." *Liar.*

"I think you did. I think you feel the same connection I do."

She shook her head. *One true thing.* "Maybe. Yes."

"Those feelings scare you."

Her laugh held no humor. "Terrify me."

"Because of what you've been through."

She nodded.

He took her hand, but she pulled from his grasp. "Carolyn, I would never hurt you."

Heat burned her cheeks. "I know. It's just…until I'm divorced, I don't feel comfortable…"

"I'm sorry. You're right."

She stood and smoothed her dress. "I'd better get back." She hurried away, leaving him sitting in the dark.

"Hey, where have you been?" Stella asked as she mounted the stairs.

"By the river."

Stella's gaze moved past her and she grinned. "By the river with JT?"

"No. Yes, he was…I didn't know he was there when I went down."

"You're blushing."

Carolyn blew out a breath. "I always blush."

~

Patsy closed her eyes as the music flowed over her. Mason was a wonderful dancer, and she loved to dance. She caught Misty's eye. She stood on the sidelines, watching with a scowl. *I'm sorry, Misty, but I'm happier than I've been in a very long time. Do what you must.* She laughed.

"What?" Mason asked, looking down into her eyes.

"If looks could kill, I'd be lying on the floor right now with my toes sticking in the air."

Mason lifted their joined hands and kissed her fingers. "Don't look her way. It doesn't matter what Misty thinks."

Patsy laughed again. "It's not Misty I'm talking about. It's Glades Benton. I think you have a secret admirer."

"Don't look her way, either. Just be happy." He looked down again. "Are you happy, Patsy?"

"You want the truth?"

A look of worry shadowed his features. "I always want the truth."

"Carolyn wrote a letter, wise words that made me very happy. In fact, the only thing that could make me happier than I already am is if you kiss me toni—"

He tasted of punch and spearmint gum, and she was lost in

him. He was the first thing she thought of when she woke, and the last thing before she drifted to sleep. Her world had changed in just a few short weeks. He made her laugh and hope and dream. He made her believe a beautiful future was possible.

"I didn't mean right now," she said, when their lips parted. "I just meant before the night was over."

"Did I embarrass you?"

"Me? Embarrassed? I thought you knew me better than that."

The corners of his eyes crinkled in the most adorable way. "Then you won't mind if I kiss you again."

She smiled right back. "Please do."

~

JT leaned against a tree trunk, watching Carolyn from a distance. She looked incredibly beautiful tonight. When he left for college, she was just a skinny girl with bright red braids. She was now a sweet, kind, very generous woman. That she flinched every time he was near made his blood boil. Her husband had tried to break her. He hoped, prayed, that given time she'd be able to overcome her fears.

Beam came down the stairs and handed him a drink. "What's with the frown?"

"What?"

"You're standing there"—Beam's glance followed his—"staring at Carolyn with a storm brewing on your face. What's up?"

JT shook his head, angry that his emotions were so visible. He straightened and looked at Beam. "Nothing."

"I noticed you watching her at the lake, too. You got a thing for her."

"No."

Beam raised a brow.

"Maybe… Yes." The words stumbled out of his mouth just as Carolyn's had earlier. "But for now, leave it alone."

"Okay." Beam chuckled. "You always were the eloquent one."

Time to change the subject. "The rebuild on the hardware store is moving quickly."

His cousin nodded. "We hired a good crew."

"Do you have the grand opening scheduled yet?"

"No, I'll give it a month. By then we should have a better idea of a completion date. Mason and I rented a warehouse in Harrisville and we're slowly filling it up with merchandise."

"I sure wish I could get whoever burned your place down."

Beam clapped him on the shoulder. "You will, cuz. There's no doubt in my mind."

"You have more faith in me than I have at the moment." He glanced at Carolyn. Rowdy was talking to her. He nodded toward the dance floor and she shook her head. Alex appeared, said something, and then pulled Carolyn away.

Beam chuckled. "You've got it bad. You didn't hear a word I just said."

"I've just got a lot on my mind."

"Riiiight. I'll let you get back to thinking."

The band changed their tune from slow love songs to 90s pop. Alex, Carolyn, and their friends hit the floor, dancing like they were back in junior high again. They laughed and gyrated to the beat, and every guy at the party was watching with a smile, including him.

⁓

*H*e was well hidden by the trees, his binoculars trained on the deck. He didn't miss Carolyn returning from the dark trail with JT just behind her, or Rowdy asking her to dance. She shook her head and he wished he was near enough to hear her refusal.

He also didn't miss JT watching her now. Was it concern for her safety...or interest? That was something he'd have to keep an eye on.

Now she was on the deck, having the time of her life. She and her friends were performing a silly dance that they must have done as teenagers. They knew the steps and had everyone on the sidelines watching and clapping along.

He wanted to be there, near her with everyone else, rather than hidden in the trees. When the music slowed, he'd pull her into his arms, and they'd dance close. He'd twirl and dip her, and she would laugh and kiss him. Everyone would sigh at what a perfect couple they made.

The music changed and Carolyn left the dance floor. She picked up a glass of something, held it in both hands, and peered over the rim as she took a sip. He followed her line of sight with the binoculars, but there were too many people to discern who she was looking at.

Sirens suddenly wailed in the distance. He lowered the glasses and ran, keeping low and moving through the trees.

CHAPTER 18

JT's phone rang at the same time he heard the sirens. He connected the call. "JT." He listened for a moment and then sprinted for the parking lot.

Gray smoke billowing up into the dark sky was visible before he reached his truck. He raced the block and a half to Town Square, where the largest pine, a tree that had graced the middle of the park since his grandfather planted it, was engulfed in flames.

The fire department already had hoses trained on the blaze and the surrounding area. He pulled across the intersection, blocking traffic from entering the square.

Soon the Harrisville Fire Department joined the Eden Falls firefighters. They aimed their hoses on the roofs of the surrounding buildings. Every shop on the square would have at least some smoke damage after this one. The tree was a loss, but they couldn't lose businesses, too.

Alex ran up to him in tears. "That's Grandpa Garrett's tree."

"Was," JT said. The fire smoldered, black smoke rolling like waves into the sky. The Harrisville teenagers came to mind and he searched the crowd for familiar faces with no luck.

"Alex, will you and Colton take a walk around the square? See if you spot any kids dressed in Goth."

"Carolyn, can you watch Charlie while Colton and I look around?"

JT turned. He hadn't realized Carolyn was behind him. Tears dampened her face and he was staggeringly glad she was here.

"Of course." Carolyn wrapped an arm around Charlie's shoulder.

He winked and she blushed while wiping tears from her cheeks.

~

Getting past her lock was harder than he anticipated. He wasn't concerned about anyone watching, since her husband had been caught and Eden Falls' citizens would be standing around Town Square for hours. He silently thanked whoever their arsonist was for giving him this sweet opportunity. His other visit had been rushed. This time, he'd move through her house slowly.

Starting in the kitchen, he imagined her at the stove cooking dinner, lifting a spoon to his lips for a taste. In the living room, he browsed through her books and framed pictures. He turned on the television to see what channel she watched. He planned to know everything from her shoe size to the color and brand of her nail polish by the time he left.

In his mind's eye, he could see himself coming home to her after work. She'd smile, her eyes lighting with joy. She'd ask about his day and listen, because she cared. She'd pull him to her for one of her sweet kisses and he'd hold her tight.

They could start their life together in this house, but, with only two bedrooms, they would have to build on or move to something larger when they started having children.

He slipped into the bathroom, picked up her bottle of perfume from the vanity and waved it under his nose. Beautiful Becca had liked citrus scents. Carolyn's taste was more floral. He read the label on the lipstick tube, Bed of Roses, and checked the brand of mascara she used.

He went through her nightstand drawer and found her wedding band. He was glad to hear through Eden Falls gossip that she met with some high-powered attorney Colton McCreed knew in college. Hopefully, her divorce would go through quickly.

You'll be mine soon.

At her closet door, he held his favorite pink sweater to his nose and breathed her in, then froze at the sound of a car door.

Quickly, he slipped into the closet just as the back door opened.

~

*C*arolyn dragged herself through the back door in pure exhaustion. She'd been at the pastry shop at four this morning, and hadn't stopped all day. Luckily, tomorrow was Sunday and Patsy's was closed.

As tired as she was, she couldn't leave the Garrett family on the square. They'd lost something important and were grieving. A part of their family history went up in flames. The tree planted by their grandfather had been used as Eden Falls' Christmas tree all her life. And now it was gone.

She walked to the kitchen sink, pulled a glass from the cupboard, and filled it with cold water. Seeing her reflection in the window reminded her of the morning she left San Francisco for good. Except, instead of being distorted, her image showed streaks of black. The soot was falling like flakes of snow, settling on skin, hair, and clothes.

Carolyn walked through the house to her bathroom, where she turned on the shower and stripped off her clothes. When they fell to the floor, the smell of smoke filled the air. She wondered if she'd ever be able to wash the scent from her hair and skin. She stepped into the shower and sighed aloud. The warm water felt heavenly as it washed the black down the drain. She shampooed her hair twice and scrubbed her skin with a loofa.

Long minutes later, she turned off the water, wrapped her body in a towel, and dried her hair with another. In the bedroom, she opened the closet and pulled a T-shirt from a hanger. An odd scent floated past, a scent that didn't register until she turned to her dresser for a pair of sleep shorts and saw her pink sweater on the bed. Terror froze her feet in place as it rippled up her spine. Robert was back. He was in her house. She pulled the shirt over her head and grabbed a pair of jeans from the hamper as she stumbled from the room.

The front door was unlocked. She hadn't noticed when she walked past in the dark. Was he still in the house? She slipped the jeans on as quietly as possible, straining to hear any sound past the rushing in her ears. She tiptoed to the kitchen, jerked car keys from her purse, then sprinted for the back door.

~

*J*T pulled his chiming phone from his pocket. The sun was just beginning to lighten the horizon, mixing the pre-dawn colors in a smoky haze. Alex, dressed as a candy corn from Halloween two years earlier, was on his screen. "Hey," he said when he connected the call.

"Sorry to bother you. I know you have your hands full, but Carolyn's at my house. Someone broke into her place."

"What?" His bark caused several firefighters to look his direction. "There is no way Richmond would be so stupid."

"I just wanted you to know she's here and safe."

"I'll be there—"

"She's fine, JT. I've already tucked her into bed."

After he hung up, he called Phoebe, who was at the station manning the phones. "Get me the number for John Hodges at SFPD."

She recited the number he'd have to put in his phone since he was calling it so often. He made the call while he watched the state fire marshal circle the base of what was left of Eden Falls' Christmas tree.

"Hodges."

"This is JT Garrett in Eden Falls."

"Don't tell me, you need us to check up on Robert Richmond again."

"Can you get someone to his house ASAP?"

"Sure, Garrett. I have nothing better to do."

JT watched the fire marshal pick something up with gloved fingers. "I know you're busy, but this is crucial. Richmond has a restraining order against him and someone just broke into the victim's house again. Call me back. Please," he added before disconnecting the call.

He pocketed his phone and walked toward the marshal. "What did you find, Chet?"

"A cell phone. There isn't much left of it, but our lab tech may be able to get something."

He held it up and JT noticed a metal skull embedded on the case. "I've seen that case before, or one exactly like it."

Chet looked up. "Where?"

"On a kid who's been hanging around town. His name is Aaron Meeks, but he goes by Blaze."

arolyn woke to voices in the kitchen. They were talking low, but she could distinguish Alex, Colton, and JT. She ran fingers through her hair and put on the robe Alex left for her.

"SFPD called back thirty minutes after I called them. Richmond was home. There is no way he could have been at Carolyn's and back at his house by this morning. When Mac questioned him, he repeatedly said he hadn't been in Carolyn's house, but I didn't believe him. Maybe he was telling the truth. Maybe it's been someone else all along."

"But who, JT? Who can break into a house without anyone noticing?" Alex said. "If it's not her husband, it has to be someone local, someone nobody would suspect."

"Someone who can get into a house with deadbolts on the doors," Colton added.

"Could her husband have hired someone?"

There was a long pause.

"I went over before I came here. The lock has scratches, but it isn't broken. So someone with know-how got in that back door."

"Like a locksmith?" Alex asked.

"Maybe. The only locksmith around here is old Henry, and his eyesight's so bad, he would have made a bigger mess of the lock."

"What about the locksmith Leo used to install the dead-bolts?" Colton asked.

Carolyn decided it was time to join in the conversation, since it concerned her. Robert had told her the same thing, that he hadn't been in her house. She, like JT, hadn't believed him. "Morning."

JT and Colton both stood from their chairs. Alex was at

the stove turning bacon. She turned, spatula in hand. "Hey, how'd you sleep?"

"Fine. Thanks again for letting me stay."

"You didn't call the police," JT said with raised brows.

She felt her juvenile blush heat the skin on her chest. "I thought the police had enough to deal with last night."

"Want some orange juice?" Alex asked, turning to the fridge.

"I'll get it," Carolyn said, glad for something to do.

JT walked over to her, close enough that she could see his bloodshot eyes. He still smelled of smoke and wore a day of whiskers. The poor guy hadn't slept, hadn't even had a chance to shower yet. "Alex said whoever was in your house might still have been there when you got home."

"Maybe. I don't know. I smelled him."

"As in he smelled bad?" Colton asked.

"No. When I opened my closet, I smelled his cologne. Then I saw a sweater that I hung in the closet. It was on the bed."

Alex leaned a hip against the counter and crossed her arms. "He may have been in the house while she was showering. Whoever this guy is, he has to be caught, and soon."

"Alex," Colton said with a frown.

Alex winced at Colton's sharp reprimand. "I'm sorry, JT. This situation just really scares me."

"I'm just as frustrated as you, Alex." JT's sagging shoulders made Carolyn wonder when he last slept. He looked Carolyn in the eye. "Sometimes we have a sense of who might be doing this deep down. Anyone come to mind?"

"I thought it was Rob." Suddenly, a thought hit her. She glanced at Colton. "Though the cologne was nothing Rob would wear. It…" She inhaled trying to put a word to the scent she'd smelled. "It was lemony, tart. And I've smelled it before…"

"Where?"

She closed her eyes, trying to recall. It was a scent so close she could almost touch it. She reached with her mind, but came up empty. She opened her eyes and shook her head.

"Have you seen anyone hanging around Patsy's, the neighborhood?"

"No."

"You told me before you felt as if someone was watching you. Is that feeling gone?"

"I haven't felt it since I got out of the hospital."

"Do you feel up to going to the house with me and taking a look around later?"

"Sure. I'm fine."

Alex set a plate of bacon and another of scrambled eggs on the table. The four of them ate in silence, each deep in their own thoughts. Hers on the biting scent of lemon and where she'd smelled it before.

JT finished first, stood, and put his plate in the sink. "Chief Brody has a suspect in Harrisville I want to question about the fire." He turned to Carolyn. "Mac and Layne are on duty today. They could come over and go through your house with you, see if anything is missing, but I'd rather be there. Are you okay waiting until I get back this afternoon?"

She nodded.

He put a hand on the table, another on the back of her chair and leaned toward her. "Don't go home until then, Carolyn."

You don't have to worry about that. After last night, she wanted to call Leo and break her lease, but was afraid whoever was doing this would simply follow her. She knew it wasn't Rob. Not because JT told Alex and Colton he was in San Francisco, but because if it had been, she'd probably be dead.

. . .

*A*n hour later, Carolyn walked around the square, which was crowded with people inspecting the damage. Seemingly afraid the inferno would reignite, everyone spoke in hushed tones.

She stopped in front of Noelle's Café and stared up at the bones of the tree that had been a part of the square for so long. The blackened remains rising tall were a stark contrast to the brilliant blue of the sky. The smell of smoke still hung in the air, an invisible reminder, as if the tree's charred, exposed branches weren't enough.

Rance and Lily Johnson stopped next to her. "It's a shame, isn't it?" Lily said.

"Yes." Carolyn watched a man walk around the tree's base and squat down, flip something over with his gloved hand. "Do you know who that is?"

"Mac said it's the state fire marshal, Chet something or other. They found a cell phone under the tree this morning, but it's not enough evidence. He's looking for more," Rance said.

Carolyn glanced across the square to Patsy's Pastries. Patsy had the front door propped open, and a large fan running. "Did The Fly Shop have any smoke damage, Mr. Johnson?"

Lily laughed. "People who fish don't care what they smell like."

Carolyn smiled when Rance wrapped an arm around his wife's waist in another sweet example of long lasting love. "Now, honey, that isn't completely true."

"How about the library, Mrs. Johnson? Any damage?"

"Luckily, we have those double doors, so very little smoke got in. Pages Bookstore, on the other hand, smells pretty bad. Maude's afraid she'll have to scrap some of her inventory."

"I hope not." She pointed across the street. "I'm going to see if Patsy needs any help with cleanup."

"Tell Patsy to let us know if she needs any help," Lily called as she crossed the street.

Patsy greeted her at the door. "Sad about the tree."

"Yes, it is. Does the shop have much damage?"

"Just smoke. I have the back door open with a fan blowing that way, too. Hopefully by Monday everything will be back to normal." Patsy threaded Carolyn's hand through her arm and looked out the window. "Did Rance and Lily have much damage?"

"Doesn't sound like it. Lily said to let her know if you need any help with cleaning."

Patsy smiled. "That's sweet of her."

Carolyn glanced at her employer. "You and Mason looked like you were having a wonderful time last night."

Patsy bit back a smile. "We did have fun."

Carolyn nodded toward the door. "Here Mason comes now."

Mason stepped inside. "Good morning, ladies."

"Hey, handsome."

Carolyn watched the tips of Mr. Douglas' ears turn red at Patsy's greeting. "I'm going to check out the kitchen."

"Lily and Rance just invited us to meet them for dinner at Renaldo's next Friday," Mason said.

"Both of us?"

Carolyn had ducked into the kitchen to give them privacy, but since the door was propped open, she couldn't help hearing their conversation and how apprehensive Patsy sounded.

Mason chuckled. "Yes, both of us. I told them I'd let them know by Wednesday."

"I'd…like that."

"Good. I thought, if you aren't too busy tomorrow afternoon, we could go shopping."

"What are we shopping for?"

"A ring."

Carolyn peeked around the kitchen door. Mason took Patsy's hand and dropped to a knee.

"What are you doing?"

She couldn't see Patsy's face, but there was panic in her voice. She pulled out her phone and touched the video button, hoping Patsy wouldn't mind when she found out Carolyn recorded Mason's proposal.

"I'm asking you to marry me." Mason glanced around the shop. "I know this isn't the ideal spot, and I don't have a ring yet, but we'll take care of that tomorrow. Don't make me stay down here long, though. I might not be able to get back up," Mason added when she didn't answer right away. "And don't say no, Patsy."

"I've already been married four times."

"This will be the last time. I promise. You make me happy, and I think I make you happy. I love you, Patsy. I want to wake up every morning with you by my side."

"I love you, too, I just don't have great staying power." A sob escaped her. "Actually, I have great staying power, but up to now, those who promised they loved me haven't."

"I have staying power. I'm old enough to know what I want. I want to marry you. I want you by my side. I want to grow old with you."

Patsy was crying now, sobs that would cause puffy eyes and red nose. Carolyn was crying, too.

"People won't like you if you marry me."

"Patsy, enough. I need you and… No, there is no *and*. It's as simple as that. I need you. I want you. I choose *you*. I love *you*. If we're shunned—which we won't be—we'll be shunned together. This is right. I think you feel the same." He smiled up at her, and Carolyn could see the love radiating from his eyes. "Say yes."

Carolyn decided she'd eavesdropped long enough. She knew what Patsy's answer would be, so she slipped out the back door. Pressing a few buttons, she sent the video to Patsy's phone, a happy smile on her face.

CHAPTER 19

JT met Carolyn in front of her house so they could walk through together. She pointed out things that were out of place in the kitchen. In the living room, a book sat back on the shelf a little farther than the others, and a vase of Mrs. Bingham's roses had been moved. These were all little things no one else would notice. But Carolyn did.

"I told you, Robert was very particular about how things around the house should be. Everything had its precise place. If anything was out of *his* order, Robert made sure I never made the mistake again."

He turned away so she wouldn't see the anger boiling under the surface. He knew once a woman got into a situation like Carolyn had lived through, it was hard to get out, but it was still beyond his understanding.

In her bedroom, a wet towel from her shower lay on the floor. She picked it up and hung it on the back of the door. The pink sweater that had first alerted her someone was in the house still lay on the bed.

"I hung it in the closet Thursday when I did the laundry," she said when she noticed him looking at it.

He glanced in the bathroom. The pretty dress she'd worn to the party last night lay on the bathroom floor where she'd dropped it before a shower. He could see the streaks of soot on the fabric.

"Whoever was in here moved my perfume bottle." She shuddered, then picked up her toothbrush, and dropped it in the trashcan. "And my toothbrush. I guess I was too tired when I first came in to notice those." She walked back into the bedroom.

"Can you tell if he took anything?"

Carolyn pulled the top drawer in her dresser open. "He went through my underwear drawer again, but I can't tell if anything is missing. I told Phoebe the last time, I don't catalog my…clothes."

She pointed to one of her two nightstands. "He seems very interested in what I read, and always moves pictures around."

He raked fingers through his hair. "Whoever is coming in knows how to pick deadbolts. He knows how to blend in, because no one has noticed a stranger hanging around. That leads me to believe he *or she* is local." He raised an eyebrow. "You didn't win the lottery and stuff the money in your mattress, did you?"

He could tell she was fighting it, but her smile won out. "No."

He sat on the edge of the bed and patted the mattress next to him, waiting until she sat. "That was in fun, but now I'll be serious. I want you to close your eyes and think of the customers you wait on at Patsy's."

She closed her eyes and bowed her head. Unexpectedly, an image of her parents' funeral flashed through his mind. She sat in that exact pose at the graveside service. JT was standing with his family. He remembered thinking she looked so terribly sad and vulnerable. He had actually rubbed his chest because his heart ached for her.

The urge to pull her close was overwhelming, so he stood. "I want you to go through a day, customer by customer. Who is a regular?"

"Colton is our only everyday customer."

"We know it's not Colton. Who else comes in, maybe not to buy donuts, but to say hi?"

Carolyn smiled. "Mason."

JT chuckled at the thought of Mason going through a woman's bra and pantie drawer. "I'm ninety-nine-point-nine percent sure it isn't Mason. Who else?"

Carolyn shook her head, her eyes still closed. "No one."

"Okay. When you go outside to clean tables, do you notice anyone standing around watching? Is there anyone in the square, anyone you see every day?"

She breathed out a sigh as she looked up at him. "I see a lot of people every day. Eden Falls is a small town."

He squatted down so he was looking her in the eye. "Is there anyone who goes out of their way to speak to you? Anyone who makes you feel uncomfortable?"

She shook her head.

"You said the cologne you smelled was familiar. Where have you smelled it?"

"I've been thinking of that all day. It's right there..." She put her index finger and thumb together as if pinching a memory. "...but I can't quite grasp it."

"Picture looking out the window. Who do you see on the sidewalk, across the square, in front of The Fly Shop or The Roasted Bean?"

Her face turned a pretty shade of pink.

"Who, Carolyn?"

"You."

She's watching for me as much as I'm watching for her.

His feelings for her had grown faster than they had for any other woman he'd ever known. His thoughts turned to her all the time. At work, he'd stand at the window facing Patsy's before he even realized he was doing it. When he walked out of the police station, he always glanced toward Patsy's first.

How could he feel as if he were falling in love with someone he'd never kissed, never even taken on a date?

He smiled as he straightened. "This isn't working."

Her face was still flushed, her freckles standing out adorably. His stomach growled and she laughed lightly. "Hungry?"

"Yes. I haven't had time to eat since breakfast." And he hadn't slept in two days.

She tipped her head toward the door to the hall. "I can fix something."

"Let's go somewhere."

"That's…not a good idea."

He knew it wasn't, but still asked. "Why is having dinner with a friend a bad idea?"

"People will talk."

He held out his hand to help her up. "We'll go to South Fork. I know a great place."

He saw the indecision cross her face before she nodded. "But I'll pay for my dinner. That way it won't be…"

"A date." He finished the sentence she'd left hanging.

At the moment, he'd agree if it meant he could spend more time with her. "Okay, but only because I'm too tired to argue."

~

They didn't talk much while JT drove to South Fork. As she watched the scenery pass, her mind ran over and over the questions he had asked, hoping someone would stand out in her memory, but no one specific made an appearance.

He parked in front of a Mexican restaurant she hadn't eaten in since she was a teenager. When she walked inside, the scents that assaulted her were familiar and oddly emotional. She took a moment to look around, noting very few changes. The comfortable feel of the place made her remember why she was so intent on coming back here when she left San Francisco.

After they placed their orders, JT studied her.

Uncomfortable with the scrutiny, she said, "I'm sorry about your Grandpa's tree. Do you have any leads?"

"The fire marshal found a cell phone. It was pretty scorched, but I recognized the cover as belonging to one of the kids creating trouble at the Fourth of July celebration." He pulled a small notebook from his pocket. "The Seattle crime lab is trying to get something from it. The kid claims it was stolen on the fourth. Phone records show it's been used since then, but we have no proof by who."

"How could that tree have been lit on fire and no one saw anything."

"More than half the town was at The Dew Drop for my parents' party. Luckily, the fire department got there quickly, or we might have lost more than just the tree."

They discussed different scenarios for her break-in and he threw out a few names. By the time they were finished eating, they hadn't come up with anything new. No names, no motives.

"I want you to stay with Alex until I get this figured out."

Carolyn shook her head. "I don't want to put Alex and her family in danger."

"No one knows you're there. Not even the police department. You can't stay alone, Carolyn. So far this guy hasn't approached you or broken in when you're home, but he's bold, and we can't take any chances. He always comes in when you're away, which makes me believe…"

"He knows my schedule." Why was this happening? All the miles she'd traveled, all the precautions she'd taken and still she wasn't safe. An overwhelming sense of dread engulfed her. Was this some form of punishment?

JT leaned forward and rested his elbows on the table. "I'm sorry, Carolyn. I don't want to scare you, but to be safe, you have to know what we're dealing with. We know it's not your husband, so who?"

She shook her head.

He released a long breath. "Tell me something, Carolyn."

"What?"

"Something I don't know."

"Now?"

He lifted a shoulder. "Why not? We've exhausted the other subject. Tell me one true thing."

She appreciated him changing the subject, trying to take her mind off of what was going on in her life. She looked out the window, trying to come up with something that wouldn't embarrass her. "If I could be an animal, I'd be an otter."

"I'd choose a cheetah."

She smiled, glad that he now reciprocated in this game he liked to play. "I've never tried liver and onions."

He laughed. "I've never wanted to."

"I've never been to a zoo."

"Really," he asked, raising his eyebrows in surprise. "We'll have to change that."

She smiled.

"I've never been sky diving."

She laughed. "Sorry. I'm not helping you change that."

"Ah, come on."

"Nope, you're on your own for sky diving." She tapped her fingers on the table. Coming up with one true thing without revealing too much was getting harder. "I wish I didn't blush so easy."

He reached across the table and took her hand. She saw it coming and didn't pull away, let his fingers lace with hers. "Don't wish that, Carolyn. Your blush is as much a part of you as your red hair. Those things make you beautifully unique."

~

He sat in his car, wrestling with his timing. He'd planned to wait until Carolyn was divorced from that scumbag husband before he approached her. He wanted to make sure she was completely free to love him. He wanted to give her time to heal from the pain Robert Richmond had inflicted. He wanted her to feel the anticipation of their first date, their first touch, their first kiss.

He also wanted time for his own healing. He wanted to be free of his memories of Becca before he slept with another woman.

There was a lot he wanted to have happen before he went to Carolyn. But he couldn't wait any longer, because JT was ruining everything.

He'd seen Carolyn in his truck a couple of days earlier and then last night he saw her and JT having dinner at Renaldo's with Alex, Colton, and Charlie.

After all his careful planning, JT was horning in and making a mess of everything, pushing him to act before he was ready, but he'd make things work. He had to for Bec— for Carolyn.

He pulled the gun from his glove box and tucked it into the waistband of his jeans, hoping he wouldn't have to use it.

He made sure his jacket covered the weapon, then climbed out of his car.

Charlie was eating dinner at a friend's. Alex and Colton left for a city council meeting, so Carolyn ate a grilled cheese sandwich alone in Alex's kitchen. She was ready to go home. She hated staying here, invading Alex, Colton, and Charlie's space. Even though they made her welcome, she still felt in the way. She wanted to work in her yard, mow her lawn, and hang the pictures she found at a flea market.

She was ready to live a new life, one free from fear and anxiety. Life had been awful for so long, she wasn't sure what normal was anymore. Not that she'd ever really known, but she was willing to find out.

She'd been here six nights and there was still no lead as to who had broken into her house. Leo came into Patsy's this morning to tell her he was having a security system installed. She tried to argue that she'd pay for it, but he refused to listen. She felt responsible for all the extra Leo was doing to keep her safe, so she planned to be at the house tomorrow to pay the installation before Leo arrived.

She put her plate in the dishwasher and straightened the kitchen. In the guest room, she picked up a book she borrowed from Alex and climbed onto the bed. Just as she opened the cover, a chair moved in the kitchen. She glanced at the clock next to the bed. It was too early for Alex and Colton to be home. She closed the book and stood. "Charlie? Is that you?"

As she reached the bedroom door, Russell Walsh stepped into view. Carolyn jumped and put a hand to her chest. "Oh, Russ, you scared me to death. I was expecting Charlie."

"I'm sorry, Carolyn" he said hesitantly.

She smiled. "It's okay. I didn't realize you were coming over. Is JT with you?"

He shook his head slowly, his expression flat.

"Did he send you over?" She looked past him. "I didn't know anyone was home to let you in. Is Charlie here?"

That's when she smelled the lemony scent. A shiver of dread worked its way down her spine. Time slowed to a standstill as a silent alarm blared in her head. Feeling eerily detached from her body, she watched him step over the threshold. Slamming and locking the door was no longer an option. She took a step back, but she had nowhere to go in the small bedroom. "How…how did you get in?"

"I came in this morning, after everyone had left for the day, and disabled the lock on the kitchen window."

"It's been you? All this time, you were the one breaking into my house?" She knew the answers even as she asked the questions.

His expression didn't change as he slowly nodded his head.

"You went to San Francisco and hurt Robert."

"I did it for you, Becca." His tone changed from monotone to hopeful.

"Who's Becca?"

He shook his head, as if trying to clear a thought. "I did it for you, Carolyn. For us."

"Why, Russell? Why would you…?"

He reached out to her, but stopped when she jerked away. He lowered his hand. "Once you get to know me, you'll understand how much we have in common."

She dared a quick look at the clock. She didn't have any idea how long city council meetings lasted. *Stall.* Her only hope was to keep him talking. "Breaking into houses isn't how you get to know someone."

"If I'd asked you out, would you have gone?"

"I'm married, Russell."

His mouth turned down almost like he might cry. "Yet you're going out with JT."

"No. We're not going out. We've been to dinner a couple of times, but those weren't dates."

"I see the way he looks at you. He's taken a personal interest in your case. So much so, that he didn't even tell the rest of the force about the most recent break-in."

Something inside told her to try and reason with him. Make him understand. "JT was just trying to protect me. We're not dating. Just discussing who's been coming into my house."

"Did you ever guess it was me?"

Carolyn shook her head, her mind working as fast as possible under the circumstances. "Why don't we go into the kitchen? I'll get you something to drink and we can get to know each other."

His jaw tensed. "It's too late now."

"You're a police officer. You're supposed to be upholding the law. Why are you doing this?"

He looked at her as if she should know the answer. "I told you, I did it for us, Becca."

"Please tell me who Becca is. Is she your girlfriend back home? Didn't you tell me once you were from Oregon?"

His expression brightened and her hopes rose...until she heard the front door open. He turned and his jacket lifted enough that Carolyn saw a gun in the waistband of his jeans. The alarm in her head grew louder. Why did he have a gun? She grabbed the footboard of the bed, her knees trembling. The sound of running feet almost had her hyperventilating. He glanced at her and she sent him a silent plea.

In answer, he put a finger to his lips and pulled the gun from his waistband.

"Please."

"Carolyn, want to get an ice cream cone with me and—"

Charlie stopped at the bedroom door when he spotted Russell. "Hi! How come you're here?"

Carolyn stepped forward, but Russell quickly held up his free hand to stop her. "Charlie." She swallowed to calm her shaking voice. "Russell and I are talking. Can you go back over to Tyson's until—"

Colton came to a halt behind Charlie. "Hey, Carolyn. Charlie and I are going to—Oh, hey, Russ. I didn't know you were here. Is everything okay?"

His glance bounced from Carolyn to Russ. She knew the second Colton spotted the gun held just out of Charlie's sight. Keeping his eyes on Russ, he turned Charlie by the shoulders and pushed him toward the front door. "Charlie, I want you to go down to Tyson's house and stay there until I come get you."

"But Colton, you said we could—"

"I know what I said, but something important has come up. You go down to Tyson's and—"

"But Colton—"

He looked at Charlie. "Now!"

Charlie jumped, his bottom lip quivering. Colton pointed and Charlie disappeared.

"You need to go with him, Colton," Russ said.

Instead of leaving, Colton stepped into the room. Carolyn's heart dropped to the floor. She would not allow her friend to become a widow for a second time. "Please go with him, Colton. I'll be fine. Russ and I were just talking."

"I'm not leaving you."

Her knees were shaking so hard, she was afraid they'd give out on her at any moment. She took another step back and Colton used the opportunity to step between her and Russell.

"So, it's been you this whole time?"

"Follow Charlie out of here, Colton."

"Why are you doing this?" Colton asked, stealing a glance at her.

Russ fisted his free hand. "Why is it so hard for everyone to understand? Becca and I belong together!"

Colton frowned. "Russ, this is Carolyn, not Becca. You have her mixed up with someone else."

Russell waved the gun. "I know who she is. Don't try to confuse me."

"You don't need a gun here. You're scaring Carolyn. She doesn't deserve this."

"Who is Becca?" Carolyn asked, trying to keep her voice gentle and steady.

"Becca is"—he shook his head in agitation—"was my fiancée, but that was a long time ago."

She took Colton's arm and pulled him back a step. "What happened to her?"

At her sudden movement, Russ pointed the gun at her and Colton held up his hands. "Whoa, whoa, whoa. Everything's okay, Russ. Relax. Tell us where Becca is. We'll get her on the phone for you."

Russ turned the gun on Colton.

"No." Carolyn exhaled the word on a breath of air, trying to move in front of Colton, but he blocked her with his arm.

Russ's expression broke, but he quickly recovered, then it broke again. He wiped his free hand over his eyes. "Dead. She's dead." Russell's voice was suddenly too calm given his revelation. "You need to leave, Colton. Now."

"You know I can't leave Carolyn. Being a police officer, you also know you won't get away with whatever it is you're planning." He held his hands up in surrender. "Put down the gun, walk away, and we'll forget this ever happened."

"No. I'm going to take Carolyn with me. We'll leave Eden Falls quietly." He looked at her. "Carolyn, get a scarf, something we can use to tie Colton up."

Colton reacted so fast, all Carolyn saw was his hand come up. Her only thought was to save him. She pushed around him and screamed when the gun exploded. Searing pain shot through her side before she fell to the floor. Her body jumped as the gun discharged a second time, then her world went dark.

~

JT grabbed the radio from the dashboard of his patrol car, trying to make sense of what Gianna was saying.

"Calm down, Gianna. Say again."

"Alex's neighbor called. There's gunfire at Alex's house."

He punched the gas and flipped a U-turn while switching on lights and siren. He was six blocks away, which might as well have been sixty miles.

"I'm on my way," Mac said over the radio. "I'm coming from the east side of town."

Minutes later, JT turned onto Alex's street. Mac was at the other end of the block coming at him. They both screeched to a stop and jumped from their cars at the same time.

"Alex, stop!" JT yelled when he spotted Alex sprinting for the front porch steps. "Mac, take the back."

JT ran up the stairs and grabbed Alex's arm, yanking her back from the door with one hand and pulling his gun from his belt with the other. "Who's in there?"

"Charlie said Colton and Russell are in the bedroom with Carolyn."

"Where's Charlie?"

She pointed toward the neighbor's house.

"Go around back and let Mac in. Then you stay out of the

house." He shook her arm to make his point. "I mean it, Alex. Stay out."

JT opened the door and glanced around. The living room and kitchen were clear. He eased down the hall, checking Charlie's room and the bathroom on his way. He peeked around the door of the room Carolyn was using. She lay on the floor, unmoving. Russ was stroking her hair, babbling incoherently. He eased around the door, his gun leading the way, willing Carolyn to move. Colton sat with his back against the footboard of the bed, a gun pointed at Russ.

"It was him all along," Colton said, when he spotted JT. "It was Russ."

JT holstered his gun, grabbed Russ's collar, and yanked him away, throwing him to the floor. Mac came in the room and pulled Russ down when he tried to scramble back to Carolyn. "Hands behind your back."

JT felt Carolyn's neck for a pulse. Faint, but steady. Relief washed over him in cold waves, causing a shiver. He keyed his radio. "Gianna, get an ambulance to Alex's house immediately."

"One is already on the way. Brandt should be there any minute."

"I didn't mean to hurt her. I would never hurt Becca. She wanted to be with me, but Colton wouldn't let us leave. This is his fault," Russ wailed, tears dripping off his chin.

"Shut up!" The gun shook in Colton's grasp.

JT crouched down in front of Colton, gently lifted the gun from his grasp, and pushed it under the bed. He'd deal with it after he was sure Carolyn was okay.

Blood seeped down Colton's left arm. "Where are you hit?"

"Take care of Carolyn. She hasn't moved."

"Alex!" JT knew his sister hadn't listened to his instructions about staying out of the house. "Get some towels."

She raced into the room carrying a stack of bath towels almost before he finished his sentence. She dropped to the floor next to Colton. "What happened? You're bleeding."

"I'm okay," Colton groaned as Alex pressed a towel to the front of his shoulder.

Russ whimpered when Mac lifted him to his feet. "Wait! I can't leave her like this. Becca, wake up."

Mac dragged him from the room.

JT turned to Carolyn, carefully rolled her to her back, and lifted her T-shirt. "She was shot in the side, but it looks like the bullet went all the way through." He grabbed two towels, placed one under the wound, one on top, and applied pressure.

"Who's Becca?" both JT and Alex asked at the same time.

"Seems Russ had a fiancée who died before he moved here," Colton said. "He kept calling Carolyn Becca."

~

Carolyn opened her eyes slowly. Disoriented, she tried to move, but gasped when pain shot around her middle. A man appeared next to the bed. She tried to jerk away, but gentle hands held her shoulders to the mattress.

"You're okay, Carolyn. You're in the hospital, again." JT's voice, soft and close to her ear, created heat in her belly that rose to her chest. "You had surgery for a bullet wound in your side. Everything went well. You're safe."

His words brought everything flooding back. Russell, Colton, a gunshot. She opened her eyes and glanced around the dimly lit room. "Russell?"

"He's in jail."

"Colton?"

"He's in a room down the hall. He was shot in the shoulder. They got the bullet out and he's going to be fine." He eased his grip on her shoulders. "Colton said you took the bullet that was meant for him."

Carolyn eyes slid shut as she remembered… "He stepped in front of me. I couldn't let him get hurt because of me."

JT enveloped one of her hands in his. "Do you feel up to telling me what happened?"

She opened her eyes and stared at the ceiling, trying to recall the details, but wanting to forget at the same time. "I was in the bedroom and suddenly Russell was there. He said he unlocked the kitchen window while we were all away from the house. He had a gun. Charlie and Colton came in." She glanced at JT. "Charlie—is he okay? He was there. I was so terrified he'd get hurt."

JT chuckled. "Charlie is physically fine, though his feelings were crushed when Colton yelled at him."

She hadn't realized JT was gently but thoroughly massaging her hand with strong fingers, relaxing her arm, her shoulders. She closed her eyes. "Colton did yell, but we were both so scared. Russell had a gun."

"Alex will explain everything to him. His seven-year-old feelings will heal."

She swallowed as images flashed through her mind. "Once Charlie was out of the room, Colton stepped between us." She opened her eyes. "He asked Russell questions, tried to keep him talking. Russell got angry and raised the gun. I thought he was going to shoot Colton, so I pushed around him. Russell fired. I remember hearing the shot and feeling a burning sensation. I must have blacked out, because I don't remember anything after that."

"Colton was able to get the gun away from him."

"I can't believe this happened." She shook her head. "Did you have any idea? Did you ever suspect Russell?"

"I suspected just about everyone but him, which was a big mistake on my part."

"I never would have thought of him. Ever. He was always so sweet and so shy." A sudden memory surfaced. "He kept calling me Becca."

"Becca *was* his fiancée, but she died of cancer before they were married. She had red hair and freckles, and he believed he could recreate what he had—what they had—with you."

So sad. Carolyn closed her eyes as the heavy clouds of exhaustion descended. JT had managed to relax every tight muscle in her body.

She felt lips touch her forehead, a light squeeze of her fingers. "Sleep now, Carolyn. I'll be right here. You're safe."

~

*J*T didn't leave the hospital or Carolyn's room until Stella arrived. Then he walked down the hall to check on Colton, who was sitting up in bed being spoon-fed ice cream by Charlie. Obviously, apologies had been made and accepted.

"Hey, Uncle JT! Colton got shot in the shoulder, so I'm helping him eat ice cream."

"I see that. Can you take a break from feeding the patient so I can ask him some questions?"

"Come on, Charlie." Alex stood up from her chair on the other side of the bed and kissed her husband. "We'll go down to the cafeteria and see what other sweets we can dig up for Colton."

JT sat in the chair Alex vacated. "How you feeling?"

"Now the adrenalin has stopped pumping through my system, I'm okay."

"Can you tell me what happened?"

"I took Alex to Town Hall, but decided ice cream sounded like more fun than sitting through a council meeting. I picked Charlie up from Tyson's. It was his idea to invite Carolyn."

Thank you, Charlie.

"When we got to the house, Charlie ran in ahead of me. Russell was there with Carolyn. I thought it was strange that he was in the house, and even stranger that he was in her bedroom, but decided you must have sent him. It wasn't until Carolyn glanced at the gun he was holding that I realized what was going on. I sent Charlie out of the house. Both Russ and Carolyn told me to go, but I couldn't leave her there."

Thank you, Colton.

"I stepped between them, trying to figure out a way to get her out of there. We both talked to Russ, but he was beyond listening. He was determined to take Carolyn with him. She said something and for some reason, he pointed the gun at her. A moment later, he turned the gun on me and Carolyn stepped between us. I think her sudden movement caused him to panic and he fired. He was so distraught about shooting Carolyn that his focus was on her. I grabbed for the gun. He was thrown off balance enough that when he fired again, the bullet hit me in the shoulder rather than the chest, but I was able to get the gun away. He didn't even fight me. I honestly think he had no intention of hurting anyone. He just wanted Carolyn."

"That was brave, wrestling for the gun."

"Self-preservation isn't bravery. Besides, Russell was so upset after shooting Carolyn, he almost handed it to me. I actually felt bad for the guy. For about five seconds."

Charlie burst into the room. "We just visited Carolyn. She can go home in a few days."

Alex sent JT a knowing smile. He returned it with a sense of satisfaction.

Carolyn was going to be okay.

He was in love.

Life was good.

CHAPTER 20

JT pushed into Carolyn's room and sank into a chair next to her bed. She was sleeping, her face free of anxiety.

He leaned forward and took her hand. As tired as he was, he couldn't leave her alone. Her sister refused to come, positive Carolyn had done something to deserve all that had happened to her.

She'd been through so much since coming back to Eden Falls, and even before she arrived. At least her husband couldn't come near her and divorce papers were filed with the State of Washington—three months faster than the State of California allowed. Then she'd be free. Perhaps not free of the memories or the hurt, but of the man.

Russ was behind bars. His parents were on their way from the east coast to try and make sense of what happened. He would be spending some time in a psychiatric ward for evaluation. Owen was working on another restraining order.

Now, if he could only catch the arsonist, maybe their little town could get back to its peaceful norm. They'd questioned Blaze, but, other than his phone, which he swore was stolen, they had no proof he'd set either fire.

. . .

*H*is eyes flew open at a touch on his shoulder. He released his hold on Carolyn's hand when he saw Patsy grinning at him.

"Too late," she said with a smirk. "I already caught you."

"Don't let it go past those doors, please. For Carolyn's sake. She doesn't need any more gossip floating around."

Patsy mimed twisting a key at her lips. "Believe me, your secret is safe. At least until her divorce is final." She set the vase of flowers she'd brought in the windowsill. "How is she?"

He stood and stretched, feeling every hour he'd slept in the uncomfortable chair. "The doctor told me she will be fine. The bullet went straight through. No damage to vital organs."

"Quiet, sweet Russell Walsh. Who would have guessed?"

Waves of frustration rolled over him.

"Don't you dare blame yourself, young man. He had us all fooled."

"Who else am I going to blame? My own officer, a man I picked, was stalking her. He could have taken her and held her captive, just as her husband did, for years."

"But he didn't, and we can all be thankful for that. From what I hear, he had her confused with a fiancée. That's a sad story. He must have loved his fiancée very much." Patsy smoothed the hair off Carolyn's forehead. "She's been through the wringer, but she's one of us now, and we protect our own."

"Yes, we do." He picked up his jacket. "I'd better go. I have to be on duty today to cover Russ's shift."

"Hang in there, handsome. Things always work the way they're supposed to in the end. By the way, I'll expect to see you when Mason and I get married next month."

"What?" He pulled her into a hug. "Congratulations,

Patsy. You've found a great man, and Mason deserves the happiness you share so freely."

~

*A*fter JT left, Patsy sat in the chair next to the bed. It wasn't long before Carolyn's eyes opened. "How're you feeling, hon?"

"Sore."

"A normal life is awaiting you as soon as you get out of here." Patsy took the hand JT had been holding. "I'm going to have one, too, thanks to you."

Carolyn's smiled. "It had nothing to do with me."

"The letter you wrote made me realize some things about myself. Despite my divorces, despite what people think, I am a good person."

Carolyn squeezed her fingers. "You're a fabulous person, Patsy, and I'm so happy for you."

"You're fabulous, too, and your chance is coming." Patsy glanced toward the door. "JT spent the night here. I suspect, most of it holding your hand."

"What?"

"Yep, he was here when I came in. Any man who sits next to your bed, holding your hand while you sleep, seems pretty serious to me."

Carolyn fought against a smile, her eyes lighting, truly lighting with joy, for the first time since she'd come back to town. Happy looked very good on her. The smile disappeared as she shook her head. "I have too much baggage. Two hospital visits in just a few weeks. A crazy husband—"

"Soon to be ex-husband," Patsy interjected.

"But still a husband, and a stalker."

"All that didn't seem to bother him too much while he slept in this hard chair all night. There is happiness out there for you, hon. I promise you'll find it. By the way, thank you for the video."

"You're welcome. I saw the opportunity and had to take it. Hope you don't mind that I was eavesdropping."

Patsy grinned. "Not a bit." She stood and looked down at Carolyn. "I have a huge favor to ask."

"Anything."

"I want you to be my maid of honor."

~

Carolyn took her place at the front of the church with Mason and Beam as the congregation stood.

Patsy walked down the aisle in a blush-colored dress that was fitted to her upper body before flaring gently to the floor. The bodice was decorated with delicate, beaded blooms.

She carried a bouquet carefully selected by both her and Mason, with Alex's help, regarding each bloom's meaning. White lilies for majesty and orchids for refined beauty, chosen by Mason. Patsy decided on pale pink phlox, which stood for "our souls are united," and baby's breath for everlasting love. Alex added a touch of blue with forget-me-nots. It was as beautiful as Patsy, whose hair was held back with lily of the valley, which meant a return to happiness.

The flowers reminded her of the violets JT left for her at the hospital a month ago. She had to ask Alex their meaning, because she couldn't remember.

Alex's smile was a little mischief mixed with satisfaction. "A violet stands for purity and innocence, a love that is delicate. My grandma always said they mean 'let's take a chance on happiness.'"

Carolyn still remembered the blush that burned up her cheeks.

Mason stood on the other side of Preacher Josh Brenner

with joy written all over his face. Misty was the only one who scowled. She still hadn't come to terms with her father marrying Patsy, but she also hadn't been able to stop the wedding. She told them at their last girls' night out that she'd be there to pick up the pieces when Patsy left Mason. Carolyn felt certain that would never happen. She saw them together daily and was sure their love was the forever kind.

She rubbed where her wedding band used to fit her finger. Her life had changed dramatically since she stood here six months earlier for Alex and Colton's wedding. She'd left an abusive marriage, moved home, found a job she loved, survived a stalker, and was now surrounded by lifelong friends.

She didn't think she and Catherine would ever be more than estranged sisters, which hurt her heart. But until Catherine wanted more, there was nothing she could do. She hadn't called or visited during either of Carolyn's hospital visits, which hurt her heart even more. After talking to Preacher Brenner, Carolyn was finally able to accept she and Catherine would never be close.

Trying not to be obvious, she glanced at JT. He sat with his family in the second pew of the church, looking as handsome as she'd ever seen him. The sight of him still made her heart thud as if she'd just run a marathon.

She turned her attention back to the wedding. As Mason took Patsy's hand, happiness flooded her. She'd asked for just one good thing when she first moved here, but her life was full of good things.

~

*P*atsy felt her cheeks quiver under her smile as she walked down the aisle on the arm of her husband. She'd held her tears at bay, even when Mason's eyes filled with unshed tears during the vows. But now that it was all over, emotions swamped her. She was married. For the fifth —and last—time.

Mason pulled her into a room off the foyer of the church and kissed her senseless until everyone had a chance to exit. He looked striking in his dark suit, and she was so filled with joy her chest hummed with pleasure.

"You are gorgeous, Patsy. So beautiful, inside and out."

She pulled his glasses down his nose. "We need to have your eyesight checked, but not until we come back from our honeymoon."

He pushed his glasses back into place. "I don't have to see you to know how beautiful you are."

"You say the sweetest things." She kissed him again. "And you look adorable in that shade of lipstick."

He pulled a handkerchief from his pocket. "Clean me off. We have to go out and make our debut as Mr. and Mrs. Douglas."

She wiped the lipstick from his mouth, and they walked outside to be greeted with hugs, good wishes, and a shower of rose petals.

~

JT found a chair at the reception where he could watch Carolyn talk with friends, accept compliments about the wedding cake, and decline every invitation to dance. Thankfully, she was completely healed from her physical wounds. He hoped her other scars would heal as quickly.

They were seeing each other socially, but only in groups. They had dinner with Alex and Colton or met up with friends at Rowdy's. Her divorce would be final in October and he was counting the days. He believed Carolyn would be the last woman he'd ever date.

He watched her from across the room. She looked beautiful in her green dress, her smile finally reaching and transforming her sad eyes.

As if she felt him watching her, she glanced his way, and their gazes connected.

He winked.

She blushed.

If you enjoyed *A Taste of Eden*, I hope you'll continue reading! The next book in the Eden Falls Series is *The Angel of Eden Falls*.

To keep up to date on new releases join my newsletter at TinaNewcomb.com.

Following is an excerpt from *The Angel in Eden Falls*.

EXCERPT FROM: THE ANGEL OF EDEN FALLS

CHAPTER 1

Mac Johnson trudged up the porch steps of the renovated Victorian house. Welcome, Owen Danielson, Attorney at Law was emblazoned on a plaque next to the door. Tempted to knock the cheerful sign off the wall, he sucked in a deep breath, hoping the extra oxygen would calm his raging heart. If only he'd skipped his trip to the mailbox yesterday. The manila envelope he carried felt like a hundred pound weight. He wanted to rip the contents to shreds or set the thing on fire, but neither option would solve his problem.

When he entered the large foyer, Owen's receptionist turned from her computer screen with a smile. "Hi, Mac. Owen is taking a call, so it will be just a few minutes."

"Thanks, Jolie."

"Can I get you something to drink while you wait?"

She made the offer as if today was like any other, but then she didn't know the envelope's contents were eating away the lining of his stomach. "No. Thanks."

Mac glanced around. He'd never been in Owen's offices before, hadn't needed the advice of an attorney in years.

"How's Beck?"

He gripped the blasted envelope at the mention of his son. "He's good."

"I bet he's looking forward to the Harvest Festival."

Mac smiled. Probably his first of the day. "Yeah, he is."

"Have a seat. Owen should be out any minute."

When Jolie turned to her computer, Mac stuck the envelope under his arm and walked across the room to a magazine rack mounted on the wall. After flipping through the pages of *Field and Stream*, which failed to grab his attention, he put it back and yanked out one on fitness. "How's Jeff?"

Jolie looked up. "He's good."

"Still in Montana?"

"Yes."

He shoved the magazine back in the holder and walked to a window, staring at nothing. "How's JessAnn?"

"She's fine."

"She lives in California, right?"

"Yes, and Jeremy is working in Spokane," Jolie said, finishing off her "J" siblings. "Mom and Dad are good, too," she added before he could ask.

He sat on the edge of a chair and glanced at his watch for the third time. He'd arrived early, praying he could get in sooner. Now Owen was five minutes late.

Jolie glanced over her shoulder with raised brows.

"What?"

She nodded at his bouncing knee, which made the wood floor under his foot squeak.

"Oh. Sorry." He wiped a palm down his pant leg. "Nervous."

Jolie swiveled her chair to face him. "Owen is very good at what he does. I'm sure he'll be able to help you, and if he can't, he'll find someone who can."

A door down the hall opened and Mac leapt to his feet,

sending the offending envelope skittering across the floor. Owen scooped it up. "Hey, Mac."

"Thank you for seeing me so soon," Mac said, shaking Owen's outstretched hand.

Owen smiled. "The way Jolie put it, I didn't have much of a choice."

"Sorry, but this can't wait," Mac said, nodding to the envelope Owen held.

"Well, come on back and let's see what's so important."

Owen led him into a spacious office with deep green walls, the bottom half covered with rich wood paneling. Built-in bookshelves lined both sides of a beautiful wooden mantelpiece. A small conference table near the bay window overlooked a garden where pots of fall flowers surrounded a fountain. Owen's massive mahogany desk faced the soothing view.

The comfortable room and setting beyond settled the queasiness that had seized Mac's stomach ever since he opened the envelope sixteen hours earlier.

Owen gestured to one of the wingback chairs in front of his desk before circling to take his own chair. "How's Beck?"

"Good." Mac sank into the soft leather and pointed at the envelope Owen still held. "That will explain my impatience to get in as soon as I could."

Owen opened the envelope, tugged the contents free, and spread the papers out on his desk. Mac watched his eyes move back and forth while he read and then reread each sheet. Mac tried to decipher his expression, but Owen's features remained neutral. When he finally looked up, Mac released the breath he'd been holding.

"Were you and"—Owen glanced at the letter he'd placed on top of the pile—"Mrs. Lynwood married when Beck was born?"

"No. We were married, but divorced before his birth."

Owen rested his forearms on the desk and laced his fingers together. "Start at the beginning."

Mac looked down at his own fingers, twisted in tension. "Our marriage was a mistake. We were college kids, dumb and drunk in Las Vegas with a group just as dumb and drunk. Dares were thrown out and, before I knew what was happening, Cheryl and I were in one of those sleazy chapels saying, 'I do'.

"We were together a week before she moved out, saying she'd have divorce papers delivered." Guilt and embarrassment of a long ago mistake tightened his chest muscles. "I don't know if she dropped out of school or what, but I never saw her on campus after that. She did send divorce papers. We shared no property, so it was uncontested. I showed the papers to an attorney, signed them, and the divorce was final. I didn't hear anything from her for a year and a half.

"Then one morning, before dawn, there was a knock on my apartment door. When I answered, I found Beck in a baby carrier with a 'He's yours' note attached with a safety pin."

Owen's eyebrows rose, wrinkling his forehead. "She left him on your doorstep?"

Mac nodded. "A bag of formula, a few diapers, and a birth certificate that had me listed as the father and Cheryl as the mother were in a paper sack next to him."

Owen reached for a legal pad and jotted a few notes. "How long were you married?"

"She sent the divorce papers about a month after she left, so a month and a week."

"Which means there was a fifty-fifty chance she knew she was pregnant when she filed for divorce."

"I don't know much about those things, but my guess is yes."

"You didn't talk to her that morning?"

"No."

"Did she stick around long enough to make sure it was you who opened the door of the apartment?"

"No. I'm not even sure she's the one who dropped Beck off."

Owen looked up and Mac saw the surprise on his features.

"I ran down the stairs and out the front door of the apartment building, but didn't see anyone."

"After Beck was dropped off, did she have any contact with him? Or you?"

"None."

Owen's pen stopped scratching over the surface of the legal pad a second time. "None? She never sent birthday cards or Christmas gifts?"

"No."

"Did you ever receive money for Beck's support?"

"Zero contact."

Owen nodded slowly and resumed writing. "What does Beck know about his mother?"

"Not much. He asks about her occasionally, and I try to be up-front without hurting him." Mac rubbed the base of his skull where a tension headache was starting to throb.

"What do you tell a kid whose mother leaves him on a doorstep when he's only six months old? I've never bad-mouthed her, but I've never made excuses either. I'm not going to lie to my son or get his hopes up. Cheryl never told me why she did what she did. She never even told me she was pregnant." He met Owen's steady gaze. "Yes to your next question. Beck is mine."

Owen ran an index finger under his bottom lip. "Do you have the paperwork to prove it?"

"Yes."

While Owen made more notes, Mac held his own questions at bay. His what-ifs and should-I-haves were lined up like little soldiers, marching through his mind. *I should have made sure there were custody papers drawn up. What if Cheryl has a case because I didn't? I should have checked with an attorney before moving to Washington. What if Cheryl takes my son away because I left California without permission?*

"How old was Beck when you moved back to Eden Falls?"

"Almost five."

"Why did you move back?"

"When it was time for kindergarten, Mom and Dad offered to help, and the police department here was hiring, so I moved. Before that I'd hired a nanny. I thought being near family was the right choice. It never occurred to me to check with an attorney before I took Beck out of California."

Owen steepled his fingers and rested his chin on top. "Why haven't you remarried, Mac?"

Mac knew the surprise had to show on his face. Of all the questions he'd imagined Owen might ask, that wasn't one of them. "Does it matter?" He noted the defensiveness in his tone. *Of course it matters. I'm a single dad. Judges usually rule for moms.* "Between work and Beck, my days were full. *Are full.* When would I have time to date, and where would I meet a woman? There isn't an overabundance of single women in this small town."

Owen held up a hand in surrender. "I was just curious, Mac. I wasn't passing judgment."

"Would it help my case if I were married?"

Owen turned his hand over, palm up as if weighing his answer. "It wouldn't hurt, but that's not why I asked. You don't still have feelings for—"

Mac snorted. "No. Cheryl and I barely knew each other. Our marriage was a stupid, immature action on both our parts. Our relationship…" He shook his head. "There was no relationship. Our time together was purely physical. Over before it started."

"Why do you think Cheryl wants custody after all these years?"

Mac sat back in his chair as the pressure in his head pounded along with his heartbeat. "I have no idea."

Owen nodded and looked down at his notes. "I understand you not wanting to get Beck's hopes up. I feel the same with clients, because anything can happen. If this goes before a judge, you never know how he or she will rule. However, you have several things going for you. Cheryl abandoned Beck, she's never tried to contact him, and she's never contributed to his support."

Mac narrowed his eyes. "I hear an another unspoken however hovering in the air."

Owen took off his glasses and polished the lenses with a cloth he pulled from a desk drawer.

He's stalling.

"However, we don't know why." Owen replaced his glasses. "There may be extenuating circumstances that a judge would find justifiable. This letter says she's remarried and has two stepchildren she cares for, which shows responsibility. Do you know anything about her family? How she was raised, if she has siblings?"

Mac shook his head.

"Why did Cheryl leave?"

Mac shrugged, too ashamed to admit his relief when she packed her bags. Grateful she was the one to leave rather than forcing him to make the decision. "Other than going to the same school, we had absolutely nothing in common. I hated the music she played. She hated mine. She was vegan. I wasn't. I could go on and on, but really, what does it matter?"

Owen tapped the eraser end of a pencil on his desk.

"I'm not letting Beck go, Owen. She abandoned him on

my doorstep nine and a half years ago. Beck was a defenseless baby and she left him with a note pinned to his chest. She hasn't called once to ask how he is, if he's healthy, or happy. She's never taken him to the dentist or a ball game, never attended a parent-teacher conference, or one of his school performances."

"How would you feel about this letter if she had?"

Another surprise question, one that made him pause. "I'm not sure. My guess is I'd still be in California and we'd be sharing custody, so there wouldn't be a letter."

Mac dropped his head back and stared at the ceiling. "I want to do what's best for Beck and I don't believe uprooting him, completely changing his lifestyle, is the answer. He doesn't know Cheryl at all and he shouldn't be forced to *live* with her because she's suddenly changed her mind." Mac met Owen's gaze. "He's happy here, Owen. He's doing well in school, plays on several sports teams, and has great friends. He's close to my parents, sees them everyday. They've played as big a part in his life as I have. The situation would be different if I was an unsupportive parent or unable to care for him, but that's not the case."

"Would you be willing to discuss visitation?"

"Do I have a choice?" Mac pressed his fingertips together, desperate to regain the control slipping away. "Yes. If Beck wants to meet his mom, I would be willing to discuss visitation, but it has to be here, in Eden Falls. I'm not going to ship him off to California."

"If you wish to retain my services, I'll send a letter to Mrs. Lynwood's attorney expressing your concerns, and your willingness to negotiate." Owen pushed up from his chair. "That willingness will go a long way with a judge, if this goes that far."

Mac assumed their meeting was over, though he felt far from the relief he'd hoped for. He stood. "I appreciate anything you can do for me, Owen. Beck is my life, has been since he was six months old. I can't just send him off with someone he doesn't know."

Owen came around the desk. "I'm sorry you're going through this, Mac. I can't imagine how I'd feel if it were my boys. We all have things in our past that seem to rear their ugly heads at one time or another." Owen opened his office door and started down the hall. Mac had little choice but to follow.

"We didn't discuss fees."

"This meeting is a free consultation. Jolie will go over my fees with you, but let's hold off until I hear back from Mrs. Lynwood's attorney. Jolie, will you make copies of these papers for Mac's file?"

Mac held his hand out and Owen shook it. "Thank you, Owen. And thank you for fitting me in so quickly, Jolie. I appreciate it."

"You're welcome." Jolie turned to the copy machine.

"As soon as I hear anything, I'll be in touch," Owen said. "Until then, try not to worry."

Mac hoped to leave Owen's office with his promise that nothing would come of the contents of that brown envelope. He wanted to feel secure in the knowledge that Beck was going nowhere, except bowling on his tenth birthday. What he got was, "Try not to worry".

A shadow fell over him when he stepped outside as clouds obscured the sun. He pocketed the sunglasses he'd just pulled out. The gloom settling over Eden Falls matched his mood.

Mac hoped bad weather held off until after the town's Harvest Festival. Rain would dampen the celebration and his nine-year-old son's excitement.

He climbed behind the wheel of his truck and headed for Town Hall where the police station was located. From there he'd change into his uniform and spend the night keeping Eden Falls, Washington safe.

*****

Noelle Treloar rubbed her eyes and yawned. Today had been good. Summer tourist season was over, but business was still bustling. She closed her laptop and stood up to stretch. If the café continued to have weeks like this, she'd be able to pay off the loan for the kitchen's new appliances by the end of the year, three months ahead of schedule, which called for a celebration.

The wall clock taunted her, its hands standing straight up at attention. The café closed three hours earlier, and she'd been crunching numbers ever since—something she missed from her previous life. Numbers had been her business.

She stretched, hands high overhead, then bent at the waist until they lay flat on the floor. She held the position for thirty seconds before slowly straightening. Time to go home.

First a victory dance, because she couldn't help herself. The idea of owning a café, even after eighteen months of actually running it, still seemed surreal. She owed it all to a distant uncle she'd never met and a letter she wrote for a fourth-grade genealogy project. After the uncle answered her questions about the Treloar family tree, their spotty correspondence continued for several years.

When her letters started coming back with Return to Sender stamped on the front, she wondered what had happened to this wandering uncle. Then she received a certified delivery from Attorney Owen Danielson. The one-page letter informed her that Jeremiah Royal Treloar had died and left her a restaurant in Eden Falls. After an internet search, she learned Eden Falls was a small town in the middle of Washington state. She contacted Owen, who hired someone to board up the place. She paid the back taxes and promptly forgot about the restaurant and Eden Falls for five years.

A few stolen clients and a backhanded business deal two years ago had her booking a flight to Seattle to escape the cutthroat company she worked for and her overly-aggressive parents, who were pushing her toward insanity. What better place to hide out for a month than an estranged uncle's stomping grounds?

She opened the door to her office and wandered around the polished-to-perfection kitchen, the accomplishment of her fabulous staff. What would she do without each and every one of them? She didn't want to find out.

Pushing through the swinging doors into the front of the café, she spun one of the red vinyl stools. The linoleum floor shone from a recent mopping. She straightened a few glasses and made sure the bin that held rolled silverware was full. She fished a quarter from the front pocket of her jeans, slipped it into the slot of her prized possession, a nineteen-sixties jukebox, and selected C-5, her go-to song when she was alone.

Kelly Clarkson's "Stronger" poured from the speakers while she threw herself into a victory dance of freedom. Gone were her days of anxiety and scrambling for the next big deal. Gone were her mother's harping words and her father's disappointed looks. She was free from stress and frustration. Free to live her life the way she wanted to live it. Suffer the consequences of her mistakes without her family breathing disapproval down her neck.

She grabbed spray cleaner, a roll of paper towels, and polished the glass on the jukebox she'd purchased on a whim. As the song wound down, she rechecked the lock on the front door. The hardware store, and then the big tree in the square, the one the town decorated for Christmas every year, were both burned to the ground recently. She knew the police chief suspected someone, but there wasn't enough evidence to convict. She wasn't going to take a chance with her baby.

After one more look around, she flipped off the lights and walked through the kitchen for her coat.

Outside, Indian summer still prevailed. It was almost balmy for the middle of October, although rain was on the way. She just hoped it held off until after Eden Falls' Harvest Festival, or a lot of people would be disappointed.

She made sure the door was shut tight, then turned as a patrol car swung into the parking lot. Handsome Mac Johnson leaned his head out the open window.

"I saw lights go out in the front of the café and thought I'd drive around to make sure everything was okay."

One of the many reasons she loved this little town. Residents—not just the police—watched out for each other. On top of the fires, there had been a loony stalker on the loose a few months earlier. He was apprehended and all was quiet again, but the events had shaken Eden Falls' residents' usual sense of security.

"Everything's good. Thanks for checking. Will you and Beck be in tomorrow night?"

"Same time as always."

Father and son were Friday night regulars unless Mac was on duty. "Albert made a to-die-for pumpkin cheesecake."

His white-toothed grin appeared in the glow of the dashboard lights. "I remember his cheesecake from last year. Choosing between that and your apple pie will be a hard decision. How about you save us one of each."

"Anything for my two favorite customers."

She waved as he backed out. The town was in good hands, patrolled by Eden Falls' finest. Everything was just as it should be.

ACKNOWLEDGMENTS

There are many who contribute to an author's book and go unacknowledged, because we don't always remember where the inspiration came from. Whether it's an overheard conversation between two strangers, a news story that captures the attention, a song, or the line from a movie or book, something sparks the imagination.

For me, it's usually travel. The road trips I take with my husband almost always trigger a story for me. Before we get home, I'm familiar with the setting and I've already met the main characters.

The Eden Falls series came to life after a vacation that started and ended in Spokane. We made a wide circle through Idaho, Montana, Canada, and Washington. Without our travels, I wouldn't have come up with the fictional town of Eden Falls. So, to my husband Rick, thank you for all the time and planning you put into our travels away from home. You are my rock!

I have to give a shout of thanks to our eight children who show their love and support in different ways. I love you all.

My beta readers are the very best. Thank you Chris Almodovar, Holly Hertzke, and Jeanine Hopping. I appreciate and value your suggestions, your feedback, and your friendships. You are amazing!

I want to thank editors Joy Clintsman of Big Sister Edits, and proofreader, Amy Dix. I appreciate your time and talent for detail.

Thank you Dar Albert of Wicked Smart Designs for the

Beyond Eden book cover. You created the perfect image to portray Eden Falls Hardware and Lumber.

Also, a huge shout out to The Blurb Queen, Cathryn Cade, thank you for your ability to whittle a manuscript down to a couple of paragraphs.

I would be remiss to not mention the members of my critique group. Dawn Annis, Mary Hagen, and Sherri Valentine. You taught me about passive voice and filter words (Yeah, still working on both). You encourage and inspire me to be a better writer. I value your talents and cherish the friendships that have come from breakfast twice a month. Hugs to you all.

As you can see, there are many who have contributed to my endeavor. I hope you enjoyed the end results.

ALSO BY TINA NEWCOMB

<u>The Eden Falls Series</u>

Finding Eden

Beyond Eden

A Taste of Eden

The Angel of Eden Falls

Touches of Eden

Stars Over Eden Falls

Fortunes for Eden

Snow and Mistletoe in Eden Falls

Rumors in Eden Falls

<u>Second Chance Romance Collection</u>

When You Love Someone

Endless Love

Rhythm of Love

Second Chance Romance Collection

ABOUT THE AUTHOR

Tina Newcomb writes clean, contemporary romance. Her heartwarming stories take place in quaint small towns, with quirky townsfolk, and friendships that last a lifetime.

She acquired her love of reading from her librarian mother, who always had a stack of books close at hand, and her father who visited a local bookstore every weekend.

Tina Newcomb lives in colorful Colorado. When not lost in her writing, she can be found in the garden, traveling with her (amateur) chef husband, or spending time with family and friends.

Follow Tina on:

facebook.com/TinaNewcombAuthor

instagram.com/tinanewcombauthor

bookbub.com/authors/tina-newcomb

goodreads.com/tinanewcomb

pinterest.com/tinanewcomb

www.ingramcontent.com/pod-product-compliance
Lightning Source LLC
Chambersburg PA
CBHW061046190726
48286CB00006B/1624